P9-DLZ-228

NATIONWIDE PRAISE FOR **ROSEMARY ROGERS**

"She doesn't disappoint."

Los Angeles Times

"Her novels are filled with adventure, excitement and, always, wildly tempestuous romance."

Fort Worth Star-Telegram

"The reigning queen of romance."

Publishers Weekly

"Pure entertainment . . . She has brought unique fantasy into the lives of thirty million readers worldwide."

Chicago Tribune

"She offers more (and better) sweet, savage love."

Family Circle

"The crème de la crème of romantic escapist fiction."

Newport News Daily Press

"A phenomenon!"

Sacramento Union

"Her name brings smiles to all who love love!"

Ocala Star-Banner

Other Avon Books by
Rosemary Rogers

ALL I DESIRE
THE CROWD PLEASERS
A DANGEROUS MAN
DARK FIRES
THE INSIDERS
LOST LOVE, LAST LOVE
LOVE PLAY
MIDNIGHT LADY
SURRENDER TO LOVE
SWEET SAVAGE LOVE
THE TEA PLANTER'S BRIDE
THE WANTON
WICKED LOVING LIES
THE WILDEST HEART

ROSEMARY ROGERS

IN YOUR ARMS

AVON BOOKS NEW YORK

This is a work of fiction. Names, characters, places, and incidents either are product of the author's imagination or are used fictitiously. Any resemblance to actual events, locales, organizations, or persons, living or dead, is entirely coincidental and beyond the intent of either the author or the publisher.

AVON BOOKS, INC.
1350 Avenue of the Americas
New York, New York 10019

Published by arrangement with the author
Library of Congress Catalog Card Number: 99-94458
ISBN: 0-380-80026-8
www.avonbooks.com/romance

First Avon Books Printing: December 1999

AVON TRADEMARK REG. U.S. PAT. OFF. AND IN OTHER COUNTRIES, MARCA REGISTRADA, HECHO EN U.S.A.

Printed in the U.S.A.

WCD 10 9 8 7 6 5 4 3 2 1

Prologue

It was quiet in the main salon, almost too quiet. He put a hand against the door, pushed it open, impatience making him careless.

The woman seated on a cushion before the fire turned with a gasp, half-rose to stand with the light behind her. Her garments swung loosely, the fire outlining her curves through thin silk. A cloud of fair hair was loose around her face and shoulders, tumbling into her eyes. Then she recognized him and her entire face changed, went from frightened to joyous, and she came toward him with outstretched arms.

"Dev! I cannot believe you came after all . . . I thought you said—"

"Did you think I would not, after the message you sent? What is so important, Maria?"

He caught her, only because she gave him no choice, and felt her familiar hands move over him, intimate caresses on face, chest, and belly. He put her at arm's length, eyed her narrowly as she wet her lips with the tip of her tongue.

Lovely, but fickle, a faithless female he would not trust for a moment. The beautiful Maria, toast of the *ton* her first Season out, blonde and petite, with china-blue eyes and luscious curves.

He curled his hands tightly around her arms until she gasped, looked up at him with reproach in her eyes.

"What *is* it, Dev? Are you not glad to see me?"

"Dammit, your message said it was urgent—but you're sitting here eating bonbons. I always wondered what women did when alone."

She laughed, a little uncertainly, put a palm against his chest; her fingers toyed with his cravat, rearranging the intricate folds his valet had worked hours to perfect. He put a hand atop hers, held it still.

"Boyle will not appreciate your efforts. I have little time. Tell me what you consider so urgent."

"I have no idea what you mean, Dev. Roger is gone, so I came here alone, hoping to find you, but your servant said you had an appointment, so—"

"So you thought it would be amusing to send an urgent message and see how long it took me to get here? Christ!" He closed his hand with casual cruelty in her hair, tugged her head back so that her face was turned up to his, watched her eyes widen. "No more of your games, Maria. It would be best if this were the last time you came here."

"Dev—wait!" She grabbed his arm when he released her, held on. "You cannot dismiss me like this—I will not allow it!"

"You will not allow it?" He laughed. "I find that rather droll, considering that your husband might protest."

"Roger doesn't care what I do, as long as he

has his precious diversions! Oh God, you have no idea what he is capable of doing! Dev—you cannot mean you are truly ending it."

He peeled her hand off his arm, gazed down at her, eyes drifting to the generous bosom half-bared beneath her filmy gown. A faint, tempting shadow flirted between her breasts, silk shrouded. He glanced up, caught the greedy, cat-like gleam in her eyes, and dropped her hand.

"That is exactly what I mean. It had to end one day, Maria. Surely you knew that."

"Yes—but not until *I* am ready. And you are not ready to end it, or you would not have come for me . . . would not be looking at me like you do, or be so—*ready* for me."

Damn her—she reached for him, hand shaping the rigid length of his betraying body, massaging him through his fawn breeches, and he grabbed her wrist. "This won't change anything, Maria—"

"Then give me one last time, Dev . . . please. If you are determined to end it, let us have one last time together."

Before he could stop her, she tugged at a lace just below her bosom, released it, and shrugged free of the thin wrapper around her. She was naked beneath it, pale curves gleaming like alabaster in the fire-glow. Rosy nipples stood up, begging for his touch, and the soft triangle at the juncture of her thighs was a nest of silky blonde curls.

Inconvenient lust pounded through him, blood drowning out the voice of caution in his brain, and he reached for her, fingers dark against ivory skin.

At the back of his mind the nagging warning

that he should stop, should end it cleanly, as he had intended to for some time, grew dim. Maria was too demanding, too careless of her husband's name and reputation. A discreet affair was one thing—blatant indiscretions were dangerous.

"Dev . . . I know I can change your mind," she whispered against his ear, but he ignored that fallacy.

Moaning, she leaned into him, whimpering when he teased her nipples into rigid peaks with his tongue. Reason slowly dissipated as she dragged her hand over him, clever fingers unfastening the buttons of his breeches, shaping him with her palm, a luxurious stroke along his length that dismissed the last of his resistance.

An insatiable little wildcat, clawing at him, moaning, her mouth on him wherever she found bare skin, tugging at his shirt, his cravat, the buttons of his breeches to free him. Rampant sensuality, erotic heat, the driving urge to end the throbbing ache in his groin drove him to possess her. He pushed her down upon the cushions before the fire, held her arms above her head to keep her from clawing at his back, then spread her thighs with his knees and drove into her with a deep, satisfying lunge.

She bucked beneath him, cried out, panting little sighs of ecstasy. There was no love in it, nothing but pure lust and the need for release.

Somewhere in the haze that enveloped him, he heard an alien sound, a click and thud, and looked up to see Lord Wickham lounging in the salon doorway.

"Ah, I see you received my message. Are you enjoying my wife?"

Book I

Journeys

London
May, 1808

Chapter 1

April rain ran in rivulets from rooftops to the street, gushed from gargoyle mouths to the gutters below and spread across paving stones to make streets slick. Deceptive puddles formed, shallow in appearance, yet hiding deep holes to suck at carriage wheels and send up geysers of muddy water as horses and vehicles splashed down Curzon Street.

Sarah, Lady Winford, watched out the window, waiting. Baxter had brought the news that Holt had returned to London, and she should expect her grandson's arrival quite soon. Natural impatience did battle with rising annoyance as the gilt clock on the mantel chimed twice. Waiting always annoyed her.

When at last Holt appeared in the courtyard below, there was no hint of haste in his movements despite the rain. He dismounted, gave the reins to the horseboy waiting; his bare head glistened, wet and plastered to his head by the rain. Lady Winford released folds of heavy velvet drape to fall back over the window, turned, and moved without haste to the stuffed chair placed before the fire. A marble hearth reflected subdued color, but flames glowed bright gold and crimson on the brass firedogs; heat and light cast erratic pools that danced across the thick carpet as she sat down and arranged sprigged muslin skirts in a graceful drape.

Age sat easily on her despite her years, and a portrait on the wall in the third-floor gallery bore testimony to the beauty she had once been. It was still evident in her erect bearing, sculpted bone structure, and eloquent movements.

Beyond the occasional pat of a slippered toe against patterned carpet, she betrayed no outer sign of impatience as she waited; Holt would be up soon enough. He always presented himself to her upon his return, whether out of duty or love was a frequent topic of conjecture. A faint smile curved her aristocratic mouth. He was too much like his father at times. Ah, Robert had passed along the same famous temper to his only son, yet with a major difference: Holt had restraint. It had been Robert's downfall, that tendency to loose his wrath on those around him, swift to anger, swift to action, thus swift to early death.

She sighed, a soft sound lost in the muted hiss of rain against the windowpanes. A draft crept across the room, insistent and chilling her feet. She stretched them closer to the fire, watching reflected light glitter in silver threads embroidered on the toes of her slippers. A silly scene, depicting dogs chasing a rabbit, but comfortable shoes were a necessity these days.

A log popped, sending up a shower of sparks; wood burned so much cleaner than coal. Perhaps it was less efficient, but it smelled nicer, reminding her of so many pleasant things. . . .

Footsteps sounded on the hall carpet, and she pulled her feet up under her chair, rearranged her skirts, took up a book from the ivory inlaid table at her side. Idly, she flipped a page, not looking up when the door swung open even before the light tap against it faded.

"Your manners need remedying, Holt," she said serenely, and turned a page. "One usually waits to be granted permission to enter before doing so."

The door closed with a solid click. "Such formality. Can it be that you missed me after all, Grandmère?"

Idle mockery, tinged with real amusement. Lady Winford pursed her lips, studied the printed pages without really seeing them. She waited. In a moment, she heard the soft thud of booted feet crossing the room, moving away from her and not closer. A surreptitious glance followed Holt to the gleaming cherry liquor cabinet; glass clinked, a muted sound as he uncorked a crystal decanter and splashed a small amount of brandy into a goblet.

Then he turned, a study in casual elegance, tall, dark, handsome in riding garb with form-fitting fawn breeches and knee-high Hessians. Oh, he did remind her of Robert when he looked at her like this, a half-smile curling his mouth, his blue eyes a faint gleam beneath his lashes. Arrogance was a family trait, inherited from his grandfather and father, but somehow even more pronounced in Holt—Robert Holt Braxton, now the ninth Earl of Deverell. *Devil* to his cronies, it was said, though of course, none but Baxter dared mention the preposterous epithet to his grandmother.

"And how is the war?" she asked, when the silence stretched too long. She turned another page, aping Holt's casual indifference.

"Long and bloody. Futile. Dangerous. How is Socrates?"

She glanced up, frowned. "Who?"

"Socrates." He indicated the book she held, a wry smile on his mouth. "A treatise on Socrates is usually best read right side up, Grandmère. Or has no one told you?"

"Curse you, Holt." The book snapped shut, was replaced on the table. There was no rancor in her tone or her words, and she surveyed him with a practiced eye. "You look as if you've been dragged through the mud."

"An apt description of my day, I'd say." He lifted his glass to her, an ironic gesture. "I suspect you are about to make it better."

"Yes, perhaps I am." The first hint of irritation crept into her tone. "We are to have guests for a time."

"More of your country vicars, I presume. God save us all from well-meaning hypocrites."

"Mind your blasphemous tongue, Holt. Reverend Smythe was quite pleasant."

"He was a horror. Is he coming back?"

"No. Though it might do you good if he were."

"It is most doubtful. I blame him and his mousy wife for your involvement in Reform. Life was much simpler before you were given a Cause, and much more peaceful. Now I am beset with vagabonds and vicars at every turn."

"Most unkind of you, Holt. Reverend Smythe

just gave me a new direction for my life." She paused, cast about for a simple explanation, found none and proceeded cautiously. "Twenty years ago, I was dear friends with a certain Lady Silverage. I'm certain you do not remember her—"

"Is she coming for a visit?"

"No, she is dead, Holt. Do let me continue." She regarded him with a faint frown; he was restless, pacing from the liquor table to the window and back, long strides like a prowling cat's, controlled impatience evident. Her resolve strengthened. "Lady Silverage's daughter had the faulty judgment to run off with a Colonial, and of course, was dispossessed for such foolishness. I remember her well . . . a nice young lady, though a bit headstrong and far too independent. She went off to the Colonies with her young man, a Captain Courtland."

"Intriguing as this bit of information is, Grandmère, I have an appointment—"

"I am trying to tell you something important, Holt. Do have the courtesy to listen, even if you have made it plain you are not particularly interested."

He came to stand in front of her. She looked up at him, annoyed that he chose today to be disagreeable, when she had finally drummed up enough courage to tell him about her invitation. Really, he could be so difficult at times, steel beneath the facade he showed her, a reminder that he was no longer a boy, but a man grown and in full possession of the power of his seat in the House of Lords.

Blue eyes regarded her intently, and the

straight slash of his mouth was bracketed in irritation. "Have you invited the Colonial and his fugitive wife to live here?"

"Do not be ridiculous, Holt. And Anna wasn't a fugitive at all. She was disinherited. Amalie—Lady Silverage—was very distraught about it, but there was nothing she could do. Lord Silverage cast her off, and that was that. No, I have not invited Captain Courtland and his wife to stay here."

"A singularly intelligent decision, Grandmère. Just whom did you invite?"

"Their children. Oh, do not look so black at me, Holt. After all, I was godmother to Anna, and kept up a form of correspondence with her for quite a while. Lovely girl. Such a pity she was so headstrong—"

"Why are their children to come here?" Ominous shadows darkened his eyes. A thin red line like a scratch marred one cheek, sweeping from his left brow to his jawline. His face sported a faint bruise, high on the cheekbone.

"Your face . . . what have you done, Holt?"

He waved a hand, sweeping away questions and alarm. "It is nothing. Why are their children to live here?"

"Anna and her Colonial are dead, killed in a tragic accident. Master Dunbar, a barrister in Norfolk, Virginia, sent me a letter from Anna, in which she asked that I care for her children in the event of her death. As dear Anna's godmother, I feel it incumbent upon me to do so, if for no reason other than duty—"

"Misguided duty, as usual."

"Holt, there is no one to take care of the poor

little things. And it might be nice having children about again. I rather miss it at times—and before you suggest leaving them there or letting Lord Silverage deal with it, I might remind you that he is dead and the children destitute. Not that it matters. I promised Anna that if anything ever happened to her, I would see to the welfare of her children, and that is what I intend to do."

Silence fell. An ormolu clock on the mantel swept hands across a pearl face with loud ticks until finally Holt said, "This is one charity that you may soon regret, Grandmère. It is not much to take in vicars and spinsters, or even those nasty little pugs that bite my ankles at every chance, but this could be a monumental mistake. I suggest you consider it more carefully."

"I have. All the arrangements have been made. Within a month, they will be here. As for the pugs, you provoke them, and I do not blame them for biting you."

Holt regarded his grandmother with exasperation. She frequently strained the boundaries of his patience. It was too late to remonstrate now.

"I would rather have teeth marks on my ankles than shrieking, bothersome children at my heels. As repulsive as your pugs can be, children are even more so. Have you thought of their needs, beyond the fact of getting them to England?"

"Baxter has ordered everything that children might require, and I shall see to their education—there must be something a boy can do these days to earn a decent wage. A barrister, perhaps, like Bondurant. Or a banker . . . yes, that would be just the thing. And the girl, I am certain she must be quite sweet, for after all, blood does tell, and Anna Silverage was very well connected. In due time, when she is old enough, we can find her a suitable husband. She is still quite young, you see . . . I cannot remember exactly, but it seems to me they are seven or eight years of age by now."

How like her, to condemn the parents in one breath, pronounce them "sweet" in the next. Lady Winford frowned slightly, and regarded the toes of her slippers with rapt intensity. Gray liberally streaked her once-dark hair, a token of advancing years, though she seemed to him ageless.

"Grandmère, I will have my barrister make arrangements for the care of these children when they arrive. While I applaud your charitable instincts, it will be too much to expect for them to stay here."

She glanced up; behind the kindly eyes lurked obdurate lights, a determination as strong as his own. He recognized the signs of resistance, obliterated them without regret.

"We need not discuss this further. I have an appointment now, and may not return this evening. I will be at my club."

Lady Winford's lips compressed into a tight line. She acknowledged his farewell with a brief bob of her head that showed no sign of surrender.

He quit the parlor, shutting the door behind him. As if summoned, Heaton appeared in the long hallway, his demeanor elegantly obsequious, as expected of an earl's steward.

"Will you be staying for dinner, my lord?"

"No. I have an appointment. Inform Boyle that I will be going out, and he may have the night to himself."

Heaton inclined his head, moved down the hallway to the sweep of wide stairs that led to the upper floor. For a moment, Holt stood still, his hand still on the parlor door handle. Grand-mère certainly complicated matters with her flights into sympathetic charity. One of these days, it would end badly if he didn't curb her tendency to grand gestures. With relations going sour between Britain and America, all that was needed was the importation of Colonial orphans into his house. Parliament might view it with more than normal reservation.

One more detail to be added to the arrangements made before he met Lord Wickham in the park. Cursed folly, for the irate viscount to challenge him—a damned nuisance. Duels before dinner were bad enough form. Killing cuckolded husbands was viewed askance by the law.

If luck was with him, Wickham would survive the encounter, and if not—was it any worse facing hundreds of Frenchmen across a bloodied field? Napoleon held Rome now, and Madrid and Barcelona, but the Corsican intended to conquer all of Europe. British forces were massing to land in Portugal, and politicians argued policy while men died. Yet another folly.

Here he was, seething in London while men under his command prepared to fight Napoleon. If not for the tangled deceit of powerful lords in Parliament, he would be with them instead of languishing impatiently while his commission was reviewed and decided.

There lurked a suspicion in his mind that Wickham was somehow involved in the Commission's decision to investigate him, sparked, no doubt, by the fated involvement with Lady Maria Wickham: a retribution for his sin of taking what was so freely offered by Wickham's wife. It might have been left at that, save for Maria's unwise confrontation that forced her husband to challenge him to this ridiculous duel.

It could not have been what Wickham preferred, no matter how great the provocation—certainly not to avenge the dubious honor of a wife indiscreet enough to blurt out publicly her anger at being rejected by her lover.

Very bad form, indeed.

He thought of Maria briefly and without regret. She was an insatiable lover, marking his back with her long, sharp nails when they made love, as if labelling him as her personal property. He was not sorry to end their affair, but irritated that she had chosen to make a public spectacle of it.

Holt descended the wide, sweeping staircase to the first floor and his study, a panelled room at the rear of the townhouse that was his refuge when he stayed here with his grandmother. No one was allowed to enter without his permission, even the downstairs maids. Heaton, a trusted employee of long years, saw to the cleaning and polishing.

Here were none of the gilded clocks or intricate curls of chairs, but solid, massive furniture, unfettered with ornamentation, and glaringly masculine. His desk was made of mahogany, the gleaming top a sinuous baroque curve in the only concession to popular style. Heavy brass handles fronted drawers fitted with uncompromising locks.

It took only a few moments to pen necessary letters and instructions to his barrister, the requisite caution of a man who had learned not to trust Fate. If nothing else, war had taught him that.

Life could be extinguished in an instant; a flash of saber, explosion of a cannon, and men were catapulted screaming into eternity. No, he trusted in nothing.

Emerging from his study, he paused in the entry to place the sealed and addressed letters on a silver tray to be posted, took the steps two at a time to the second floor and his apartments in the east wing of the house. Best not to chance meeting his grandmother again; there was no reason for her to be aware of the duel and worry needlessly. If it went as usual, he would return in the morning freshly shaved and rested, honor and Wickham a little worse for wear, but alive and satisfied.

Late shadows pooled under towering oaks, squatted along the road that led from London, shrouded spectators in misty grayness. The rain had stopped, leaving behind a blanket of mist that permeated clothing and nerve.

"Wickham is a fool," David Carlton, Viscount Stanfill muttered to Holt. "All of London knows you're a dead shot."

"I think he hoped for the épée."

Holt's dry tone summoned a reluctant grin from David, his appointed second in the duel.

"He would have been misled in that choice as well. He should have insulted you so badly you would have been forced to call him out for it. Then he could have chosen weapons and terms as he liked."

"I do not think it matters much to him. Here. Give me that. Your hands are shaking too badly to be any good to me."

Stanfill relinquished the pistol, glanced at Holt, uncertainty written on his face. "I don't know whether I should admire your nonchalance or curse it. Wickham means to kill you. This is not to satisfy any notion of honor—half of London has slept with Maria Wickham and boasted of it." He shook his head, a frown pleating sandy brows. "No, this is too deliberate, the challenge too public to be merely insult or honor-driven."

"That hardly matters now." Hands steady, Holt loaded the pistol with swift efficiency then handed it over to the mediator to inspect. It was pronounced sound, as was Wickham's, and the mediator turned to Wickham to give him a final opportunity to withdraw his challenge.

Wickham looked blank, face pale beneath a spray of tan freckles that stood out like blotches on sharp cheekbones and nose. His second, the Honorable Mister Dalton, had to ask twice before Wickham turned to look at him, eyes opaque with some inner struggle.

"No."

"And you, my lord Deverell? Do you wish to offer an apology or refusal to continue?"

Holt briefly met the mediator's eyes, smiled slightly. "I wish merely to be done with this. I am expected at my club for supper."

Seconds and mediator withdrew, moving away to stand with the surgeon on the edge of the field. The world smelled fresh, new, the sweet spice of May trees drifting on the light breeze. Holt lifted his hand, arm bent at his side, pistol pointed skyward, and waited for the mediator to count off the agreed upon distance.

Pistols at twenty paces. It would take a man with a cool head and steady arm to hit his mark. Steps were counted off—"Eighteen, nineteen"—and before the final number was called, Lord Wickham turned in a blur of white lace cuffs.

Holt glimpsed motion and the brief ellipse of orange flame, felt the burn in his side. It spun him around, sent him to one knee; he flung out a hand to keep his balance. Intense pain threatened to swallow him in black clouds. Air left his lungs in a harsh grunt. Somehow he was on his feet again, pistol slowly lifting, vision wavering as he focused on Wickham, so far away, a solitary figure in white shirt and black trousers, a beacon against blurred green.

Noise assaulted him from all sides, a clamorous ringing as of church bells shrilly tolling; gradually, a voice came out of the blur, distinct, demanding he sit down on the grass.

"I am the surgeon, Lord Braxton. Let me inspect your wound."

"No." He shook off the insistent hand on his arm, then gave the anxious Stanfill a push away, ignored his protests.

"Damme, Dev, as your second it is my duty to keep you from fighting when wounded!"

He focused briefly on Stanfill, saw the worry creasing his face, shook his head, an act that nearly unbalanced him. "No, I have not yet fired my shot."

Chaos quieted, grew deathly still. A strange emptiness crept through him, made him light-headed. Stanfill's words drifted through a thickening haze to him; he perceived the gist of them, a plea that he let it go until later.

For a moment the haze cleared; he saw David distinctly now, noted without surprise the blood on his hands and knew it was his own.

Calmly, as if from a distance, he heard his own voice, surprisingly coherent: "I am not hurt. Stand back. This play needs an ending."

As they moved back, Holt turned slightly, ignored the throbbing torment in his side as he lifted his arm. Wickham stood helpless, waiting, staring his death in the face as the pistol did not waver but levelled steadily. Not a tremor betrayed Holt, not a flicker of an eyelash or twitch of his mouth relayed the pain that spread from his side to his back and then his throat. It was encompassing, alive, a ravening beast that ate at him with relentless savagery but did not dilute his intent.

Silence was suffocating, the mist insidious and damp, muffling sound so that all he heard was his own heartbeat and ragged breathing. Slowly, his thumb pressed the hammer of the pistol, drawing it back with a click that sounded as loud as a cannonade.

Wickham watched with devastated eyes; his mouth worked soundlessly. Pale light gleamed soft on the nine-inch barrel of the pistol, a dull, deadly glow.

Holt waited. Fear was a palpable thing, a live

creature that slowly came to life until Wickham began to shake, hands at his sides, the useless pistol dropping from suddenly nerveless fingers to thud on the crushed blades of grass at his boots. One shot only. That was the rule. And Wickham had taken his.

But I am not yet dead . . . a bad choice, my lord Wickham.

A faint sobbing sound reached him through the gathering mists, and he realized it came from Wickham. At last. He had broken, disgraced himself by firing before the count was done, and now would be forever branded as a spineless coward for weeping. It was a far better fate than he deserved.

Ever-encroaching shadows crept closer, nibbled at the edges of his vision, infiltrated into fading reason to lap at his tight hold on consciousness. Instinct guided Holt now, prompted the steady squeeze of curved trigger that summoned instant recoil in his palm, rocked him back.

Bereft of balance and sight, he went to his knees and the pistol slipped from his hand. Cacophony burst around him, a babble of indistinguishable sounds that melded into one continuous hum.

Dimly, he felt a vague sense of regret that he had not said farewell to his grandmother. She deserved better from him.

The shadows rushed him greedily, gray turned to black, claiming him even as he resisted. From a distance, he heard Stanfill calling his name, a sound like the rolling rush of ocean waves washing against sand, then oblivion.

Chapter 2

Tidewater, Virginia
1808

Brisk winds blew off the Atlantic, pungent with the spice of ocean salt and fresh water that spilled from the mouth of the James River; fragile fingers of sea-oats lay in a scalloped fringe along the curving shore, tickled by the winds to a light dance. Spindly loblolly pines, stands of oak and sweetgum staggered at intervals up the shoreline. Sandy marshes along the estuary nudged ragged banks into languid pools rich with aquatic life, and bluish spires of pickerel weed decorated receding banks of a small tributary.

Seventeen-year-old Amalie Courtland stood knee-deep in the water; a long-handled net sprouted from her small fist, and nondescript brown skirts were pulled between her thighs and tucked into the confines of a belt around her waist. She vibrated intensity, straight brows furrowed over her eyes as she focused on the water; silt stirred up by her bare feet clouded the surface. The salty pool sucked at the edges of a bank bristling with tall grasses.

Nestled underwater, blue crabs hid in grassy feet. A flash of movement alerted her to their hiding spot, and she bent, swept the net along the bottom, scraping them into the trap with an expertise born of experience.

Triumphant, she lifted the dripping scraper to the surface; angry crabs struggled against the confines.

"I knew I'd find you here," came the observation from the sandy bank, and she glanced up, not surprised to see her brother. Wind ruffled dark hair the same intense hue as her own; familiar features were a masculine version of the image she infrequently glimpsed in her own mirror.

A faint smile curved her mouth. She brandished the heavy net. "A little while in the shedding float and these will be ready to sell."

Christian did not answer but stepped into the shallows to help dump the net filled with crabs into a floating cage tied in the reeds. When it was done, he knelt on the bank to peer into the tank of woven willow. The straight slash of his brows lifted, and he shook his head with a grin that transformed his lean features from sober adult to youth.

"You've had a better day with a dip net than Master Covington has had with a hundred crab pots."

"I'm not surprised." She felt his glance, ignored it as she clambered up onto the bank. Her skirts were wet despite being tied up so high; she freed the tucked ends, gave them a shake to dislodge sand and debris. The soggy hem clung to bare ankles, a clammy weight of brown cotton. "Master Covington prefers indolence to industry when it comes to his own day's work."

Amusement edged Christian's reply: "A harsh assessment of his character."

"But true. Help me sort busters from peelers. I think there are a few softshells as well."

Silence marked their work as they separated blue crabs that had already begun to shed their old shells from crabs on the verge of shedding. The muted clack of pincers as the crustaceans scuttled busily about the tank was familiar.

"Look at them," Christian said with a laugh when they were done, "pulling each other back into the cage. Just when one makes it to the top, the others drag it back down."

"Rather like some people I know." Amalie stood up, scrubbed her hands down her skirts. For a moment, nothing was said. Overhead, gulls were feathery arrows, white-winged grace gliding on air currents; high, lilting cries drifted earthward.

It was quiet, a rare peace, when not far away lay the village of Newport News. Yet here it was desolate, barren, familiar. A reassuring constancy in her life, when all else was in turmoil.

"Did they send you after me?" Her abrupt question earned the answer she expected.

"Mistress Covington said it is not proper for a young lady to wander about unescorted. People will talk."

She snorted, an unladylike exclamation that would have earned rebuke if Mistress Covington heard it. "It's not often these days I have time to *wander about*. Besides, people always *talk*. About me. You. Mama and Papa. . . ."

Her words trailed into sudden silence; it was still awkward, painful to mention, devastating to remember.

Silence stretched thin, broken finally by the heavy beat of a heron's wings as it dove for a fish in the tidal pool. A loud *plash* made ripples widen, spreading out then fading as the heron came up several yards away, a fish wriggling in its beak as it took to the air.

Amalie looked at her brother, saw in his dark eyes the same anguish she felt, managed a smile that felt stiff and tortured on her lips.

"Mistress Covington can wait a bit longer. She'll forget why she sent you after me when she sees the crabs."

Clouds skimmed the sky, seaming ocean and horizon into a solid line; they walked to the beach, silent, familiar with the other's thoughts. Amalie sat upon a sandy hillock cushioned with grass, stretched out her legs in front of her, and gazed at the ocean.

Bare toes dug into sand heated by the sun, made small furrows like mouse tracks, warm against the soles of her feet. Booming surf crashed with rhythmic familiarity against the beach, scattering debris on sand and rock: bits of seaweed, shards of brine-soaked wood, a few shells glistened in the fading light. Foamy breakers rose, receded, vanished into the endless space of ocean again, ceaseless tide, mysterious, old as time—and as indifferent to human frailties and needs. Uncaring ocean, folding back on itself, disappearing into anonymity.

If only I could disappear as easily. . . .

Wind pushed back dark hair from her forehead, tangled silken skeins down her back. Green eyes narrowed against the prick of bright sunlight reflected on sand and water; lashes made lengthy shadows on cheeks that had acquired a faint gold sheen from frequent walks on the beach. Now her face was pinkened by wind and sorrow.

It dogged her days, invaded her nights when she should be asleep in her own familiar bed with her parents not far away. All gone, changed irrevocably in the blink of an eye, in the careless tilt of a coach wheel on a soft verge—an accident, it was said, but it seemed to her a monstrous act of Fate that left her and Christian alone, orphaned in a world that cared little for what happened to them. Six long months now. . . .

Nightmarish days rendered them bewildered, grieving for dead parents, then evicted from the only home they had known to be left at the mercy of indifferent authorities. Papa had not planned well, had not thought of death when he loved life so much . . . foolish, endearing man, too confident of his own future to consider such an abrupt end.

For Christian, it was different; he was almost of age. But she was left without prospects, dependent upon the Covingtons, a family with six children under the age of ten. She had a place to live, if not a warm welcome.

"We will endeavor to overcome the evil of their upbringing and endow them with a proper sense of God and all that is holy," Mistress Covington liked to say, a self-righteous smirk contorting her plain, gaunt features. "It will do them good to see how *decent*, God-fearing folk live."

Decent! As if Mama and Papa had been immoral, wicked people! *Oh, how I miss them!* No more joyous family outings, no ready laughter at silly things . . . gone, rent asunder in an instant to leave them bereft in a town peopled with reserved Tidewater inhabitants who had scorned Captain Courtland and his aloof, haughty wife.

Haughty? Mama? Not the woman she had known, a soft-spoken, often dreamy-eyed lady with a sometimes sad smile. It wasn't until after her death that Amalie had found the bundle of letters in a small teakwood box, correspondence that had ended long ago. A youthful Anna had penned words of longing, of wistful friendships severed by distance and disappointment, pouring out her heart in letters never sent; they were still carefully tied with a silk ribbon and locked away in the box with the few letters she had received. Poor Mama. Love for Papa had cost her dearly.

Christian hovered for a moment before he folded long legs to sit beside her on the flat stretch of sand; tall and gangly, the promise of manhood was yet awkward on his lanky frame. His boots pushed up grainy hillocks beneath scuffed heels; he smelled faintly of rich tobacco—and spirits.

"You've been at the docks again." Calm statement, not accusation, and her brother shrugged it off.

Lazily, he propped his weight on his elbows to regard her with arrogant affection. His posture was negligent and unconcerned. Wind pushed back his dark hair; light gleamed in eyes a riveting green as he grinned at her with masculine insolence. "You're becoming a scold, Amie."

"Don't call me that." She lifted a brow, gave him an imperious glance. "My name is Amalie."

"Amalie Sarah Anna Courtland—far too much name for a smidge of a girl no bigger than a gnat's foot."

It was true. She was thin, graceless, with skinny arms and legs, a despairing reality. Her mirror gave back relentless truth. Dark hair framed a face with high cheekbones, with green eyes slanted at the outer corners like a gypsy's, and her generous mouth was too large.

Christian leaned forward, teasing, "It will be all right, Amie. I'll take care of you when you're a spinster."

"How can you take care of me when you cannot even take care of yourself?" Bare toes dug into sand, propelled her to her feet. She shook grains from her skirts, spattering him in a stinging shower. "You are a man. Almost. No one will stop you if you want to escape. I am bound to stay with the Covingtons until I rot. I do not think I can bear it!"

Teasing lights faded, and his eyes narrowed slightly at the trembling emotion that was more than grief.

"What is it, Amie?"

A seagull screeched, swooped, a graceful drift of white in a lazy suspension against blue sky. Sparse tufts of sea-oats bent in a rustling whisper; wind pressed drab brown skirts against her legs, softly outlining slender thighs. She looked away from him, took a deep breath that pushed out the front of her gown. Plain cotton conformed to her body, rounded and firm over small breasts, flattened against the swell of belly and hips she considered despairingly angular.

"Amie." He surged to his feet, put a hand on her shoulder. Warm strength flowed from him, a comfort and a question: He hesitated, indecision written on his face, then said softly, "I miss them too. . . ."

Despair clogged her throat as she shook free his hand, took three steps away, sliding a little in the loose sand that swept to the sea. "It's not just that . . . I don't know what is the matter with me. I feel . . . I feel lately as if I am about to explode. I don't know why."

That isn't true—I know why. I have all these strange feelings inside me, but no one to talk to about them . . . oh, if only Mama were here! She would know how I feel, would know what to say to make it stop. . . .

She took another step away, caught up her skirts in one hand, pointed toes in powdery sand and made a pirouette that Mama had taught her. So long ago . . . ballroom dancing lessons in a small parlor, remnants of a life long past, the gentle pleasures of Mama's youth lent to her daughter with a poignancy she had not recognized then.

Closing her eyes, Amalie swayed to remembered melodies carefully plinked out on the old harpsichord in their parlor on winter mornings. She could almost smell the beeswax that made the furniture gleam, could hear her mother's laughing tones remonstrating that she was to step lightly, not stomp her feet like the militia: *Do you want men to fall in love with you, or fall over you, my darling?*

Sunlight was still warm on her face and bare arms, sand gritty and heated under her feet, flying up in spraying arcs as she danced over graceful tussocks, emulating the bend of the long grasses, arms over her head, moving to silent music and desperate sorrow.

Christian regarded her somberly. For the first time, he noticed female curves. When had that happened? Amie had always been his younger sister, sweet-natured, often a pest, but not to be regarded as—well, *womanly*. It was disconcerting.

She paused finally, breathless from her exertions, face flushed pink, sand-crusted skirts lifted to expose bare, slender legs to the knees. With her hair in disarray, freed from the confining braid and tumbled over one shoulder, she no longer resembled a child. In the slanted eyes lurked a female awareness that was startling. All his perceptions of her crumbled, disappeared like seafoam. He felt adrift, floating aimlessly without a rudder to steer his way.

He put out a hand, awkward and uncertain, then let it drop to say simply, "I'll help you carry the crabs."

They hid the shedding float among the tall grasses, away from prying eyes, and put only the crabs for Mistress Covington into a pail. By the time they reached the house, it was nearly dark. Lights blazed out from windows of the downstairs parlor that was never used. A strange carriage was drawn up at the gate; fading light gleamed on polished black leather and red-painted wheels.

Amalie drew in a sharp breath, put a hand on

his arm and squeezed tightly. "Kit—that carriage belongs to Master Dunbar. The barrister who told us about—Papa."

He exchanged a swift glance with her, put out a hand as if to shield her, then dropped it. "It is never good news that brings out men like Master Dunbar."

Christian set down the crab pail; live crabs scrabbled against the wooden sides, forgotten as the front door swung open and Master Covington was framed against the light behind him. Short, wide, he blocked out the view, so all that could be seen was his waistcoated figure topped by a bristle of thinning hair. He gestured to them.

"Past time for both of you to be back. Come into the house, please."

Apprehensive at this unusual courtesy from a man who preferred barking commands and direct orders to normal conversation or request, Kit found himself standing in front of his sister as if to protect her from a blow.

"What is it?"

"You'll see soon enough. Come inside."

Impatience edged his words this time, but still held a hint of deference that was totally unexpected.

When they entered the parlor, Kit's gaze went at once to Mistress Covington. She sat primly in a high-backed chair, spine as stiff and unyielding as her nature. She beckoned Amalie forward.

"Come here, child. Look at you—the stink of the sea on your gown and your shoes—I can imagine what you've been up to this time!"

"Wife," Covington cautioned with an ingratiating smile that only slightly wavered, "Squire Dunbar wants to speak with the youngsters."

"Yes," Dunbar interrupted, and rose to greet them. "It is expected that we will have privacy for our discussion, I presume, Master Covington."

"Privacy? Oh, to be certain, Squire, to be certain!"

It was obvious it had not occurred to Covington, and just as apparent that neither of them wanted to leave. But Dunbar was inflexible, remaining silent until they left the parlor. Then he crossed the room to close the door, pulled it firmly shut with a decisive click.

Turning, he regarded them gravely. Gray tufts of brow like a ledge shadowed deep-set eyes, and his long thin nose swelled into a bulb on the tip that quivered like the inquisitive snout of a small forest creature. Kit tried to look elsewhere, but his gaze returned involuntarily to the barrister's nose, lingered much longer than was polite.

Dunbar gestured with a curiously elegant hand, and Amie took a seat to stare up at him with eyes wide as saucers; the earlier impression of burgeoning maturity was vanquished by anxiety now, her mouth pressed into a firm line that betrayed her with an adolescent quiver.

"What brings you here after all this time, Master Dunbar? It has been over six months since—surely, Papa's estate is settled?"

"Most definitely." Wry amusement lit his eyes, altered his appearance from sharp to indulgent. "There was little enough estate to settle once outstanding debts were paid. Captain Courtland was a kind gentleman, but not farsighted in financial matters—but that is not why I am here."

He paused, cleared his throat, moved to stand by the hearth with its collection of cheap pottery arranged on the mantel. Two brass candlesticks nudged several china dogs, Mistress Covington's prized pieces purchased in Norfolk on their last visit.

Dunbar touched a blue-and-white dog with one finger, then turned to gaze at them from beneath the shelf of his brow. He put his hands behind his back, rocked forward on the balls of his feet, feet shifting slightly on the thin, worn carpet as his mouth curved into the caricature of a smile.

"I have received correspondence from your godmother. You are to join her in England as soon as arrangements are completed."

"Godmother?" Amie sounded bewildered, hesitant, and glanced up at Christian with a frown. "I do not understand what you mean. . . ."

"Understandably, this must be a shock to both of you. I was unaware until receiving her correspondence that the Lady Winford to whom I sent notice of your parents' deaths as stipulated in Captain Courtland's will is your godmother. A badly written will it was, too. He should have allowed me to draw it up properly, which only proves my contention that laymen should not act as their own attorneys. Ah well. It is behind us now. Yes, Lady Winford is your godmother, and has made the necessary arrangements to care for any children of your late mother. It is all proper, handled by her London barristers." He paused, glanced around the shabby parlor, then added kindly, "I think you will be much happier with Lady Winford than here."

Silence descended on the parlor; outside, muted noise of children could be heard, punctuated by an occasional bark from one of the dogs. But in the small, stuffy room with its collection of china dogs, there was only the faint rasping sound of quiet breathing.

Amalie sat very still, looking as fragile as one of the china statues, as if any movement would shatter her into a thousand pieces. Finally she said softly, "I think that will suit us quite well, Master Dunbar. *Quite* well."

Chapter 3

It was the sudden cessation of constant noise that woke her at last; only the rhythmic creaking of ropes penetrated a silence that was both heavy and oppressive.

Amalie stirred, a little dazed with sleep, and rolled to one side cautiously. The bunk was narrow, hardly more than a shelf with thin mattress; on the wall directly over it was a porthole beyond which only gray ocean waves stretched for miles. A greenish film clouded the thick glass, kept open until the interminable spray that dampened cabin and garments became more annoying than the lack of fresh air.

Then she would go up on deck, in a usually futile search for Kit. While she merely endured, he thrived on board the clumsy vessel. It was a tub of a ship, not at all the fast, sleek clipper that she would have preferred, but the Embargo Act of 1807 forbade American ships to sail to foreign ports, compelling them to take passage on a Dutch merchant ship instead. The *Success* originated in Holland, yet its captain was American, a subtle thwarting of the embargo restricting trade with Britain or France.

A nuisance, but necessary, Kit insisted, as the U.S. frigate *Chesapeake* had been fired upon by a British ship the year before, and several American seamen had been killed and others impressed into the Royal Navy.

"It all has to do with the French," he had explained, "as Napoleon closed French ports to the English. Now British regulations require any vessels going to ports closed by France to stop first at a British harbor and pay a duty on its cargo. It might not be so bad, but now the British are seizing ships that refuse to comply, and France seizes those that do. America is caught in the middle."

So now they were on a Dutch ship out of Newport News, bound for London.

It was still like a dream . . . after months of bleak despair, to learn that there was hope for their future was as rewarding as the realization they were to finally meet family. Well, *almost* family. The short personal note from Lady Winford was warm, extending a welcome to the dear children of her beloved goddaughter, Anna.

Amalie had tried to recall her mother mentioning Lady Winford, and thought she could remember a little; at the time, it had not made an impression. It was only later, rereading the letters tied with a silk ribbon and placed carefully in the teakwood box, that she had realized how very much they meant to Anna Courtland. Small pieces of trivial information were detailed, usually about ballgowns, outings in Hyde Park, or the newest pug dog. On some, the ink was faded, almost illegible in places, paper creased and worn, as if opened and read many times.

How little I knew her . . . how lonely she must have been, Amalie thought, with a tinge of sorrow for the mother she had not really known. Not that way. She had seen her only with the eyes of a child, never understanding the despair of a woman cast off by her family.

She lay quietly, watching a beam of light shift across the cabin floor, flecks of dust hazing the air. The ship rocked, rose on a swell, hung there a moment, then dropped into the trough between waves again. It was strangely quiet now, when usually there was the constant thud of feet, men's voices, and slap of wind pushing out canvas sails.

For the past three days, Kit had been too busy for her; he loved it aboard ship, though not at all certain he wanted to go to England.

"There's nothing there for me, Amie," he had admitted at last when she asked why he was so quiet about Lady Winford's generosity. "I have other plans for my life."

"But you will go, won't you?" She hadn't been able to keep the fret out of her voice, yielding to sudden panic at the thought of facing strangers alone. "I don't think I can bear it if you aren't with me."

He had been quiet for a moment, then sighed, put an arm on her shoulders and said, "I'll go."

Feelings of guilt were assuaged with the assurance that he really wanted to go, after all. Perhaps he only wanted to be coaxed, as when they were children and he sulked because of some trivial concern, until Mama or Papa teased him out of it.

Still, it had been a relief to see him so happy

at being on board a ship; he even looked the part of one of the crew when stripped to the waist with loose cotton trousers and bare feet, hauling ropes under the watchful, bemused gaze of the captain and his first mate.

Even the language he spoke was different, the phrases incomprehensible to her:

"Lift up the skin, put the slack of the clews into the bunt . . . haul the bunt well up on the yard, smooth the skin and bring it down well abaft. . . ."

Captain Yarbrough was indulgent with Kit as a paying passenger, but she had taken notice of his harshness with the crew. It would certainly not be the exciting, adventurous life Kit envisioned, but he dismissed her concerns with a shrug. It was inconceivable to her that he should find the stench of tar and irregular hours enthralling, but he did. Perhaps by the time they reached London, the novelty would have palled, and he would realize that life on the seas would not provide the life of adventure he craved, but more of drudgery.

A sudden lurch of the ship heaved her to one side of the bunk, and she clutched at the wooden post fastening it to the cabin wall. As the vessel righted, she swung her legs over the edge of the bunk, put her feet on the floor, and waited a moment to adjust to the constant motion.

She had learned to ride it a bit, bracing against the moment when it would rise beneath her like a living beast to lift her into the air with an eerie sensation of flying. She didn't mind that, but hated the abrupt drop when it seemed as if she remained airborne an instant too long, then the swift crunch as her body settled, always in the wrong place.

Sighing, she grabbed at the back of a chair, felt it slide away from her, and fumbled for the table edge; it was bolted to the floor, a stable object in an unstable world.

Above, feet thundered heavily against planks, orders were shouted, and a whistle piped. She clung to the table, reached for the gown draped from a peg on the wall. The cabin was so small she could almost touch all four walls by standing in the middle and stretching out her arms.

It was growing warm now, heat seeping down from the upper decks, bringing with it the pungent scent of cargo; cinnamon and cedar were recognizable, an aromatic blend bound for the London docks. The hold was filled with rich carpets, spices, wood, and other goods, Kit had told her, a variety that would bring the Dutch shipping company a tidy profit, once sold in England.

Struggling, Amalie managed to wriggle into her gown, then swept her loose hair into a single twist over one shoulder. A tiny square of polished tin was the only mirror, hardly necessary, but a luxury in a cabin with the barest of conveniences. The chamber pot was stowed behind a small sliding door in the wall, an embarrassing necessity the first time she'd used it and set it outside her door as instructed. It was awkward being the only female on an entire ship filled with men; eyes followed her every time she went above deck.

Dressed at last, she crossed the dipping floor to open the door. A narrow ladder led from the passageway to the main deck, the square of light above her a beacon to guide her from the musty shadows. As she reached the top, blinking against the strong light and press of wind, she was struck by the air of frenetic motion.

"Amie—"

She turned blindly, squinting as her eyes adjusted, and saw Kit loom in front of her. He put a hand on her shoulder, gave her a little shove downward.

"Get back below for now."

"No." She shrugged off his hand, a bit irritated at his domineering attitude since they had been aboard. "I have not eaten, and I'm tired of staying in my stuffy cabin. Besides, if you—"

"Amie. . . ." He caught her arm, urgency penetrating his tone. "There is no time to argue, dammit. Go to your cabin and bolt the door."

"Bolt—?" She looked beyond him, recognized now grim purpose in the activity on deck. Guns were being wheeled to the rail, fastened into place, decks sanded and sails unfurled. Her fingers tightened on the rail of the ladder. "Kit, what is it?"

"The captain isn't sure. The lookout spied a ship approaching under full sail. It isn't flying colors yet, so he cannot be certain. . . ."

"Cannot be certain of what?"

He looked away, frowned, then glanced back at her. "Pirates. We are only a few days out of Newport News, so it's most likely nothing more than another merchant ship. Still, Captain Yarbrough is cautious."

Crewmen in various stages of panic scurried over decks, scrambled up rope rigging, and hauled lines, loosing sails to catch the wind; cargo was strapped down.

"So I see." She hesitated, caught his gaze, put a hand on his arm; muscles tensed beneath her fingers, and she knew he expected her to plead with him to hide with her. Instead, she said softly, "Be careful, Kit. You're all I have left."

He lay a hand gently against her cheek, the backs of his fingers curled on the cushioned curve of skin and bone, and smiled. "I'll be fine. Don't worry about me."

She wondered, as she went back below and bolted her cabin door, how many wives, sisters, mothers had heard those very words. It was chilling to consider.

Amalie huddled, apprehensive and with growing fright, as the *Success* plowed through waves with growing speed; she had grown up in a coastal town, knew all about pirates, had heard tales her entire life. Some were legend, like Cook and Blackbeard, delicious terror incited at the mention of their names. The reality, however, was far worse, the facts of their depredations glossed by fictional deeds of heroism that made them seem not so evil, but more like naughty boys playing at dangerous games.

Yet she discerned the truth from the fiction, and hoped that the approaching vessel was no more than a passing brig or schooner. After the recent law prohibiting slave trade, slave ships and pirates had been swept clean of these waters, pursued by government cutters until it was safe once more to sail the Atlantic. The worst that might happen, was that the ship would turn out to be French, at war with Britain, and in no mood to be charitable to any vessel breaking their embargo on English ports. Yet they were still so close to American shores. . . .

A thundering broadside erased any thought that the ship was friendly; the *Success* rocked wildly, shuddered as the huge guns on deck fired a reply. Amalie fell forward, went to her knees on the pitching floor of the deck, curled her fingers into wood, and panted with fear. Her ears hummed, assaulted with terrible alien noises, cries, and grunts, the dreadful booming of guns, and distant thudding splashes . . . it was a nightmare, conjured from too many tales told round a fire at night while winter winds whistled down the chimney.

Terror gripped her, an urgency that prodded her to action, to anything but waiting in the belly of a ship for it to slide beneath the waves. If she was to die, she would rather be with her brother when death came.

Lurching to her feet, stumbling, grabbing at anything to remain upright, she made her way to the door, fumbled at the bolt, slid it back, and swung open the door. Immediately, smoke and sulphur stung her eyes and nose, a thick fog like clouds rolling down the open hatch and into the narrow, dank passageway. Only a vague square of light could be seen above now, and she moved toward it, heart pounding so loudly she could hear it above the rattling roar of guns.

Feet like lead shuffled across bucking planks toward the ladder, and she reached for it, fingers closing around a thick wooden rung when the light from above was suddenly darkened, obliterated. Instinctively she fell back, pressed her spine against the damp wall, blinked in confusion as a heavy bundle of rags plummeted through the hatch to land at her feet with a sickening thud.

She thought she heard someone scream, but her throat had closed on any sound; haze shifted, dissipated, and the bundle of rags took form, coalescing into the shape of a man. Head flung back, eyes stared up at nothing, glazed in death, his mouth open, and blood a bright crimson gash across his throat and chest.

Nausea rose, stung her throat and nose, heaving in her belly as she fought for control. Tears stung her eyes from the effort, and she moved on shaky legs past the poor devil on the decking, scaled the ladder to the top, driven by the need to know that her brother was not sprawled in his own blood, his life seeping away.

Pandemonium greeted her as she emerged from the hatch, a scene straight from hell. Sulphurous smoke wreathed the deck in thick layers, lending a nightmarish quality to the sight of dead and dying men, the bright orange and yellow flares like tongues of flame licking at the sea. Reeling as the ship pitched, she grabbed at a line to keep her balance, felt it come loose in her hands and slither to the deck in a coiling slide like a striking snake. Rigging severed by the blast of pirate guns hung frayed and ragged overhead, draped across the deck in a hazardous tangle to trip men.

She coughed, choked, forced her way across the littered deck in a desperate search for Kit. None of the men looked familiar, sweaty, soot-streaked, working feverishly at loading guns, powder burns leaving painful red streaks on bare arms and chests.

Sliding on something slick, she did not look down, not wanting to know what it was as she worked a path over strewn belaying pins, smashed wood, and limp forms. When she found Kit, he was standing by one of the huge twenty-four-pound guns, looking grim and intent as he helped the gunner.

"Kit. . . ."

She thought he had not heard, for it seemed as if his name came out in only a rusty croak, but he glanced up, saw her, and immediately left the belching gun.

"What are you doing up here? I told you—"

"I don't want to die alone."

Black soot smeared his face, sweat-grimed and thick. He put a hand out, took her arm, pulled her to him. She felt the trembling vibration in him, knew he was as frightened as she was, and the realization was suddenly calming.

"At least we are together," she said, and saw in his eyes a spark of anguish.

"Yes. Listen to me, Amie, I want you to hide behind those barrels. Don't come out until I tell you to—or until you know you must." He put a quick hand on her cheek, a soft stroke, and managed a smile. "We may come through this yet. Don't count us out. Yarbrough's an old hand at this, and we're still afloat. I have to get back—the main gunner is dead, and they need all the hands they can get."

It was agony, hiding behind wooden barrels lashed to the deckhouse with ropes, watching

Christian work the gun, a little slower than the rest, but efficient enough.

Dampened by sea spray, choking on smoke, Amalie huddled in fear, unable to tell which way the battle went as it raged interminably. It seemed like hours—days—before it ended, not with a resounding bang, but with a final whimper.

When the pirate ship sidled close, grappling hooks dug into wooden rails and men clambered aboard the *Success* in a jubilant wave. Resistance was brief and decisive; numb with fear and despair, she watched as the men were rounded up to the middle of the deck. It was quiet now, smoke drifting in gauzy layers across the deck, smearing the air with sulphur.

Kit went quietly, not glancing toward the barrels where she hid, his stiff posture a warning and appeal to her to remain out of sight. The smell of charred oak was rife, rough wood beneath her palms abrasive as she leaned forward in an effort to see, anxiety raking across nerves stretched taut enough to snap.

Inaudible orders were given, only an occasional word distinguishable where she hid, and she crouched with aching muscles, afraid to move, paralyzed with the certainty that she would have to emerge before long. It was inevitable that she would be found; where was there to hide aboard a ship? And could she sit quietly if Kit—

Her mind refused to travel there, to the possibility that he might be harmed. It was inconceivable.

Laughter came in snatches of sound, rough

and cruel, and a man cried out before his shriek died with an abrupt gurgle. She put her hands over her ears, squeezed her eyes tightly shut, strained to hear a familiar voice.

It was Captain Yarbrough she recognized, however, his tone a cool reply. More laughter sounded, broken by the thud of cargo and scrape of iron tackle on decking. Ropes creaked and groaned, and the skid of two ships bound by grappling hooks was a loud screech that sounded almost human.

Her heart thudded; perhaps they would just take the cargo and leave. It was possible. *Please, God, just let them go and leave us alone . . .*

But that prayer was swiftly denied, hope crushed by the swarm of men over the ship. Inevitable that they should find her; a laughing discovery, delight etched in his teak-brown features as the pirate pulled her from behind the barrels to drag her to the main deck.

Coarse laughter, avid eyes, a glance of resignation from Yarbrough before her gaze found Kit, caught his eyes with a beseeching despair that prompted him to step forward.

"Leave her alone!"

Astonished mockery answered his demand, and one of the pirates pushed him roughly to his knees, a wicked blade held at his back to keep him there.

One man, broad of shoulder, garbed in red satin coat and breeches that were incongruous with the brace of pistols slung across his chest, was obviously the captain of this piratical band; he regarded Amalie with a dispassionate black gaze, then turned to Kit.

"Is she your wife?"

Kit shook his head; his mouth thinned to a taut slash in his face. "No. My sister."

"Ah. Your sister." A faint smile touched edges of the hard mouth, and he gestured to the man holding her. "Bring her to me. Yes, come here, my pretty. You seem frightened. Do you think we will hurt you?"

Coarse laughter rippled through the ranks of men, those who were not transferring cargo to the pirate ship crowding closer, eyes greedy and hot. As Amalie was prodded forward, her unwilling feet stumbling over charred rope on the deck, several suggestions were made as to her fate, some of them couched in terms she could only decipher by the expression on Kit's face and the calm protest from Captain Yarbrough that she was a young lady of quality, not accustomed to the vulgar talk and touch of a man.

"Ah, you are a virgin, then, are you?" the pirate captain said softly, and put a hand out to trace her cheek. She trembled under his touch, repulsed and terrified.

No man had ever spoken to her like that, or looked at her as these men were doing, as if she were a toy for their entertainment.

"Take 'er wi' us, Cap'n Jack," one of the pirates said with a leer, "an' we can teach 'er a blanket jig."

"Yes, I imagine we could." Captain Jack's hand fell away from her face; he studied her a moment in the fading light and smoke, his dark eyes hooded and a faint smile on his mouth.

Amalie had not spoken, uncertain if her lips would even form words without breaking into sobs; the hand on her arm was tight, the grip cruel and unyielding. There was nowhere to run, nowhere to turn, even if she could find the courage.

When the pirate holding her shifted, his free hand moving to graze her throat, then spread down to her breast, she tried to shake free but was held fast. Hot breath that smelled sour wafted over her cheek, and the pirate captain watched impassively as her captor cupped her breast in one hand, squeezed painfully until she cried out.

Christian jerked free, surged to his feet, lunged at the man holding her. Two pirates leaped in a half scramble and grab for weapons, putting hands on him to hold him. A blade flashed in sunlight, a yellow glow that cast faces in harsh light and shadow, gleamed on the weapon as Amalie cried out a warning.

"Kit, no! Oh God no, it's all right . . . don't hurt him—please don't hurt him. . . ."

To her relief, Captain Jack put out a restraining hand, waved the men back, though they still held Christian fast, forced him again to his knees, head jerked back with fists tangled in his dark hair, baring his throat.

"Touch her and I'll kill you!" he raged, panting, eyes hot with frustration and fury.

The pirate leader laughed. "You are rather at a disadvantage, young master. It seems that we have the upper hand at the moment, in sheer number, if nothing else. Now here, let us reconsider, shall we?"

Even in the midst of her terror, Amalie recognized the tone of control, the clear enunciation of education, and had a brief, wild hope that the pirate had once been a gentleman.

Was it too much to hope that he might listen to reason? To a calm plea for mercy?

"Captain," she said, dragging his attention back from Christian, "my brother and I are orphans, alone in this world save for each other. Do not fault him for wanting to protect me, for he is accustomed to it."

"Is he, now?" Impassive eyes flicked toward the men loading cargo, surveyed the debris and bodies littering the decks, then returned to Amalie. "Would he make *any* sacrifice for his sister, do you think?"

She hesitated. Behind the curved mouth and impassive eyes lurked a malevolent purpose. The impression of him as a former gentleman was swiftly revised, altered to the sinking realization that he was a pirate, after all, a leader of men accustomed to murder and thievery. How naive she was, to think she could negotiate with a man who possessed no honor.

"Yes," Christian snarled before she could reply, "I would do anything to keep her safe from swine!"

Captain Jack barely flicked a glance at him, his gaze still on Amalie. "How old are you, child?"

A hesitation, torn between truth and deception, then a grudging admission as she realized it would make little difference, "Seventeen last September."

Close scrutiny made her flush as his eyes raked over her, lingering on her breasts a moment, then moving to her face again. "Seventeen. Nearly a woman. Many maids are wed at your age, with a babe or two clinging to their skirts."

She did not answer. The deck lifted, ship rising on a swell, and the pirate ship bumped against it with a scraping screech of wood on wood. Captain Jack turned, gestured, and Kit was hauled to his feet, hands balled into fists at his sides. A cord was swiftly looped around his neck, pulled tight so that it dug into his flesh, but did not strangle him.

It was suddenly quiet on deck, a heavy silence that was ominous and expectant. A chill shivered down her spine, turned her blood cold; Amalie stared in horror, helpless and agonized as the pirate leader stepped close to her brother, his voice a soft mockery.

"Young master, you speak boldly. Let us see if your courage matches your tongue. Several of our number have been killed today—do you have the mettle to live aboard a ship flying our colors, or do you prefer to allow your sweet sister to join us instead?" His glance toward her was light with mockery, his tone lazy. "Women aboard ship are known to be bad luck, as was proven today, I believe, and even if only idle superstition, women provide too much distraction and inevitable arguments. I would prefer a willing hand to a squalling female. What say you—are you man enough to take her place?"

Christian met his eyes, a steady gaze that belied the shaking of his hands. The cord around his throat made his voice hoarse, rusty: "I will go with you, though I never thought to put to sea with pirates instead of true sailors."

Captain Jack looked around him with an amused curl of his lip. "True sailors? If you refer to these poor sods, you will soon learn better. Captain Yarbrough is not unknown to me, a harsh taskmaster, it is said, who prefers flogging a man to death rather than straining the quality of mercy. But you will learn, you will learn. Lively, now, boys, put him aboard, with any other unmarried man who would rather live free than as slave to the unlikely compassion of a merchant captain."

Disbelief welled in her, and Amalie surged forward, grabbing at the pirate leader's arm. "No! Do not take him, I beg of you. . . ."

"I do not take him unwillingly. He was given a choice." Brittle light glittered in his eyes, the curve of his mouth a cruel mockery. "Should you care to take his place, my crew would prefer you to him, for however brief a time you might survive."

"Amie—" Freed from the cord around his neck, Christian came to her, took her arm, his hand cold and shaking as he drew her into his embrace. "I will get word to you as soon as I can," he murmured into her ear, fingers splayed against the back of her head to hold her hard against him.

She felt his heart pound in his chest, the slight quiver of his hand stroking her hair with awkward, clumsy comfort, and recognized that he was as terrified as was she . . . oh, it was too much to bear!

Clinging to him, she could not speak for the lump in her throat, the heavy weight in her chest an acute pain like a sharp blade.

And then he was gone, over the rail to the pirate vessel breaking free, prow rising on a swell as wind filled canvas sails with a hollow thumping sound. There was no sign of him as the *Success* pulled away, crewmen scrambling to clear the decks, reef sail and shroud bodies to put into the sea.

Vaguely aware of the activity around her, Amalie stood at the rail long after the pirate ship had disappeared on the horizon, until finally Captain Yarbrough escorted her gently from the deck to her cabin below, forced a cup of brandy to her mouth, and waited until she had emptied it.

"He's young," Yarbrough said heavily, "and strong. He is not the first lad impressed into the service of pirates. If lucky, he can escape soon enough."

With her empty stomach heated by the potent brandy, she felt lightheaded, dizzy. She looked up, fingers still curled around the tin cup. "And if he is not lucky?"

There was no answer, and she closed her eyes. After a moment, she heard the cabin door close behind the captain. Alone, she thought that this was much worse than when her parents had died, for at least she had known them at peace. Oh God, what would happen to Kit now? It was her fault, for forcing him to come with her when he wanted to stay behind . . . grief welled, choking her, and tears flowed at last, silent and futile.

It was a long time before she slept, only to dream, of days when life had been kind.

Chapter 4

London was much larger than Amalie had ever dreamed it would be, and dirtier, with a haze of soot from chimneypots hanging above the city like thunderclouds. A gentle rain that was more of a mist fell, drowning the light, though it was only early afternoon. She stared out the window of the coach as it rocked along narrow streets, leaving the chaos of the waterfront behind.

A carriage had been sent to the docks to meet her, "Every day for the past week, Miss," the coachman, a kindly man with a round face and pleasant smile, had said to her when he met the *Success* as it limped into port. "Lady Winford began to worry."

"An extra week was less than it could have been, with tattered sails and a short crew," Captain Yarbrough declared, with a smile of satisfaction that was as enraging as it was peculiar. How could he consider the voyage a success when his cargo was stolen, his crew impressed into piracy, and his vessel damaged? It was a miracle they had survived at all, and she might never see Christian again—it might not mean much to anyone else, but she felt as if she would never be able to smile again.

Now, perched upon luxurious velvet squabs inside a coach of gleaming black with a driver on top and two footmen clinging to the boot, she thought how much Kit would have relished this. Familiar grief rose, was pushed down with determination, too painful to acknowledge.

As a diversion, she tried to determine the nature of the tall, impressive buildings they passed, with towering spires and ornate cornices, some obviously churches, others not so obvious in design.

Finally the coach came to a halt on a quiet street lined with tall, elegant houses. Feeling very much the country mouse, Amalie leaned back so the coachman would not see her with her nose pressed against the glass like a bumpkin, and waited. In a moment, the door opened and the step was set down for her. Stiffly, her feet found the narrow steps, her balance still uncertain on land after so many weeks at sea.

A helping hand was offered and she took it, glad of the valise she carried that helped hide the nervous quiver of her hands. Suddenly she was afraid of meeting this Lady Winford who had offered a new life to two strangers. In the weeks after the pirates had taken Kit, she had spent hours in thought, trying to make sense out of the recent tragedies.

Perhaps Lady Winford was alone and lonely, as she was now, with no one else in the world to care for and who cared for her. It would be nice if they could be friends, if she could repay somehow the generosity that had changed her life.

Yet she was terrified as well, afraid she would be a disappointment, that Lady Winford would find her unsuitable in some way—or be like the Covingtons, only wanting free servants. What a terrible thing it was, to be dependent upon the kindness of strangers.

"Miss, if you will come with me?"

One of the footman waited, polite, but with a guarded expression on his face, as if not quite certain what to make of her.

Amalie gathered her courage and dignity, inclined her head with distant courtesy, as she had seen her mother do to ladies of the village when they gawked at her rudely, and moved past him up the short walk to the door. The other footman rapped firmly, and the door swung open immediately, as if they were waiting for her arrival.

A silver-haired man clad in black coat and trousers stepped to one side, greeting her, "Welcome, Miss Courtland. We have been expecting you."

"Yes, thank you." She hesitated, uncertain how to address him, for it had been so long since Mama had taught her etiquette. And of course, there had been no reason then to think she would ever have a use for such rules, for Captain Courtland was only an officer in the American Army, and his family did not get invited to homes where servants wore evening dress in the daytime.

Gleaming white-and-black tile floor met her eyes as she stepped into the entrance hall; a wide staircase at the far end swept up to the second floor. The scent of lemon oil and beeswax was rife, everything bright and clean and shining as if new. The man holding the door cleared his throat softly and she flushed, realizing that she was barring his effort to close it by gawking in the portal.

Heat rose in her face, burning cheeks and eyes. What a goose she must seem!

"Shall I take your valise and cloak, Miss Courtland?" he asked, when she entered and he closed the door with a discreet click. His voice was cool, cultured, with precise diction.

"No." It seemed rude not to qualify her refusal, and she added lamely, "I—am chilled from the damp."

"Lady Winford will be down shortly," the man said in the same cool monotone, "and has directed that you should be served refreshment in the parlor."

He seemed to expect that she follow him, and she did, feeling more intimidated by the moment as their footsteps echoed with ringing clicks on slick floors. She felt very young, very simple, and very uncomfortable as she followed him. How did she ask his name? Or did she? Did one address servants familiarly? And he might not even be a servant, but an old uncle, or family friend. . . .

"Lucy will see to your trunks, Miss Courtland," he said, as he paused in a doorway, his stance indicating that she was to precede him into the room, "and Dora will serve you refreshment. Is there anything you require?"

"No—" The single word came out in a husky quiver, and she stifled a nervous burst of laughter. *Lucy* would not find any trunks to *see to*, as all she owned was in the valise she still held. But she had no intention of saying anything so gauche, and cleared her throat to say firmly, "No, thank you. I will wait here for Lady Winford."

A faint smile pressed at the corners of his austere mouth, and he inclined his head slightly in acknowledgment. "Very good, Miss. Should you require anything before Lady Winford arrives, you may ring for it." When she did not reply, he nodded toward a tapestry banner hanging discreetly against the wall by the fireplace. "Just use the bell pull should you need it."

Then he was gone, and she was alone in the parlor. A fire generated heat under a marble mantel that bore a huge gilt clock; tiny china figurines that were far different from the cheap china dogs that Mistress Covington collected lined the mantel. They were dainty, delicate, too fragile to touch, and she contented herself with distant admiration. Her feet were cushioned by thick wool, a carpet of intricate pattern and rich color covering the floor. Several couches and upholstered chairs offered comfort, and crystal lamps on gleaming tables shed soft light. Heavy draperies framed tall windows across one wall, holding back gray light. Gilt-framed paintings hung on panelled walls, landscapes and cherubs seeming to be a favorite subject.

Ill at ease, uncertain and nervous, she set her valise on the carpet by a chair, then moved across the room to gaze at a painting of a woman and cherub; it was lovely, invoking a deep sense of appreciation for the artist. She leaned close to inspect it, touched the ornate frame with a finger.

"The Snake in the Garden."

Startled by the masculine voice and comment, she whirled around, blinking. Silhouetted against the brighter gray of window light, a shadowed figure took a casual step forward, then paused, still dark against the light.

Amalie was unwillingly reminded of pirates, with no good reason for it. Apprehension rose, rendered her mute. In the heavy silence, the clock on the mantle loudly hummed away the time. She felt his eyes on her, a faint gleam in shadow, his voice faintly mocking and a bit impatient.

"The painting. It's called 'The Snake in the Garden.' By Sir Joshua Reynolds. Rather appropriate, I think. Were you admiring it, or planning to steal it?"

Appalled, she sucked in a sharp breath, not knowing how to answer the insulting accusation.

He moved into a pool of light that illuminated only one side, leaving half his face in shadow. She had a brief impression of height and sardonic amusement, felt his raking scrutiny and heard the contempt in his tone.

"Since you are hardly the sort of female who usually comes for tea, I can only assume that you are here to steal it, little gypsy. I might warn you that it would be a singularly foolish error, but then, it might amuse me to see how you plan to get it from the parlor. It's quite heavy, you see.

"Ah, no," he said, when she made an abortive move as if to leave, "that would be just as unwise. You will stay right where you are until I have summoned the Watch to take you away."

Dismay filled her, replacing outrage with the dawning realization that he thought her a thief. A thief! If she were not so weary and frightened, perhaps she would just laugh and explain who she was, but the strain of the past weeks coalesced into a tight knot of distress that held her in its grip.

Amalie could only stare at him, her feet lead weights and any coherent explanation unformed. Not even when he took another step toward her, moving as stiffly as a marionette, did she move or speak, but stood silent.

Until he put a hand on her.

It was only a light touch, warm and not harsh on her shoulder, but the flashing memory of the pirates returned in a rush to ignite panicked outrage. For an instant, she was on board the *Success* again, subjected to the indignity and terror of the pirates, of the hand on her throat and breast, hot and heavy, a threat.

All the pent-up terror and rage of the past weeks were in the vicious shove she gave him, the heels of her hands a sharp force against his ribs, catching him by surprise and sending him several steps backward. He bent double with a grunt of pain.

Panting, near hysteria, she said through clenched teeth, "Do not *dare* touch me! Ever! I am not a plaything—"

"Damn . . . little bitch!"

The menace in his curse penetrated her hysteria like a dash of icy water. She paused, then backed away as he let out an unsteady breath and slowly straightened, and in the light from the lamp she saw the ferocity in his face. It sent a chill down her spine, fingers of fear motivating her to retreat. Would anyone hear her if she screamed?

Three more steps took her up against the wall by the fireplace, cool marble unyielding on one side, a table on the other. Something dangled next to her, a narrow strip of tapestry that she recognized as the bell pull. Her hand closed around it, yanked frantically, once, twice, three times, but there was no sound of a pealing bell, nothing but the advancing threat of her accuser. She tugged again.

"Stop pulling that, or you'll have the entire staff up here with fire buckets," he grated, and reached for her.

Desperate, she gave it another wild tug, then ducked under his outstretched arm. But he was too quick for her, catching her, swinging her about, and shoving her up against the wall again, one arm holding her easily despite her struggles.

At last she screamed, a ripping sound that hurt her throat and made him swear again. Frantic now, she kicked at him, and he caught her by both shoulders and leaned into her, pinning her like a butterfly against the wall.

"For a thief," he muttered, "you show a remarkable lack of self-preservation."

"I am *not* a thief!" She freed one hand, aimed it at his head, a glancing blow that he easily avoided. He snared her free hand, imprisoning both her wrists with a harsh grip, his fingers squeezing until she gasped with the pain.

"Be still. I have no desire to hurt you, but it will be inevitable if you continue to struggle.

Here. Let's get this ridiculous hat off you so I can see your face. . . ."

His fingers were swift efficiency, tugging at the strings tied beneath her chin, pulling the bonnet free to toss it aside in a careless twist. She felt the burn of his eyes on her, but refused to look up, smarting under the lash of contempt, terrified of what he might do.

"Foolish chit . . . who sent you here? What are you really looking for? Christ almighty, they pick children to do their dirty work for them now!"

It was difficult to breathe with his weight leaning into her, pressing her against the wall, his face only inches from hers. He smelled faintly of tobacco, an elusive fragrance that a native Virginian would recognize anywhere, rich and aromatic, a good quality. His eyes were narrowed, dark beneath his lashes—black, pitiless pools. She forced her body to relax, head tilting back against the wall.

Her hair had come loose from the neat braid she had pinned atop her head that morning, an effort to make herself as presentable as possible. Now it straggled around her face as she faced this madman—it was obvious that he lived here, just as obvious that he expected something to be stolen from him.

If not so weary and frightened, she might have been more curious. But now she was intent only upon escape, flight from this parlor an imperative.

He was staring down at her, his face oddly pale beneath normal color, and deep grooves framed his mouth, set as if he was in pain. Brows were a black slash over his eyes, dark menace in his probing gaze.

"Who sent you?" he demanded again, softer this time, but no less determined. His hand came up, cradled her jaw in spread thumb and fingers, held her face still. "You're not the sort I would think they'd send. But then, I made the mistake of underestimating them before, and it cost me two good men."

Confused, she put out a tongue to wet her lips, to deny that anyone had sent her, but his hand on her jaw increased the pressure until her face began to ache. Beneath the soft, silky purr, menace vibrated, deadly and terrifying. Tension knotted her stomach, made her heart pound so loud she was certain he must be able to hear it . . . a terrible weakness oozed through her, made her legs tremble and the hands in his harsh grip quiver uncontrollably.

Finally, she got out between pinched lips, "No one sent me . . . no one."

"Little liar. I suppose you mean to tell me you walked in through the front door. Hardly the sort Baxter would allow in, I think."

Chagrin raced through her, heated her face, scoured her with shame. She knew how she looked: dowdy in a simple blue gown of light cotton, suitable for shipboard but not London society, of course, inexpensive and plain. But she was clean and neat, her shoes of good quality and her upbringing that of a young lady, not a common thief.

Summoning her scattered wits, she managed to say, "Yet he did allow me in. Ask him."

"A ready bluff," he said coolly, and straightened. "I intend to do just that."

As his grip finally eased, she seized the moment and pulled free, evading him as she raced toward the door. It was half-open, and she grabbed for it just as a blur of white and clink of metal appeared on the other side.

Even as she plunged through the door, she recognized a startled female face with a teapot on a tray, but it was too late to stop. She collided with the maid, sending silver tray, hot tea, cups, and cake to the gleaming floor in a tremendous clatter of breaking crockery and metal plate.

At that moment, doors burst open and the entrance hall filled with chaos: uniformed men and women, a babble of voices all speaking at once, punctuated by what sounded like a hundred yapping dogs. Bundles of fur exploded into the hall, accompanied by an irritated demand to know what the blazes was going on, and "Is there a fire?"

"Who rang the bell like that . . . ?"

"Where is Baxter when he's needed?"

"I am here, my lady," came the unruffled reply, though the silver-haired man who had admitted Amalie to the house wore an expression of dismay and astonishment. "I believe Miss Courtland must have rung. . . ."

All eyes turned to her. She stood rooted to the marble floor, aware of how she must look as she searched for words to explain.

It was unnecessary.

Behind Amalie, a sardonic voice said, "Ah, can it be that your Colonial has arrived after all, Grandmère?"

Grandmère? She turned, stared in horror at the man leaning in the open door to the parlor; he regarded her with hooded eyes, a faint curl of his mouth acknowledging her alarm.

As everyone turned to look at him, the noise abated, so that there was only the incessant yapping of what looked to be dozens of small, furry dogs with curly tails and snubbed muzzles.

Only Lady Winford seemed unfazed, moving through the tangle of dogs and servants to greet Amalie. "Oh my, you are much older than I thought. Rather inconvenient. Baxter will have to return so many clothes. I see you've met my grandson. Do not glower, Holt. I will explain all later. You were hardly in any condition to be bothered with such details."

Amalie was very aware of him staring at her; eyes she had thought black were a dark blue glint in the light, but no less hostile. Moving stiffly, he gave his grandmother an ironic bow, then turned to fix Amalie with a cool gaze.

"We will meet again, Miss Courtland," he said, and stalked across the entrance hall to disappear through a doorway.

Lady Winford smiled reassuringly. "He's not so fierce as he seems. He is recovering from an accident, and rather disagreeable at the moment. *Down*, Toby! Now, come along, and Lucy will show you to your room—*stop that*, Sophy! Baxter, do let the little darlings back into the garden. I am afraid this is a bit overwhelming for Miss Courtland—may I call you Amalie? It was your grandmother's name, you know."

"No," she said faintly, "I didn't. Yes, of course

you may call me Amalie, if it pleases you, my lady."

"None of that, now. You may call me—Grandmamma. Yes, that will do nicely. But wait—aren't there two of you? Where is your brother? Isn't there a boy, Baxter? I was certain the letter said there were two children. . . ."

"Yes, my lady, it did indeed. It is my understanding that there was an *incident* aboard ship. I am certain Miss Courtland will explain it all to you when she has rested."

"Oh yes, of course." Behind the swift spate of chatter, kind eyes regarded Amalie with unexpected shrewdness. "Poor child. Come along. After you are settled in, we will have a long chat. You are the image of your mother, I think, though it was so long ago when I saw her last . . . you must have more tea."

Numbly, Amalie followed Lady Winford while the dogs were shooed outside and one of the maids knelt on the black-and-white floor to clean up shards of crockery and smashed cake. It was a most bewildering arrival; more bewildering even than Lady Winford's habit of leaping from topic to topic without a breath between was the unexpected hostility from her grandson.

Yet, Lady Winford—*Grandmamma*—made an obvious effort to smooth over her grandson's rudeness as they moved through a confusing succession of hallways.

"This will be your chamber," the dowager said, showing her to a spacious room in the west wing of the house. It was obvious from the toys and dolls set carefully about the room that they had expected a much younger visitor, a child.

Lace dresses were draped over a chair, pretty garments far too small for Amalie. She stood a bit uncertainly until Lady Winford turned, smiled softly as she assured, "I am quite pleased that you are older. If you do not like this chamber, we will find you another. But I thought you might like this because it has a view of the gardens. I love the gardens—oh, look, there are my precious beauties. See them below?"

Dutifully, Amalie moved to the window, gazed out to view neatly trimmed hedges, flower beds in brilliant bloom, and a seething mass of dogs.

"Yes," she said, "I see them. Are they all yours?"

"Oh my, yes . . . it's cruel the way some people cast off an animal when it begins to bore them, never thinking it has feelings. I take them when no one wants them. At first, I thought I might find them homes, but that is not so easy to do at times. And people are so careless. Quite so." She glanced at her, smiled and said softly, "But we can talk later. Do you like this chamber? Good. The bed is quite comfortable, I am told. Lie down, and I will have Lucy bring you tea. Dinner is at nine, if you are up to it. If not, I will see you in the morning."

Feeling rather as if she had been sucked up into a brisk wind and then deposited in a strange land, Amalie managed a smile and a nod, uncertain whether she should express her gratitude for Lady Winford's concern.

At the doorway, the dowager paused, turned back, and said warmly, "I am very glad you came to stay, my dear. I get lonely at times."

Before she could form a reply, the door closed softly behind her, and Amalie stared at it with swimming eyes. It was just as well Lady Winford left when she did, because any attempt at a response would have ended in embarrassing tears. She turned back to the window, gazed out without seeing the lovely garden.

If only Kit were here . . . then I think we could be happy. But he was not there, and she did not know if she could be happy when he might be suffering.

Pressing her forehead against the window glass, she closed her eyes a moment, shuddered at the spasm of pain that wracked her when she thought of him. The entire structure of her life had crumbled in less than a year. Had it been only a year before that she'd thought her life would never change? Oh, she had known that one day she would meet someone and marry, have children, and be content like her parents, but it had always seemed to be in the future. Now the future was here, stretching before her, irrevocably altered.

Opening her eyes, she squinted slightly; the sun had come out from behind the clouds, brightening the gardens, casting a glare against the window glass. A blur of motion at the far end of the garden caught her eye, and she recognized Lady Winford's grandson. He stood in a small area behind a hedgerow; he held something in one hand that caught sunlight in silvery runnels, brief splinters that flashed and danced across the window panes.

A sword . . . Holt—a last name? First name?—swept it up, held it out, made several passes through empty air with it. Deft, efficient, murderous, the blade was instant reminder of the battle aboard the *Success.*

Heart pounding with remembered terror, she pressed closer to the window, watched in horrified fascination. He wore only trousers, boots, and a wide swathe around his chest. Light gleamed on bare shoulders and chest, a damp sheen playing over taut muscles and lean power. Her fist pressed against glass as she recognized the swathe around his middle as a bandage... she thought of his grunt of pain when she had pushed him away, recalled the hard feel of his body beneath her palms. Had he been wounded in battle?

It seemed unlikely. He wielded the sword with vicious intensity, skewering an invisible opponent with a sudden lunge that was both graceful and lethal. She shivered. If *he* had been aboard the *Success,* no pirates would have been able to take Kit away. None of the men she had seen fight had this air of ruthless competence....

She rubbed idly at her wrists, still chafed from his harsh grip. He had frightened her with accusations of theft when he had not even bothered to ask her name. An assumption that she was there to steal from him told her more than he would have liked—a man with secrets, it seemed, convinced there were those who meant him harm.

Strangely, she was not afraid of him now. Perhaps it was because she knew he was Lady Winford's grandson. While he might have been rude, even frightening, she might have reacted the same if she thought an intruder was in her parlor.

Surely, now that he knew Lady Winford had sent for her, he would be more gracious and welcoming.

~

Dinner was served precisely at nine, as usual, and yet there was no sign of Miss Courtland. But then, Holt had not really expected her to come down.

"She is a rustic, Grandmère. You cannot change the color of a horse."

"She is not a horse, Holt. She is a child—almost a young woman. Besides, I do not want to change her. She is delightful."

"Really." His brow lifted; he gazed at her across the linen draped table lit by three candle racks. "If you deem as delightful this Colonial chit skinny as a rail with an appalling lack of manners, then you should be well satisfied indeed. She looks more like a gypsy. And, might I add, she certainly seems older than seven or eight."

"Yes, well, of course she is older. I suppose time went by more swiftly than I recalled. No matter."

He tore apart a chunk of bread, looked up at her. "It would very much interest me to know why you did not deem it important enough to tell me that you had sent for them after I made other arrangements."

"The arrangements you made were unsatisfactory to me. Besides, you were wounded and raving. I could not upset you."

"No, that would not do. Much better to wait and let me confront the little baggage in my front parlor and accuse her of being a thief." He dropped the chunk of bread on his plate, sat back in his chair with growing irritation. "Christ, it could have been worse than it was. What if I'd sent her off with the Watch? I shudder to think of the scene you would cause at the police station. All of London would soon know we're harboring Colonial gypsies. And I did not rave."

Unperturbed, Lady Winford cut a small portion of meat and chewed it slowly, not answering. His jaw set.

"Grandmère, if you insist upon her remaining here, at least see that she is properly schooled. With remedial training and a modicum of manners, she can be married off within the next six months."

She did not look up. "You are hardly the arbiter of proper manners, I would think. After all, I seem to recall something about a certain Lady Wickham that led you to the edge of disaster. It is only by the grace of God that you did not kill her husband and hang for murder."

"Manners and morals are entirely different subjects. I did not kill Wickham because it was much more satisfactory to let him live as a disgrace. It was his own decision to sit in his library and put a bullet into his head."

She looked up at last; candle-glow reflected in her eyes. "You are in danger," she said softly, "of becoming a very callous man. It is unbecoming."

"So it is. Unfortunately, tender hearts have a deuced hard time serving His Majesty's interests in battle. Or out of it. I thought there were two Colonials belonging to *dear Anna*. Where is the second one?"

She pursed her lips, nodded slowly. "Yes, there are two. Most interesting. Baxter told me what happened. Pirates."

"Pirates. And how would Baxter know about pirates?"

"Just as Baxter knows everything else. He inquires most discreetly. At any rate, the young man was impressed into service by pirates. A Captain Jack, I believe. Distasteful business. Do see what you can find out, Holt, and get him back. It will never do to have dear Anna's son at the mercy of pirates."

"Judging from his sister, it may be pirates at the mercy of dear Anna's son."

She frowned. "You are being very disagreeable again. I do wish you would recover quickly. You are quite unbearable in this mood."

"It is a condition," he said coolly, "that is unlikely to abate until I have my house free of unwanted guests."

"Does that apply to me as well?"

"No, it does not," he said sharply, "and you know that very well."

"Do I? This is, after all, your house now. You inherited it, along with the title, a seat in the House of Lords, and the vile temper." Candlelight gleamed on her fork as she stabbed another chunk of lamb, lifted it, looked at him over plate and table. "Perhaps it is time I returned to my own home, as I suspect you no longer want me here."

Angry that she would even suggest it, he

scraped his chair back from the table, waved the footman away with an impatient hand. "Do not be foolish, Grandmère. This is your home as well. I simply require it to be as peaceful as possible."

Stubborn lights glinted in Lady Winford's eyes, and she carefully set down her cutlery and leaned back in her chair. "I see your manners are not as perfect as you would like to think. A gentleman does not rise from the table until the lady is ready."

"Nor does a gentleman tell his grandmother that she is behaving foolishly, even when she is. But we are agreed that I am no gentleman. Send the chit off to a school, or to the country."

"No. Do you think me so docile that I will dismiss my own wishes simply because you do not want to be bothered with the child? I am not so agreeable."

"How well I know," he murmured dryly. "Nonetheless, it is what will be. For the love of God, Grandmère, I am not suggesting you put her in a sack and drown her like an unwanted kitten. You feel an obligation, it is obvious, so see to her welfare. But do not burden me with her."

Silence fell; candlelight flickered, muted and soft on the silver dishes and gleaming tabletop. After a moment, his grandmother looked down at her plate, said inflexibly, "I do not condone the drowning of kittens. Nor can I oblige you in this, Deverell. Amalie and I will leave this house as soon as is possible. Baxter, of course, will come with us. Since we are a burden and inconvenience to you, we shall remove ourselves from your sight."

Deverell. Not *Holt*, nor even *Braxton*, but his title, a subtle gesture to remove herself from him in mind, if not in distance. Anger battled with astonishment that she would so swiftly take the Colonial upstart to heart, yet he remained silent. She would not leave. She never did, though she threatened to on occasion, usually when he was in a temper because one of the pugs had eaten one of his boots or chewed on a table leg. It would be the same now.

But it wasn't.

Within the space of three days, Lady Winford and Amalie Courtland had abandoned the house on Curzon Street, removing themselves to the country, along with all the pugs, a half-dozen cats, and the long-suffering Baxter.

Viciously, Holt thought they deserved one another. He lent himself to an entire week of gaming; he would be gray and withered by the time he was thirty, if he allowed his grandmother to dictate to him, and by God, he did not intend for that to happen.

But after a week, even debauchery began to pall. He considered going to the country to face his grandmother again, force her to see sense.

Then Britain invaded Portugal, there were uprisings in Spain, and Holt returned to his regiment, leaving the townhouse vacant, with only a small staff to maintain it.

It remained that way for three years.

Book II

Homecomings

London
September, 1812

Chapter 5

London was still jubilant after Wellington's victory at Salamanca in July. Napoleon's army was purged from the Spanish city, and celebrations were planned in Whitehall Chapel, an elaborate military ceremony that the earl of Deverell would much rather avoid. His perceptions of war and the men who planned it had altered radically in the past three years, giving him a broader spectrum and more cynical outlook on any affair which celebrated men dying in great agony.

It was a recent idiosyncrasy that was not, he had noted, shared with either Parliament or the general public, neither of which had stood on the burning deck of a frigate in His Majesty's Royal Navy while the rigging collapsed and cannon shot separated men from life with amazing ease. Worse were the days spent in hand-to-hand combat under the blazing Spanish sun, dragging an army over barren plains while the gentlemen in Whitehall argued about pence and shillings. It was no comfort to him that he had survived, nor that he was to be honored with a hero's welcome.

It was a discomfort that he decided to appease with a visit to his club where he would be certain to find entertainment in the form of whist or faro, preferable to dull speeches meant to incite patriotism and gratitude that there were men who would die to ensure England the liberty to pursue debauchery in whatever form it was desired.

A singular notion, of which he intended to avail himself with little delay. After the heat and stink of Spain and crowded ships, the smell of depravity would be welcome.

Night shadows blanketed narrow streets and provided discretion for those who did not wish to be seen coming and going from the unremarkable house on a quiet side street of London. A single knock at the unprepossessing door earned the swift opening of a peephole to identify the visitor before it was opened to allow admittance.

Inside, it resembled a rather luxuriously furnished gambling hall, peopled with familiar faces of the *ton* and a sprinkling of foreign diplomats. Most of the ladies wore masks, bejewelled creations with netting that did little to conceal their identity, but served to give them the security of disguise in order to behave more boldly than normal.

He was met by Madame la Marquise, ageless, weighted down with jewelry and elaborate makeup.

"My lord Braxton, it is so pleasant to see you again," she said in her husky voice. Lamplight glittered on diamond pins tucked into her high powdered wig, an affectation she had not abandoned, it seemed.

Bending over her hand, he murmured, "It is my pleasure, Madame L'Aigle."

A throaty laugh accompanied her invitation to join one of the gaming tables. "I believe that your friend Lord Carlton is still here. He expects you, I understand."

Stanfill knew him better than most, he thought with grim amusement, and entered the salon she indicated. A haze of smoke layered the air, shifting as he passed green baize tables and made his way to the far end of the room. As he paused beside the table, David glanced up with a grin.

"You're late. I expected you hours ago."

"So I see." A wry smile acknowledged Stanfill's pile of coin and half-empty glass. A nearly nude woman draped over his shoulder, her bare breast nudging his ear. She looked up at Holt, smiled as unselfconsciously as if they were in his grandmother's drawing room, and drew her fingers over the viscount's hair in a light caress.

In response, Stanfill turned his head, flicked out a tongue to tease her rouged nipple to a rigid peak, then left off to glance back at the cards spread upon the faro table.

Strains of music drifted down a wide stairway from a screened gallery above, and unobtrusive butlers replaced emptied glasses of wine or champagne as quickly as they were consumed. The Damnation Club deserved its reputation for wickedness; play here was steep, the betting book as large as at White's, where fortunes were won and lost on the most trivial wagers.

"Care to play?" one of those seated inquired, and stood up to indicate Holt could replace him. "I'm foxed, and in no mood to lose more when I've got a bit of muslin waiting on me upstairs."

The restless mood that had brought Holt here prompted him to sit down. For a time, his concentration was on the play. He won easily, disgusting Stanfill, who quit the table to take the bare-breasted doxy with him to a brocade couch in a shadowed alcove. No one paid them the least attention, beyond a casual glance.

By the time Stanfill returned to the table, Holt's stack of coins had doubled. He played efficiently, gauging the odds with an expertise born of long experience.

"Do you mean to attend the fête Lady Winford is giving for Miss Courtland next week?"

Holt shoved a stack of coins forward, watched intently as the dealer drew a card from the faro box. "I was unaware there is to be a fête. But then, I have not spoken to my grandmother in over three years."

Silence greeted that remark, and it wasn't until Holt had risen from the table, that Stanfill said, "It might be worth your while to go. Damme, Braxton, you needn't give me a look like that! Gives me a qualm, reminds me again why they call you 'Devil.' "

"Keep that in mind, should you be tempted to involve yourself too deeply in my personal affairs," Holt replied with a curl of his mouth that did not diminish the warning in his tone.

Stanfill recognized it, and did not presume to offer more advice. They talked quietly for a time, until finally Holt chose from among several available Cyprians that the delightful Madame L'Aigle employed for the sole purpose of satisfying the well-heeled gentleman who visited the Club.

They disappeared up the stairs to one of the rooms, the doxy delighted to be selected, laughing gaily as Braxton escorted her with a minimum of talk, his replies betraying impatience as she attempted to engage him in conversation.

Lord Carlton watched idly until they disappeared from sight. There was a change in Holt since his return, a hardness that had not been there before. Oh, he had always been reckless, with a ruthless streak when it was necessary, but since coming back from the Peninsular Wars, there was an edge to him that warned a man not to tread too close or too hard.

He wondered again, as he had three and a half years before, if it was true that Lord Deverell was mixed up in the scandal involving a certain Minister of Affairs, who had been accused of treason. Proof had been obtained, and the minister had quietly resigned his position, gone home, and shot himself in the head—much as Lord Wickham had done after the duel that had cost him his honor and his reputation.

Not that the duel was acknowledged, of course, for it was still against the law, and men had been known to survive a duel only to hang for it at Tyburn. No, none of that was admitted, nor had Braxton ever indicated by word or deed that he knew anything at all about Whitworth and the old scandal. The proof—if it existed—had disappeared, along with several known officers of the British Navy. It was still a matter of conjecture who—if anyone—had gained the incriminating evidence against the minister and many of the cabinet.

Yet it was odd that not long after his recovery and the invasion of Portugal, Holt had received his coveted commission and left England. It had come hard on the heels of his quarrel with his grandmother, as well.

Ah, he would relish being present when Holt saw Miss Courtland again! The little Colonial had—blossomed.

But it was not judicious to mention it again, and he would have to be content with hoping to be allowed to tag along, for it was certain that he would be issued an invitation to the birthday gala planned for Amalie Courtland the following week. It was well known that Lady Winford could never stay angry for long, and it was obvious she felt a great affection for her grandson. Yes, she would extend an invitation, and he resolved to be certain Holt attended.

It would be too delicious an occasion to miss!

A fête. It was so good of Grandmamma to organize it for her, but Amalie could not help but wish she had chosen a more private celebration of her twenty-first birthday. After all, it was not as if she were an acclaimed beauty, or an heiress, or even *wanted* to drink champagne and dance under the stars.

"Be still, if you will, Miss Amalie," Lucy said with another sigh, and tugged at the hem of her gown again, a rather hard pull that settled the muslin around her ankles. "It is this train—it will not drape as I wish, and every time you move—"

"My apologies, Lucy. I'll be still."

She glanced up, sighing, gazed at her reflection

in the mirror with a critical eye. Fashion was simple for the most part now, and the sheer white muslin gown embroidered with tiny gold stars was flattering on her tall, slender form. A bit too tall, she thought, but Grandmamma had said, *Oh no, it is quite lovely to see a young lady who does not look as if she has been stamped out with a cookie press. . . .*

"All alike these days, crowding Almacks with blond hair and tiny, petite figures, not a brain in their heads, I'm afraid, but there you have it—men *will* prefer a fair face to intelligence every time. I've always said it."

Smiling at the memory of Lady Winford's unintentional cut, Amalie looked more closely at her reflection. Perhaps she was not a conventional beauty, but really, the white gown set off her warm skin tones and dark hair very nicely, and flattered her figure. A gold satin sash crossed under her breasts and matched her satin slippers, while matching ribbons were wound into the dark shimmer of curls piled atop her head in an artful arrangement. Madame LeFleur had taken great pains to torture wisps of hair into soft curls to dangle on her high forehead and at her temples.

"Like a Greek goddess, yes?" she had said with a laugh, and Grandmamma had been most delighted.

"Lovely, just breathtaking, Amie dear," she had agreed with Madame. "You are quite the thing."

It was no good to tell her that she was not at all *the thing*, for it would make no difference. Grandmamma heard only what she wanted to hear. It was one of her more endearing—and maddening—virtues.

Long gloves were donned; she took up a silk fan and delicate lace shawl spangled with gold, dabbed a touch of rouge on her lips and high cheekbones, and she was ready.

"Come along, my love," Grandmamma urged, "for you must stand beside me in the receiving line and it is almost time. Do not look so martyred—everyone will only compliment you and say how charming you are. Ah, this will be the most talked about affair of the small Season, I just know it. The invitations were quite well received, and I think—oh, it would be *so* fortunate if he would come, though he does not usually attend such functions. Far too tame, you see, far too tame . . . but I have syllabub and sirens present this evening, so you just never know what he might do—"

"What *who* might do, Grandmamma?" she interrupted, as they descended the wide staircase to the first-floor ballroom. Below, on the ground floor, lights blazed, and outside the open doors and windows she could hear the arrival of coaches and rumble of conversation. Beacon House was a hive of activity this evening, transformed from their usual winter lodging to a fairytale castle.

For some reason, she was suddenly nervous, and barely heard Lady Winford's reply, until a familiar name caught her attention:

". . . and of course, I sent an invitation to Holt, though I daresay he will not come. He detests these things more than the Prince does—my dear, are you unwell?"

Amalie recoiled, but quickly recovered and managed a smile. "No, no, I am fine. Just nervous."

"Ah, you will be most well received, do not worry. And look, already there's a line of carriages in the street that would do the Countess Lieven proud. . . ."

Dorothea, Countess Lieven, recently arrived in London with her husband, Count Christopher Andreievitch, who was the Russian ambassador, was an acknowledged beauty of the first water, and had created quite a stir with her arrival. To be included in her company was high praise indeed, Amalie knew, and acknowledged her godmother's compliment with a fond squeeze of her arm.

Some of her dismay at the discovery the Earl of Deverell had been invited and might make an appearance faded. Perhaps it would not be awkward; after all, it had been nearly four years since he had greeted her so rudely, and he must have changed. He was an Acclaimed Hero now, a decorated veteran of battles fought under Sir Arthur—no, it was *Lord Wellington* now, a recent elevation to viscount earned for his courage and prowess against Napoleon.

Well, a returning hero deserved a warm welcome from his family, and she would extend the olive branch of peace to Deverell despite the estrangement with his grandmother. After all, Grandmamma did miss him, though she pretended not to be distressed at their estrangement. Yet it was obvious from her delight and barely concealed excitement that she was anxious for all to go well with him tonight.

And really, what would it hurt to be gracious? If he had not bothered to visit his grandmother in so long, it was between them. Truthfully, Deverell had cause to resent her, as she was the bone of contention between them. She would make an effort to be pleasant to him if he did, indeed, attend the celebration. It was the least she could do for her godmother.

They reached the entrance hall and it all became a blur, hours of welcoming guests, making small talk, trying to remember names and titles and proper address, small *on-dits* of information to personalize each greeting, all the while holding her head high, her back straight, watching her diction. The hours of instruction she had suffered just to play such a charade!

But it made Grandmamma happy, which was her goal, after all, for she owed her so much. The only flaw in her life was the apparent disappearance of her brother.

Christian—no sign of him had ever been found; those who'd searched for him reported with regret that it was most probable he had died soon after being abducted by the pirates.

Grief had eased with the passage of time, but she had not forgotten Kit. Every night before she fell asleep, she thought of him, prayed that his death had been easy, and silently thanked him for his sacrifice.

A small compensation, but it eased the feelings of guilt that overcame her at times when she blamed herself for causing his death.

"Miss Courtland, may I present my nephew, Charles de Vane. . . ."

Brought back to the present with a jerk, she

smiled, acknowledged the introduction, focused her attention politely on a tall, thin young man with spots and a nervous twitch of one eyelid. He stammered a bit, so that she had to concentrate to understand him, and replied to his effusive greeting that she hoped he would enjoy himself.

"Oh, I sh-sh-shall, Miss C-C-Courtland, I sh-sh-shall!" He followed this assurance with a request that she include his name on her dance card, for he would be most delighted to lead her in a waltz, at which point his doting uncle tactfully intervened to move him down the line.

Relieved, and with the beginning of a headache, Amalie turned to greet the next guest, held out her gloved hand, and glanced down the line to see with gratitude that it was almost ended. Soon, she would be able to take a glass of punch, and a rest, perhaps, before she must do her duty and open the dancing.

"I see that Stanfill was right, Miss Courtland," a deep voice murmured, and her gaze snapped back to the man whose hand she held.

Deverell. . . .

The years had changed him, lent a wariness to him now that had not been there before. He seemed even taller than he had then, and much leaner, features sharp as a knife-blade. Skin that was naturally dark was burned by the sun to deep brown, eyes an intense, piercing blue. He radiated confident masculinity and an air of danger, a honed edge to the man he had been before.

He regarded her gravely; when she did not reply, but only stared at him mutely, the slash of his brow lifted in a sardonic amusement that she recalled far too well.

"I think you have forgotten me, little gypsy," he said then, an edge of mockery to his tone, and she removed her hand from his grasp.

Sensitive to any hint of ridicule, she regarded him more warily.

"No, my lord, I have not forgotten you at all. Your grandmother will be most pleased at your arrival."

"I take that to mean you are not?"

"If you are asking if I am unhappy you are here, it would be most rude of me to say yes." *How disconcerting—he is still angry at my presence even after so long. . . .*

Because she didn't know what else to do without being too obvious, she turned away to the next guest in line, a deliberate rebuff that earned a soft laugh from Deverell.

He did not pursue the moment, but instead moved away to greet his grandmother with the same easy manner, as if he had been gone only a few weeks, instead of nearly four years.

Well-remembered irritation resurfaced at his cavalier behavior. The least he could do was be conciliating, instead of brazenly rude. In all this time, there had been no word from him, save the few scribbled missives he'd sent to Lady Winford through his solicitor. Grandmamma had pined dreadfully for him, castigating herself most unmercifully for allowing her temper to drive him away.

"He is all I had until you came, Amie," she had said more than once, wistfully, "and though we have quarreled before, I have never known him to stay away this long. I should have curbed my horrible temper, but he irritated me so, with his arrogant assumption that he could tell me what to do and I would just obey—as his father used to do, and even his grandfather, the earl. Why, not even my second husband was so overbearing at times, though I suppose Holt meant well—do you think he did, Amie? Do you think he meant only to protect me?"

Her reply was always a soothing affirmation, of course, though privately Amalie thought nothing of the kind. Still, she could not have wounded Grandmamma like that, not when she was already so distressed over her only grandson's defection.

And now he was here, waltzing into Beacon House as if he had only just gone to Brighton for the week, his eyes as bold as ever and his manner still arrogant. All her good intentions withered. He'd made it very apparent that he still regarded her as an interloper.

Even while she greeted the Viscount Stanfill, she was far too aware of Deverell talking with Grandmamma, his voice a deep murmur, his proximity unnerving.

Lord Stanfill gently squeezed her fingers, bringing her attention fully to him. "Reunions are always pleasant, do you not think, Miss Courtland?"

"I am certain some of them are, my lord."

Brown eyes crinkled in amused appreciation. "Ah yes, there was a bit of bad blood between the two of you, I believe."

"I'm afraid I am quite unaware of any bad blood with anyone, my lord. You must excuse me, for my memory is one of convenience. I refuse to recall unpleasant things."

Before he could pursue the subject, she asked if he intended to enter a horse in the race for the Brighton Cup.

Immediately, he was diverted, and spoke of a blooded animal he had recently purchased that was a certain to take all the money this year.

"A prime bit of blood, worth every gold sovereign wagered, I do not doubt."

"Then perhaps we shall have the pleasure of seeing it run, my lord," she said politely, and removing her hand from his, let her attention shift to the next and final guest in line.

At last it was over, and the receiving line dissolved. Usually, Amalie never drank spirits, for they always went straight to her head, but tonight she felt the need, and took a tall glass of champagne from the silver tray a footman held out. It was cool, bubbly, tickling her throat and cooling her.

Heat was generated in the crowded rooms, and fires were lit even though it was still warm outside. A sticky film of perspiration dampened her face with a misty sheen, and the thin muslin of her gown clung to her body in damp folds that were uncomfortable and a bit immodest. It might be the fashion, but she was not quite as daring as some, who actually went so far as to dampen their gowns to cling quite closely to their bodies.

Outside, the gardens beckoned, promising cooler air and relief from the press of the crowd. Avoiding Grandmamma, she slipped through the throng of elegantly clad guests, all laughing and talking at the same time so that even the music was blurred, and made her way onto the veranda, where the air was fresh and cool.

Supper was to be served as a buffet, later, after the dancing ended, and as she did not wish to go back inside and risk being cornered by an eager guest, she ignored the faint rumble in her stomach and appeased it with another glass of champagne. Why not? It was, after all, her birthday celebration, and she should be glad that she was here, glad that her godmother cared enough about her to plan such an elaborate gala in her honor.

Listening to the subdued babble inside, she leaned back against the cool stone of the veranda railing, smiling a little as a feminine shriek of laugher drifted up from the bottom of the garden. Apparently, some of the guests were taking advantage of shadows and privacy.

A tempting diversion, and she thought of Sir Alex, tall, blond, very handsome tonight in his blue velvet coat and white silk cravat; frilled ruffles on his shirt were visible at his wrists, and instead of the more formal knee-breeches, he wore snug pantaloons that skimmed muscled legs most attractively.

She allowed herself a brief moment of fantasy, a rush of pleasure at the thought of being married to Sir Alex. He was a baron's younger son, well-born but not so high up that he was unattainable, and she had met him two years ago at the very first ball to which she had been taken by Grandmamma. It had been a terrifying experience that Sir Alex had made bearable with his attention to her. She had never forgotten it or him, and at every opportunity, she did her best to be in his company.

Sir Alex was a *true* gentleman, not like Deverell, who seemed as unsuitable for the role of *gentleman* as one of Grandmamma's pugs.

Her fingers tightened on the slender stem of the glass she held, the champagne making a slight hiss; the scent of late flowers drifted on the breeze, sweet and slightly pungent. The night would be interminable, now more so with the earl's acerbic presence. If only Sir Alex would approach, do more than smile at her from across a room, it might be bearable.

He was always so remote, indulging in only polite conversation when they chanced to meet, a frustrating torment to her when she found herself dreaming about him at odd times of the day. Though, oddly enough, at night her dreams were often of a man with dark hair instead of light, a figure always in shadow, a face hidden, a mysterious presence that eluded identification.

Moonlight sparkled in the champagne, and she lifted it to her lips, let it slide down her throat with cool ease. Two glasses! She was becoming quite reckless lately.

As she set down the empty glass, another was thrust out to her, amber liquid catching light from lanterns and moon. Startled, she glanced up, stiffened when she saw the earl.

"More champagne, Miss Courtland?"

Was that laughter she heard in his voice? Mockery again?

"No," she said coolly, "I find that I am no longer thirsty."

"How convenient, for I am." He leaned against the stone edge of the wide railing, regarded her through hooded eyes with an intensity that she found unnerving. He lifted the glass to his lips, drained it, his eyes not leaving hers. Then he lowered it; a faint smile pressed the corners of his mouth, drew her reluctant attention.

"You have changed a great deal, Miss Courtland," he said abruptly, his voice a lazy drawl that hovered between amusement and insolence.

"Am I to regard that as a compliment or as a regret, my lord? Forgive my confusion, but I am unaccustomed to such personal remarks from strangers."

"Ah, but we are hardly such strangers, after all, now, are we?"

Carefully she set down the glass she still held, heard the muted clink of glass against stone, and used it as a delaying tactic. To insult him directly might very well anger him, and while she did not mind for herself, it could cause another rift with her godmother. That she *did* mind.

She looked up, met his eyes, and held his gaze for a long moment. "As we met only once, and for a brief moment, I do not think we could consider ourselves more than remote acquaintances, my lord."

"A pity."

"You do not sound as if you find it to be so terribly distressing. I admire your ability to mask your anguish." She paused, clenched her teeth to hold her tongue. These years with Lady Winford had taught her more than clear enunciation of her words and how to wear her hair; she had learned plain speaking, which while acceptable in a lady of her godmother's stature was not at all permissible in a young lady of few connections.

Yet Deverell laughed softly. She shivered, suddenly chilled in the light press of the breeze and moonlight. A burst of music from the ballroom cascaded through the open doors, the strains of a popular waltz recognizable.

She took a step away, felt compelled to be courteous enough to go through the motions of proper manners, and said, "I must go back. Grandmamma will be wondering where I am, as I am to start the dancing."

"Ah yes, *Grandmamma* most definitely will wonder where you are if you do not return. I will escort you—"

"No!" Sharper than she'd intended, the refusal did not perturb him.

"I am afraid, Miss Courtland, that you are obligated to begin the dancing with Lady Winford's grandson this evening, and we would not want to flout protocol, now would we?"

"I have never heard of—"

"I imagine there are countless things you have never heard of, not that it is of great moment now. It has been announced. Did you think I sought you out for reasons of my own? We are to begin the dancing, as you know—unless you wish to go inside and declare that you refuse."

Coolly amused, he waited, a brow arched in that infuriating way he had, knowing that she could not very well refuse without causing comment.

"What are you afraid of?" he asked softly, when she did not respond. He moved toward her now, efficient grace in his stride, a single step that evoked images of a stalking cat. He put a hand on her arm, the remembered touch making her shiver again as he held her lightly. "It is only a dance."

Only a dance. . . .

No, it was much more than that, and she suddenly knew it. It was a challenge.

Primitive male, confident in his success, expecting her either to run away or fall foolishly into his arms. Well, she would do neither.

"Very well, my lord, if we are committed to a dance, I will do my duty. It is, as you said, only a dance."

But she was wrong, she realized, when the music began and he swept her into the elegant pattern of the steps. *A waltz!* Unprecedented—oh, he must have chosen it, of course, for Grandmamma would never be so careless, though the dance had come into favor recently. No, it was just an excuse to hold her much too closely, ignoring her subtle withdrawal, his hand against the small of her back a hot pressure that kept her near. They danced alone, as was the custom, the first dance belonging to the honoree, and she felt hundreds of pairs of eyes on them.

Her face flamed, and a vague flutter of alarm ignited in her belly; he must know that people would talk, that if he made a spectacle of her, it would ruin any chance she might have to marry well. Outwardly composed, she did her best to keep him at arm's length.

He danced well, smoothly, with fluid, easy motion that was effortless. Yet there was a faint vibration in the muscles beneath her hand, the light pressure of her palm on his shoulder detecting tension.

Beyond them, the room was a blur of color and

loud conversation, sensed rather than seen and heard as she concentrated on the steps and tried to ignore the heat of the lean body so close. She had danced the waltz before, but not so closely, and not with *him!*

It ended finally, after what seemed an interminable time, and the polite smile on her face felt frozen, as if it would not ease without her entire face cracking. Not a word had passed between them during the dance, and now a *polonaise* was playing as others moved onto the floor.

Still silent, she did not demur when he escorted her across the ballroom, but kept her hand lightly on his arm as if it were the most natural thing in the world. It was only when they reached an alcove and she glanced up at him to see the mockery on his face that she yielded to anger.

"If you please, my lord," she said tautly, "I would like to speak privately with you for a moment."

Amusement glinted in his eyes, acknowledging the request as he reached behind her to twist a knob and swing open a door leading into a small antechamber.

"After you, Miss Courtland."

She entered the room, waited as he shut the door and turned toward her. Trembling with anger, she opened her mouth to tell him what she thought of his shameful trick, but he moved swiftly, pulled her hard against him, one hand cupping the back of her neck to hold her as he kissed her with a ferocity that stole her breath. There was no tenderness in the kiss, no gentle desire, but a searing heat that scorched her lips.

Shocked, she tried to push him away, but there

was no give to him, nothing but hard solid muscle, unyielding beneath her palm. Confusion roiled, and anger, and the appalling recognition that he was too strong for her. She felt helpless under the onslaught.

It wasn't until he released her, stepping back with an abruptness that left her slightly off balance, that she recovered her wits and breath. She stared at him, outraged and unpleasantly reminded of their first meeting.

The blow of her open palm against his cheek was unexpected, catching him by surprise before he could duck. It did not hurt, of course, but it was not meant to. It was meant to anger, and it succeeded.

He caught her wrist, a swift reaction, and held it tightly in fingers like iron. "What the devil—?"

"Yes, the *very* devil! How dare you, sir, hold me up to ridicule, to be so contemptuous of my reputation as to attempt some petty vengeance for what happened between us almost four years ago! It is contemptible, and I will not allow you *ever* to place me in such a position again."

"*You* will not allow? I do not think you are in a position to allow anything, Miss Courtland." His cold tone belied the hot rage in his eyes, but he kept his voice low, as did she. "If you did not want to be kissed, you should not have invited me to a private corner."

"I invited you in here to tell you just what I think of you, not to solicit your touch! Are you so vain you think that every woman who speaks to you privately intends such an invitation? How droll!"

He released her wrist suddenly, gave a harsh

bark of laughter. "No, but I did not request the waltz, either."

"I doubt very seriously that anyone else would be so presumptuous as to do so, and certainly your grandmother would not—"

"Christ. Grandmère. She said *you* requested the waltz. I should have recognized her fine hand in this. For some reason of her own, she apparently wants us to be friends."

"I fear Grandmamma is doomed to disappointment, my lord."

"So it seems."

"Everyone will be whispering about us around the morning breakfast table tomorrow. If you have not done irreparable harm to my reputation, you have certainly managed to incite gossip. You should be quite proud of yourself, my lord, for you have no doubt succeeded in your intention."

His eyes narrowed slightly. "What do you think my intentions were?"

"Vengeance, of course, for a mistaken belief that *I* was the cause of the estrangement with your grandmother. It is quite clear that you have never forgiven me for being here."

For a long moment, he regarded her with a brow lifted and his eyes' dark scrutiny, then he gave a shrug of one shoulder. "It seems that you are even more naive than I imagined, Miss Courtland."

"I hardly think so. It is not naive to recognize an act of vengeance when I see one."

"Is that what you call it?" One corner of his mouth tucked inward. "You confuse vengeance with a far more elementary incentive, it seems, but I am not surprised."

Uncertain, she stared at him for a moment. "I don't understand. . . ."

"Don't you? I think you do." He put out a hand to touch her lightly on the cheek. "Poor little Colonial. A gilded bird in a cage, the plain sparrow changed somehow into an exotic nightingale—but you are still in a cage."

It was true—oh God, he knew the restless yearning that she had shared with no one, the inescapable feeling that she was trapped, albeit in a silken web of comfort and gratitude—but he somehow knew.

There was a brief, ironic twist of his mouth, a glance from dark blue eyes that told her he recognized the truth, and he turned away, moved to the door, and left, closing it softly behind him.

And she remembered then the dreams that haunted her slumber, the vague impressions of restless yearnings, the unfulfilled aches that often woke her in the night. Those dreams left her agitated, the shadowy figures mysterious and promising a pleasure that always eluded her, left her even more unsettled than before.

Now it struck her that the voice she heard in her dreams belonged to Deverell, the hands that touched her and never quenched the hunger were his . . . the sense of danger that always accompanied the dreams came from him.

As music penetrated the small antechamber lit by only a single lamp, she stood rooted to the floor, listening to the silence of collapsing illusions.

Chapter 6

Mozart's melodies swirled around him, spliced with a continuous babble of indecipherable conversation in loud, shrill tones of inebriation, Holt made his way to a French door that opened onto the veranda. For September, it was hot and stuffy inside, due to the press of bodies reeking with perfume and gaiety.

There was no sign of Grandmère, though it was not surprising. She would avoid him until his irritation faded to exasperation. It was wise. He had not enjoyed making a fool of himself, and it rankled that the little chit would be so insulted at his mistake. Damn her. She had regarded him as if he was some loathsome toad—a reaction he had not expected nor relished.

While he was not vain enough to presume all females would welcome his attentions, neither was he so naive as to ignore the fact most young women would realize the advantage inherent in being singled out by a member of the peerage at her birthday celebration. In some cases, it would be enough to assure a prosperous Season, even the small one, and there had been enough anxious mamas throwing their plain daughters at his head through the years to know that his favor was greatly desired, if for no other reason than his rank, wealth, and the nebulous possibility of an advantageous marriage.

Yet the upstart little Colonial had reacted with utter horror at his touch and presumption in even casual conversation—as if she was an Acclaimed Beauty of the *ton,* not a young woman dangerously near being left on the shelf. Twenty-one was not old, but neither was it young enough not to be aware of the stigma of *spinster* that might be attached to her before long.

What kind of game did she play? Was it honest dislike, or the feigned reluctance of a coquette, the cunning farce he had endured from women before, who had only pretended indifference? Subtle reasoning, perhaps, that hoped to intrigue and trap a man—useless tactics, for a man well versed in such machinations.

One hand curled into a fist atop stone as he leaned against the wide railing of the veranda. Beacon House. Grandmère's London folly. It was too big, too drafty, too expensive to maintain. She had her own money, of course, and to her credit, had not drawn on the amount his solicitors settled upon her once a month. That had surprised him, for she was notoriously spendthrift; her damned charities cost more than this monstrosity of a house.

"My lord?"

He turned, irritated until he recognized the red-haired man standing with stiff military bearing in the shadows.

"Lord Cochrane . . . I thought you reassigned

to a command in the Baltic by now."

Captain Sir Thomas Cochrane, son of a Scottish earl, managed a grim smile and shake of his head. "In light of my unpopularity in Parliament at the moment, I doubt that will be granted me."

"A shame," Holt said, and meant it. "It is my opinion that any man Napoleon names *Le Loup des mers* should be given his own fleet to command."

The faint smile of agreement was accompanied by a glance around them, as if expecting to be interrupted. Then Cochrane said, his voice low and slightly blurred with a Scottish burr, "I saw you on the dance floor. I must talk to you. Is there a place where we may be private?"

"It seems to be my night for private conversations. Yes, I know of a small chamber."

Curiosity more than anything earned agreement; Cochrane was a brilliant tactician and courageous naval officer, the aptly named *Sea Wolf*, undeserving of the humiliation he'd received at the hands of His Majesty's Royal Navy.

As the door to the chamber he had so recently occupied with Miss Courtland closed behind them, Holt gestured to the small table against one wall; crystal decanters gleamed with amber and burgundy hues in the soft light. "Brandy or port?"

"No. Nothing. Deverell—I am in a dilemma and I think you can help me."

It would be decidedly tactless to state categorically that he detested dilemmas, especially someone else's, so he stalled by crossing to the small table of mahogany to lift a decanter. He poured, felt Cochrane's intent gaze on him, and took a long swallow before he relented.

"Nothing disastrous has occurred, I trust, no female troubles that you want to ask my advice on solving."

The light note went unnoticed. Cochrane took a step closer; his voice vibrated with tension. "There are men out to kill me."

"I take it you are not referring to Bonaparte's vast legions." Holt lifted a brow, studied Cochrane a moment before saying carefully, "Is it because of your independent reform policies? If so, Members of Parliament have grown more vicious in my absence—"

"No. Not for that. I designed a new weapon to use against Napoleon." He paused, blurted, "I was shot at last week—barely missed me. Yesterday, a coach-and-four nearly ran me down and never stopped. These are not accidents."

"Have you spoken with anyone else about this? Who sent you to me, Cochrane?"

"I am not at liberty to say. As the prince and his military advisers were not interested in the new weapon I designed, I doubt they would be interested in keeping it—or me—safe from harm. All they require is my silence."

Holt waited; he rolled the glass between his fingers, watched idly as amber liquid sloshed up concave sides like rich silk.

Cochrane raked a hand through his hair, took a step closer. "You were there at Aix Roads three years ago. You said then it was a good idea."

"Ah. The fire ships."

"Not fire ships. *Explosion* ships. A stink vessel. I've been working—you know my father specializes in chemistry—I have been working on my technique, perfecting it. I know how to create a sulphur ship loaded so that when detonated, it will spread out over a wide area and fall on the enemy with very precise accuracy. If properly handled, just three ships could saturate a half-mile-square area with six thousand missiles—enough destructive force to cripple French squadrons even if they lay berthed within an enclosed anchorage. You see, clouds of noxious effluvia would be emitted, enough to send the enemy running away to escape the choking gas. Then British marines could land, secure otherwise unattainable positions and establish footholds on the beaches."

Holt set down his glass, eyes narrowed slightly. He saw the possibilities, yet said cautiously, "I recall your last effort—"

Impatiently, Cochrane waved away the reminder. "It was working well enough until that idiot Admiral Gambier tried to stop it. Surely you remember!"

"Yes, but I also remember that the French set up a boom to stop the fire ships."

"I have modified my design extensively. This time, not even a protective boom would save them. Christ, man, it will renovate warfare, turn the tide in our favor, and destroy Napoleon's forces."

"Then why isn't the Prince interested?"

Cochrane blew out a disgusted snort; he was tall, over six feet, and with his red hair and brilliant blue eyes, seemed younger than his thirty-six years.

"Damned advisers—you know Sir William Congreve and his son, and the Duke of York.

They formed part of the panel of *experts*—for the love of God, *experts!* The only men really qualified to judge the value and possibilities were the admirals, Lord Keith and Lord Exmouth. Oh, they agree the scheme has merit, but say such radical devices are not exactly *conventional.* For Chrissake, they argued that if the enemy gained such knowledge, they could use it against us! It's enough to make a man weep at their narrow-minded fears, when if they would just—" He broke off, took a deep breath, then grimaced. "But that is not why I am here. No, I had no intention of letting any of this get out. It isn't safe—I agree with them there. If Napoleon knew, he might very well use it against us."

"If the French do not know, then who is trying to kill you?"

Cochrane looked at him with a lifted brow. Ruddy cheeks glistened with perspiration, and his mouth twisted. "I want you to help me discover who it is—I trust few men. We were shipmates, brothers in arms, and you stood up for me when I was involved in Gambier's court-martial after the disaster at Aix Roads."

"I only spoke the truth." Holt frowned. Outside the chamber, strains of a waltz provided a momentary distraction as he listened to the music. The frustrations of earlier began to fade; even the stinging memory of the contempt and disdain in Miss Courtland's tone was forgotten as he focused on Cochrane's problems.

Damned awkward, if Cochrane was right. If the French knew there was a new method of warfare available, they would have no scruples in using it against British forces.

Cochrane suddenly said aloud what he was thinking, his voice utterly devoid of emotion: "There are those in England who would rather see me dead than risk letting Bonaparte discover how to create new weapons systems. The French would like nothing better—yet they supposedly know nothing."

Holt nodded calmly. "Who else knows about your work, except for the Prince and his panel?"

"No one. I told no one."

The implications were obvious.

Holt set his empty brandy glass on the small mahogany table. "I don't know what I can do to help, but I'll make my inquiries."

Relief flooded Cochrane's face, but he said nothing beyond a solemn nod and, "I appreciate your help, Deverell."

"It would be best if we were not seen in conversation, I think. I will contact you when I learn something."

They left the room separately, Cochrane first, slipping out the door and closing it softly behind him. Holt poured another brandy, held it thoughtfully as he considered the dangers of Cochrane's position. He had known him for some fifteen years, served with him at Aix Roads. It had been a fiasco, made more frustrating by the mulish obstinance of Admiral Gambier, earning the loss of British ships and men.

Cochrane had shared the blame with the admiral, but not been as fortunate in his acquittal. The personal humiliation Cochrane suffered tainted his position in Parliament as an independent but reform-minded member for the village of Honiton. It also earned him numerous political enemies, and delayed his reappointment to another command afloat.

If attempts had been made on his life, it could be anyone.

A sound at the door earned instant attention, and he looked up, hand tightening on crystal as the door swung open and a familiar figure stepped inside.

"There you are! Running off like that—" Lady Winford eyed him, then said abruptly, "Are you unwell?"

"Why would you ask that, Grandmère?"

She waved a hand and said, "No reason, except that you were there one moment, gone the next, vanishing into thin air again like smoke—where is Amie?"

"I have no idea who or where she is—"

"Amalie. Miss Courtland. She was with you."

"You needn't look at me so suspiciously. I have not done away with her."

"You were in here together, were you not?"

His eyes narrowed; he decided to be deliberately obtuse. "Yes, as a matter of fact, we did speak privately for a very few moments."

"Oh." Silence fell; the din in the ballroom was still loud, chaotic. She drew in a breath that made rows of rucked lace on her bodice quiver. "I expected you to take better care of her, Holt. Did you frighten her?"

"I think," he said dryly, "that she frightened me much more than I could ever frighten her. She does not seem like the kind of woman to frighten easily."

Lady Winford laughed with obvious delight. "No, she is not at all a missish sort of girl, is she?

I've been quite pleased with her. She is so eager to please me, so eager to learn, and such a pleasant, soothing kind of person—quite a delight, actually, and I cannot think why you took such an instant dislike to her."

"At the time, Grandmère, I mistook the young lady for an intruder. She did nothing to alleviate my concern, but only reinforced it."

"I see." Some of the pleasure faded from her eyes, and she regarded him with the intense interest of a watchful bird, her head tilted to one side. "And so you are still set against her?"

"I did not say that."

"But it's what you meant. Oh, you are so like your father in ways, Holt, forming prejudiced opinions that nothing short of tragedy can change—but this is not the time nor the place to indulge in this discussion. Come along, there are so many people here who seem to find you a fascinating character, a hero, if you will, for all your exploits in Salamanca. Is it true that you captured a strategic French position?"

"I did have some assistance," he murmured with a faint smile, and allowed her to take him by the arm and guide him to the door, her hand seeming suddenly frail and weightless on his arm, skin pale as parchment and as thin. Blue veins spidered her hands with evidence of age, yet there was a vitality to her that he had not remembered.

She moved through the crowd easily, pausing to make introductions on occasion, ever gracious, the epitome of the *grande dame* when she chose to be. Such a contradiction, flighty as a child at one moment, with her interminable, ridiculous charities, and the very essence of regal aristocracy the next. It was irritating and endearing, and he realized that he had missed her.

After all, she was the only constant in his life, the only other survivor of a family obviously bent on ruination and damnation. It seemed to be a family trait.

Thousand of candles illuminated the ballroom, glinting silver and gold, enhancing the gathering that was equally brilliant. Jewels glittered around white throats, on ample bosoms, and on male jackets, while the women were like so many fluttering birds in satin ballgowns and blazing gems.

Walls were hung in silk, interspersed with garlands of fresh flowers that gave off a cloying scent to rival the tempting aromas of excellent food and exotic perfumes. It had grown warmer, and all doors were thrown open to the wide veranda for the overflow.

He battled impatience, allowed his attention to drift as his grandmother engaged a dowager countess in trivial conversation about innumerable charities. It occurred to him that Miss Courtland had disappeared quite effectively, for he did not see her anywhere in the crush of guests. An extraordinary chit! Most young women of her background would make the most of it, would set her cap for the most eligible man there and do her best to snare a husband. He admitted his error in believing her responsible for the waltz, as Grandmère had slyly suggested.

It was obvious his grandmother plotted ways to bring him to excellent terms with Miss Courtland, but he had no intentions of cooperating. Her machinations were futile.

Miss Courtland had done nothing to change his mind. If she intended to wheedle her way into his good graces, she certainly chose a disagreeable method. There was no attempt to accommodate him—rather, she made it obvious she viewed him as detestable.

A novel approach, if unsuccessful. It left him with the irritating impression that he did not measure up to her expectations. While he was weary of adulation given current heroes—men who had only done their duty—he had the uneasy feeling that Miss Courtland saw beneath the facade, knew what a great, bloody charade it all was, knew that he had hated the blood, the dust, the death, the useless waste of life in the heat of a burning sun, men dying all around him while he urged them forward into cannon blast and sabers. . . .

Instead of admiration, her assessing green eyes, direct and discerning, had pierced his barriers and left him, for a brief, alarming moment, vulnerable. It was not a comfortable feeling.

"Deverell, you know Lord Exmouth, of course."

He turned, met the cold, dark eyes of the man mentioned by Cochrane just a short time before, and inclined his head briefly. "I do."

Exmouth smiled, a gesture that did not reach his eyes. "England is fortunate to have such a great hero return to us once more, my lord Deverell."

"Hardly heroic, surviving when so many did not. Merely a matter of chance, I would say, a cannon ball exploding aft when I was fore."

"Such modesty. And yet it is said that you

fought most viciously in close quarters, and earned General Wellesley's recommendation and a royal commendation—though I did not see you at Whitehall for the ceremonies."

"I had a previous appointment, I am afraid."

"More important than an expression of your country's gratitude? I admire your *savoir faire,* Deverell. Tell me, do you intend to accept the proffered commission to lead a fleet against American forces, or will you remain in London to keep other—appointments?"

"For the moment, I am at leisure, my lord Exmouth. My civil duties require my attendance, as I have been absent some time." The implied criticism raked his temper, and he added softly, "I understand that the American frigate *Constitution* destroyed our *Guirrière* last month. American privateers swarm the Atlantic, and have taken dozens of British vessels. Should you not be more concerned with that front, now that Napoleon is busy invading Russia?"

Exmouth, who had only recently been appointed to the commission in charge of destroying the American threat, gave him a cold shrug, then turned to Lady Winford. "So pleasant to see you again, my lady. I must leave, however, for as your grandson so kindly reminded me, I have much to do. I am not allowed the luxury of dancing attendance on ladies at balls, alas."

When he departed, Lady Winford said with a trace of annoyance, "You do know how to alienate people, Holt. A most undesirable trait."

"Do you think so? I consider it most convenient." His dry comment earned a reproving glance, then a sigh.

"Well, he *is* rather a bore, I suppose, always so dour and serious . . . ah, there she is. Come along, now, for it is time you did your duty, a much more enjoyable obligation than dealing with insufferable lords—Amie, darling, where have you been? I was getting quite concerned, for it is not like you at all to just disappear without a word, and not even Baxter could find you . . . Holt, dear, another dance would be just the thing. You must give her all your attention. People are watching, and since the prince did not come—I had so hoped he would, for it would be such a coup, but there you have it, he is not at all dependable in these things, for he is so busy, and—where are you going?"

A glance at Miss Courtland's rebellious expression was enough to convince him he would find more welcome among the pugs than with her, and he paused to give his grandmother a brief bow.

"I will visit you soon, Grandmère. Like Exmouth, I find that duty is suddenly much more agreeable than questionable pleasures."

The swift glance and flush of chagrin from Amalie Courtland at his cut direct should have been extremely satisfying. Christ! She was an interloper, no doubt a scheming little tart who planned only to inveigle her way into his grandmother's life, use her as a stepping stone to society.

So why did he find the scheming Miss Courtland so damned appealing in spite of it? It could not be her looks, for she was really quite ordinary, if scrutinized with detachment. Dark hair in Grecian ringlets was the fashion this year, it seemed, for every other proud mama's daughter sported them; no, it wasn't that, nor her large green eyes that were striking in a pale face—she was tall, slender, with a willowy grace that reminded him of a ballet dancer he had formed an attachment for when he was still at Eton, yet it was not even that he found tempting. Nor was it Grandmère's far too obvious attempts at forcing them to cordiality if not familial intimacy.

He was damned if he knew what it was, or why it should matter to him that she viewed him with such obvious dislike. The fact that it did matter was unnerving enough to put him in a temper.

It did not help that his grandmother chose to be obstinate.

"No, Deverell, it is not at all the thing for you to take your leave from us now. There are too many eyes, too many ears, and it is simply far too much to expect for me to have to endure scandal at my age. Now do as I ask, if you will be so good as to remember the rudimentary manners you were taught as a boy, and do not make a scene here when I have tried so very hard to make all right between us again."

Though she injected as much coldness and rebuke into her tone as she could, she was not at all certain he would capitulate. Oh, he was *such* an implacable man at times! And she had worked so hard, in a fever these last weeks with all the preparations, and darling Amie so obviously unwilling but dutifully obedient—sweet child, so like her dear mother at times. Now Holt threatened to ruin it all, with his cold face and angry eyes, while people stared at them and would whisper that Miss Courtland had been given the cut direct by the earl. . . .

"You are a shameless charlatan, Grandmère," he said, with a faint smile that relieved some of her apprehension, "and do not deserve my cooperation. Can Miss Courtland not dance with someone else? Surely, there are enough eligible men here to sign her dance card—"

"Excuse me," Amalie interrupted, "but I do not care to be discussed as if I were a vase or a lamp. And Grandmamma, you know my dance card is quite full, and I am to dance the quadrille with Colonel Whitworth next, so do not use me to coerce your grandson into staying here with you. If the earl is so remiss in his affections and duty, involving me will not help you at all."

"No, no, you have misunderstood—" Lady Winford stopped before she blurted out the truth, and turned to Holt with a smile that felt frozen and stiff. "Perhaps she is right, my lord Deverell. I should not attempt to keep you here if you have a previous engagement."

Whether it was her sudden capitulation or his desire to stifle the gossip that would inevitably make the rounds, Holt put out a hand to Amie, and said in a voice that was lazily indolent, courteous, and yet challenging, "Miss Courtland, do me the honor of the next dance, if you will."

Whatever the reason, Lady Winford watched with relief and hope as Amie hesitated, then put her hand into his with a stiff nod of agreement. There were, she thought with a sigh of satisfaction as they moved onto the dance floor, certain advantages to being the object of so much public interest. It was a double-edged sword. Amalie might not like Holt now, but to create a scene would be disaster, and the girl was smart enough to realize, that even if she did not care for herself, it would reflect badly upon her sponsor. So she agreed; and for whatever reasons of his own, Holt had given in—yes, it would be so very agreeable if they saw their way to forming a more permanent *friendship*, for whether he knew it or not, Amalie Courtland was just the kind of wife Holt needed.

And they looked lovely together, both tall, with Amie so graceful, and Holt so darkly masculine. He needed someone like her, soft and amenable yet strong and confident—not at all like those horrid dancers he frequented, or one of the scheming girls from Almacks. She had despaired these last few years, certain if he did wed, it would be to someone entirely unsuitable. And then Amalie had dropped in her lap like a gift from the gods, her childhood friend's granddaughter, well connected—except for her mother's indiscretion, and really, Captain Courtland had been the grandson of an English knight, so it wasn't as if he was so *terribly* unsuitable for poor Anna, after all—she had told Lord Silverage that, too, quite emphatically, but he had not been a man to relent, and poor Anna had died in that horrid, uncivilized country where savages and wild beasts roamed freely, forsaken by her family, by all she had known.

Well, *she* would see to Amalie, as Anna had begged, and while there had been nothing she could do about Anna's son—a dreadful fate at the hands of pirates—she could think of no better future for Amie than to wed her to Holt.

For all his outward arrogance, he was really quite a nice young man—not so young now, perhaps, at thirty-two, but still young enough to make a decent husband. It was her duty to see him wed, to ensure the continuation of the line, as dear Robert would have wanted. For all that he had been dead so long, he was still the only man she had truly loved, and while their son had been weak, their grandson was not. He reminded her of Robert at times, especially when he came over all arrogant and cold—oh, he had the Deverell streak of ruthlessness in him, after all! Yet so had her beloved Robert.

It would take a strong woman to handle Holt, as it had taken a strong woman to handle Robert.

Lady Winford smiled, watched as her grandson escorted Amie onto the dance floor, and nodded in satisfaction. A good match. A very good match indeed.

Chapter 7

For Amalie, this was the final, crowning insult to an evening that had become rife with tension and aggravation. All due, of course, to the appearance of the Devil Earl, as she had heard him called, a likely appellation that he had certainly earned, in her opinion.

If she was not so terribly fond of Grandmamma she would have refused out of hand, but of course, that action would have caused a scene, and her godmother embarrassment. So now she was dancing with Deverell, when she had sworn not an hour before never to let him touch her again! The only saving grace was that it was a quadrille, so at least she did not have to endure his arms around her again, holding her close as he did the last time.

It was too unnerving, coming so hard on the heels of her realization that he was the man she had dreamed about for nearly four years. Not even her brief, childish infatuation with the man she had thought him then was a good enough reason for her sleeping mind to conjure up such vague, restless images . . . and it was appalling to think she had so little control over her dreams.

They were spared the polite fiction of making idle conversation by the steps of the dance, formed in a square with other couples. To her extreme annoyance, the other women seemed to find it exciting that the earl formed part of their set and made every opportunity to flirt with him, with sidelong glances and pert smiles, an accidental brush of hands and breathless laughter that Amie found ludicrous.

Yet men always seemed drawn to that sort of thing, like flies to honey, never noticing the yearning behind soft eyes and smiling lips. A complete waste of time with this man, of course, for Deverell was polite but not receptive, remaining coolly aloof.

Of course, he must have women throw themselves at him all the time, she thought as they joined hands again in the dance, a brief clasp then separation, and she glanced back only to find him watching her.

There was the devil's own speculation in that gaze, an assessment that seared her to the bone, shocked and unnerved her. Brief, intense, as scalding as heat from a lightning bolt, the dark blue glitter scattered her wits and rendered her clumsy.

She stumbled, murmured a swift apology to her current partner, then continued, all too aware of Deverell's gaze. Witless reaction! she scolded herself, when she was wide awake and in control of her brain and body. After all, he did not deserve even charitable thoughts. The years had changed him, but not for the better.

Whispers were still voiced about his tawdry

affair with the wife of a marquis—or was that a viscount? Not that it mattered; he was dead now; killed, some whispered, by the shame of his wife's affair with the Devil Earl.

Thankfully, the music halted, the quadrille was over, and she moved away without waiting for Deverell.

Then he was beside her; with deceptive negligence his arm shot out, iron-hard fingers curling around her wrist to hold her.

"It would be remiss of me not to ask you to dance with me again, Miss Courtland. You do enjoy the waltz, I think."

The words were an amused drawl, another challenge, the gauntlet thrown down. She forced herself to look up at him with a calm she did not feel, heard her own voice sound remarkably steady.

"You are ever so kind, my lord, but it would be remiss of *me* to ignore my duties by excluding other partners. If you will release my arm—?"

"Ah, did you not hear my grandmother's instructions? I am to direct all my attention on you tonight—perhaps to keep away the wolves."

Instead of pulling away when he held her so tight, she moved closer, closing the gap with a single graceful step. "My lord earl," she said softly, so that only he could hear, "you are the only wolf in attendance tonight. Unless it is your wish to embarrass your grandmother, release me."

Ignoring her demand, he slid a hard, muscular arm around her waist and held her firmly. His other hand grasped hers, giving her no chance for escape or polite withdrawal as he swept her with him into the steps of the waltz.

He was much too close . . . it was constricting, being held so tightly. His movements were graceful for so large a man, a lean power emanating from him as he guided her through the steps with one hand at her back. She felt the heat of his palm through her dress, distracting and unnerving. He swung her around and leaned close, head bent slightly to stare into her face.

"I must say, Miss Courtland, you've done very well for yourself. You have my grandmother right where you want her, it seems. Ah, ah, don't glare at me so fiercely, or you will create a nasty little scandal that will contradict your pretense of being a lady."

She sucked in a furious breath, deliberately trod on his foot with all her weight. If it pained him, he did not betray it; he simply shifted his arm more tightly to lift her in a swirl above the floor, giving all the appearance of a practiced step.

"Vicious little thing," he murmured, but there was a sudden harsh note in his voice that made her shiver. "You do not weigh enough to do much damage."

"A pity."

His arm tightened until she felt lightheaded from lack of air; ribs constricted by his ruthless embrace ached. Her hand was on his shoulder, and she dug her nails into the skin above his collar. He gave a startled grunt.

At last she had his attention; he loosened his hold, and she removed her nails from his neck. This time when he looked down at her, there was a wariness in his gaze, and the dawning of respect.

"You are indeed a vicious little cat, Miss Courtland."

"Thank you, my lord. I believe the dance is ending. You may return me to Grandmamma."

"And if I do not?"

Music ended with a flourish; the crowd was a blur of flashing jewels and satin seething around them. But it seemed the world had narrowed to just the two of them. The air between them was alive with tension; it crackled, hissed, sparked into something unexpected.

Her tongue felt weighted, clumsy, but she managed to say, "You hardly resemble the hero you pretend to be. But then, you must know that."

This time he did not try to hold her, and she turned away with all the dignity she could muster. To leave the floor unescorted invited gossip, but it was better than enduring another moment with such a man—oh, thank God, there was Sir Alex in front of her, a perplexed expression on his handsome face.

He looked to her like an angel as he held out his arm, blond and beautiful, with gray eyes as clear as rain and as opaque . . . she put her fingers on his arm, saw him look up and past her, knew that Deverell must have gone.

"Sir Alex, a gallant knight come to a lady's rescue, as usual," she said, and his gaze shifted back to her, polite as always, and as always—remote. She stifled a sigh, forced a note of gaiety into her words: "I seem to have become separated from my dancing partner, and was adrift—will you be so kind as to escort me to my godmother?"

"Of course, Miss Courtland."

He escorted her quite impersonally, with exquisite courtesy and impeccable manners. Sir Alex always did just the right thing; there had never, to her knowledge, been any hint of scandal attached to him.

Now he smiled as he handed her to Lady Winford, who was looking at her with a slight frown, and to forestall inevitable questions she saw trembling on the dowager's tongue, she said quickly, "Sir Alex, would it be too great an imposition to ask you to fetch me a cool drink? It is quite warm tonight."

"No imposition at all. Shall I bring some punch for you as well, my lady?"

Grandmamma gave a deft flick of her ivory and lace fan that sent a small current of air over her face. Powder caked fine creases around sharp blue eyes. "Yes, that will be most welcome, Sir Alex."

With a slight bow, he left, and Amalie stared at his blue-velvet back with longing. If only Sir Alex would decide to pay her court. . . .

"Where is my irrepressible grandson?"

Reluctantly, she turned, said calmly, "I have no idea. He left me on the floor."

The fan paused almost imperceptibly, then fluttered a little faster. "Indeed. How very like him."

"Is it? I find it quite annoying, Grandmamma. Forgive me, but I think it best if I avoid him. He is your grandson and I feel awkward even suggesting it, yet perhaps he would feel more comfortable seeing you when I am away."

"Away?" Lady Winford's eyes widened. "Where would you go, child?"

"To the park. To the end of the garden, if you like, when he comes to visit, but we seem to bring out the worst in each other. I am sorry. I know you would like for us to be more cordial."

"Yes, that is true." She looked at her with suddenly shrewd eyes, then smiled slightly. "But it is also true that one rarely gets what one wants in life without a bit of trouble over it. Ah, here comes Sir Alex with our punch. A handsome young man, though rather weak-chinned, do you not think?"

There was not enough time to give that observation the reply she thought it deserved before Sir Alex arrived with two cups of punch. Unwillingly, Amalie found her gaze riveted on his chin, and was quite irritated to discover that there *was* a certain weakness to it, a lack of resolution, perhaps, in the rounded curve. Even more annoying, the image of Lord Deverell's chin popped into her head, the square set of it not weak at all, but rather forcefully strong—inflexible, it could be said without exaggeration.

"Thank you," she said to Sir Alex, and took the proffered cup of punch with a smile that she hoped conveyed her admiration of him. "I trust you are enjoying yourself tonight?"

"Immensely." He reached into the pocket of his waistcoat, withdrew an enamelled snuffbox, and flicked it open with an expert flick of his thumb. The pungent scent of tobacco was familiar yet different. "Quite a gathering tonight. Do you partake?"

He held out the snuffbox, a very pretty one,

white with gold trim, and she shook her head. "No, it is not a habit of mine."

"Nor mine," Grandmamma said brightly, "though you would think our dear Amie would enjoy it, as she is from Virginia, where they grow tobacco. They do grow it there, do they not, Amie darling?"

"Yes, but I cannot say that I was much acquainted with it as a child. I was more interested in the immediate benefits of crab pots."

"Intriguing," Sir Alex murmured, a tawny brow lifted in languid contradiction. "This is my own mixture, made from a new shipment. No one else has this particular blend, nor does anyone know what my secret ingredient is—a secret I shall keep, as even Prinny vows he cannot detect its origin."

"Ginger," said Lady Winford, nodding wisely. "I can tell you that there is ginger in it. Am I correct?"

For a moment, Sir Alex just stared at her; his eyes narrowed slightly, then he gave a small shrug and took a pinch of snuff, sneezed, and flicked closed the enamelled box. "You are quite astute, my lady. That is one of the ingredients, though there are others, of course."

"Aha. I knew it. Tell me, Sir Alex, how is your father of late? I have not seen him in some time."

"Well enough, I suspect. He does not come to London anymore, but prefers the country. Since my mother's death, he remains at our Kent manor. It was her favorite, you see."

"Yes, I can understand how he must feel. And your brother? He is well?"

Amalie allowed her attention to drift as they

discussed people unfamiliar to her, and she took a sip of punch. It tasted slightly bitter; not surprising, in that the fruits available since the embargo were often old or not yet ripe.

Now, with war declared on England by the United States, so many things were unavailable or of poor quality—or priced so high because of blockades and the high cost of smuggling that it was ridiculous.

"Did you say that your snuff blend is from a new shipment?" she asked Sir Alex. "I thought there was an American embargo."

"Yes, of course there is. That does not mean that it is unavailable, however. There are those who still get a small supply in on occasion, and I have my contacts."

There was a wariness in the cool gray eyes, though the smile on his face was quite pleasant as he regarded her with an indulgent expression.

"Really, Amie darling," Grandmamma said then with a soft laugh, "you are not so naive as to think it patriotic to suffer needlessly?"

"No, but I had not considered a dearth of snuff to be a cause of suffering for patriotic Englishmen." She caught her tongue at the same moment Sir Alex frowned, realized she had just implied that he was unpatriotic or worse. "I do not mean to sound unsympathetic, but we had discussed the ravages of war at Miss Dutton's soiree, and I recalled how you said then that there is a lot of needless suffering because of Napoleon."

"Yes, so I did, Miss Courtland. It is most flattering of you to remember my simple comments. More punch?"

There was a constraint in the conversation now, and it degenerated rapidly. It was not at all surprising when he expressed his regrets, and murmured that he must leave the gala early.

"It has been a lovely evening, and as always, I'm pleased to have seen you again, Miss Courtland."

Amalie made the appropriate remarks, smiled, and watched as he left, silently cursing her wayward tongue. How awkward!

"Come along, Amie darling," Grandmamma said, either unaware or simply ignoring the situation, "I see Don Carlos de la Reine, and you simply *must* make his acquaintance. . . ."

Don Carlos, she discovered, was charming and very attentive, a balm to her bruised pride. Though not a young man, he was still handsome, with swarthy good looks and hot, dark eyes. He paid her close attention, flattered her, and was obviously smitten.

"You are very beautiful, Señorita Courtland. I admire you all the evening."

Flattering, to be complimented so, and she privately admitted that it was a balm to soothe her wounded pride, yet Don Carlos was so fervent, his gaze so intense, that she found herself holding him at arm's length.

"You are too kind, sir," she murmured.

"No, not at all kind. *Soy honesto sobre su belleza*—I am honest about your beauty, lovely lady."

"Please, Don Carlos, you embarrass me."

"It embarrasses you for a man to admire you? Ah, perhaps because the English are more restrained in their admiration, yes?"

"Yes, perhaps that is it."

"Ah, these English, very polite, but so reluctant to state the obvious." His hand shifted slightly, moved to the small of her back to guide her onto the dance floor, a light touch that did not encroach or demand.

"Tell me," she said, to ward off effusive compliments, "how do you find England in comparison to your native land?"

"Ah, Spain!" His eyes lit up, and he spoke fervently of the beauty of his country, the villas and vineyards, the rolling hills that were being destroyed by the war. When the music stopped, he escorted her to the veranda, where it was cooler, and gave a soft, deprecating laugh. "But I bore you."

"No, not at all, Don Carlos. I am most intrigued by Spain, and have always longed to visit. Perhaps when this dreadful war is over, I shall."

He smiled, a flash of white teeth in his dark face, and said, "I cannot now say I am sorry there is a war. If not for Napoleon's invasion of Spain, I would not have met you. It is most refreshing to meet a young woman who will listen to a man's loneliness for his homeland."

It was, Amalie thought, a distinct pleasure to be talked to as a woman of some intelligence and spirit, not at all as Deverell regarded her, or even Sir Alex, who no doubt would avoid her now after her faux pas. Still, despite Don Carlos's rapt attention, she longed for an end to the night.

The rest of the evening passed in a blur of faces, music, and rather nauseating glasses of punch, and it was late when she was finally free and alone in her room.

Reflective, she stood barefoot and pensive, gazing out the window of her room into the garden below. The muted sound of pugs punctuated the night, and she smiled as she heard Grandmamma's cooing tones urging the little dogs back inside.

A kind heart, loving nature, and rather eccentric outlook characterized Lady Winford, and she still felt so very fortunate to be here. Yet now that the earl was back in London, the uncertainty returned. He disliked her; he made it plain that he thought her a fortune-hunter of some kind, as he had once called her, a "gypsy thief" out to rob them all.

And now she had alienated Sir Alex, the only man she had yet found sufficiently interesting for even idle conversation. Save perhaps Don Carlos.

Thank heavens, it was over, her birthday behind her, another year past. She should really contemplate her future most carefully, despite Grandmamma's promises that she would be well cared for, that dear Anna's daughter would not be cast into the cold without protection. Nothing in life was secure. She had learned that lesson well.

And if the Devil Earl had his way, she would most definitely be cast out into the streets should anything happen to Grandmamma.

Abhorrent, that her very survival depended upon the goodwill of a man, and she suddenly understood the fervor of certain ladies like Elizabeth Fry, who condemned the strictures placed upon women. Grandmamma had recently made her acquaintance, as they were alike in their goals, though Mrs. Fry focused more upon social reforms than the needs of animals. Yet still they had formed a friendship of sorts, an understanding between them.

Oh, how uncertain life could be! And how frightened she felt when she thought of her future. There were even times she wondered if she had been meant to survive—and then she thought of her brother, with yearning and implacable sorrow.

Poor Christian. He was past all the uncertainties of life, lying in a watery grave somewhere in the Atlantic, and she was so selfish to give in—even for a moment—to despair. No, she would hold her head high, would continue on, for to yield would make his sacrifice for her in vain.

But it was so difficult at times. . . .

Chapter 8

"Where is darling Amie?"

Lady Winford appeared in the parlor doorway wearing a brocade pelisse that was unfastened and hanging loose around her, a pug tucked under one arm. Holt looked up just as a thin yellow stream hissed, darkened the brocade, and formed a spreading pool on the floor at the dowager's feet.

"Your pug just piddled, madam," he said, ignoring her question. "Shall I fetch Lucy to clean it up for you?"

"Yes, oh my poor little darling—she is breeding, you know."

Halfway to the bell pull, he paused, turned around, and looked at her, startled. "I beg your pardon?"

"Breeding—*you know*—pregnant. Don't look at me like that, Holt. It is a perfectly acceptable word, at least in privacy and not in public, but good heavens, you'd think no one ever used it or knew what it was. Silly, for people to be so proper about certain words when they do the most heinous things behind closed doors. But there you have it. Most people of my acquaintance are hypocrites, doing one thing, saying another, and blaming those who are caught at it as if they have never done it themselves. Shameful, in my opinion. Don't you agree?"

He continued to the bell pull hanging discreetly against the panelled wall, gave it a sharp tug, then went back to his grandmother. He eyed the fat, wriggling dog in her arms for a moment, then said, "I am presuming you mean either Lucy or this dog is breeding, Grandmère."

"Yes, of course. I'm certainly too old for such things. Who did you think I meant? Oh, not Lucy . . . it's poor Sophy. Look at her—she keeps leaving puddles and I am afraid she is in some kind of distress."

"I am hardly qualified to judge."

"Dogs are not much different from those horses you tend all the time, or, for that matter, people. Not when it comes to this. Doesn't she look distressed to you?"

Grudgingly, he looked more closely at the dog. Brown eyes bulged, but they always bulged; the black snout was dry and the lips pulled back from snaggled teeth, giving the dog an odd expression, if dogs could be considered to have expressions.

But the little animal was panting, her tongue a pink ribbon at one side of her mouth, and there was a swift, erratic quality to her breathing. He put out a hand, took the dog, cradled it in his arms, and felt along the distended abdomen. It was taut to the touch, with irregular lumps beneath the skin.

At his touch, the pug whimpered, and his

grandmother exclaimed, "I am *certain* she is in distress!"

"It's entirely possible. Summon Johnny from the stables. He's accustomed to this sort of thing."

"It's his day out and I sent Trent to the market for Reverend Botkin, as he should not be out in this weather. Much too cold, even for November. He is ill, you know."

"No, I did not know." Relinquishing the panting pug to his grandmother, he stared down in some distaste at the damp stain on his waistcoat. "I don't even know Reverend Botkin."

"Of course you know him, he—never mind. Sophy is most important now . . . you must do something, Holt."

He looked up, frowned. "Christ. What do you expect me to do?"

"Whatever it is one *does* in these situations. You should know. After all, you have horses and your hunting dogs in the country—"

"In case you haven't noticed, they're a lot bigger than these bits of fur and teeth. And I'm dressed for the opera—which you were to attend with me—not to nurse nasty little dogs."

But she was staring at him with such pleading eyes, and the little dog in her arms made such pitiful whining sounds, that he found himself giving in and ending up in the warm environs of the kitchens. While he settled the dog into a basket, his grandmother fluttered about, making cooing noises and generally getting in his way, nearly as distressed as the pregnant pug.

"Grandmère, you're only making things worse. Where is Lucy? Or Baxter?"

Wringing her hands, Lady Winford shook her head. "Lucy faints, silly girl. And Baxter is worse. Oh, why did I allow Johnny the day out? And with Trent gone and even Cook at her sister's—"

"Grandmère, you have more than five servants. Where the devil are the others?"

She looked up at him, her chin thrust out in a stubborn tilt. "I gave them up. You needn't look at me like that. I had to conserve my money while you were off running about Spain and everywhere."

"Bloody hell; if you had taken the money I sent you through my solicitor—"

"No, I do not accept money from men who are angry with me, not even my grandson."

He glanced back down at the dog. "You should take lessons from Miss Courtland, then, for she seems to have no qualms about accepting money."

"Whatever are you talking about, Holt?"

"Nothing. I think the first pup is coming." The dog gave a high-pitched howl, then a grunt, and in a moment a pup slid onto the thick blanket behind the bitch. It did not move, and Lady Winford gave a sharp exclamation that he ignored. Sophy looked back at the still, tiny form on the blanket, and struggled to her feet, ignoring it. The birth cord stretched taut and she gave a sharp yelp.

"Damn stupid dog . . . bite it in two, will you?" But Sophy was too anxious to reach his grandmother, and he had to hold the dog before she dragged the lifeless pup with her. He cut the cord with a kitchen knife, then, using a rough towel, rubbed at the still creature. It lay in a stiff curve on the blanket, unmoving. Such a small thing, never to have taken a breath. He rubbed a bit harder with the towel, silently urging the motionless puppy to life as he cleaned it. After a few moments, he detected the faint twitch of a foot.

"Here, you silly mug," he muttered, eying the panting bitch, "your turn."

"Oh God, Holt, I think it's dead."

"It needs to know its mother is here." He gave the bitch a nudge toward the puppy, but she flinched away from the basket.

His grandmother moaned, "It must be dead, poor thing. It's not moving at all!"

"I can see that, Grandmère. Put Sophy back into the basket." He lifted the palm-sized pup in his hand, stroked it with the towel, until finally the mother took interest. She sniffed it cautiously, a bump of her nose against the tiny head, then began to lick the pup with long swipes of her tongue. At last it began to stir beneath the gentle washing.

"It's all right, Grandmamma," a soft female voice said behind them, "Sophy knows what to do now."

Holt glanced up, saw Amalie with an arm around his grandmother, a comforting caress. She did not look at him, but eased Lady Winford to a low bench near the stove.

"It's going to be fine, Grandmamma, do not distress yourself, or Sophy will be too distracted to do what must be done." She looked at Holt finally, a clear-eyed glance from beneath her lashes. The lace cuffs of her dressing gown fell over her hands, and she began to roll up the sleeves to her elbows. "I'll fetch another basket, and you wait here while I prepare something for the puppies. When they're all born we'll put them back in with Sophy."

At that, Lady Winford nodded. When the pup was finally cleaned, it was placed gently into the other basket while Sophy gave birth to another. This time, the little dog needed minimal help, so that Holt had only to stroke the newborn with a towel until the mother began to lick it to life.

He looked up, chanced to meet Amalie's gaze, held it for a long moment before she looked away.

"I'll make tea," Amalie said briskly, "for it won't be long until there's another puppy. Do you take tea, my lord?"

"On occasion."

"Is this an occasion for tea?"

"It seems more likely an occasion for brandy, but tea will do for now."

He sat back on his heels, observed Amalie as she put out clean cups and a china pot, folded towels atop a small tray with calm efficiency, just what was needed to defuse the tension. The kettle came to a boil on the stove in a shrieking alarm, and she poured hot water into a teapot, then served the tea. When he took his cup, his fingers deliberately grazed her hand and she looked up, startled.

A faint flush brightened her cheeks, and she moved away to sit primly beside his grandmother on the bench. Silence was not uncomfortable as they waited.

In only an hour, four puppies were born, wriggling with tiny whimpers on the clean blanket near the stove while Lady Winford smiled delightedly.

Still kneeling on the cold tiles of the kitchen floor, Holt stood up at last, stretched cramped muscles, and looked down at his trousers in disgust. Streaks of blood smeared the legs where he had held the puppies against him, and his waistcoat was stained yellow.

Though she had remained in the kitchen the entire time, Amalie had not said more than a dozen direct words to him, concentrating instead upon her godmother and the dogs. Now she rose to her feet, looking wearied, dark hair tangled into silken skeins down her back and in her face.

Pushing aside dangling curls, she glanced up and met his eyes; corners of her mouth pressed into the faintest of smiles.

"You have obscure talents, my lord."

"So I've been told."

It was suddenly as if it were just the two of them in the kitchen, with its high ceiling and brass pots hanging from hooks, reflecting dull light from the fire that was never allowed to go completely out. The smell of herbs and spices was subdued.

"Here," she said, a soft murmur as she held out a wet cloth, "I'll help you clean up. Your clothes are ruined."

He allowed her to rub at the stains on his waistcoat; her brow was furrowed with concentration as she raked the cloth over his chest. The faint scent of perfume came to him from her hair; elusive fragrance, exotic and sensual, a promise.

The artless movements of her hand against him were seductive and arousing, a potent reminder of how long it had been since he'd been with a woman.

As if sensing the direction of his thoughts, she stopped abruptly, held out the cloth to him.

He took it, his fingers curling around cloth and her hand to hold her. She quivered, but did not jerk away, and he realized that his grandmother was gone. They were alone in the kitchen, with only the pugs for company.

It seemed to close around them, become intimate; he pulled the cloth over his waistcoat again, her fingers still within its damp folds, his eyes holding hers.

"My lord . . ." A faint whisper, breathless, uncertain, shadows in her eyes as she looked up at him.

His gaze drifted to her mouth, lingered. Her lips parted, breath a soft rise and fall of her chest, her hand slightly trembling as he dragged it over his chest. His body responded, a swift, throbbing erection that was disruptive.

She gazed at him, put a hand against his chest, her fingers splayed in a light pressure. He put his free hand over hers, held her palm against him, felt the quiver in her muscles. It seemed only natural to kiss her.

Unresisting, she leaned into his loose embrace, let him kiss her mouth, the slope of her cheek, then the pulse that throbbed in her throat. Flexing his arms, he pulled her more closely against him, his hand shifting to press into her back to hold her.

Erotic torture, to hold her like this, to feel her breasts against him and the quick little drags of air into her lungs as his mouth traveled from her throat to her ear and lingered; he blew softly, felt her shudder.

It had grown darker in the kitchen now, light from the fire and a single lamp providing the only illumination in the room. High windows shed a pearlescent glow; December shadows swiftly melded to early dusk.

When she pulled away, he let her go, watched as she moved to the cabinet and took down a small decanter. She turned, held it out, her smile uncertain.

"Sherry, my lord?"

"Sweet or dry?"

"Sweet, I'm afraid. Cook uses it in sauces."

"Then I shall decline, thank you." He realized he still held the cloth, went to lay it atop the sturdy wood table in the kitchen's center, turned to watch as Amalie poured a small amount of sherry into a plain tumbler.

She held it up, amber gleaming in thick glass, met his gaze with a lifted brow. "This is for Grandmamma. She likes a small amount in the evenings with her supper."

"If Cook is gone, who will serve supper?"

"I am capable enough. I usually do it when Cook has gone to her sister's for the day."

"I see that I have been remiss in my attention to details of the house."

"Yes. You have." A pause, then hesitantly, almost shyly, "Now that you're back, perhaps things will be better."

"I wouldn't place a large wager on that." He

watched her as she sliced bread, placed it on a tray with some cold meat, deft movements of her hands graceful.

Mundane details, idle chatter—unimportant and irrelevant. His body throbbed; scoured with importuning lust, he ignored the fierce surge of need that rocked him.

Damn her, he thought without rancor. She had somehow managed to blunt his suspicion and dislike; he wasn't at all certain how. In the past two months, he had grudgingly relented in his determination to rid Grandmère of her, but he still had his reservations.

She glanced up at him, lips slightly parted and wide green eyes speculative. He didn't blame her; he must look a rare sight in bloodstained evening clothes, and no doubt the ravages of suppressed desire in his eyes.

Then she surprised him by saying, "What is it like, being a hero?"

"Bloody hell!"

It was an exclamation, but she seemed to take it as an answer, and nodded.

"I thought it must be rather awkward. People expect so much of you when they've already formed an idea of what or who you should be."

Dryly, "Yes, deuced awkward it is."

There was honesty in her level gaze and slight smile of commiseration. "I feel the same at times. Not, of course, that I am familiar with heroics, but because people form opinions of me that are unjust. Now that Britain is at war with America, it is worse. Being *one of the enemy*, I mean."

"I imagine it is." He studied her, the faint flush on her cheeks, the gravity with which she regarded him, and suspected that she intended it as a gentle message.

He had no intention of allowing her to take him down that particular path, and said, "It is hardly heroic to stand amidst the carnage of battle and realize that you're alive only because the cannon ball hit a few yards to the left instead of to the right. It's a matter of luck, a turn of the card, a toss of the dice."

"Yes . . . I can see how you would feel that way." She looked down, rearranged a chunk of cheese on the silver plate. Her face was in shadow, hair tumbling forward to hide it from him, seductive and loose, a silken drape.

Suddenly tired of playing the gallant, he reached for her, slipped his hand around hers, and turned it up, his thumb raking across the cup of her palm. Then he lifted it to his mouth, pressing a kiss against the heel of her hand before working down to her wrist.

Practiced seduction, performed a hundred times in a hundred different ballrooms and bedrooms. He felt the beginning of surrender in the slight quiver of her hand, the tremble of her fingers in his clasp, and glanced up.

Far too easy with Amalie Courtland, who stared at him with widening eyes; easy to put his free hand behind her head, bend his fingers around the slender column of her neck, and draw her slowly to him. She made no protest, only a slight exhalation as he kissed her again.

This kiss was not gentle like the last, but harsh, demanding; need beat a fierce song, dismissing any notion of gentle seduction.

His hand slid downward, exploring the curve

of her spine, his mouth more demanding as he realized that she wore nothing beneath her dressing gown but the thinnest of female undergarments. His palm pressed against the small of her back, urged her into his embrace even as he leaned into her, wedging her against the edge of the long table.

Using his weight to hold her, solid, insistent, he spread his fingers over fabric, closed his fist in a wad of muslin to draw it upward. She gave a faint sound of protest that he ignored; it was his experience that most women felt compelled to protest even when they didn't mean it for a moment. Easy enough to tell the difference, and Miss Courtland's protest was halfhearted at best.

Sliding his hand around, he opened it to cup her breast, thumb and finger closing on the hard bud of nipple he felt through the muslin.

The halfhearted protest became real, exploded into firm resistance, and with a faint sense of regret, he let her go. She stumbled away a step, stared at him with wide eyes that held conflicting emotions. If he pressed her, this would end differently.

But it came to him as he stood there with desire beating hot and hard, a heavy ache in his groin, that he was in his grandmother's house and his grandmother's kitchen, and it didn't matter a damn if Miss Amalie Courtland was willing or unwilling—there would be hell to pay.

Christ, she looked up at him as if he really was a hero when he was far removed from even remote resemblance. There was only one thing for it, for if she gave him the chance, he would be only too glad to forget everything but the pressing need to take her.

Deliberately cruel, he said, "I've no desire for gentle romance and sweet kisses, Miss Courtland, so unless you want to find yourself in my bed, stay away from me."

Green eyes widened, went dark. "Is this an attempt to frighten me, my lord? Or do you merely intend to prove how rude you can be?"

"In my experience, mademoiselle, the women I meet encourage more than a few kisses. We do not waste our time on playful flirtation. If you're intelligent enough to take my advice, you'll forget what just happened. Search elsewhere for a lover, Miss Courtland. I make a damned bad suitor for curious virgins, though if you're insistent, I will be more than glad to oblige you."

Only the telltale flush spreading across high sculpted cheekbones betrayed her anger and embarrassment. He could have told her it was the kindest thing he could have done for her, but he did not. It was a lesson she would have to learn for herself.

Chapter 9

January winds howled around gray stones, spit snow that frosted bare tree limbs and cold pedestrians. Amalie alighted from Lady Winford's coach, wrestled with bound packages belonging to her godmother, and looked up gratefully as Baxter opened the front door to admit them.

Lady Winford bent to greet the throng of pugs that scratched across the floor with demanding clicks of toenails on tile, yapping delight at her return, while Amalie prudently stepped around them to keep from being entangled. More than once, the pugs had nearly sent her tripping to the floor in a sprawl, and she had learned to avoid this first moment of enthusiastic greeting.

As she set down the packages for Baxter to retrieve, and slipped out of her warm pelisse, Lucy appeared, round face a bit harassed, and said above the din of pugs, "Tea is already being served in the parlor, Miss Courtland."

"Oh, do we have a guest?"

A hesitant glance, fraught with meaning, and Amalie relinquished her pelisse to the maid and turned toward the open parlor door.

Lounging in the doorway, arms crossed over his chest and his expression one of cynical amusement, Deverell met her gaze calmly.

"Another shopping expedition, I note. How gratifying, to see money well spent."

"A novelty for you, I would imagine," she said with a lifted brow, and turned toward Lady Winford. "I find that my headache has returned, Grandmamma, so I will not be joining you for tea. Please excuse me."

"Oh no, Miss Courtland," Deverell said smoothly, and came toward her in long, lithe strides to take her arm, "it would not be the same at all without you joining us. I will begin to think you sickly, as you so frequently take to bed with a headache when I visit. Can it be that you are avoiding me for some reason?"

"I cannot imagine why you would think that, my lord."

"Can you not?"

Black lashes lowered slightly over eyes of an intense blue, reminding her with his disconcerting gaze that he was well aware of her restraint. It was necessary, a wary barrier between them that she had erected after the night in the kitchen. That night had cracked the hard outer shell he cultivated, given her a glimpse beneath to the man he tried to hide from those around him. It had been an illuminating discovery, a revelation that put into place all the disturbing discrepancies she had seen in his nature, the crudeness vying with unexpected compassion.

It would have to be Deverell who breached the distance, for she would not attempt it again. Let him court his illusions, his denials, but he must be the one to come to her. She would wait. Foolish, and perhaps only dreams of her own, but of all the men she had met, he was the only man who lingered in her thoughts.

How foolish I am, to think he might ever be mine, but no other man has fascinated me as he does. . . .

Before she could form a response, he turned to his grandmother, said smoothly, "Detach yourself from those nasty little dogs for a few moments, Grandmère. I have news of interest for both of you."

"News?" Lady Winford gave a joyfully wriggling bundle of fur to the unflappable Baxter, then turned to Deverell with a lifted brow. "How marvelous. Come along, then. We shall have tea while we talk. Amie, darling, come along."

It was a gentle, implacable nudge, and with a sigh of surrender, she joined them in the parlor, perched upon the settee near the hearth. A fire burned warm welcome in the grate, a pool of heat that spread across thick carpets, glinted in gleaming brass firedogs and on china cups arranged on a silver tray.

The earl moved to stand by the fire; he was garbed in riding clothes, knee-high boots polished to a mirror-finish, gleaming with reflected flame. Fawn riding breeches fit his long legs snugly, outlining strong legs that needed no padding to appear muscled. A claret coat with tails and sloping front edges emphasized his broad shoulders, the elegant style of an idle gentleman making his morning calls.

A strange tension gripped her, as it usually did when Deverell was near, an odd tightening in her stomach and lungs that made her awkward.

The china cup clattered in its saucer with a faint chink of sound, a slight vibration as she sipped her tea and tried to ignore the earl.

Must he always make her feel so gauche, missish, and clumsy? Even when his attention was focused elsewhere—as it was now, answering Grandmamma's questions about the war and Napoleon and Russia, all intriguing subjects to her under normal conditions—he had the effect of making her unsettled and agitated. It was a relief when he finally moved to take a seat near her godmother, his lean frame sprawled in a dainty chair that seemed as if it must bend beneath his weight as he said, "Now that Russia's embargo on England is over, and Napoleon's Russian Campaign is in retreat from Moscow, the war with America has escalated, Grandmère. It is not so easy to get information."

Interest renewed, Amalie looked up, found him watching her with narrowed eyes, took a sip of tea to disguise the sudden quiver of her hands. A faint curl of his mouth signified that he noticed, and she set the cup down with a decisive thud to meet his silent challenge.

"President Madison was reelected, I understand."

"Yes, Miss Courtland, he was. Madison's Warhawks will not surrender easily, I am certain."

"Or at *all*, my lord Deverell." She held his gaze with her own, a familiar debate that dared him to deride her homeland again. It was a recurrent battle, enjoyable for the most part on the occasions when she allowed herself to be persuaded to join his company, the earl caustically denigrating America, and Amalie rising to the defense without defaming her adopted country.

"We shall see, little Fire-eater," he said with a cynical lift of his brow. "Now that Parliament has declared a blockade of the Chesapeake and Delaware Bays, it will not be so easy for American troops. Or pirates. Which brings me to my news—with war on both sides of the Atlantic, it was very difficult to trace your brother, Miss Courtland."

Blood drained from her face, and despite the warmth of the fire, she was suddenly chilled. "Yes, so I was made to realize, my lord. Am I to understand that now you may have received some word of his fate?"

"It is quite possible." He paused, rose to his feet, went to stand before the fire, leaning against the mantel to gaze down at her with a faint frown. "In matters like this, reliable sources are not always—reliable. But my grandmother is not one to accept rumors, and since my return to London, I have done my best to learn what I can about your brother."

This pause was pregnant with foreboding, and her hands curled into tight fists in her lap, knuckles white with strain and impending doom. Yet her voice was calm enough, a trick learned through constant practice.

"Pray, my lord, do not keep me in suspense any longer. If you have news about Christian, I would hear it."

"Sources tell me that the men impressed from the *Success* were hanged as pirates in Jamaica two years ago. A regrettable error on the part of the authorities, but most captured pirates claim to be under impressment, so the policy is simply to hang them out of hand. I regret the necessity of bearing such news, Miss Courtland."

It was shattering, and not even the note of true regret in his words alleviated her instant anguish. She stared into the dancing flames, silent, misery turned inward, her shoulders hunched as if warding off blows. Hot tears stung her eyelids—amazing, when she had not even wept as the pirate ship had disappeared on the horizon.

Yet now her face was suddenly wet, drops spattering her tightly clenched hands. She was oblivious to the murmuring sympathy of her godmother fluttering about her with soft sounds, oblivious to everything but the blurred tongues of fire licking at the logs.

"A milk posset is the thing," Lady Winford insisted, and had the earl ring at once for Lucy, "and of course, off to bed. This has been a shock. Good God, Holt, could you not have found a more subtle manner of telling her?"

"Of all people, Grandmère, you should know there is no subtlety to bad news." He tugged the bell rope twice, sharp rings that would summon Lucy swiftly enough, and moved back to stand before the fire.

He had considered sending his barrister with the news, but had changed his mind. As uncomfortable as the scene would be, Miss Courtland deserved to hear it from him, not the unemotional recital of a man more used to dealing with dry documents than with living human beings.

At least she did not go into hysterics or swoon, quite unlike most of the females he knew. And oddly, this private grief was all the more heartrending for its depth and silence.

The strange compulsion to comfort her was somehow unnerving, left him on edge and irritable. It would be an unwanted gesture, far too awkward coming from him; let Grandmère, accustomed to offering compassion even to the undeserving, soothe her with one of her famous milk possets, a concoction with enough brandy in it to intoxicate a French sailor. Besides, he was an outsider here, a male in a feminine world of pugs and possets.

Experience had taught him that he was an unnecessary and undesirable nuisance at moments like this, and he let himself out the front door quietly, paused for a moment to glance up the street with a frown. A swift shadow, quickly obscured by the corner of a building, caught his eye. It was hardly surprising, in light of the inquiries he had been making recently, but still annoying that he had made little progress in the matter of investigating the recent attempts on Cochrane's life.

The only certainty was that there had been attempts made, the last a matter of poisoned wine that had nearly succeeded. It was obvious that there were men who wanted the new weapon for their own reasons, and would not hesitate to kill for it.

"Your horse, my lord," the hostler said, shivering in the cold wind that whipped down the empty street with a low moaning sound. "He seems a bit fresh today."

"So he does, Johnny. Perhaps he needs a run in the park to settle him."

The bay gelding snorted wetly, pranced on icy paving stones in a loud clatter of hooves as he mounted with an ease born of long practice. A run would do them both some good, and he had time before he was to meet Stanfill.

Hyde Park was nearly deserted, bare tree limbs making a faint clack of sound in the wind; the only signs of life were birds and the occasional squirrel searching among fallen leaves for a forgotten acorn. The smell of snow was in the air, and traces of white edged walkways and slopes under the trees. Even the Thames was near frozen over, and the days grew still colder.

He took a main road, tree-shadowed and gently sloped, to let the bay run. Muscled power bunched, surged forward, icy wind an assault, like needles in the lungs. Hooves dug into dirt frozen to rock, propelled forward. Frost clouds of breath were thick vapor streaming behind like smoke.

The release of energy after weeks of inactivity cleared his mind. A blur of impressions took form, some sharper than others; Cochrane's safety was assured for the moment, with the viscount contentedly ensconced in a house outside London to work on projects dear to his heart. The secrets of his new weapons were known only to him, which increased his danger. If he was taken by the enemy and forced to divulge the formulas he had worked out in his father's chemistry laboratory, Cochrane's scheme could bring about England's downfall.

It had been nearsighted of the Prince and his advisers to refuse to use the weapon, though he understood their reluctance. It was dangerous, and with Napoleon now trudging back from his disastrous attempt to conquer Russia, perhaps even unnecessary. With the Corsican in retreat, the war with America could be dealt with more easily, a victory to regain Britain's supremacy.

He slowed finally, the restive animal snorting resistance, and leaned forward to pat the steaming neck with a gloved hand. A subtle popping sound accompanied a sudden sharp stinging on his cheek; the horse plunged and wheeled, until he calmed it with a firm hand. Warm liquid like melting snow trickled down his jaw, and he put up a hand, frowning as his glove came away wet.

Impossible, but it was crimson as blood—he looked up, saw nothing beyond the furry flick of a squirrel's tail disappearing beneath the sharp spines of a hawthorn bush.

To a veteran of combat, being a target was hardly a novelty, but it was unexpected here, in Hyde Park instead of on the heaving deck of a ship.

Old enemies, perhaps? It would not be surprising. The days in His Majesty's service as a courier had earned him more than a few silent enemies. It would not be likely they would have forgotten him after only a few years, nor had he forgotten them.

Stanfill, when he met him at White's an hour later, expressed alarm. "Damme, Dev, this is getting dangerous if men are after you as well as Cochrane now. We *have* to find out who is behind this—any ideas at all?"

"I have a lot of ideas, but unfortunately, nothing to prove or disprove them. What do you know of Don Carlos de la Reine?"

"Ah, the Spanish count. Not much, I'm afraid, just what most know—displaced because of Napoleon, he has been here trying to persuade certain members of Parliament to use their influence to restore his lands, now that the Corsican has been driven out of Salamanca."

"And has succeeded, to some extent. Yet Spain is not secure, by any means. There is always the French threat."

Frowning, he put a hand up to his face, fingers testing the bloodied crease along his jawline. It was no longer bleeding, but still raw, a reminder that he had been foolish enough to relax his guard—a mistake that could have cost him more than a scarred face.

"Oh," Stanfill added, "and I also know that Don Carlos has been a frequent visitor at Beacon House. To see Miss Courtland, of course, though he has been discreet."

Deverell looked up from his brandy, recalled with chilling clarity the mysterious shadow when he had left his grandmother's house, and his mouth tightened.

"Has he? Odd, that no one has mentioned it to me by now. I usually hear endless details about pugs and vicars, yet not a word has been said about Don Carlos de la Reine. I find it most intriguing that her liaisons are not mentioned."

"Well, she was an Acclaimed Beauty last Season, it is said, with a host of admirers. For a time, it was thought she would accept the suit of Lord Tunbridge, for he was quite infatuated with her. There was a hint of scandal, but then, there are people who will misconstrue even the most innocent of situations. It was barely averted by the generous Lady Sefton, who granted her vouchers to Almacks."

"Lady Sefton is notoriously kind-hearted."

"Yes, but not foolish." Stanfill eyed him a moment, then grinned. "And now she is in demand again. Apparently, your favor has greater benefits than I would have thought for a man with your reputation."

"I hardly think my influence is a lure to Lady Sefton or to Don Carlos."

"No, but perhaps there are those who may think your approval is equivalent to money, since your grandmother is Miss Courtland's godmother."

It was a thought that had occurred to him as well, and he stood up, scraping back his chair. It was time he got answers to some interesting questions—and past time that Miss Courtland found a husband or a new benefactor.

Chapter 10

Night shadows huddled on the stairs, lounged in the hallways, slithered around corners and up walls, fleeing the wavering light from a single candle as Amalie made her way down the stairwell. It was cold; her bare toes curled up from the icy floor as she crossed the wide expanse of the entrance hall to the library.

It was not as large a library as some, but substantial enough, with shelves of leatherbound volumes that had not been opened in years, dusted by the maids and kept because Lady Winford's first husband had enjoyed them. Amalie had wondered once whether her second husband, Lord Winford, had liked constantly being reminded of the former earl, his predecessor in nearly everything.

Silence shrouded the house, enveloped it in unusual peace. All the pugs would be with Lady Winford, tucked into beds along her walls, or even in the wide bed where she slept. The half-dozen cats preferred baskets in the warmth of the kitchens, or even cozy nooks in the stables, to vying for space with the pugs, and Amalie did not blame them.

Despite the heavily laced posset, she had awakened. A thick haze could not cloud the pain. While it had not been unexpected, the confirmation of Christian's death was shattering. Now, groping, desperate for something to take her mind from the horror of his fate, she hoped for diversion in the pages of a book.

She placed the single candle in its stand upon a table, turned to gaze at the shelves that rose from floor to ceiling around her, interspersed with a set of multipaned windows behind velvet drapes, flanked by a pair of ladders to reach the topmost volumes. So many books, all neatly categorized.

Yet she stood shivering in the middle of the library, while the candle-flame danced eerily on dark walls, staring at the shelves without direction. The tick of the clock on the mantel was loud, the wind outside the house a constant moan, as if in anguish or pain, a moan that she felt to the very marrow of her bones. It was overwhelming.

She dropped suddenly to her knees. White muslin flowed around her, a pool against the dark wine-and-green-flowered carpet; she put her face into her palms, helpless to stem the rising tide of despair that surged through her like a dark river. Loose hair shifted over her shoulder, a gleaming black ribbon against her white nightdress, stark contrast in soft gloom viewed between her fingers.

Never had she felt more alone than she did at this moment, the confirmation of Kit's death reminding her that she was the last of her family alive, the only survivor to remember them. Who would remember her? There was no one, for in the natural way of life, she would be alive long after Lady Winford, who was the only one she had now, the only person who cared, truly cared, for her.

In the dark solitude of the library, she faced years of loneliness, emptiness without end stretching ahead of her, and for the first time, could not see the light. For what seemed hours, she knelt there on the thick carpet, staring at nothing, feeling nothing beyond black sorrow.

"Belle dame, pourquoi êtes-vous préoccupée?"

The words were soft, husky, warm, and almost intimate, summoning her reply as she looked up, vision blurred by brandied haze and grief as she recognized the tall shadow visible in the pale flickering glow of the guttering candle.

"Puisque la vie peut être si triste, mon seigneur. . . ."

It did not seem at all strange when he moved into the wavering pool of light that he should be here; he had been here earlier, the bearer of grievous tidings, and he was here now, a dark angel come to her in the night, calling her *beautiful lady,* and asking why she was so troubled, when he already knew. . . .

"Grandmère's education has been complete, I see." He knelt beside her, smelling of cold and snow; tiny flakes still littered his dark coat with white, melting slowly in the chill of the house. He put out a hand, touched her cheek. "You're cold as well as sad. I'll light the fire."

She made no protest, offered nothing beyond mute acceptance of his presence, and he moved away from her to light the fire, using the spill of paper curls and a long lucifer stick, the scratch and sharp smell of sulphur lost swiftly in the familiar scent of burning wood as the fire caught.

"Handy things," Deverell mused, replacing the lucifer sticks upon the mantel before he shed his coat and turned back to her. He did not ask, or demand, but came to her, took her by the arm, and lifted her to her feet.

Stiffly, her legs cramped from being in one position for so long, she allowed him to seat her upon the settee and draw a small wool coverlet over her legs. Reaction set in with the chill, and she shivered suddenly, flesh awash with prickles, shudders racking her body so that the small settee trembled.

"Bare feet in January," Deverell commented. "Suicide. Here. No, don't pull away. Your feet are like blocks of ice, for Chrissake. If you were outside, I'd treat you for frostbite."

Oddly, his slightly acerbic no-nonsense comments brought her back from the edge of despair. Silent, she watched as he knelt and took her right foot between his hands, rubbed briskly, and ignored her soft gasp as needles of pain pricked her. As feeling returned to that foot, he took up the other one, rubbed it to life as well, his hands competent and indifferent.

Finally he looked up at her; his back was to the fire so that she saw him only in silhouette, features darkened by encroaching shadows the candle could not banish. Yet she felt his gaze, almost as if it was a touch of his hand on her face. It warmed her, lent heat to the chill inside, spread from her toes upward, a flush that made her belly quiver and her breasts tingle.

Confused by this reaction, by the almost gentle, certainly uncharacteristic ministrations of the earl, she arched her foot when he pulled it toward him, and he said into the gloom, "Don't turn shy on me now, my barefoot little gypsy. That was what I thought you were the first time I saw you, you know—a gypsy, with that cloud of dark hair all loose around your face. Your skin then was gold, a color almost like ripe peaches."

Strong fingers stroked upward, firmly rubbing the arch of her foot, then her heel, smooth motions that were both exquisite and arousing somehow, and she could not find the strength to pull away, to stand up and leave the library with all due dignity and speed.

Instead, she let the delicious sensation expand, the odd, dreamlike sense of suspense sweep her along with the earl's husky voice, his words low and mesmerizing.

"Sadness does not have to be forever, little green-eyed gypsy. Haven't you learned that yet? I would have thought you knew it well by now."

Fingers worked upward to massage her ankle, then the back of her calf, kneaded flesh in circular motions that eased her knotted muscles. He propped her foot against his thigh, the soft buff breeches warm beneath her sole as she curled her toes against him. Steadily, his hands moved over her, up to her knee beneath the edge of her gown, and she drew in a sharp breath at the touch of his hand upon her thigh.

But then he abandoned that leg for the other one, beginning with her toes, impersonal and efficient. It felt so good, so wonderfully relaxing, this soothing touch and the murmur of his voice, an unexpected and astonishing absence of hostility. It must be the remnants of the hot milk posset that was more brandy than milk that helped to relax her. It seemed so natural for him to be here, to be holding her . . . she curved her toes into his palm, sighed softly as his thumb pressed into her ankle with small, circular motions, then skimmed up the curve of her leg in a seductive glide. Heat beat through her, warm and welcome, a flowering awakening of her senses that he seemed to recognize.

Something changed, a subtle shift from impartial massage to arousing caresses. He glanced up at her, a speculative scrutiny from beneath his lashes, the gleam of his eyes a faint sheen in the glow of fire and candle. Rose and gold shadows leaped on carpet and walls; his hair gleamed black in reflected light. His hands paused, rested against her knees, exerted slight pressure to spread them.

Slowly, he slipped his hands under the edge of her gown, palms cupped against bare skin. His fingers flexed, dug into her thighs with gentle, insistent pressure, thumbs working small circles into the inner folds of her knees.

Erratic beats of her heart were a loud rush in her ears, her pulse escalating into mad rhythm; she drew in a sharp breath, lifted a hand to push him away, a lethargic gesture that went unheeded.

His hands moved upward, inexorable, a steady progress over quivering flesh. Somehow her gown was pushed up almost to her waist, her thighs a pale gleam in the dim light, his head a dark contrast as he bent to press a kiss where his hands had traveled. She gasped, tangled her hands into his hair, but he ignored her, his mouth tracing a fiery path over trembling thighs.

The wool coverlet slipped to one side, discarded as he caressed her, kissed her, slid his hands up under her gown to lift it. His mouth covered hers when she gasped again, a protest smothered beneath his lips.

Until Deverell, her experience had been limited to light, exploratory kisses in the garden, gentle exchanges that had aroused no more than a vague curiosity that did nothing to explain restless urges she was too embarrassed to acknowledge.

Now, the same restless sense of urgency came alive, a powerful wash of anticipation and unfamiliar yearnings that made her breasts tingle and ignited a throbbing ache in the pit of her belly and lower. Depleted lungs worked for air; her sluggish brain struggled to make sense, but her body seemed to have a will of its own.

Deverell touched her breasts beneath the muslin, an expert caress that made her arch toward his touch. She ached for more, and the throbbing between her legs grew stronger, insistent, a quivering anticipation with each stroke of his hand.

He said something, but it did not penetrate the haze in her brain; then her gown was gone, the coverlet spread upon the floor, and she was lying upon it, looking up at him as he leaned over her. Hot, fierce, his tongue washed a fiery trail over taut nipples, teased them to rigid peaks, his lips tugging at them as she twisted beneath him. It was all warmth, heated where he touched, cold held at bay.

Then he was gone, mouth and hands deserting her, and the cold crept in, illuminating and terrifying. She struggled upward, but he was suddenly there, words a low murmur of comfort, his hands on her again, clever fingers seeking and finding the ache between her thighs.

"Oh no," she said softly, hand reaching out to grab his wrist, "no. . . ."

"Too late now, *chérie,*" he murmured in a slow drawl accompanied by the upward stroke of his hand, a delicious, relentless caress that summoned exquisite shivers. And he was right, really, for the sweet release burst upon her in a white-hot light, shattering belated resistance.

Depleted, shocked by the intensity that rendered her boneless and shaking, she felt him bend over her again, and realized dimly that his shirt was unbuttoned, his trousers open. The significance eluded her until he moved between her thighs, lowered his weight on her, his hands tangled in the long skeins of her hair to hold her head still as his mouth found hers again.

Kissing her lips, her cheek, her brow, and then her mouth again, he lulled her into passive response. She kissed him back, lifted her arms, slid them beneath the open edges of his shirt to caress bare skin. Then he shifted, his hips pressing into the vee of her thighs, his body hot and hard against her.

Perhaps she was ignorant of intimacy, but she was not so naive as to be unaware of what came next. Yet did it really matter? If it was a dream, it would shatter too quickly. And if it was not—life was so short . . . and she was alone. So alone.

But then indecision was too late anyway, because he pushed forward, a sudden lunge of his body that took her by surprise and arched her upward, the shock of his invasion swift and unforgiving. Pain splintered through her body, dissolving any latent pleasure his hand had given her, and she pushed at him with both hands.

What had happened? The intense urgency shattered at this knife-thrust that felt as if he had torn her in two; she curled her hands into fists, pushed at his bare chest with panting resistance.

"Get . . . *off!*"

"Christ!" he muttered harshly, a startled oath. For a moment, he hung there, braced on his arms over her, his expression gold and crimson shadowed by the fire glow. It was unbearable to see his face, the narrowed scrutiny in his eyes as he stared down at her.

Misery rose to replace that wonderful expectation, the reality harsh and annihilating as she closed her eyes against him.

A soft laugh accompanied his rueful observation: "A virgin gypsy, after all. . . ."

"Yes," she replied, an inadequate response, but all she could form at the moment; the effort of speech was almost too much . . . the assaults of emotion and confusion, the abrupt change from erotic sensations to this sharp pain that was slowly ebbing, left her floundering.

"Too late to stop now, little gypsy. The damage is done."

Damage? Oh yes . . . I suppose he is right . . . but it is nothing like I thought it would be, nothing at all. . . .

Gentle now, he touched her cheek with one hand, held himself taut, his body stretching her almost unbearably, it seemed, as he bent to press light kisses on her face again, murmured soft endearments, held her close to him with his heart a rapid thud against her bare breast.

Slowly, the harsh impact of his penetration faded to a faint ache and he began to move, a steady friction that was uncomfortable at first, but soon eased. Slightly dazed with reaction, she put her arms around him obediently when he murmured a command, rocked her hips up to meet his thrusts, let him set the rhythm as the discomfort slowly faded.

As if she was someone else, she knew how they looked there on the library floor, the earl so dark and her own body a pale flame, the seductive dance of love without music, an erotic melody. *Love* . . . of course, it *must* be, or he would not kiss her so gently now, his voice a tender concern, his caresses arousing.

The tempo increased, a driving rhythm, his sudden fierce thrust and deep groan followed by another kiss, and he rolled away from her, pulled her into the angle of his arm and side to hold her close to him. Slowly, the rapid thud of his heart slowed beneath the palm she put against his chest, steadied to an even pace.

A feeling of serenity settled slowly, the tempest over now, the urgency gone, the pain fading. He held her against him, kissed her cheek again, then her brow, his voice a soft, husky assurance.

The sense of illusion seemed stronger than ever now, the dream vivid as she wavered between sleep and reality. He murmured something else to her, and she put up her arms, allowed him to slip the nightdress back over her head, tug it down around her hips.

Then he lifted her to her feet, half-carried her from the library, moving with blind assurance through the dark hall and up the stairwell. The creak of her door swung open into her room, and he took her to the wide bed beneath a bank of windows, tucked her beneath the covers and pulled them up to her chin. It was comforting.

Drowsily, she put a hand upon his cheek, fingers moving over a rough furrow along his jawline.

"You've been hurt," she murmured, and he took her hand between his palms.

"Go to sleep, little gypsy. God, I think you must be half-drunk." A sound like a strangled laugh accompanied the kiss he pressed upon her brow. "The damned posset. I should have known."

There was nothing to say to that, and she slipped into a light slumber, awakening later to wonder if it had all been a dream after all, then knowing it had not by the evidence of bloodstains on her gown.

No, it had not been a dream at all, and she wondered what the earl would have to say when he saw her again.

Book III

Deceptions

Louisiana
February, 1812

Chapter 11

Sixty miles south of the city of New Orleans, a swampy indentation known as the Bay of Barataria cut into the Louisiana coastline that was separated from the Gulf of Mexico by Grande Terre and Grand Isle. At the northern end of the bay, a dozen bayous led deep into murky swamps of tangled cypress and alligators, a labyrinth to any who were not familiar with the waterways.

Dangerous to wander alone in these waters, fatal to be caught by the inhabitants, whether alligator or man.

On Grand Terre, a fringe of trees screened illicit activities from the Gulf and passing revenue cutters.

Thick trees and knobby roots jutted up from turbid water lapping at the edges of the swamp. It was a remote wilderness, an outpost of civilization; yet inland, thatched cottages were strewn along rambling lanes of ocher and umber; gambling-houses, cafés, and bordellos thrived, while enormous warehouses stored stolen booty.

An air of commerce thrived here, laughter accompanied by the muted clink of money discreetly pocketed, orders given for merchandise to be delivered to New Orleans.

Kit Silver, as he was now known, watched idly, his back against the stout bole of a cypress. The man at his side watched with great satisfaction as merchants from New Orleans' thriving stores emerged from the brick and stone mansion in the center of the colony, blinking in the warm winter sunlight that filtered through tree branches hung with moss. Guests of the Lafitte Trust, wealthy merchants brought generous commerce to Barataria.

"Ah, Kit, business is good," Pierre Lafitte said with a faint smile.

"What of Governor Claiborne's proclamation?" Kit eyed him with a lift of one brow. "He has warned the citizens of New Orleans to have no more dealings with anyone on Barataria."

"Claiborne is annoying." Pierre squinted against the bright prick of sunlight, glanced at Kit with a Gallic shrug of one shoulder. "Jean returns to the city with me today. You should come as well."

"I've been to New Orleans. Besides, I have other business."

"Ah yes, I remember." Pierre studied him with dark eyes; the long mustache that swept across his thin face gave him the look of a pirate that his expensive garments belied. "You have decided at last to search for your family, yes?"

"Yes—and no. I have no family, only my sister. She is in London, as far as I know. By now, she must be convinced I am dead."

"Ah, but you are, *mon ami!*" He laughed at his

own jest, gave a wink. "That man had to die, or he would die for certain at the end of a rope. Not a pleasant death, I think, to dangle and kick for the amusement of the governor. But then, death in any form is not so pleasant, heh?"

Kit did not answer the last, but gazed across the busy square as the Bos sauntered down a paved walkway at the side of John R. Grymes, the District Attorney for the Parish of Orleans. Here, Jean Lafitte was in his element in the empire he had created out of ragtag pirates and rivermen. Influential men frequented Barataria; it was not unusual to see elected politicians bringing their wives to shop, for the Lafitte brothers operated an excellent "import" business.

Jean Lafitte—the Bos, he was called by those who followed him—cultivated friends among the gentry as well. Tall, with fair skin, a clean-shaven face and black hair and eyes, he presented the picture of a perfect gentleman; erudite, fluent in four languages, he was first and foremost a businessman. He knew who to flatter, who to cajole, who to intimidate.

A slight smile curved Kit's mouth; only last week the pirate leader had issued a proclamation to answer Governor Claiborne's posters, an offer of fifteen hundred dollars for the arrest of Governor Claiborne and the delivery of his person at Grand Terre. It was a bold reply to the earlier proclamations Claiborne had posted in prominent places throughout New Orleans, offering a reward of five hundred dollars for the arrest and delivery of Jean Lafitte to the Sheriff of the Parish of Orleans.

As yet, neither of them had been delivered.

"Bah," Pierre was saying, "look at Grymes. He is to protect us from men like Claiborne, yet we are hounded. It is difficult to do business when we must waste time with foolish revenue cutters and trivial seizures."

"One day," Kit said, "it will not be so trivial."

"Perhaps not. But now it is a nuisance."

Kit pushed away from the tree, turned toward the path that led down to the water. It would be time soon; he had been preparing for this day for two years, ever since he had escaped Captain Jack's ship after a fierce battle with Lafitte, who had protested the former's encroachment on his territory. Defeated, standing amidst battle debris, he had been impressed by Lafitte's cool demeanor and demands that Captain Jack "shop" elsewhere for plunder. Rashly, he'd made a bold bid to join Lafitte, and he'd not regretted it since. A providential decision, as it turned out, for the crew who sailed with Captain Jack were soon after captured by revenue cutters and hanged, and the pirate leader killed.

Now he had his own ship, earned with his share of the booty captured from Spanish vessels taken in the shipping lanes of the Gulf. Lafitte had a thousand men under his command, and fifty ships flew the flag of Cartagena, a privateer's flag, with letters of marque from Colombia. It was not a bad life, but he was restless. It could not last forever; Claiborne was only the first crack in the security of the thriving trade from Barataria.

When he reached the shore, he saw that the tide was coming in. When winter waned, it would be time to sail. His ship was fitted out and provisioned, ready for the Atlantic. It would be his first voyage as captain of her.

Cacafuego was a small sloop, fast and bristling with guns, hence the name. The polite translation was *Spitfire*, but the crew affectionately used the literal interpretation of *Shitfire* when referring to the vessel. A sweet ship, and his, now that the original owner—or, he should say, *last* owner—had been killed.

Originally, the ship had belonged to Spain; now it rode the sea as one of Lafitte's Trust, the company formed by pirates and privateers.

Sometimes he thought of the days in Newport News when he had been young and naive, thinking that life at sea would be adventurous and exciting. In reality, it was sheer terror at times, punctuated with hours of back-breaking labor made more difficult by searing sun or lashing rain. Yet it had its rewards: he was still alive.

For a time, his fate had been doubtful. Those first months with Captain Jack had come close to destroying him. If not for the timely intervention of Jean Lafitte, he might well have died and his body been given to the sea.

As it was, he was alive, and now he intended to let Amalie know he still lived. He just wasn't certain how to manage it without being apprehended and hanged. It would hardly do to invite her to his hanging.

But it had been over four years now since they had been separated. Everything had fallen into place at last and the time was right. He would find her, and he would give her the choice to come with him, though it was not a life for someone like Amie. Still, he could settle her in New

Orleans, make her swear not to tell anyone he was her brother, and perhaps she could find happiness there.

He thought of her so often, wondered if she was happy, if she was married, if she ever thought of him. He just wanted her to know he had not forgotten her, or his promise that he would return.

"Lover, *amante*," a voice purred at his side, and he turned to see Rosa smiling at him. Black eyes and hair, a luscious body, and a willing nature enlivened winter nights when the heavy rains came and it was hard to tell where land, sea, and sky separated.

He put an arm around her, felt her snuggle close to him, her hand touching him intimately. "Bold little cat," he said in Spanish, and she laughed.

"Ah yes, but you like me that way, do you not?"

"I do. . . ." His hand slid upward, cupped her full breast in his palm, squeezed gently as she sighed and rubbed against him in invitation. Idly he caressed her until she squirmed, his mind not fully on the passionate little creature, but straying instead to details of his upcoming voyage.

There was always the chance that Amie had already been wed, and would be horrified at his sudden intrusion into her life; he would not blame her. After all, a pirate as a brother would be an inconvenience and an embarrassment. Would she be appalled at his choices? But life did not always present good choices, sometimes offering only the option to survive.

Rosa slipped her hand into the waist of his

trousers, cupped him in her palm, and his attention was diverted to her as he laughed. "You have no shame. Do you want me to take you here on the dock, where all can see?"

"If it pleases you. . . ." She rose to her toes, nipped him lightly on his neck, then licked the small bite with the tip of her tongue. "You ignore Rosa, when I want you to pay attention to me."

"Greedy bitch," he murmured, but surrendered to the deft strokes of her hand on him, and with a soft oath, curled his hand into her long, loose hair and dragged her head back to kiss her with harsh, savage intensity.

Frustration and uncertainty could be forgotten in the arms of a woman, even if only for a short time, and he took her into the dubious privacy of the trees, threw her to the ground, and heard her sighs and moans of pleasure. Rosa liked it rough; it excited her when he used her like the whore she was, and he obliged, shoving up her long skirts and pushing her down into a tussock of long grass.

Panting, she wrapped her legs around him, arched her back as he freed his erection and impaled her in a swift, hard thrust. Her teeth scored his neck, stinging pain that he ignored, closing out everything but the erotic shudders that wrapped around him like a heated fist.

It was, he thought later, when passion was spent, an indictment of his character that he was so easily distracted by a woman. But then, he had changed greatly since leaving Newport News, and not for the better.

Would Amalie even recognize him? He did not recognize himself most of the time, the man he had become a stranger in the mirror. . . .

Chapter 12

Deverell was in a foul temper, one of his black moods that always made Stanfill wary. The viscount waited, sipped excellent French brandy that had no doubt been in the earl's cellar for a hundred years, and idly watched flames leap behind brass firedogs.

The reason for Dev's mood was unknown, but he suspected it had to do with a woman. To be precise, Miss Courtland. After all, he had gone to his grandmother's house with the intention of confronting them both with their association with Don Carlos de la Reine; Lady Winford should know better, for he was a scoundrel of the first water, a rogue and a fortune-hunter, with only a title and questionable family antecedents to recommend him. Yes, no doubt the interview had gone badly with them, as it frequently did when one was dealing with Lady Winford.

Now, *there* was an exasperating woman! Aristocrat, wed twice to powerful men, yet flighty, and prone to involving herself with country vicars and packs of pugs. He had been treated to the little dogs more than the vicars, and was not at all certain which was the worse. Both he found obnoxious, but perhaps the pugs had redeeming qualities, for at least they could be rented out to ladies eager to have their portraits painted with a dog, but loathe to own one of the popular breed.

Ah well, it was Dev's problem and not his, thank God, for he had his own to deal with. Pressure increased for him to marry and provide an heir, as it seemed his brother, the present heir, was loathe to dally with females, much preferring the company of pretty young men. If not for the fact he was looked to for the provision of an heir, he would find great satisfaction in thwarting his brother. They had never, after all, liked one another.

"Damn her," Deverell said into the silence, and he looked up at him with a lifted brow, waiting. In a moment the earl glanced at him, grimaced, set down his empty brandy glass with a thud. "I'll have to speak to Grandmère in the morning."

"I take it the interview this evening did not go well?"

To his surprise, Deverell gave a harsh bark of laughter that rang much too loud in the quiet study. His mouth curved into a cynical smile.

"Oh no, it went much better than any man has a right to expect. That is the problem." He rose to his feet, went to the fire, and stared down at the flames, silent again; he was in a bad mood, indeed. The clock on the mantel chimed the midnight hour, sonorous tones that faded into gloom.

After a moment, Stanfill rose to his feet, stretched, and yawned. "I think I shall make an early night of it. You will be there tomorrow, I trust—at Portland House?"

"Yes, I'll be there. If I'm late, wait for me. I have a man working on some of the investigations for me, and he is not always dependable when it comes to telling time."

"Ah." He grinned. "Jemmy Taylor, I presume."

"Yes, a rascal and a rogue, but able to ferret out almost anything we need to know." Deverell turned, smiled a little. "He is more reliable than most Members of Parliament."

"I'm not at all certain that's any consolation. But if anyone can find out who is behind the men stalking Cochrane and now you, it's Jemmy."

It was, Stanfill thought, as he left the Curzon Street house, a pity, when a former Bow Street Runner had more integrity than men who ran the country. He shivered, pulled up the edges of his coat, stepped into the warmth of the waiting hansom and out of the frigid air. It rocked forward, hooves a muffled thud on ice, cautious footing as wheels crunched over frozen ruts. More snow would fall before long, and the Thames was already a solid sheet of ice thick enough to provide footing for a Frost Fair.

An idea occurred to him, and he almost halted the cab and turned back, but thought better of it. Tomorrow would be soon enough.

Snow thickly blanketed ground and streets. Traffic had slowed to a crawl in places, and carriages moved sluggishly; cautious pedestrians picked careful paths.

Holt dismounted in the stableyard of Beacon House, gave strict instructions for the care of the bay, and made his way across ice-coated pathways to the house. Smoke curled from chimneys in sharp-scented wisps to mingle with lowering gray clouds. Huge flakes fell in a steady curtain, a soft drape over trees and bushes already bent beneath the weight.

Baxter met him at the doorway, took his coat, waved him toward the morning room.

"Lady Winford is at breakfast, my lord."

"And Miss Courtland?"

"I believe the young miss is having breakfast in her room today."

Just as well. He was certainly in no mood to see her yet. Of all the fool things he had ever done in his life, the yielding to temptation in his grandmother's library had to rank at the top. It had not been planned; he had gone to Beacon House with the express intention of taking his grandmother to task for allowing the attentions of Don Carlos, and berating Miss Courtland for encouraging them. He had certainly not expected to find everyone else retired for the night, and the chit on the floor in her white muslin gown, with hair loose and seductive.

Nor had he expected desire to hit him so strongly, a hammer blow that smashed any good intentions he might ever have had in his life; now, for the first time, he felt a sense of regret for something he had done.

Imperturbable as always, Baxter, if he knew anything about his late night visit, did not reveal it by word or expression, but said merely, "I believe Lady Winford is expecting you, my lord."

His mouth tightened. Not unexpected; it was likely the girl had gone straight to her with a tale of woe. Just as likely that Grandmère now waited to give him a dressing down. Not undeserved, perhaps, but unwanted.

Lady Winford glanced up at him when he entered the breakfast room, a bright-eyed gaze that revealed nothing.

"Ah, you are here at last. Sit down, sit down. We'll eat while we talk."

She waved a hand toward the chair next to her. As usual, a swarm of dogs gathered under the table, waiting with impatient expectations for the occasional tidbit she fed them, an act that was usually accompanied by yaps and a sporadic quarrel among the pugs.

He eyed them. "I do not dine with dogs, Grandmère."

"No? That is not what I heard, but then, your latest bit of muslin is more of a cat, if rumor is correct. Trent, remove the dogs, if you will, and be certain Cook gives them treats."

"Yes, my lady," the footman replied as he regarded the pugs with resignation.

It took a few minutes, but the breakfast room was soon cleared of dogs and Holt took a seat in the chair beside his grandmother.

Her gaze was swift and sharp. "Your face—have you been involved in another duel? No doubt your current bit is married as well. You court disaster, Holt."

"A small accident in the park left this," he said as she lightly tapped the boiled egg perched in a delicate cup. "You listen to too much gossip, Grandmère."

Her spoon paused; she glanced up at him, smiled, and shook her head. "Not at all, dear boy. I'm far too busy. Mrs. Fry—do you recall her, by chance? She is most charming, a woman of great energy and ideas. Of course, she is more interested in social reform and the revolutionizing of the prison system, while I crusade for more humane treatment of animals, but we have similar goals, after all, and get on quite well. She keeps me quite busy, much too busy to indulge in idle rumors. Yet gossip seems to find me despite my full days. Such a trial at times."

"Baxter can be quite informative, I am sure."

Unfazed, she acknowledged his sardonic comment with a vigorous nod of her head. "Yes, he is marvelous. Knows everything that goes on in London. I have no idea how he does it. Yet there are some things even Baxter cannot manage for me. Holt, I am concerned about Amalie."

He sipped hot, strong chocolate the footman served him, cynically waited to hear the barrage of indicting euphemisms that would all lead to the inescapable truth that he had taken Miss Courtland's virginity.

But instead, she frowned, spoon poised over the egg cup as if it were a dagger in her hand, and said severely, "It is Don Carlos de la Reine's suit that alarms me."

"His suit?" He set down his chocolate, leaned back in the chair. Gray light from the tall window behind his grandmother left her face half in shadow; there was no hint of subterfuge or censure in her eyes, nothing but this grim tone in her voice as she went on about the Spanish nobleman.

"Not at all the thing, somehow; I do believe he is not what he seems. Oh, I do not know why I think this, and Baxter has heard only that he is an emigré because of that nasty Corsican who is ravaging countries like a voracious wolf, but there you have it—I *am* concerned. What do you think of Don Carlos? Do you think him suitable for our darling Amalie?"

Carefully, he replied, "I have met him only a few times, Grandmère."

"Yes, but you usually know when a man is what he claims to be. You have an instinct about these things. So I implore you to find out what you can about him, for I do believe he means to offer for our Amalie."

His brow rose. An unexpected solution—and a problem. It would be too easy to allow Don Carlos to wed her and absolve him of any guilt for removing her maidenhead—but he did not trust the Spaniard, though he had no definite proof for his misgivings.

"Why do you think Don Carlos means to offer for her?" he asked, instead of committing himself out of hand. "Has he approached you about it?"

"Not directly, but Holt, there are *signs*. Surely, you must be able to recognize when a man is in love, though I daresay *that* firsthand knowledge has always managed to elude you, somehow. Still, there is hope that one day you will be fortunate enough to find a woman who is suitable for not only your position, but your nature."

Dryly he replied, "I shudder to think who that might be, Grandmère, for as you are so fond of reminding me, I am not exactly a congenial sort."

"True, but there will be a woman who can soften up those hard edges of yours—if you will only be clever enough to recognize her."

"We were talking about Don Carlos and Miss Courtland, I believe."

"How tiresome you can be. Yes, of course we were, and I really want you to do what you can to learn all that is important about him. I want our darling Amalie to be happy, after all, and while a good marriage is essential, there is no reason why it shouldn't be to someone quite suitable, don't you think?"

It was obvious that *darling Amalie* had said nothing to Grandmère yet about their intimacy in the library. For a moment he toyed with the notion of telling her himself, to blunt the effect this revelation would have on her, but then discarded the temptation.

It wasn't something he relished doing. He still didn't understand why he had succumbed to the sudden overwhelming desire to possess the little Colonial. She was certainly not the first woman he had seen in a thin nightdress—or without one—nor was she the most beautiful. In fact, he had not thought her beautiful at all, with her mass of dark hair and those preposterously large eyes that always regarded him with such disdain—he'd considered her a gypsy-child, rustic and naive despite her tart tongue that could flay him to the bone and render him furious in the space of a heart's beat.

Yet despite that, despite his irritation at what he considered her presumption in settling herself on his grandmother as she had, he had found his sympathy ignited by her unexpected vulnerability the night before. His usual impression of disdainful gypsy had softened, so that he saw only a woman in need of comfort. Sympathy had slowly altered to an unanticipated reaction as he'd stroked warmth back into her chilled limbs, but desire was no less potent for being unexpected.

It still amazed him, that he had forgotten himself so much as to ignore the inescapable fact Amalie Courtland was his grandmother's goddaughter, and that she was—even if indirectly—under his protection as well. He might have flouted convention all his life, but this was inexcusable.

"Well?" Grandmère demanded, eying him with a slight frown, "What do you think of Don Carlos wedding Amalie?"

"I think," he said with deliberate indifference, "that she is getting no younger. She definitely needs to be married to someone. Not Don Carlos, but to the first suitable man we can find."

Lady Winford replaced her spoon on the saucer beneath her egg cup with a slight clatter, sat back in her chair to look at him. "Do you? How interesting that you have concerned yourself with her future, Holt. I find that most heartening. Can it mean that you are thinking of someone other than yourself?"

"As amazing as that may seem to you—yes." He met her surprised gaze with a faint smile. "I am thinking of you. I have made no secret of the fact that I've never approved of your affinity for taking in waifs and strays, and Miss Courtland is certainly a tenacious lodger. But it is time you relinquished her care to someone else. Get her married off, and the sooner, the better."

"How pompous! Just when I begin to think you might have a heart after all, you spoil it with autocratic demands."

"Miss Courtland is a liability, not an asset. It is time you faced that fact, Grandmère.

"Good God, Holt, I thought we had an understanding by now. Amie has brought me great joy, and she has been here with me, something my own grandson does not deign to do. I merely wish to see her happy, as she has made me happy. If you do not wish to make inquiries about Don Carlos—"

"I fully intend to make inquiries about Don Carlos," he said, "and I fully intend to find a suitable husband for your gypsy waif. What I do *not* intend to do is allow her to embarrass you with a scandal."

"Oh no, that would be a bit redundant, wouldn't it, when you are already so adept at it?"

"There's a vast difference," he said softly, "between a man's occasional acquisition of a mistress and a lady's indecent behavior."

"Is there? I wonder if the mistress feels that way."

He shoved back his chair, rose abruptly to his feet. "I see that our conversation is in danger of becoming a debate on social reforms. Let us end it on a pleasant note rather than on disagreeable terms, shall we?"

Dull light through the tall casement windows gleamed on the pearls around Lady Winford's throat, created a hazy aureole around her head as she stared up at him with a lifted brow.

"Yes, we shall, though I find it most intriguing that you always end the conversation when it is disagreeable to *you*. Never mind. Discover what you can about Don Carlos, though I do think Amie should not accept his suit when he offers. You may deal with Don Carlos as you see fit. Shall I send him to you with his offer for her?"

"By all means, do that. I'll have her married off to him and shipped to Spain within the week."

"You needn't be so offensive, Holt."

"No, and you needn't throw your little Colonial in my face, either. I weary of *darling Amalie* and her damned problems. And you don't need to look at me that way—you know how I feel, how I've felt since you took her in as if she's another goddam pug, slobbering on your shoes and at your heels all day. For Christ's sake, Grandmère, if you wanted another lapdog, why didn't you just get another pug? I'll be more than glad to see the last of Miss Courtland, and if it takes marrying her off to a Spaniard or even a Bow-bell Cockney, then I'll do it, by God—though if you had as much sense as compassion, we would all be better off."

He hadn't meant for the vicious note to creep into his tone, but it had, and he saw from his grandmother's suddenly pale face that he had hurt her again. Dammit, he wished to hell she had not taken in the girl. Matters had not been right between them since.

"Deverell, do lower your voice," Lady Winford said at last, her tone even, "as the servants have ears and I do not wish this to be repeated all over London."

Her meaningful glance toward the breakfast room door was ample reminder, and he turned, but saw nothing beyond a slight sway of the door. He looked back at her, said in a more reasonable tone, "Grandmère, I came here with the full intention of warning you about Don Carlos. I don't need to make inquiries about him. If he thinks Amalie has access to your money, he will make an offer."

"Then you can disabuse him of that notion, I daresay."

"I daresay." His hands curled over the curved back of the Sheraton chair, pushed it forward a bit. "Now I must leave for an appointment. Give Miss Courtland my regards, and remember what I said about getting her married to the first suitable man who offers."

"Oh, I most certainly intend that she marry someone suitable. I have my own notions of who will suit, however."

"I do not doubt that at all." He paused, then said, "I will settle a small sum on her as a wedding dower, but do not expect more of me."

He ignored the surprise on his grandmother's face, and her murmured exclamation, and left the breakfast room. One of the maids disappeared around a corner, the hem of her white apron briefly visible as he entered the hallway. Grandmère's assessment of prying servants was irritatingly accurate, it seemed.

It was, he thought, as he strode across the entrance hall and waited for Baxter to retrieve his coat, a damned unpleasant way to start the day.

He was glad it was over. And even more glad he did not have to face Amalie Courtland and be reminded of what he had done. Marrying her off was the kindest solution he could think of to solve her problems, and his own. With a tidy sum settled upon her, the loss of her virginity should matter little to a prospective husband, and he would see that it did not. No, he owed her that much, a generous sum to ensure that she married well.

It was the least he could do.

~

In the shadows just off the hallway, Amalie pressed her back against the wall; her heart thudded, and in the pit of her stomach, a dull weight settled like a stone. It was all she could do to keep rising nausea from choking her as she huddled in the corner, the memory of Deverell's words a harsh ring in her ears: *I weary of darling Amalie and her damned problems. . . .*

A ruthless assertion. A scalding evaluation—*you know how I feel, how I've felt since you took her in as if she's another goddam pug, slobbering on your shoes. . . .*

How humiliating . . . why ever had she thought, for even a moment, that he might care about her feelings? He did not, of course. His compassion had been only a prelude to what he really intended, a ploy to discredit her in front of her godmother. And oh God, what must Grandmamma think of her now? What would she see in her eyes when she must face her again—condemnation? Disappointment?

At this moment, she thought she had never

been so humiliated in her entire life. The Devil Earl, an apt name for him. He *was* a devil—and she had allowed herself to be duped into believing him redeemable, to thinking he might harbor a fondness for her. And oh, what was worse, she had not stopped him, or even tried to stop him, but allowed him to have her so easily . . . she could not even blame the posset, for surely she could have summoned the presence of mind to evade him if she had not been so used to having him in her dreams . . . another folly.

The dream version of Deverell was far more human than the reality of him.

Now she must face the consequences of her action—or inaction. Steeling herself, she stepped from the shadows into the faint glow of a wall lamp that illuminated the hallway, and walked to the breakfast room. If she was to be evicted, best get it behind her now.

Chapter 13

Lady Winford frowned. What *was* dear Amie babbling on about? And how unlike her, to be so out of countenance—the poor girl looked as if she was about to burst into tears at any moment, and was making no sense whatsoever. But of course the discovery that her brother had been hanged for a pirate must have a dreadful effect on her.

"Shall I have Lucy prepare you another posset, my darling?"

Amalie sat down abruptly in the chair next to her. "No, Grandmamma, it was a posset that—no, I do not think I would care for another one."

She rose, put a hand atop her shoulder, and smiled gently. "It will be all right, my child. Now, come along, unless you wish to eat something—? No? Very well, come with me into the parlor. You look quite haggard this morning, and I know you cannot have slept well at all after Deverell was here. Ah men, they lack compassion at times, though I know he meant well—Trent, do see to my precious darlings, will you? I don't know why Holt does not care for them, for they are such loyal creatures."

"Grandmamma . . ."

She turned, a little surprised at the note of urgency in Amie's tone. "Yes, my dear? What is it? Are you unwell? Oh dear, did the posset make you ill?"

A sound between laughter and a sob came from Amie's lips, and she put a hand over her mouth as if to press it back. Truly concerned now, she went to her, led her into the parlor, and sat her down in the stuffed settee before the fire.

"My darling Amie, whatever is the matter? This is frightening, seeing you like this—can't you tell me?"

"Grandmamma, I've been *trying* to tell you, but—oh, you really don't know, do you? I thought he would tell you about it—I should have refused, but I—did not."

Lady Winford's hand stilled for a moment on Amalie's hair, where she had been gently stroking it back from her forehead. An uneasy suspicion formed, and she studied the pale face for a long moment. Tragedy lurked in the wide green eyes, dark shadows that she had seen before on faces of girls who had made grave errors in judgment. It was not unknown, nor was it that rare, sadly.

Yet with Amalie, it was astonishing. She had shown no interest at all in any man, save Sir Alex, and *everyone* knew that he preferred beardless young men to females when it came to certain acts . . . could she have been foolish enough to get involved with him? But no—impossible. She was not blind, and must know of Sir Alex's habits.

Besides pretty young men, Sir Alex had a penchant for gambling, and would no doubt find a penniless young woman quite unnecessary, *de trop*. No, even if Amie were willing to behave foolishly, Sir Alex would not be interested.

A horrible thought struck her—surely Amalie had not done something foolish with Don Carlos! Oh, that would ruin everything, for she had just succeeded in getting Holt to notice the fact that the Spaniard had been paying court to Amalie—a ploy designed to make him also notice *Amie*, of course, as a most desirable young woman. Oh, it would be too terrible if she had . . .

Delicately, she said, "My darling, you must know that you can tell me anything. I am quite loyal to those I love."

"Oh, I know that." She looked up, managed a smile that wavered unsteadily. "I really do, but this—I do not understand it myself, I truly do not. All this time I have had those dreams—silly dreams, but it made me think of him when I had no reason to, and then when he came here—well, he was so *aloof*, and I realized that my dreams were only illusions. It seemed so romantic when I was young, all gallant and daring, to know that he fought a duel over a woman. I should never have indulged myself, but it seemed harmless, and after all, who knew that anything would come of it?"

Appalled, Lady Winford realized that she meant Holt. It explained his vehemence earlier, and his wary expectation. She had wondered about it, but it was always best to let people tell you things in their own time. Yet to allow Amie to confess what happened would force her to acknowledge it, and that might ruin everything. *No. . . .*

"My dear, I know that you are overwrought about your brother. And I also know that you would never do anything to hurt me or yourself." Deliberately, feeling a bit guilty but determined not to let this ruin all her plans for them, she forced a smile to her lips, patted Amie on the cheek gently. "It would devastate me to think that you would ever do anything to embarrass us. You have far too much honor, and you know that I would feel betrayed. No, I trust you to do the right thing. You will never disappoint me."

It was difficult not to look away from the desperate despair in Amie's eyes, but at last she lowered her gaze and nodded, her voice a faint whisper: "No, Grandmamma, I would never do anything to hurt you."

Pangs of guilt were smothered with the determined reassurance that this was all for the best, that once Amie and Holt were married, nothing else would matter.

More snow fell, a steady *chink* against the window panes. Amalie watched it silently, the despair inside much colder than the growing white drifts that piled against the house.

She could not tell Grandmamma the truth. If it was to be told, *he* would have to do it. Oh, what a coward she was, a spineless, weak coward! If only she could forget all the things the earl had said, but they haunted her: *I'll be more than glad to see the last of Miss Courtland, and if takes marrying her off to a Spaniard or even a Bow-*

bell Cockney, then I'll do it, by God. . . .

Her hand closed into a fist against the glass windowpane; cold seeped through glass into her hand and up her arm. Despair churned, spread through her, insidious and pervasive. Yet it began to harden into desperation, to take on another form as she stared out the window.

Perhaps there was a way out, after all. Marriage would solve her problem. She thought not of Don Carlos, but of Sir Alex. After all, even though she had committed a faux pas with him, he still called on her occasionally, and seemed content to be in her company. They had mutual interests, and he encouraged her to talk of America and her life there as a child.

Sir Alex was handsome, kind, and not at all abrasive in his manner. As a younger son he was in need of money. Since Deverell stated his intention to settle a sum upon her—another humiliation—she would not be foolish. She would take it, use it as her dowry for a marriage to Sir Alex. Oh, it would be so difficult to broach the subject, as he was so remote, but surely he would not be *too* averse to the notion of wedding her? It was done every day, marriages of convenience performed for much less reason than the lack of money, and she really did like Sir Alex, and he seemed to like her.

Yes, that was what she would do. Loathe as she was to take anything from the earl, she would allow him to settle a generous dowry upon her. Deverell owed her that. As she would have to live with the consequences of her actions, the least he could do was pay for his.

With hope strengthening her resolve, she put

away the despair that threatened to annihilate her. It would not help to surrender to it. As soon as weather permitted, she would pluck up her courage and call upon Sir Alex. It was not exactly *the thing* to call upon a gentleman, but to a woman who faced utter ruin, that was as unimportant as a flea bite.

For a long time, she stared out her window, watching snow whirl in the wind that buffeted London. It echoed her mood, this cold emptiness inside her, the frozen wasteland of shattered dreams and hopes.

She thought of her brother with grief and regret, and prayed that Kit had forgiven her before he died. If only she could forgive herself. . . .

The storm that raged outside Beacon House subsided the next night; snow piled high and the Thames was frozen over between the dilapidated piers of London Bridge and the newer Blackfriar's Bridge. Despite bitter cold, half London turned out to play upon the river, an impromptu fair upon the frozen surface.

It provided the perfect opportunity for Amalie to leave the house.

"Lucy will accompany me," she said calmly when Grandmamma voiced protest at her proposed venture. "And I am certain many of my acquaintance will be there."

"But my darling Amie, so will cutpurses and thieves."

"I do not propose to carry a large sum of money with me, Grandmamma, so you needn't worry that I shall be at risk. I weary of remaining in the house, cooped up like a bird—" She halted, unwillingly reminded of Deverell's mocking assessment of her situation at Beacon House.

"Oh, young people have so much more stamina these days," Lady Winford said with a sigh, and stretched her feet closer to the sitting room fire. One of the pugs yapped sleepy protest at her movement; she put a hand atop the furry head in a languid stroke. "All that frigid snow and ice—why, Baxter told me that people have already set up booths on the ice, with skittle-alleys and even Punch and Judy shows."

"Yes, much like last year's. At any rate, I intend to stay briefly, and only as a spectator. I found it quite entertaining last year."

"So did the chimney sweeps and gin-wives. Oh dear, I do sound quite intolerant, don't I? Mrs Fry would be very disappointed in me, but really, one must be cautious when going about London these days, as it is difficult to know who can be trusted not to hit you in the head for a few baubles or your purse. You will be careful, won't you, Amie darling? Take Trent with you as escort. He is a sturdy young man, and anyway, he absolutely adores our Lucy, and it would please them both, I think, to be together."

"You are a kind soul, Grandmamma."

"Not at all, just practical. If I appeal to your good heart for Lucy's sake, I am much more likely to get you to agree. Now, do bundle up warmly, if you insist upon this reckless venture. Oh, do not mind Sophy, she is so jealous when anyone gets near me. . . ."

Amalie avoided the yapping pug that took umbrage at her proximity to Lady Winford, and pressed a kiss upon the dowager's cheek. A surge of guilt at her deception tempted her to confide the true reason for her outing, but such a confession would only hurt her godmother.

Yet when she alighted from the carriage in front of Sir Alex's townhouse, she almost turned back. Sudden apprehension gripped her, made her clumsy as she picked her way up icy steps to the front door with what she hoped was casual composure.

Lucy had been surprised at the detour, but willing enough to remain in the carriage with Trent.

"A short visit to drop off a card," she explained to the maid with a blithe self-assurance she did not feel, and Lucy had accepted it without demur.

If the elderly butler who admitted her to Sir Alex's domain was surprised by the visit of a young woman without escort of even her maid, he did not reveal it as he showed her into the small parlor.

"Please wait here while I see if Sir Alex is in, Miss Courtland." He bowed slightly, a stiff courtesy, and left her in the parlor to take her card up to Sir Alex.

The parlor was gloomy, with little light filtering through heavy draperies flanking tall windows. No fire burned in the empty grate, and there was an air of musty finality to the room that not even a cheery fire could have eased. It was cold, the chill pressing down on her so that she shivered with it, tucking her hands deeply into the plush warmth of the fur muff she carried. Nor did she push back the hood of her bright red wool cloak, much preferring warmth to propriety. Besides, the red suited her, and the silk lining was a soft rose color that was very flattering.

It was disconcerting to discover that she was as vain as some she knew, thinking of her appearance at times of stress, but it might be important to Sir Alex that she be considered attractive, given the nature of her visit.

Oh God, what am I doing?

Nervous, she wondered wildly what she would say to him when—and if—he accepted her card and call. How *did* one propose marriage to a man who had never even kissed her hand? Oh, this was insane . . . she should not have come, should not have let herself become so desperate even as to consider such an improbable scheme. It was foolish beyond sense. If he said no, she would look a fool and worse. And if he said yes, how would she ever live with the knowledge that she had literally sold herself to him?

No, not even to save Grandmamma embarrassment can I stay here and debase myself so. . . .

Swiftly she crossed to the parlor door that had been left slightly ajar and put out her hand to open it, but it swung open before she could touch it.

Sir Alex halted in the opening, lifted a pale brow in faint surprise. Tawny hair tumbled onto his forehead à la Brutus in careful curls, and the sleepy gray eyes regarded her intently beneath half-lowered lashes.

"Why, Miss Courtland, were you about to depart?"

"No—yes. I thought perhaps I was disturbing you and should leave. . . ."

Her words trailed into awkward silence as she struggled for composure. Despite the chill of the house, her cheeks were flushed with heat. She tucked both hands into the depths of her fur muff to hide their sudden quiver, managed a smile that she hoped disguised her panic.

His smile was reassuring, a practiced curve of his lips. "No, you could never disturb me. I am always pleased to see you. Would you care for chocolate, perhaps? I could have—"

"No, Sir Alex, it was really forward of me to come here like this, and I realize it must seem extraordinary to you, but I—I wondered if you still have that copy of Maria Edgeworth's book on London social life. Do you recall that we discussed it?"

"Yes, of course I recall. A witty novel." He regarded her with his faint smile, his gaze almost lazy as he reached out to take her arm. "The book is in my library, a much warmer room than this. Merton should not have put you into such an inhospitable room—why, you're shivering, Miss Courtland. I insist you come with me."

Coward, she berated herself, as she allowed him to guide her from the parlor to the library. His hand on her arm was comforting and she thought again of the difference between Sir Alex and Deverell. Such dissimilar men, though they shared similar backgrounds.

Perhaps she could summon the courage after all to propose her bargain to him—an arrangement that might well benefit them both.

A fire warmed the library, a dark-panelled

room with comfortable settees and chairs, shelves of books from floor to ceiling. Lamps threw small pools of illumination over tables, and carpets that had seen better days were a bit thin underfoot.

"Stand here by the fire, Miss Courtland. You're still shivering."

It wasn't the cold but tension that made her shiver, but she moved obediently to the fire. She felt his eyes on her, intent, curious, and turned to face him, screwing up her courage.

"Sir Alex, it is my thought that we have gotten on rather well since we met."

"Indeed we have, Miss Courtland. Of all the women of my acquaintance, I daresay you are the most congenial. Did you say it is the latest Maria Edgeworth book you want? *The Absentee*, I believe it is called?"

"Yes, I believe that's it—Sir Alex. It's not just the book I came here to talk to you about." She drew in a deep breath, gripped the fur muff tightly with both hands.

"Is it not? How intriguing. Why, Miss Courtland, you seem unnerved." A look of concern creased his face and he came close, gripped her by the shoulders to stare into her eyes. His voice was suddenly soft, intimate, and her heart leaped with hope. He put his hand against her cheek; it was warm and soft. "You have not been yourself since the earl returned from Spain. Brilliant victory, Salamanca, yet I understand Deverell prefers not to speak of it."

"I am not close enough to the earl for him to confide his emotions about the war, Sir Alex."

"No? Yet he is frequently at Beacon House, I

would think. Does he not speak of it? Or of his plans?"

She hesitated, dismayed by the direction of their conversation but uncertain how to bring it back around without seeming rude. After inadvertently offending him at her birthday celebration, it would ruin all if she did so again.

"I have heard him speak of the war, of course, usually to my godmother. If he has stated his plans, I've not heard them. Sir Alex—"

"Odd, do you not think, that Deverell did not go with Wellington to winter at Portugal? One would think he would want to remain with Lord Wellington after that marvelous victory against the French."

"Really, Sir Alex, I do not know nor do I care what the earl does!" Sharper this time, she succeeded in gaining his attention. "I came for another reason."

"Ah yes, the book. Let me—"

"No, not just the book. Sir Alex, this may seem forward and precipitate, and you have certainly given me no reason to believe you might encourage such feelings, but I am convinced that we have a solid friendship."

A brow lifted, and he gazed at her with a faint frown on his handsome face, the beautiful features arranging into a wary mask. "Indeed we do. Pray, go on, Miss Courtland."

His hands dropped from her shoulders, fell to his sides, and he looked unapproachable again, as remote as he had across a ballroom floor. She hesitated, floundered in the chill of his gaze. It seemed suddenly more than just brazen to be here, but she was committed to her course.

"Sir Alex, circumstances lately have left me somewhat in a predicament, and I wished to ask you—"

A brief movement beyond Sir Alex caught her eye, and she paused as an unfamiliar gentleman halted in the open door of the library. He seemed surprised, and hesitated with a hand still on the door latch.

"Oh. Sorry. Had no idea you were busy, Maitland. Shall I come back?"

"No, not at all. Miss Courtland, you no doubt know Lord Carlton."

"We have been introduced." Dismay battled with relief that she had not gone further before this unexpected interruption, and she regarded the new arrival with a frozen smile.

A mistake to come here, a disaster if it is repeated.

Silence fell; the three of them stood awkwardly. When the silence stretched too long, Sir Alex prompted, "Miss Courtland, you wished to ask something of me, I think."

"Yes, I did. But it seems foolish now. Forgive me, Sir Alex. I have wasted your time."

"A man's time is never wasted when it is spent with a beautiful woman, Miss Courtland."

A gallant phrase, smooth and practiced, the kind of thing men said to naive girls—it irritated her, when she should be flattered.

"No, I am certain it is not, Sir Alex. Now, if I may borrow the book, please, my maid is waiting for me."

Not until she was back in the safety of the carriage with a wrapped brick at her feet and Lucy all flushed and agitated at her side did she look down at the book in her hand. Then she laughed ruefully. It was an entirely different book, *Sense and Sensibility*, written *By a Lady*, an anonymous writer. Apparently, Sir Alex was as flustered as she had been, to give her the wrong book.

Perhaps Lord Carlton's arrival had been for the best. It might have been a grave mistake on her part not to prepare Sir Alex better for what she intended to ask. Next time, she would think it through more thoroughly. The fact that he had been receptive to her visit was heartening; she must find a way to break through his reserve.

Chapter 14

Long before the carriage drew near London Bridge, the roads were jammed with vehicles and occasional wrecks. The icy roads were hazardous, yet it looked as if all of London had turned out for the Frost Fair on the frozen surface of the Thames.

Still agitated, Amalie regretted the necessity of a pretense that brought her there; if she did not go, Lucy might think it odd, since that was her professed reason for leaving the house on such a frigid day.

An odd sight indeed, the Thames was packed with booths: bookstalls, peddlers, pie-men, oyster wenches, and fruit sellers vied for space and customers, jammed in together on the ice, elbow to elbow. A festive air greeted them as they picked their way cautiously over slick surfaces and snowbanks, Lucy laughing at anything the footman had to say, and Trent doing his best to divide his attention between Amalie and the ruddy-cheeked maid.

Tempting smells of hot bread loaves wafted across the ice; brandy balls, gin, beer, and other hot potations warmed patrons of certain booths, who seemed not to mind the bitter cold at all. Gambling booths staggered along the fringes of snow, hastily erected between wooden posts sticking up like jagged teeth.

They moved slowly through the crowd, and at one of the booths, Trent purchased hot meat pies for all of them, greasy concoctions that were surprisingly good. The pastry was filled with chunks of beef and onion, held together with thick suet gravy, strongly spiced. Laughing a little at her inability to keep the pie from dripping down her gloved hand, Amalie realized she was hungry, when she had not been able to eat in nearly two days.

Perhaps getting away from the house was the best thing she could have done for herself today, even if she still had no idea how to solve her problem. At least here, where swarms of Londoners came to forget the harshness of their lives for a few hours, she could be one of them, could lose herself in simple pleasures.

"Oh look, Miss Courtland," Lucy said, a little breathless from the exertion of walking down the steep slope, "a Punch and Judy show. Shall we watch?"

A booth had been set up, red curtains framing the puppets that were by turn bawdy and clever. Puppets with outrageously distorted faces were manipulated by unseen hands, squabbling in clever commentary of everyday life, of mundane events and of the notable. Amalie found herself laughing with the crowd, amused by the often ribald references to everything from politics to the royal family.

"Acquiring a taste for the vulgar, Miss Courtland?"

The husky tones of the familiar voice behind her needed no identification; she knew it far too well, and stiffened with dismay. Of all people to chance meeting in such a crowd!

Slowly, she turned, gazed at Deverell with all the coldness she could muster in her reply: "I have, more often than I like been thrust into the company of certain vulgarities, but at least this is innocent amusement."

"Do you think so?" One corner of his mouth quirked into an imitation smile that did not reach his eyes. He looked darkly sardonic. "Not so innocent for many here, I would think."

"I am not surprised. You prefer thinking the worst of people."

"And I am so often right." Dark blue eyes fixed on her with a gimlet gaze that seemed to see right through her charade, as if he knew where she had been and why. Oh, must he *stare* at her like that? It was unnerving.

"Excuse me, my lord, but we were just leaving."

"How fortunate. So am I. I shall escort you home, as I have business with Grandmère."

"That is hardly necessary, my lord. The carriage is only a short distance away."

"Excellent. My companions left without me, and I dislike hired hacks."

Without being obviously rude within hearing of Trent and Lucy, she had little choice but to give in and allow the earl to accompany her, but it was infuriating.

When they reached the carriage, Deverell sat

next to her on the velvet squabs, entirely too near, his large frame a solid, heated presence that seemed to fill the entire space. On the seat across from them, Lucy perched like a bright little bird, her piquant face still aglow from cold and the handsome footman.

The rattling jolt of wheels on rutted ice and slush as the carriage jerked forward was a relief; upon reaching Beacon House, Amalie would be able to flee.

But now, next to him like this, unwelcome memories returned to leave her flustered; she thought of the night in the library, details vague as if only a dream, but the reality stark and painful. Must he look at her like that, his lean form sprawled on the seat in lazy indifference, blue eyes regarding her with amusement?

Distractedly, she noticed the scar on his jaw; it was red, new, a curved gash along the bone that lent him a wicked aspect—a *more* wicked aspect, she amended, and jerked her gaze from the earl to the window. Snow-frosted lanes and buildings lent London a pristine facade it did not deserve, hid the ugliness beneath.

"You seem to enjoy courting danger, Miss Courtland."

She dragged her gaze from the window reluctantly, gave him a brief glance. "I hardly see how you would think that, my lord."

"To visit this area unescorted is not only foolish, it's dangerous."

"I hardly think that in broad daylight—"

"Apparently you've forgotten the Ratcliffe Highway murders."

She drew in a sharp breath. "No, I have not

forgotten at all. But that was over a year ago, in the East End."

"Not that far from here. We're close to the new London Docks. Wapping and Bermondsey are close as well, and rife with drunk sailors, lightermen, coalheavers, lumpers and prostitutes, any one of whom would be quite happy to part you from your purse—perhaps even your life, if drunk enough."

"A rather sweeping condemnation, my lord. If I remember correctly, the Ratcliffe Highway murders were committed by an acquaintance of one of the families."

"Oh, he hanged for it, but some say others were involved."

Lucy made a strangled sound, her face as white as the snow weighting tree branches and streets. Irritated, Amalie said, "I believe we can dispense with conversation, my lord. I find the subject tiresome."

Deverell seemed content to lapse into silence. Images wheeled by the carriage window in anonymity, though her brain registered a few details: St. Paul's Cathedral, the intersection of Blackfriar's Road and Farringdon. . . .

Too soon they were at Beacon House, and Trent was opening the carriage door for them. Amalie accepted his hand to step to the ground, ignored the earl's offered arm, and moved up the steps and into the house.

Baxter greeted them, unflappable as always, taking her red cloak and murmuring that Lady Winford was in the downstairs parlor before he turned to Deverell.

"My lord, the countess will be most pleased to see you, I think."

"No doubt. Ah no, Miss Courtland, do not run away so quickly." He caught her arm, held it tight, his fingers an iron grip around her wrist. His smile was pleasant, but behind the congenial facade lurked grim determination. "You will join us in the parlor, I trust."

"I must refuse, my lord." She met his gaze, a dare to make a scene in front of Baxter. "The day's exertions have wearied me."

"Yet I insist."

Aware of Baxter still close by, she hesitated, wondered what Deverell would do if she flatly refused, then decided it would not be to her best interests to find out.

"Very well, my lord, since you obviously have something of importance to impart."

Her insides knotted with tension; his hand on her arm was heated, an unwelcome reminder of the night in the library, of his horrible words to her godmother the next day. It was difficult just being in his company, when the echoes of his comments were cruel taunts.

When he opened a door, she entered the room, halted at once as she belatedly noticed they were in the library and not in the parlor where Lady Winford waited.

His hand was inexorable pressure at her back, nudging her forward a step, and she heard the click of the closing door and whirled around to face him.

"What do you want, my lord? It's obvious that you have something private to say, so do so quickly, as I do not want to be in here alone with you."

Crossing his arms over his chest, he leaned back against the door, surveyed her with glittering blue eyes that were unnerving.

"A little late for that precaution, I think."

"Yes," she said briskly, "but not too late to prevent another . . . occurrence."

His laugh was soft, insinuating. "Do you suggest that I might be agreeable to a repetition?"

"No, I suggest nothing of the kind!" *Oh God, he makes me say things so badly, puts me so ill at ease . . . I wish he would not look at me, would just leave me alone!*

But Deverell obviously had no intention of leaving her alone. He watched her like a cat watched a bird in the garden, with the lazy confidence that at any moment the game could end.

"A pity." His eyes raked over her as if he could see beneath the layers of clothing she wore. "We both made a mistake, Miss Courtland. There may be consequences. I am prepared to deal with them."

"Are you?" She tilted her head to one side; he did not look away from her gaze, did not offer an apology or explanation, or even sympathy. But what had she expected? He was not a man accustomed to admitting fault or offering justification.

"Yes, of course I am." He pushed away from the door, ran an impatient hand through his hair. It had grown long, she noticed, strands looped over his forehead to brush against his eyebrows. In the back, it grazed his high collar, black against the pristine white of his neckcloth, an intricate fold under his chin that was simple and yet elegant.

"If you're breeding, arrangements must be made."

Her attention shifted from his neckcloth to his face again, lingered. That had not occurred to her; of course, it was a distinct possibility. Why had she not thought of it?

"What sort of arrangements did you have in mind, my lord Deverell?" she asked calmly, while inside the rage began to build and build, white-hot and volatile.

"Marriage is usually the best arrangement in such a case." His dry tone added to the building fire; he eyed her narrowly, then gave a lift of one shoulder. "I am certain we can find you a suitable husband, one who will not mind terribly that you are—no longer pure."

"Or that I may be bearing a bastard, of course."

His mouth tightened. "Yes, that would have to be addressed if it should prove true."

"Then you have thought of everything."

"Not exactly. I have several candidates in mind, but I thought you might prefer to choose."

Feeling brittle, as if she might break in two if she moved too swiftly, or spoke too loudly, she turned slowly and moved across the library to the fire. Right there, on the carpet in front of the narrow settee, she had lain in his arms, a wanton, unresisting, even encouraging the touch of his hand on her. She remembered most of it, could recall with sizzling clarity the warmth of him against her, the heat of the fire, and the thudding beat of his heart against her bare breast.

Only two days ago? Three? A lifetime. It did not take long to ruin one's future with a careless action.

She turned to face him; he was watching her warily, as if expecting her to attack him. It was not a serious threat, for he was far too big, far too agile, a man used to warfare. No, there were ways to assault a man without physical force, though most men seemed ignorant of them.

A woman's best weapon was often her tongue.

"I hardly think you capable of making decisions for me, my lord, when you cannot even make them for yourself. I am not so big a fool as to think you qualified to judge me, or you would not enjoy the dubious reputation you now have. Was there not something about a duel, a wife, and a suicide? Yes, I believe there was—why would I trust *you* to make a decision about my life when you have so fully ruined your own?"

For a moment he only stared at her. She heard the thud of her own heartbeat, loud in her ears, the faint hiss of the fire in the grate, and the interminable tick of the small case clock on the mantel.

"Pull in your claws, little tiger," he said at last, but there was a taut look on his face that betrayed the accuracy of her barbs. "We are speaking of you, not me."

"No, we are speaking of how you can best shirk your share of the responsibility, I believe."

"Damn you, I'm here to shoulder my share of the blame for what happened. I'll see that things are made right."

~

"Why my lord Deverell, is this a marriage proposal? I'm flattered—but alas, I must decline. I've no wish to be wed to a man with no scruples."

In two strides he was at her side, his hand on her in a harsh grip, his tone vicious. "If you think I have no scruples, then you are fool indeed to provoke me. I fully intend to settle a generous amount on you in compensation for your loss, and that should purchase you a goddamn husband with enough scruples to satisfy even Parliament. I suggest that you hold your tongue before you find to your sorrow that you've gone too far."

"What *is* too far with a man like you, my lord?" She did not flinch, even when his hand tightened painfully on her wrist, squeezing the bones in a brutal vise. "Would it be too far if I said that you are the most morally depraved man of my acquaintance? If I pointed out that you took advantage of me in a fragile condition? Oh, I do admit to my own liability for my actions, but ultimately, I am the one to suffer for what happened. You will go blithely on your way with no consequence whatsoever, just as you did when Lord Wickham shot himself in his library."

Fury darkened blue eyes almost to black, and white lines carved deep grooves on each side of his mouth. He looked dangerous, feral, and for the first time she felt a flutter of real fear.

But then he released her arm, moved to the mantel to lean against it and gaze at her with a disdainful curl of his lip. "Whoever said that females are the weaker sex never met you, Miss Courtland. Your tongue is wicked. If there was truth in your venom, it might be lethal. While pointing out my faults is certainly entertaining, it does not solve your problem. You are ruined. If I chose to be cruel, I could see to it that you spent the rest of your days hiding in a convent. Unfortunately for you, the world does not view my actions in the same light as yours."

It was true, of course. He would be viewed as a Man About Town, while she would be viewed as a Harlot, ruined beyond redemption, a Fallen Woman. Girls were often ruined by no more than a chance kiss or being seen in the company of a man without a proper chaperone—and she had done far more.

Her chin lifted slightly, a gesture of defiance against the earl and society's damning rules.

"Be that as it may, I will not be sold to the highest bidder as if a horse at Tattersall's. I have made my own choice."

"Have you?" A cynical lift of his brow was maddening as he regarded her with the same disdainful curl of his lip. "And who might that fortunate gentleman be? You need not pretend modesty now, Miss Courtland, for after all, your generous dowry will come out of my pockets."

When she remained silent, he said with a soft laugh, "As I thought—you have no choices."

"That is not true."

"Is it not? Then tell me the name of your betrothed, Miss Courtland, or will he be calling on me in the near future?"

Her hands curled into small fists at her sides, and she said stiffly, "I would prefer he come to you himself."

"No doubt. Which means you are merely delaying the admission of a far too obvious truth."

"Not at all . . . but my friendship with Sir Alex is not your affair."

"Sir Alex—Maitland?" Incredulity tinted his voice and lifted his brows. "Good God, you cannot mean *Maitland!* Not even *you* are that witless."

Stung by his ridicule, she snapped, "Sir Alex is not at all like you—he is kind, generous, and gallant. He's an educated man, and appreciates good conversation to tawdry affairs."

A tight knot burned in her throat; must he stare at her like that? Oh, she should not have said his name, but surely Sir Alex would live up to her expectations of him, if not for friendship, for the money Deverell offered. It was obvious from his somewhat shabby home that he was not financially secure, and he *had* said he enjoyed her company more than any other woman's, so why would he not agree?

"Oh yes," Deverell drawled, "Maitland is the soul of discretion. No tawdry female entanglements."

"That is well known, my lord." She wove chill disdain into her tone, desperate to retain as much dignity as possible under the circumstances.

"Poor, naive Miss Courtland . . . are you the only one in London who does *not* know about Maitland? Of course, that may make no difference to your plans, but somehow, I think you are unaware of Sir Alex's true inclination."

An uneasy suspicion began to form, and she turned away from his gaze to cross to the settee and perch upon the edge of the stuffed seat.

"Don't be ridiculous," she said stiffly. "I am

well acquainted with Sir Alex's preferences."

"No, Miss Courtland, I do not think you are." His laugh was softly mocking. "You see, Sir Alex prefers the company of handsome young men to that of women, but by all means, if you think he'll marry you, do so with my blessing."

Despite her reluctance to believe him, she knew it had to be true. It explained so much. And now she was bereft of any hope . . . how humiliating, that Deverell should be the one to tell her, to be watching her with those cynical eyes that seemed to know even the secrets of her soul.

Chapter 15

What a hopeless little charlatan she was. Holt regarded her with an almost affectionate cynicism. Ever surprising, Amalie Courtland was the most exasperating, infuriating, intriguing woman he had known. There were, beneath her careful dignity, ample signs of fraying composure. Had she really thought Maitland might wed her? Preposterous, of course.

Even now, confronted with the knowledge, she clung to her unraveling web of deception with a feeble argument.

"Sir Alex seems to have earned your enmity, my lord."

"No, he matters not in the least to me. Apparently, he does to you."

Pushing away from the mantel, he crossed to the settee where she perched like a nervous dove, halted her flight with a hand upon her shoulder. She flinched away from his touch; deliberate, he curled his hand beneath her chin, lifted her face to look at up at him, watched her eyes grow wide and dark with distrust.

"Don't be a fool, Miss Courtland. Life is harsh

to fools. Be sensible enough to accept my recommendations."

When she offered no protest, he released her chin, saw the faint red marks of his fingers like small bruises on her flawless skin.

Silence stretched between them, heavy and thick with tension. He thought of her as he had first seen her, an awkward, uncertain girl, shabby and provincial. The years had made a marked improvement in her appearance, if not her temperament. How had he ever thought her plain?

There was an understated elegance in her delicate bone structure and wide green eyes, in the dark beauty of thick hair pulled back into a decorous knot on the nape of her neck. Graceful, eloquent even in her silence, she was not at all the rustic girl she had been then.

Easy enough to understand why he had abandoned any sense of caution or restraint—even now the memory of her shadowy curves first glimpsed through the sheer film of her gown had the power to affect him. The memory of how she had felt in his arms sent the blood pounding through his body in a heated surge.

Ridiculous, to let himself court even a moment's doubt as to what should be done, but for an instant he wondered if there was another solution. She looked so unhappy, vulnerable in her misery. Christ, what a cur she must think him, for taking advantage of her weakness that night to seduce her. It was not something he was proud of doing, and he still could not answer his own questions as to his reasons.

Lust was easily slaked with any of the all-too-willing doxies to be found in and out of society's fashionable ballrooms. He had learned that at an early age, accompanying his cousin Adrian to a convent where the Abbess had an entire stable of nubile young girls eager and ready to introduce a youth to the pleasures of the flesh. It had been a memorable experience, more for the fact that he had witnessed his older cousin in bed with three of the unclad lovelies at once, a tangle of arms and legs that had fascinated and appalled an impressionable boy.

But that was a long time ago, and he should have learned to curb his baser instincts by now; it was not at all comforting to suspect that he did not always have his body under control.

Like now, when he wanted to kiss her again, to feel her lips part beneath his mouth, to taste her softness and sweetness . . . he turned abruptly away, returned to the fire to stand with his back to it, surveying her with outward detachment.

"There is a Master Cordell whom I think quite suitable for you, Miss Courtland. He is young and presentable and has excellent prospects. At the moment, he is employed by my barrister, with every opportunity to rise in the firm to a substantial wage. I suggest you encourage his acquaintance."

"You are more than kind, my lord."

"Am I?" He held her gaze for a long moment; green eyes like jewels gleamed in the fire's reflection, and rosy light played across her face and down her body. He remembered how she felt beneath him, long limbs silken and heated, the plush feel of her soft skin, and small, firm breasts that had fit perfectly into his hands.

Abruptly, surprising himself, he said, "If marriage does not suit you, perhaps a house in the country might. Of course, if I install you in a house, I would expect certain—privileges."

She rose at last from the settee, her face closed and remote, eyes distant and not meeting his. The sudden change from fiery anger to this cool detachment was suspicious. He stood still, watched warily as she came toward him, three steps across the carpet where they had lain a few nights before, her feet silent on the thick cushioning wool.

When she was only inches away from him, he recognized the glint in her eyes as she raised them to his face, and caught her hand before she could lift her arm.

"Do not," he said harshly, "strike me again. It would earn unpleasant results for you."

Her brow lifted. "No more unpleasant than listening to your insulting suggestions. But you are mistaken, my lord—I have no intention of striking you, though you certainly deserve it. I only wanted to be close enough to ensure that you hear me quite clearly—*I will solve my own problems, and do not require your assistance.*"

"Then by all means, do so." He released her arm, but fully expected her to lash out at him.

Her lips curved in a faint smile, slightly mocking, as if scorning his expectations. It was not comfortable to realize that she guessed his thoughts, knew him well enough now to predict his reaction.

Softly, she said, "Be prepared to be generous

with my dowry, my lord Deverell, for I do not think you want the truth of what happened in here known any more than I do."

He had no intention of admitting to that, and stood with an impassive face, betraying nothing.

"After all, your grandmother is my godmother," she continued, "and it would not be well received at all if it was known you had taken advantage of her ward under her very own roof—would it be legally regarded as incest, do you think? No matter. With your already tarnished reputation, it would be believed quickly enough. Do they still muster men out of His Majesty's army for unlawful cohabitation? I am ignorant of the laws, but I am certain there are those who are not."

She turned away, then paused to glance back at him over her shoulder. "Poor Grandmamma, her hero grandson would be known throughout London as a scoundrel, a man without the least shred of honor."

"Be careful, Miss Courtland," he said softly, "or you may find yourself residing in Covent Garden with the other jades who thought themselves above reproach."

"If I am to be ruined, I will not go quietly."

It was her parting shot, and he let her go, watched her leave the library without glancing back again, her spine rigid and her head held high.

Damn her. She was far more clever than he had given her credit for being.

He heard her speak to someone in the hall, recognized his grandmother's voice, and was not surprised when the library door swung wide.

"Ah Holt, there you are. Baxter informed me of your arrival, and I have been waiting far too long for you to join me. Whatever did you say to darling Amie?"

"What should I say to her?"

"Oh nothing, it's only that she seemed so strange just now, almost upset, though she mentioned nothing about it—are you certain you did not say something awful to her again?"

"I would be the first to know." He propped an arm on the mantel, bumped one of the small Staffordshire dogs lined up in a haphazard row, eyed it with distaste, and looked back at his grandmother.

Lady Winford stood in a square of light slanting through the window; she stood still and watchful, and something in her expectant gaze prompted him to say, "It might be the discussion of marriage that upset her."

"Marriage? Our Amie?"

"*Your* Amie. And yes, there was a mention of upcoming nuptials, I believe. It might be beneficial were you to talk to her soon."

"Oh yes—um . . . of course, of course . . . marriage." She paused for a moment, eyes slightly narrowed and a faint, mysterious smile on her lips. "I don't suppose there is something *you* might wish to say to me, Holt?"

"Yes, as a matter of fact, there is, Grandmère." He crossed to her, put his hands on her shoulders, and pressed a kiss upon her brow. "I'm leaving. Goodnight."

He crossed the entrance hall just as Baxter sent the footman, Trent, to summon a hansom cab for him. The front door closed on an icy gust, and Baxter turned to him.

"I trust that is suitable, my lord."

"Yes, but a bit unexpected."

Heels tapped on the tile as his grandmother crossed the hall, her voice imperative. "But Holt—wait, this is so peculiar, did you not come here to see me today?"

"No," he said, and took the greatcoat Baxter held out to him. "I came to see Miss Courtland."

"Ah." A beatific smile spread on her face, and she gave a nod of satisfaction. "Excellent."

Holt eyed the elderly butler with a frown. "How is it that you always know when I'm about to leave, Baxter?"

Baxter met his gaze for a moment, impassive as always as he said, "I know everything that goes on in this house, my lord."

"Do you?" He tugged on the greatcoat, slid his hands into his gloves, and smiled. "I imagine you know much more than you would ever deem expedient to repeat."

"Indeed, my lord. That is quite possible."

"I always suspected it. Good day, Baxter."

"Good day, my lord."

It was not, Deverell thought as the hansom rocked along icy streets, to be unexpected. His grandmother was more astute than she pretended most of the time, and he had always known Baxter was extremely observant. No doubt the details of his night with Miss Courtland had been kept confidential; Baxter would do nothing to hurt the dowager.

Yet he began to suspect that Grandmère might not be as dismayed as he'd first thought if her *darling Amie* were to be unwise enough to form an alliance with him. After all, marrying into the family would certainly keep her near, and he had seen how much Grandmère had come to depend upon the little Colonial.

Christ. Why had he been fool enough to follow his urges instead of his common sense? There had been nothing but trouble since. It was becoming a damned bloody nuisance.

Viciously, he thought that Miss Courtland deserved whatever husband she chose.

Amalie was still shaking with a combination of fury and anguish, pacing the floor of her bedroom with quick, angry steps, back and forth, feeling like a caged cat. *No,* she corrected herself, *a caged bird. That is what he said, and that is what I am. . . .*

How dared he dictate her future? As careless and callous as if she were one of his horses, or a dog to be bestowed upon a new master. She had been wrong about him, terribly wrong, to think he might possess any decency or consideration. He did not. He had made it quite plain that she meant nothing more to him than as an inconvenience, a *problem* to be dealt with. . . .

And oh God, she had thought—hoped—that perhaps Sir Alex might prove the answer to her dilemma, but she was wrong in that, too. What a fool Deverell must think her, and she was suddenly grateful to the unexpected arrival of Sir Alex's guest that had prevented her blurting out what would certainly be regarded as an impertinent suggestion, at best.

There was little she could do; it was plain to her now that she must make her own way, and not dally any longer with the vain hopes that some miracle would occur to rescue her from the consequences of her action.

A light tap on her door jerked her from meditation of her plight, and she paused in front of the fire to call out permission to enter.

It was Lucy, her small face curious as she asked if she should bring up a tray for supper.

"Lady Winford is concerned that you have not come down, Miss Courtland, and asks that you join her if you have recovered from your headache."

"I am still unwell, Lucy. Inform her ladyship that I prefer to take supper in my room tonight, but I will see her in the morning, after I've rested."

She would think of something before morning to tell Grandmamma. But perhaps she already knew what she would say, what she must say. There was really no other option for her now, for all choices had been eliminated.

It would be so much easier to go on as she had, to forget that night in the library with Deverell, to pretend it had not happened. But it was just as obvious that she would not be allowed to do so. He intended to force her out of his grandmother's house and into a marriage, and if she tarried too long, she would find herself trapped.

No, best make her own choices. Besides, how could she remain here now, after all that had happened? It seemed as if the earl would not return to his commission, though Napoleon's army had struggled back from Moscow in defeat, losing over five hundred thousand men in their retreat. A disaster to the Corsican's plans, a boon for his enemies. Yet even with Britain's war in America still raging, the earl lingered in England.

And she had once thought him a hero, even asked him how it felt to be so admired!

What a fool she must have looked . . . he was no hero. He was only a man.

Yes, it was time she accepted the decision she must make. There was little else she could do without confiding in Grandmamma, and that she would *not* do. It was her fault that she had ruined herself, and she had no intention of hurting her godmother with a confession.

Feeling suddenly weary, she moved to the window, stared out into the night-shrouded garden. Moonlight silvered the ground, glittered on pristine drifts of snow that looked pure and white, lovely and so cold. She put out a hand, touched the glass, icy beneath her fingertips as she dragged her hand down the pane.

She recalled her first day in London, and how she had stood in a room at the earl's townhouse and watched him at the far end of the garden, the feint and jab with a rapier catching sunlight on the lethal blade. She had thought then he was ruthless. Now she knew it for a certainty.

And she could not even hate him for it.

Closing her eyes against the pain, she began to compose a mental note to Don Carlos.

Don Carlos de la Reine peered through the gloom of the room enclosed in heavy velvet draperies and dense shadows. Discreet as always, Madame L'Aigle had shown him to this room on the second floor of the Damnation Club to meet his English contact, then departed. It was quiet, his own breath sounding much too loud in his ears as he strained to identify the voice coming from the thick folds of hood that obscured the man's face.

"Take the cover off. It is too soft, your voice," he said in clumsy English, and was startled and gratified at the fluent Spanish that answered him.

"No. Secrecy is a protection for both of us. Do you have the information that was requested of you?"

"Yes, but it is trivial."

"Nothing is trivial. Give it to me."

Don Carlos reached into his coat, withdrew a thick packet, held it out. A gloved hand emerged from the folds of concealing cloak to take the papers.

"Excellent. You are more adept than I was given to understand. And the other? You are making progress?"

Spreading his arms out to the sides, he shrugged, then thought that in the dark, the man could not see him, and said, "It is difficult to know. She is reserved, like all you English."

"She is not English, but American. It has not been my opinion that she is very reserved."

"Then you have certainly not attempted to form a close alliance with her," Don Carlos retorted. "These virgins are very guarded against a man's attention. But I visit her often, flatter her, express my admiration. It is not so very difficult to do, that, as she is not what I expected, but intelligent and obliging."

"It would be helpful if she were to be extremely obliging."

Another shrug. "I would not mind it as well."

"I daresay you would not. Miss Courtland is very charming and lovely. But remember, you are to draw the earl's attention to you without being obvious. It is imperative he be distracted. His interference may yet ruin it all."

"I do not see how—"

"No, but it is not your place to see. It is your place to follow orders."

It was not, Don Carlos thought grudgingly, what he had expected when he'd agreed to accept the part he now played. But it was not so bad, as he had said, for Amalie was very lovely, and he was not a man to refuse an opportunity when it was given him. No, he would not mind being the cause of a great distraction for Deverell, for he found the earl to be too arrogant, too contemptuous of him, as if he were no more than the dirt beneath his feet.

That was enraging, when if it was not for the Spanish revolt to distract Napoleon and divide his forces, it was likely the English would soon be under Bonaparte's rule. No, Deverell should be more grateful, and should return to his commission rather than put his nose where it did not belong and endanger the delicate balance of power. If the French took England, all of Europe would be lost, and he had no desire to live under the Corsican's dictates.

"The earl is getting too close to the truth," the voice from the hood murmured. "If he cannot be lured from England and his investigations, he must be stopped with a more final method. That is not desirable at this time."

"It is not so much the earl who is getting close, as that Cockney ferret he employs. He has become dangerous."

"I have personally handled Jemmy Taylor. He will not be giving Deverell, nor anyone else, more information."

Don Carlos laughed softly. "It is said that the Spanish are ruthless, but I think it is the English who can be most terrifying. There is no passion with you, only an obsession."

"Your opinions are of no matter to me. Just do what is required, and you will receive ample compensation."

"My title and my lands must be returned in whole. I will accept no less—this Wellington, he is inflexible in his insistence that his armies occupy my estate. It is intolerable."

"Not," the voice said dryly, "as intolerable as losing them to Napoleon. Keep that in mind. If we are not successful, the French may yet achieve victory."

"I do not know how that is possible, or why it is so imperative that the earl be diverted from his intention."

"It is not your business to know. It is your business to continue what you are doing. Use Miss Courtland any way you can to keep Deverell distracted. His return to England came at a most inconvenient time, and if there was another way to get him to leave the country until—but that is not your concern. Just do what must be done. Marry her, if you must, but get her to leave

England with you, and the earl will most certainly follow."

Don Carlos recognized something familiar in the intractable voice, but then the man was gone, the door opening briefly, a swift flash of light from the hallway lamps, and only a glimpse of a hooded figure before the door was shut again. He stared into the shadows, uncertain if this game he played was too dangerous. But what recourse did he have? These English, they were as adept as any Spaniard at weaving intrigues, but for some reason were hesitant about killing Deverell, which seemed to him the most expedient method of dealing with any threat.

Ah well. He would renew his efforts to court the lovely Miss Amalie, an added benefit to the prospect of regaining his lands and title that Wellington threatened with his occupation. It was not at all disagreeable to think of how he might best win her affections.

Chapter 16

Unbearable cold gripped the city, and Deverell stood with growing impatience and freezing feet as he waited for Jemmy Taylor to arrive. The Cockney was late, far later than normal. Nothing stayed Jemmy from keeping his appointments, greed being a far too great impetus. But now he was over an hour late, the Bow bells having rung the time. Now it was apparent he would not show, and Deverell left the corner where he waited.

By the time he reached Beacon House, he was in dire need of a brandy to warm his insides and a fire to warm the outside. As Baxter took his coat, he asked after his grandmother.

"She is out with Mrs. Fry, I believe, my lord."

"Good God, in this cold?"

"Yes, my lord. It seems there is a matter of grim conditions at one of the prisons."

"Christ," he muttered, "she'll end in her grave if I don't put a stop to this nonsense. I'll wait for her in the library. Is there a fire?"

"There is not, my lord. It is Saturday."

"Saturday—ah yes, the day out for servants. If

she had more than five in her employ, there would be enough here to build a fire when needed."

"Her ladyship is practicing conservation of her resources, and does not waste wood or coal where it is not needed, but I will make a fire for you, my lord."

"That's not necessary, Baxter. I'm perfectly capable of building a fire. I'll ring for you if you're needed."

He crossed to the library and closed the door behind him, his mind shifting to the mystery of Jemmy Taylor's failure to keep their appointment. He'd come from Cochrane earlier, frustrated at the man's obstinance in refusing to return to his home in Scotland, where he would be safer. It was not coincidence that he had been set upon yesterday on his return from visiting Cochrane—men were watching, and somehow, he did not think it was the French.

A growing suspicion had formed, but it was too ugly to lend credence. Yet why else would persistent efforts to have him return to his commission continue? Yesterday's attack had only confirmed what he'd suspected, and he had the cynical thought that it was far more inconvenient for the British government to allow Cochrane free agency than it was to keep him in hiding for his life.

Intimidation of the worst sort, an excellent method of rendering Cochrane impotent with fear and inaccessible to betray the secrets of his new weapon. Which meant, of course, that he was a damned nuisance in protecting Sir Thomas when it would be much preferred that the inventor cower in some dark, hidden corner.

But what would happen when it became clear that the intimidation was not working? He wondered how far it would go, if the government would resort to murdering one of their own to safeguard a potentially disastrous secret from getting into the wrong hands.

He knelt by the cold fireplace, struck tinder to dry paper curls from a spill, waited as it caught. The tiny blaze was slow, paper curling into black ash before it set fire to the wood shavings. A noise behind him caught his attention, and he turned, still crouched on his heels, to see Miss Courtland enter the library and shut the door behind her. She moved to the desk across the room, opened a drawer, and took out paper and writing utensils.

Silent, he watched, waiting for the moment she noticed him, and appreciated the view from his vantage point. She wore a thin dressing gown, ruffled down the front and at the cuffs, far too flimsy for the cold. It suited her, a rich rose color that was bright contrast to the dark hair pulled back from her face and tied carelessly to fall over one shoulder.

Light from the windows across the room formed cold gray bars on the floor and desk, outlined the curves beneath her gown as she pulled a chair to the desk to sit down. Soft silence shrouded the house, the usual noise of servants cleaning and going about duties absent today.

With his back warming from the fire, he watched her intently, one corner of his mouth tucked inward with wry humor that she was so absorbed in what she was doing that she had not noticed him. She fit nib into pen, opened a bottle of ink, and spread a fine sheet of vellum upon the desk surface and began to write, pausing on occasion to dip the pen into ink again.

Rising to his feet, he walked to the desk, his boots sinking into the thick carpet, noiseless as a cat. A faint luscious fragrance emanated from her, and he stood for a moment, strangely touched by the vulnerability of the back of her neck where hair draped to one side, leaving it bare as she bent over the desk, the pen scratching feverishly.

Then his eye caught a name at the top of the page—*Don Carlos*—and he reached over her shoulder to take up the paper.

With a startled gasp, she whirled, pen falling from her fingers to clatter on the desk. "How *dare* you! I insist you give me back my letter—"

Despite her disheveled appearance and the flimsy wrapper that revealed more than it hid, she retained an air of dignity that he found disconcerting. Dark hair framed her face, lustrous and tempting, curling down to lie upon her breasts, an invitation to memory that was very distracting.

"This letter," he said calmly, gaze lifting to meet her angry green eyes, "is unnecessary."

"You cannot dictate to me, my lord."

"Can I not?" His eyes narrowed, raked her up and down with a slow thoroughness designed to remind her of the last time he had seen her in a dressing gown. It must have succeeded, for she crossed her arms over her chest, pulling together the edges, her chin lifted defiantly under his probing gaze. He laughed softly and crossed to the fireplace with the letter. Deliberately he fed it to the flames, watched as it burned to ash.

"That is hardly effective, my lord," she said with a contemptuous curl of her lip. "There is more paper and ink in the desk, and if I choose, I can write a letter at any time."

"You are quite wrong, Miss Courtland. You will not write Don Carlos. Christ, are you so desperate to marry that you'd choose him? An impoverished nobleman with questionable motives for being in England is hardly suitable for a young woman who so obviously desires to rise above her station in life."

"And I suppose your suggestion that I be *your* mistress in some country cottage far from London is more in keeping with my station?"

"It would be a step up the social ladder from your origins, arriving penniless on our doorstep, fresh from the Colonies, and with parents already shunned by society."

It was cruel, and he knew it; he saw from the swift intake of her breath and widening of her eyes that his barb had struck home. Driven by anger and a desire to make her see reason, he crossed to her in three long strides and grasped her by the wrist, tamping the desire to shake sense into her.

"Listen to me, you witless little goose, Don Carlos is not the man for you. Neither is Maitland, but I think you've realized that by now. Why the bloody hell will you not listen to me? Christ, I should have known better than to give in to momentary need. It's caused nothing but trouble, and you won't listen when I try to help you."

"Help me?" Her voice broke on a high, quavering note that sounded dangerously close to hysteria, and his eyes narrowed warily. "*Help me*—you must think me fool indeed, my lord Deverell, if you think for one moment that I'll believe you care enough about anyone else to try to *help*. You care only for yourself and your own selfish needs, not mine or even your grandmother's—no, you needn't glare at me like that, because you know it's true. And God, I must be the fool you name me, because once I thought you a hero, a noble knight of the realm, with England's Cause keeping you away from London and an old woman who needs you. Yes, a fool indeed, for you never gave her a thought while you were gone, almost four years with the barest of messages from you, and most of those through your solicitor. Oh no, my fine lord Deverell, you are no hero at all. . . ."

"I never pretended to be. Christ, it's not heroic to stand in the midst of dying men with your guts dissolving in fear and your brain registering horror—it's hell, Miss Courtland. Man-made purgatory, wars started by tyrants and waged by politicians, with the poor bastards who are truly noble dying by the droves as cannon fodder. No, I'm no hero, but then, I never pretended to be what I was not. What of you? This pretense at being a lady, the Season my grandmother gave you in order to find you a rich husband and comfortable life—you're a fraud, a Colonial chit with gypsy eyes and a soul to match."

He caught her hand when she swung it toward his face, his fingers digging harshly into the delicate bones of her wrist. "See, I recognize who you are, what all the fine clothes and fancy dress balls don't disguise—you cannot hide it from me, because I've seen you as you really are."

She struggled to free herself, her breath an angry sob in her throat, and her wrapper gaped open, exposing the smooth round thrust of her breast. He felt her skin slide like silk under his open palm, cupped his hand over her breast, and raked his thumb across her taut nipple.

Instant desire exploded inside him, a response to the pent-up need he felt whenever he was with her. He groaned with it, muttered harshly, "Damn you for making me want you, green-eyed little witch. *Damn you!*"

Flexing his arm, he drew her to him abruptly, swallowed her soft gasp as his mouth closed over her parted lips, one hand behind her head to hold her still. His fingers spread through her hair, bunched it in his fist as he tasted her mouth with a ferocity he had too long denied. She grew still, her struggles ceasing as his tongue probed with fierce thrusts. Christ, it was insane, this driving, importuning lust he felt for her every time he was with her, the memory of another night in this library returning with regular inconvenience.

It was a damning indictment of his character that he could not keep her from his thoughts, when no other woman had ever lingered. But then, no other woman had looked at him as she did, with such a challenging disdain in her eyes, daring him to change her mind, to make her want him.

He crushed her to him, felt her body quiver

against his, barred only by her thin wrapper from his searching hands.

Deliberately, he moved his hand with leisurely thoroughness over her quivering body, ignoring her efforts to avoid his touch, fingers exploring all the sensitive female places with an erotic attention meant to quell her resistance. Soft skin like satin beneath his hands, warm and yet shivering, her muscles taut as he slid his palm from the delicious weight of her breast down her rib cage to the small, flat mound of her belly. The wrapper parted, opening to allow him access, and he scooped her into his embrace and half-carried her to the wide settee arranged before the fire.

A scream would have brought Baxter to investigate, but she made no sound as he bent her back to lie upon the cushioned seat, pushing her down with his weight, his lips seeking the vulnerable spot below her earlobe.

"Christ, Amie," he muttered, heat scouring him as he kissed her again, put his tongue into her mouth, heedless of anything but the overpowering need for this one woman.

A log popped, sent up a sudden shower of sparks, heat spreading out into the room. He sat back, legs folded under him as he surveyed her lying in the tangle of rose-colored wrapper, her body a slender pale flame in a bed of muslin. She was beautiful, face flushed and eyes wide as she gazed up at him, and he put both his hands upon her breasts, teasing the taut nipples to peaks, watching her face through half-lowered lashes. A wanton—a gypsy, after all, lovely and refined, but with the passionate soul of a woman just awakening.

His hand moved in a teasing drift from her breasts to her belly, and he heard her soft gasp as he tangled his fingers in the rich crop of curls at the juncture of her thighs.

"Open your legs for me, Amie," he said softly, and when she did not, pushed them gently apart, hand sliding up her pale inner thigh until he touched the damp crevice beneath the dark curls. Before she could voice protest, he bent to kiss her mouth, stifling any argument, his hand stroking and caressing, sliding over velvety folds with increasing rhythm until he felt her thighs open wider for him, and heard strangled moans in the back of her throat.

"You make me crazy . . . Christ, you're all I think about now, holding you like this, touching you here . . . and here. You've bewitched me, my green-eyed gypsy witch. . . ."

Inviting heat, delicious female . . . he moved one hand to the front of his breeches, tugged at the button closure impatiently to free himself. Rampant urgency filled his palm; he slid his body across the damp melting center of her, replaced his hand with heated strokes of his swollen body that freed him to cup her breasts, tease her nipples until she was gasping and writhing beneath him.

Strangled sighs of pleasure emanated from her, a soft lilting sound. She moved artlessly, untutored desire straining against him, hips arching into his strokes.

He tangled a hand into her hair again, his kisses harder, his mouth almost bruising. She felt his tongue slip between her lips, seeking, as the hard pressure slid over her with arrant sensuality, heated strokes that sent shivers down her spine. Resistance dissolved under his determined assault, had faded away at his frustrated confession: he wanted her, thought of her even when he tried not to—it was a scalding realization.

When he shifted, sliding into her, an uncomfortable invasion, she opened for him, her arms curling around his neck to hold him, surrendering body and heart in that moment, giving him all. It was a leap of faith. It was the most daring thing she had ever done.

She moaned and twisted under him, drawing him closer, deeper, needing the contact, the confirmation that he was part of her in more than just body. Deverell looked down at her, his eyes blue-shadowed, fierce lights making them bright as he settled deeper until she could no longer think of what to do or say or feel, but only answer with an arch that brought the heavy fullness even deeper, a blend of ecstasy and raw friction. Suddenly she couldn't breathe for the ringing tumult of her senses, the clamor of sensation that flooded through her in a rush of heat and quivering bliss.

She gasped out his name, a breathless plea as he drove into her, thrusting his hips against her with rough, frenzied motions that ignited a shattering response. A white-hot release knifed through her as the universe spun, wheeled, splintered in fiery explosions, and she was vaguely aware of his own hoarse mutter, the last thrust of his body into her before he went still, holding himself rigid inside her as he shuddered.

For a long, awkward moment he held her, a moan caught deep in his throat, his face pressed into the curve of her neck and shoulder, his breath warm against her bare skin. As the world slowly righted again, she was aware of her weak limbs and quivering aftermath.

Slowly, he propped himself on an elbow, stared down at her with a strange expression, one finger tracing a path from her brow to her mouth.

"Passionate little gypsy . . . you are a revelation I did not expect." He kissed her on the lips, surprisingly gentle, then drew back to mutter, "You know that I have no intention of letting you go now."

She smiled, tenuous joy spreading wings outward, a bit shy at this new turn of events. "Yes," she agreed softly, "this does change things."

Silence settled, comfortable now where once it had been awkward; he tugged at a curl of her hair, wound it around his finger, frowning a bit. The scar on his jaw gave him a dangerous look now, made her think of pirates and highwaymen. But then, he had always reminded her of the dangerous side of life.

He sat up at last, watching her through half-lidded eyes, helping her when she fumbled with the sleeves of her dressing gown, and kissing the nape of her neck as he tied her hair back with the ribbon again.

"Tomorrow," he said abruptly, "I will send for you. Don't bring any clothes with you. I'll buy what you need when we get there."

She raised her eyes to him, a little surprised. "Tomorrow? But . . . but where are we going?"

"We can hardly stay in London and announce that you're my mistress. It's going to be difficult enough to tell Grandmère."

A cold chill seized her, froze her to the marrow, so that the tentative smile on her lips remained in an ugly parody. His eyes narrowed slightly, and he reached out to put his hand beneath her chin, lifting her face.

"What did you expect, little gypsy?" he asked softly. "You know I want you in my bed."

She found her voice, and was amazed that it was so calm. "Yes, I understand that now. Your bed, but not your heart. Is that what you mean, my lord?"

"*My lord*? A bit formal now, I think . . . yes, I guess that is what I mean. I cannot give you what I do not have to give. Don't expect it. I offer you a place, but not my name."

"I see." And she did see. He was right, and she had been foolish to think he offered more. It was only a childish dream, after all. She nodded, turned away to move to the fireplace and stare into the flames. She felt his eyes on her, heard the silence close in around them as if a tangible thing, heavy and forbidding. He waited, and whatever answer she gave, she knew he would accept it with indifference. It was annihilating to admit.

She turned, met his steady gaze. "It is not enough for me, my lord. I must have respectability. You may find that amusing, in light of what has happened between us, but a life on the fringes of acceptable society is abhorrent to me."

"I see my grandmother has instilled in you a most inconvenient rectitude," he said dryly.

"No, my lord, this is not something learned. It is who I am. But then, you would know nothing about that, for you are concerned only with your own wants. So it is with no regret that I must inform you that I decline your offer to be your mistress, as appealing as some may find that proposition."

He regarded her from hooded eyes, his expression revealing nothing, only the familiar impassivity that she knew so well. The Devil Earl, a dangerous combination of sophistication and ruthless indifference . . . how had she been so foolish as to forget that?

It was little comfort that he offered no argument, but let her leave the library with only a murmured observation that her scruples were misplaced.

"Don Carlos is not the man you think him," he added, "and you would be wise to take my advice."

It was, she thought, as she closed the library door behind her, a gesture as final as the death of her dreams.

Chapter 17

A fire blazed, yellow and orange tongues of flame licking greedily at logs, sending curls of smoke up the chimney, filling Lady Winford's parlor with warmth and the scent of burning oak. On the mantel, a gilt ormolu clock ticked steadily, counting the minutes with inexorable persistence as she waited for Holt's reaction.

It was gratifying.

"Damn her, she cannot be serious."

She gazed back at Holt with more calm than she was feeling at the moment. "I understand that she is quite, *quite* serious. I have been in despair this last week, as you have not been kind enough to reply to my frantic summons until today. What do you intend to do about it?"

"Christ." He curled one hand into a fist, brushed it against the carved wood of the mantel so carelessly that a small jasperware ornament tumbled to the hearth and shattered into pieces. One of the shards landed at her feet, and she recognized the head of a shepherdess staring up at her with sightless eyes.

It seemed fitting.

She looked up at her grandson, said coldly, "Holt, you must do something to stop this before it's too late."

"What do you suggest, Grandmère? A duel? Pistols at twenty paces? That would solve everything. But then, Don Carlos may prove to be a dead shot."

"Even in jest, that is not amusing."

"No," he said, "it is not. But you did give your blessing to this union." His eyes were hard, his tone cold. "I seem to recall you telling me how pleased you were that Don Carlos was calling on your darling Amie, and that she could do much worse than to wed such a charming gentleman, do I not?"

"Perhaps I was precipitate. Must you always remember things I do not want you to, and forget all that I prefer for you to recall? You're a most annoying man."

How contrary of him to recall that, when he recalls nothing else I say!

It would never do to admit to him that she had only meant to make him jealous, to point out that other men found Amalie quite attractive and desirable, and that really, it was past time he thought of marrying and producing heirs. How annoying, that Charlotte Mandeville had died so young, and that Robert had not had the foresight to see that Holt was betrothed to another suitable young woman before he grew old enough to object. Silly of young people these days to make such a fuss about being in love before they wed. Why, she had met her Robert only twice before their wedding day, and had not been at all certain she liked him. But she grew to like him, then to love him, and missed him still, especially on days like this one, when all seemed to be unraveling before her very eyes.

"Holt, you simply must not allow this marriage."

"For once, we agree on something, though I don't think for the same reasons at all." He looked at her, his fist grazing his chin, his eyes narrowed and so cold as to look like chips of ice. "I have every intention of putting a stop to this farce."

Relief flooded her; he was so much more competent at these things. She nodded. "Good. It's not that I do not want her happy, you understand, but Don Carlos—as I told you, he is quite charming, but I feel she would not be content with life in Spain."

"There are times, Grandmère," he said, with that same frosty tone to his voice that so intimidated her at times, "that you contradict yourself. If you feel it necessary to play at intrigues of even the most insignificance, you must keep your lies straight."

Indignant, she glared at him, but did not bother to deny it. He had seen through her subterfuges, after all—how irritating.

He gave her a short, ironic bow and took his leave, pausing at the front door to speak in low tones with Baxter while she remained in the parlor. She could hear them, and knew that her trusted servant would confide in her later, if it was important. He was fiercely loyal and devoted, and she trusted him above all men.

And even Deverell at times, though she knew he would never hurt her. It was just that he was so *mysterious* about things, when it could not be so very important *why* he had resigned his last commission, could it? Men must eventually tire of war, after all—even heroes. Ah, no matter. At least he was to remain in England, and she fully intended to arrange his marriage to Amalie. It was more obvious to her now than ever before that they would be quite content together, for she had certainly not expected they would actually do what they had done, though heaven knew she had done her best to ensure they spent as much time together as possible . . . no, that was unexpected and not quite what she'd anticipated, but not so very terrible after all. It put the cart before the horse, so to speak, but theirs would not be the first marriage under such circumstances. All should turn out well. . . .

Unless, of course, Amalie went ahead with her foolish and dangerous plan to marry Don Carlos, then all would be a catastrophe. Oh, why couldn't Holt *see* that she was only upset and desperate? Amie must feel all alone at the moment. With a sigh, she wondered if she should abandon her pretense of ignorance. It would never do to have the girl feel forced into a marriage of convenience, when a bit of patience would gain all.

It was just so delicate a situation, and any misstep might end in disaster. Then it occurred to her with a pang of alarm that Holt might very well be provoked into unwise reaction if Don Carlos was insulting in his determination to wed Amalie. . . .

Deverell met Stanfill at White's, finding him waiting with barely concealed impatience at one of the tables near the bow window. The usual bow window set of Beau Brummell, Lords Alvanley, Mildmay, and Pierrepoint, were in position, dressed in the first stare of elegance, situated to be seen by everyone who passed by.

As he entered the room, Lord Alvanley caught his eye, a subtle invitation to join them if he so desired.

"The Unique Four are in rare form," Stanfill observed, as Deverell merely bent a nod of greeting in that direction and pulled out his chair. "Every dandy and buck in London would give a small fortune to be included in that set, yet you dismiss them with only a nod. I admit to being green with envy at your savoir faire."

Amused, Deverell took his seat. "I have no time at the moment for idle talk and serious drinking. What did you find out from Jemmy?"

"You were right, it seems: Don Carlos has been seen in the company of Maitland, and even my brother, though the last confounds me. I had not thought him so careless of his position. But there you have it—" and he leaned closer to say softly, "He is an agent, as you suspected, or he would not be able to travel so freely between Spain and France, and even England. It is incomprehensible why he has not been stopped, but of course, it may be because it is far easier to keep an eye on his activities here than it would be if he was across the Channel."

"I can see Palmerston's logic on that." It was an assumption that Palmerston knew about Don Carlos, but then, as Secretary of War, Lord Palmerston generally knew everything important.

Gloomily, Stanfill remarked, "A sad state of affairs, when a prime minister can be shot and killed in the lobby of the House of Commons without warning, yet the most minute of details are known about a villainous spy."

"Mr. Bellingham was hardly predictable, I think."

"Why not? It was well known that he blamed Perceval for ruining his business."

"The Luddite riots in Nottingham did more damage than anything poor Spencer Perceval managed. Times are grave in most quarters, with exports down over thirty percent, poor-law expenditures up by six million, and prices nearly ninety percent higher than before the war. It was the Orders-in-Council decision to halt and search American ships that provoked this damnable war with the United States, and we are saddled with a mad king and spendthrift Regent—hardly a favorable state of affairs, and certainly more damned important than the arrival of another spy with dubious motives."

Stanfill stared at him with a lifted brow. "Do I detect another reason for your ire this morning?"

"Yes. You do."

"Ah, then I shall have Georges lay out appropriate clothing for either a funeral or a duel—or is that a bit redundant?"

Deverell regarded him with a faint smile, and ignored his last comment. "You have the necessary proof of Don Carlos's current involvement, I presume."

A furtive move of Stanfill's hand, white square

of linen a brief flutter as he laid it atop the table, and when Deverell reached for the handkerchief a few moments later, he felt the solid evidence of doubled papers within the folds.

"A pity, that ofttimes couriers fail to reach their destinations," Stanfill said, and the congenial, ingenuous expression on his boyish face never altered.

It was, Deverell thought, as he regarded the young viscount, one of the chief reasons he was so damned good at what he did. He had absolutely no scruples and no conscience, and if the need arose to eliminate a man who had become a liability, Stanfill saw that it was done.

"Will you be at Amy Wilson's house this evening?" the viscount inquired, as he flicked an imaginary speck of lint from his sleeve. "She asked expressly after you last night, and was most disappointed that you did not join us."

"I leave it up to Alvanley and Brummell to entertain the lovely Amy and her sisters," he said dryly. "A hundred guineas for a few hours of dalliance is too steep a price when there are other Cyprians far more lovely and just as lively."

"Ah, I had forgotten. Your opera singer." Stanfill looked up at him with a wicked gleam in his eye. "Or even the lovely and charming Miss Courtland, perhaps? You seem to spend much more time at Beacon House than is required for even the most attentive of grandsons."

"You seem to center far more attention on my concerns than would be healthy for any other man." His oblique warning lifted Stanfill's brow and summoned a cheeky grin that was not at all intimidated, and Deverell rose from his chair. "Today was the first time in nearly a week that I have visited Beacon House. And the opera singer was two months ago."

"Oh?" Stanfill's brow lifted in a languid arch. "I began to think you had formed an attachment for Miss Courtland."

"On the contrary, I would like nothing better than to marry her off, even to Don Carlos."

"How crushing," he murmured, "I had such high hopes for another duel."

"You are doomed to disappointment, unless Don Carlos should challenge Miss Courtland, which is highly likely."

Stanfill's soft laughter followed him as he left the club, stepping back out into the cold of the London street to summon a hack. He had not been idle in the past week, but had managed to apprehend a culprit skulking outside Sir Thomas Cochrane's hidden residence. No amount of questioning had gained useful information, but he had removed Cochrane to another house to safeguard him. It was damned baffling that wherever he put Cochrane, his enemies seemed to find him. Another project for Jemmy Taylor, once he contacted him again. It wasn't like the former Bow Street runner to remain out of touch this long when working on a venture, and he would have to hunt for him once the interview with Don Carlos was behind him.

The rented house where Don Carlos resided was on a narrow backstreet off the Strand in central London. It was a bit shabby in appearance, its former elegance faded and neglected. No one answered the first imperative raps upon the door, until it was finally opened after a rattling thud of his closed fist upon the surface.

Then it was just opened, enough so that he could see an eye peering out at him.

"W'at d'ye want?"

Hardly a proper butler, sounding more like the cook, he thought, as he took the initiative and pushed the door wide. With a startled squeak, the woman stumbled backward into the entrance hall, gawking up at him with obvious fear in her eyes. Strands of gray hair straggled from a cap atop her head, and her voice quavered.

"I'll call th' Watch, I will! Gi' out o' this 'ouse afore—"

He cut across her high-pitched screech impatiently. "Summon your master. I am here to see Don Carlos."

"Gi' on wi' ye, naow, or th' Watch'll 'ave at ye, I swear it. . . ."

"Madam, I am not an intruder, as even the most witless of blind chimney sweeps could see. Is Don Carlos in?"

"D'ye mean 'at bloody Spaniard? 'E ain't in, an' ain't likely ta be in ag'in."

A glance around the entrance hall provided details he had not first noticed, and his mouth tightened. The house had that vacant feeling about it, and he could see the drift of white dust covers on furniture in the small parlor off the hall.

"It's jus me 'ere, it is, come ta clean an' earn me six shillings for it, an' paid by 'at fine gennulman, too, 'stead o' 'at Spanish cove—'ey!"

He stalked past her, moved from room to room in a swift assessment, then turned back to the glaring old woman. "When did he leave?"

"On th' mornin' tide, I wa' told, the *Scrutiny.* Took 'is new wife wi' 'im, too, but—thankee, m'lord, thankee!"

The scowling features brightened as he tossed her a coin. "If anyone asks, you have no idea where Don Carlos left or when, or who was with him. Am I correct, madam?"

"Aye, 'at ye are for a fact, m'lord." She bit down on the edge of the coin with one of her three remaining teeth and smiled when it proved genuine. "I ain' no gabster, but can tell ye right enow 'at Spaniard was a nip cheese wi' 'is blunt. Full o' Spanish coin, 'e was to 'is new wife, though, and 'er fine as a fivepence, too, much too good for th' likes o' 'im, I can tell ye, m'lord."

"A tall lady, with black hair and green eyes, by chance?"

"Aye, an' ye've met 'er, then." A shake of her head accompanied the lament, "She looked in th' megrims, she did. Ah, but I shouldn't put me oar in it."

It was not what he had expected, Deverell thought with growing fury, and he doubted very seriously they had sailed yet. It was hours before the high tide, plenty of time to find their ship and drag Miss Courtland off before she made the biggest mistake of her life.

Christ above, if she was so damned intent upon marriage, he would marry the green-eyed chit. It would make his grandmother happy and save him from more of her goddamn stupid farces.

Viciously, he had the thought that it was infinitely preferable than telling Grandmère that her *darling Amie* had run off to marry Don Carlos.

When he got his hands around that gypsy wench's neck, he might very well do something he would regret. He had never felt so much like hurting a woman as he did now, and it was not a comfortable feeling.

He left the house, paused for a moment on the top step as the door closed behind him. He had taken off his gloves and pulled them on now, flexing his fingers to smooth the leather.

"My lord Deverell?"

He looked up in surprise at the sudden appearance of a man beside him, then instinctively ducked to one side as the flash of light gave him a warning. His arm came up to take the brunt of the blow, deflecting the knife-thrust, and he retaliated with a vicious blow to the jaw, his gloved fist a muffled smack against flesh. There was a grunt and the man went down, sprawled on the steps in a daze.

Gray light fused into shadows, surrounding him in a blur. Instinct made him fight, even as he recognized the odds were against him; hands grabbed and held him, voices grunted in pain as his fists found vulnerable targets, rough oaths curled into the air.

"Bloody 'ell, 'e's a rum cove, gov—watch 'im, now!"

Deverell slammed brutally into one of the men, heard his sharp exhalation of pain, and almost fought free of the hands on him. Then white lights exploded behind his eyes and the world was plunged into instant darkness.

He woke slowly, pain a drumming thunder in his head. It was dark, the smell familiar; it was a smell one never forgot after serving aboard a ship. Furtive noise echoed in damp waves from the hold, and the clink of chains was a muted warning.

"Christ," he muttered, and his tongue felt thick and swollen, "where the hell am I?"

The voice came from the dark, resigned and hoarse. "Aboard a bloody ship, the *Fortune*, that's where, mate."

Squinting, he felt the back of his head cautiously for the lump that throbbed incessantly. His hair was damp and sticky with dried blood. He shifted, felt the weight of chains on his wrists and ankles, winced at the sharp stab of pain that action summoned.

Slowly, the sounds of a ship at anchor penetrated his consciousness; there was a sharp chop to her, and as he listened, he heard the groan of anchor chains through the hawsehole. They were weighing anchor, wherever the hell he was, and he was about to find himself at sea again.

"I've got to get out of here," he said, and grunted at the pain the effort of moving cost him. His companion, barely visible now in light streaming through the hatch high above, laughed softly.

"Aye, mate, so do we all. But ye ain't likely to get outta here so quick—not alive, anyway."

Ignoring him, he shouted toward the hatch, his throat raw from lack of water, but the only response was a weary request from the hold to shut up.

"Bad enough we got to be impressed on a wallowing Dutch frigate without some bloody blighter makin' it worse with a bunch of noise," the man grumbled.

Deverell understood then; it came to him in chilling clarity that he had been taken up by an impressment gang. It had not been accident that he was chosen, for even press gangs did not rove elegant streets knocking lords on their heads, nor did they know the names—someone wanted him out of the way badly enough to resort to this.

It would be just the kind of nasty trick a Spaniard might plan to delay having an elopement interrupted. Christ above, he felt a bloody fool. He knew what the man was, and had let anger blind him to the dangers. And had let lust blind him to Amie's true nature. It occurred to him that she had set a trap for him, and, when he had not offered marriage, retaliated. Behind those cool green eyes lurked the soul of a scheming little bitch. He itched to be free, to find her and expose her to his grandmother before he put her on a prison ship to Australia. It would be vengeance of the sweetest kind.

Once they were under way, the first mate would come down to release the impressed men, and he would inform them of their mistake. It was unlikely they would keep an English peer of the realm aboard a Dutch merchantman.

But in that, too, he discovered Don Carlos had planned well. The bo'sun was British, but heard only two words before he cuffed him with a marlinespike, sending him to the deck bleeding and half-conscious, his cheekbone laid open.

Kneeling beside him, the crusty ship's officer peered at him with a jaundiced eye and advised,

"Listen, mate—it don't matter to me none who you claim to be, as long as you do what you're told. Keep your gob shut and your hands busy, unless you want a taste o' the cat. . . ."

It was a signal lesson.

The desire for vengeance was born then, a hot flame ignited by the knowledge that *darling Amie* had duped him, and stoked by a determination to survive long enough to see that she was repaid for her treachery.

He would find her—and when he did, she would regret that she had ever been foolish enough to cross him.

Chapter 18

Gray-green water hissed past the bow of the ship as wind-filled canvas sails to push it closer to Spain. Don Carlos leaned against the rail, eyes half-closed as he watched his lovely young bride.

In the four days they had been at sea, she had acquired a tint of color to her skin; it suited her, made him think of the dusky-skinned women of San Sebastian.

"You will like my country," he murmured, when she finally turned to look at him, "for it is beautiful. Now, of course, San Sebastian is not so lovely, for your Lord Wellington has sacked the city, but it will recover. On a hill overlooking the bay, you will be able to see Miramar, where Spanish royalty spend their summers."

A smile briefly curved her mouth, but her eyes remained sad and shadowed, as they had been since she had accepted his proposal that they wed. It had shocked him, that she would so readily agree, when he had been prepared to offer arguments to persuade her. It had not been as easy to convince her to wait until they reached Spain to wed, however.

"I am a Roman Catholic, you see, and will not be considered married unless wed by a priest. Here, English law says the marriage must be performed by an Anglican. But we shall obtain a special license, and as soon as we reach Spain, we shall have two ceremonies to satisfy both our concerns. . . ."

It had been a convincing argument, and she agreed at last, another surprise. It was as if she could not bear to stay any longer in England.

Now, with the proper documents hidden in a small casket in his cabin, he would be able to retain his title and his lands, and would most enjoy presenting to the arrogant Lord Wellington the missive from Lord Palmerston that gave him back all that had been taken from him. It would give him great satisfaction. Then he would rebuild—so much to do yet.

Studying Amalie, he let his gaze drift from her sad, pensive face lower; she wore a thick pelisse, fastened against the wind and cold. But he knew what charms lay beneath her garments, had glimpsed them briefly their first night aboard ship, when he had gone to her cabin to take her a glass of sherry for her nausea.

Since then, he had been able to think of little else but the lush curves he had seen beneath her thin muslin nightdress, the dark-rose aureoles of nipples against white material, and the vague outline of slender hips, thighs, and buttocks. It might not be so disagreeable to be wed to her after all, though he had not thought of marrying again since his first wife, Maria—may the Holy Mother keep her soul safe—had died.

"Come, my little dove," he coaxed, "and I will

take you to your cabin, where it is much warmer. It is cold out here when the sun is behind the clouds."

"Yes, it is," she said at last, and looked past him toward the endless motion of the sea. Swells undulated all the way to the horizon, where gray clouds replaced the sun and blue sky.

"We have been fortunate to have such good weather, but now I think we shall see a storm. We are not far from the Bay of Biscay, and it is always stormy there. Now, come below, my dove, and let me bring you a hot drink to warm your blood."

A shout from above caught his attention, and he tilted his head back as the lookout stationed in his lonely crow's nest high above the dipping decks bellowed out a warning: "Sail-ho!"

Don Carlos turned to look for the captain, and saw him standing on the bridge with a brass-bound telescope in his hand. He held it up to his face, squinting into it. They had not encountered many ships, as British and French warships patrolled the waters of Portugal and down to the Mediterranean, a new game of cat-and-mouse since Wellington had captured Salamanca and sacked San Sebastian so near the French border.

Beside him, Amalie shivered, held her pelisse more tightly around her as she trembled.

"No," she whispered, and he looked at her sharply, saw her face grow pale beneath the newly acquired color, "no, do not let it happen again!"

"Let what happen, my dove? It is only another ship, do you see the flag?" He glanced over the ship's rail, then blanched. It was not Dutch or

Portugese, for it sat low in the water and bore a triangular sail—like an Arab dhow.

A puff of white smoke and distant booming sound made the *Scrutiny* rock wildly, sprays of water shooting up in geysers to drench decks, rails, and anyone standing near. Amalie gasped, blinked against the salt water, tightly gripping the rail with both hands, heedless of his hand on her arm urging her below.

When she turned at last, he saw a strange light in her eyes, and she said inexplicably, "It is how it should have happened last time. This was my fate, and I cannot escape it. I should not have tried."

"Come below," he urged, impatient now with what were obviously female hysterics, "until we see what they want."

"I know what they want."

But she went obediently, allowed him to drag her across the deck and below into the musty air of the passageway outside her cabin. He heard another boom, and the unmistakable cries of injured men, and said grimly, "If we are boarded, you are my wife, do you understand? It will help if you tell them you are the granddaughter of a countess, for then they will ransom you."

She just stared at him, green eyes wide and shiny as jewels, and he reached around her to open the cabin door and shove her inside. "Stay here, and do not come out until all is quiet."

Then he was gone, leaving her to go above deck. She stared after him, shaking. There was no point in hiding. They would find her. So she waited, in the dim, musty closeness of the narrow passageway, lit only by the square of light from above. She felt the ship's pace slacken as sails were hauled down, heard a grinding scrape and muted roar of indecipherable voices, then the entire vessel shuddered with the thunder of feet.

It was her nightmare come alive, memories of the last time returning with painful clarity—only this time Kit was not here to comfort her. This time, she was more alone than she had ever been in her life.

Closing her eyes as the nightmare descended, she held onto the side of the wall, waited for inevitable fate. It was all so familiar, the screams, the shouts, the clang of steel, over so quickly, falling away into eerie silence.

As if a heavy shroud had fallen over the ship, only the constant creaking of ropes and groan of wet wood penetrated the hush. It was stuffy, damp, and chilled in the closed passageway; the ship rocked on rising swells, settled sharply. A high-pitched scream shattered the silence, then died away, and she opened her eyes.

Long minutes passed, and the scuff of feet against decking was a steady whisper. She looked up, saw a slide of color pass the open hatch, heard laughter and a thud. Then bare feet appeared on the top rung of the ladder, stepped down; multicolored robes swirled around brown legs, and a figure crouched, peered into the shadows.

She stared at him, saw white teeth flash in skin burnt nearly black by the sun, and knew that this was much worse than the last time. These were no American or English pirates, or even French, but Arab corsairs, the scourge of the seas. Her heart pounded fiercely, and her mouth was too dry even to scream. She made no sound at all as he dropped from the top of the ladder into the dank passageway and reached for her.

He put out a hand, rough against her skin, touched her on the cheek, and grinned as he said something in a soft, strange language that sounded almost musical. When he put a hand on her arm, she went with him without a fuss or protest. It was as if someone else inhabited her body, a stranger, calm and accepting.

Above decks, more Arabs swarmed like bright plumaged birds, climbed rigging, descended into the cargo holds, while the crew were bunched into a huddle by the mainmast. She saw Don Carlos, looking terrified, in with the crew. A few bodies lay sprawled on the deck, and while she watched, they were scooped up and tossed overboard into the ocean as carelessly as if bundles of rags.

Impassive, she allowed the Arab who held her arm to take her to the rail, and in a moment, she was grabbed up and swung to the next ship, a sleekly built vessel painted in bright colors. More captives were brought aboard, all of them females she recognized from the days spent aboard the *Scrutiny*. Most were too frightened to speak, but two of the women screamed and wept, until one of the Arabs took them away. She did not see them again, even after the pirate ship removed the grappling hooks that held them bound to the *Scrutiny* and cast off, and did not want to think about what might have happened.

It was all a blur of incomprehensible language and fear, of sharp commands and gestures that she followed in numb silence. Instead of wallowing atop the water, as the *Scrutiny* had done, this ship cut through the water like a heron, graceful and swift.

She was vaguely aware of being fed out of a shallow bowl and using her fingers to eat a strange dish, then drank a thin, sweet liquid that looked like watery milk. None of the women talked much, but stared apprehensively at their captors.

It rained that night, a steady pounding that rocked the ship from side to side, sent pirates scampering up rigging with abbreviated robes tucked between their legs. Amalie didn't sleep; she crouched under the canvas awning on the deck and watched as rain slid in runnels through the scuppers and lightning cracked the black sky in two.

In the morning, blinking against the sun that seemed far too bright after the storm, Sarah Purcell, whom she had been introduced to aboard the *Scrutiny*, said suddenly, "They'll sell us, you know."

Amalie turned to look at Sarah and wondered if she looked as bedraggled and tired, then decided she must. She made no reply to the comment, not even when one of the others began to weep softly. It was likely true. She was a little surprised still to be alive, for she had not expected to survive this long.

"What will happen," an older woman asked hesitantly, "when we are sold?"

"I don't know. I heard my husband tell the story once of what happens to women the Arabs take—I think they are made slaves of some sort."

A pause, then more softly, "Or worse."

It was daunting, and Amalie closed her eyes and tried not to think about what would happen when the ship reached land. None of the pirates molested them, seemed not even to notice they were there, except to bring food or buckets to use for their personal needs. The buckets were brought and left, their purpose made clear by gestures and sharp commands in that strange language that they were to empty them over the rail when through.

On the third day, land was sighted; huge rock cliffs jutted up from the sea like rough shoulders. Sarah said they were entering the Mediterranean, that she had come here before with her husband.

"Not so long ago," she said softly, "when he was sent to Greece. It was lovely then."

Amalie turned away from the wistful tone. It was warmer here, the sun bright and heated against her skin. Her gown was filthy, torn, damp, and uncomfortable. No attempt had been made to give them water with which to wash, and she itched.

She thought of Grandmamma, and wished she had not left without telling her good-bye. What a fool she was, for not confiding in her. She would have understood. Instead, she had let humiliation and anger provoke her into making yet another mistake. Or perhaps she was just a coward, too unwilling to see the condemnation and disappointment in Grandmamma's eyes.

If she could honestly blame Deverell for her actions, she would, but she could not. He had taken advantage of her, but only when she'd let him. She must bear her part of the blame. That same honesty forced her to examine her own emotions, to admit that she had thought when he'd first returned to London that perhaps he might take notice of her. The years he was gone, he had been in her dreams, and when he had returned a hero, she had allowed herself the luxury of pleasant daydreams.

Silly, of course. He was not a hero.

A sudden hum of activity aboard the sloop caught her attention and she looked up, frowning as the pirates began to clear the decks. Then she saw the other sail.

It was hard to starboard and coming fast, almost seeming to fly across the water. Her heart leaped with hope that it might be English, or even American. Then she saw the flag and tasted sharp disappointment.

"Cartagena," Sarah said in a flat, emotionless tone. "A Colombian ship. Cartagena revolted against Spain, and flies her own flags. They also give letters of marque to privateers who are supposed to attack only Spanish ships, but most of the time, the privateers are really pirates who attack any ship they can."

Irrational, but Amalie felt suddenly like laughing. It must be hysteria, of course, but she found herself curiously amused by the fact that apparently, they were to be attacked by more pirates. She thought of the time in Virginia when she had caught a fish on her line, and upon landing it, discovered that the fish had swallowed a smaller fish, and that fish had swallowed a smaller fish, so that she had envisioned an entire line of predatory fish swimming in a line and eating and being eaten.

It was how she felt now.

Orderly chaos erupted aboard the Arab vessel as the other ship fired a warning shot across her bow, and sails were set to catch the wind. She saw that they meant to outrun the other ship. Huddled close together beneath the canvas awning, the women waited, though the outcome might not make any difference to their fates.

In the end, the Arab ship was overtaken, and the now familiar sound of grappling hooks digging into wood as they came alongside was loud. Several men clambered aboard and were met with resistance, but it was soon quashed with brutal efficiency. Amalie watched with growing alarm, for this lot of pirates looked even more disreputable than the last.

Her apprehension proved correct as one of the men sauntered over to peer beneath the canvas, gave a shout of delight, and grabbed for the closest female he could reach. It was Sarah, and she cried out when he pulled her roughly from beneath the awning, hauling her out by her long hair.

Speaking in French, he boasted to his comrades that he had found a prize and meant to keep them all to himself as part of his booty. Sarah struggled as he put his hands on her, ran them over her squirming body, and laughed when she tried to get away.

When he pushed Sarah back to the deck, his intentions were obvious as he held her down on her back while he tossed her skirts up to her waist.

It was the final indignity, and before she quite knew what she was doing, Amalie leaped from beneath the canvas to land upon the pirate's back. Pent-up terror and fury erupted in mindless rage, and she was vaguely aware that she was screaming at him in his own language, calling him the son of a dog and a swine, striking him on his head and back with her bare hands.

With a roar of anger, he straightened up and threw her off so that she landed on the deck with a jarring crash. For only an instant she lay there, then scrambled to her feet, grabbing at a belaying pin lying near a coil of rope as she stood up.

This time when he came at her, she brought up the pin and cracked him across the head with it. He went down like a sack of wet sand, collapsing at Sarah's feet. Amalie took a step closer to him, panting, still outraged, and lifted the pin to strike again.

Someone grabbed her arm, fingers a steel vise around her wrist, squeezing until she was forced to drop the pin.

As it hit the deck she turned, lashed out with one foot to catch her captor hard against his shin. He grunted and yanked, tugging her off-balance so that she landed at his feet. Breathless now, her arm still held by the pirate straddling her, she looked up at him defiantly.

Lungs already deprived of air emptied fully, so that she heard a distant ringing in her ears. Hovering above her was a face she had seen a thousand times in her dreams these past four years, different, but still familiar and beloved. She could not speak, but could only gape up at him.

Tall, broad now where once he had been a gangly youth of slight build, he did not even notice her stare as he gave an order to the pirates crowding close.

"Seize him up and toss him below in the brig. And if any of you has any similar ideas to abuse these women, you can discuss them with me across three feet of steel."

Harder now, with the face of a man instead of a boy, Kit glanced back down at her and hauled her to her feet. Then he paused, black brows snapping down over eyes the same green as her own, and peered closely into her face.

"My God—Amie?"

For the first time in her life, Amalie fainted.

Book IV

Conflict

New Orleans
1814

Chapter 19

August sunlight spread heat over crowded streets and close-packed houses of the *carré de la ville*; heavy scents of Spanish jessamine and rosemary were rich and sweet even on the balcony of the house at the corner of Toulouse Street and Rue Chartres. Amalie leaned over the iron rail that edged the balcony, idly plying a lace fan to stir up a cool breeze.

From where she stood, she could see the spire of the cathedral rising high above the Cabildo and roofs of the city; just beyond the cathedral were the booths for the sale of oranges, bananas, *bière douce*—the ginger beer cooled in large tubs—and *estomac mulâtre*, or ginger cake. The tempting fragrance of burnt sugar and nuts that formed the chevalier's *pralines* teased the air. Across from the Place d'Armes, small huts lined the waterfront, selling oysters wholesale or on the half-shell, supplied daily by luggers tied to the posts opposite the markets.

Today she was bored, and regretted refusing the invitation to ride along the river road with that handsome Creole, Philippe Duverné.

Though it was well past the early morning hour when he usually arrived, Kit was to visit today. Already the hot sun made shimmering waves of heat rise from the streets, and she could almost smell the boards of the *banquettes* that edged the street, baking under the relentless glare.

It would have been much cooler riding in an open curricle with Philippe, perhaps visiting the *Café del Aguila* on St. Ann for a chocolate, or buying an ice from a Greek vendor near the Place d'Armes. She always found Philippe amusing, for he flattered her, cajoled her with entreaties that she always refused but enjoyed hearing.

She had become a terrible flirt, Kit said, but always with a smile, and she thought perhaps that he was right. It was much easier to flirt than to take seriously any man's attention—a lesson she should have learned a long time ago.

Now, she listened to compliments, smiled, and ignored them. There were many men who came to the house on the corner of Toulouse and Rue Chartres, a lovely two-story brick house that had been built after the fire of 1788. It had been difficult for her at first, and for months she had not come out of this house Kit had rented for her in the heart of New Orleans, afraid of every shadow.

Finally, the nightmares eased, and she found that as the sister of a well-to-do sea captain, she enjoyed a certain popularity. Such a farce, but Kit insisted she act the part, and she had agreed. While influential citizens of New Orleans might acquire their goods from privateers who provided exquisite cloth, furniture, paintings, and objects d'art, they would not socialize with them.

So she was Amalie Cambre now, grateful for the French lessons Grandmamma had insisted she learn, employing a discreet facade to keep her brother's secret safe. It was not so difficult, and with the new name she felt almost like a new person, abandoning the restrictions of her other life. Here it was not as rigid as in London, though she must, of course, take her maid everywhere she went, and observe all the proprieties of a genteel young lady of good birth. So much had changed in the past year and a half that sometimes she felt as if she did not know herself any longer.

But New Orleans was so exciting, wicked and pious by turns, now part of the United States, yet crowded with Americans, French, Spanish, and Creoles.

Oh yes, and pirates, she reminded herself, squinting a little in the burning light as she saw Kit round the corner of Rue Chartres. While Jean Lafitte resembled a gentleman, with his expensive garments and charming insouciance, *he* looked more like a pirate, oddly enough. It was hard to reconcile the boy she had known with the hard-faced man she knew now, who spoke so casually of taking ships and outrunning revenue cutters.

Kit was so different, harder, his expression and voice sometimes reminding her of Deverell.

Deverell . . . painful memories, harsh reminders of hope so quickly destroyed. In the first months in New Orleans she'd pondered the emotions that had driven her to accept Don Carlos's proposal and flee London without even a proper farewell to Grandmamma. She had come at last to the inescapable conclusion that she could not bear the thought of being near Deverell. He would continue to visit Beacon House, and unless she left, she would have to face him, knowing that he cared nothing more for her than as a casual tumble.

It was, she thought with a ragged sigh, the night in the kitchen with the pugs that had sealed her fate. That night, despite his deliberate rejection of her, she had seen the man beneath the outer shell of arrogance and indifference. At that moment, he had seemed the man who had lingered in her dreams, the illusion coalescing into a tangible hero . . . a horrible mistake.

She wondered if Kit guessed; he said little, but she caught him gazing at her on occasion with speculative eyes, a brooding stare as if he saw through her pretense at indifference. Yet she could not confide in him, could not tell him what she had done, could not tell him about Deverell.

Oh, he knew about Grandmamma, of course, and how wonderful she was, generous and loving, and no doubt most distraught over what she must surely think was the death of her beloved goddaughter. She had stated her intention to write her at once, to assure her that she was alive.

But in that, she had found her brother inflexible.

"No," he had said, not harshly, but with a cold finality in his tone that reminded her again of Deverell, "to send her a letter would only make it worse. Leave it, Amie, and she will reconcile herself to your absence soon."

"But Kit, she is old and cares deeply for me. It

is too cruel not to tell her that I am alive and well, and I can be discreet. She needn't know where I am, after all."

"It would be dangerous."

That was all he would say about it, and finally she had ended the discussion. But she was no less determined; a simple letter without divulging her whereabouts would be harmless, and she had penned a brief note to Grandmamma, telling her that she was alive and content, and though she could not return in light of all that had happened, she would think of her always with great kindness and love.

It was very likely that the letter had never been delivered, as the war between America and Britain had escalated since Napoleon's abdication in March. Blockades of American ports were thick now, with privateers the only ships getting through, and the Lafitte Trust grew richer. Yet it was even more dangerous for the pirates.

Turning from the balcony, she went downstairs to greet Kit as he entered the courtyard of the gracious house. He wore a loose white shirt, trousers, and boots to the knees, cooler in this sultry heat that pressed down like a fist on the city. When he crossed the tiled court, he came to her with an affectionate embrace, as he had when they were children.

"I began to worry about you," she said, drawing back a little to look up at him, "with reports of British ships in the Gulf, and Claiborne's determination to rid Louisiana of pirates."

"Unexpected business," he said, with the slow smile that made him look younger than his twenty-five years. "Lafitte has a new client for his merchandise, so I took him by pirogue to Barataria."

Tucking her hand in the crook of his arm, she teased, "A fat, wealthy old man is more important than me?"

"Wealthy? Perhaps, but not fat or old. Bos has shrewd instincts, but this time, I think he may be disappointed."

"Oh, Kit, I do hope you're cautious. I hate it when you come into New Orleans, and worry that one day you'll be arrested. It could happen, you know. Look at Pierre."

"I am not as well known as Pierre, you must admit," he said dryly. "I like it that way. To Claiborne, I am just another face, one of the hundreds dealing with Jean Lafitte. Pierre owns a store and is easy to find."

"Still, it worries me," she murmured, and then gave a sigh when he changed the topic, but surrendered to the inevitable. He would do as he wanted, just as he had when they were children and he had frequented the waterfront despite her parents' and then the Covington's demands that he stay away.

She sent her maid, Solange, for chilled fruit juice and fresh pastries, and a glass of the strong liqueur Kit preferred to wine or juice, then turned when Kit said, "You may be pleased to know that our house is nearly finished." His brow lifted to watch her reaction; because he sounded so proud, she agreed, though she was reluctant to leave New Orleans.

"Of course, I'm pleased, though it has been quite pleasant here in New Orleans. I've grown to love this city. It's charming and exciting here."

"You'll love it on the island more. I don't want you here during the bad time, when yellow fever hits without warning. It's that way late in every summer, and you'll be safer on Belle Terre than here."

She sobered, remembering the year before when the yellow fever raged, and New Orleans was deserted as those who could, fled to their plantations outside the city. All the houses had been closed up and left, shuttered against the heat and the overpowering smells from gutters that ran thick with refuse.

Slaves had taken the brunt of the fever, dying like flies, sickened by the thick vapors that rose from the swamps that surrounded the city and hung above the river.

"Besides," Kit added, "I can come and go on Belle Terre without notice or arousing suspicion, or the risk of Claiborne's wrath."

"Kit—" She put a hand on his arm. "Don't you think it's time for you to leave? We could go back to Virginia, if you like, or—"

"Christ, Amie, are we going to go through this discussion again?" Impatient now, he moved away from her, crossed the tiles of the courtyard to sprawl in the iron comfort of a chair placed beneath the delicate fronds of a palm tree. "I have no choice but to do what I'm doing. Once Captain Jack took me aboard his ship, I was considered a pirate like the rest of them. If it had been me they'd caught in Kingston, I would have been hanged in Port Royal with the others. Poor Clement—he paid the price for me, his neck stretched on good King George's gallows for crimes he was forced to commit. I was damned lucky to be taken on with Lafitte."

"So lucky that every time you come into New Orleans, I fear you'll be arrested," she said, more tartly than she meant. "Oh Kit, it's just that I worry about you, and what will happen one day. This cannot continue forever, you know."

"Of course I know that." He regarded her from beneath black brows drawn into a scowl. "I'm not like the others, spending what I get as soon as it's in my hands. I've been saving it, and now I have my own house on my own bit of land, though it's not quite what I want. One day, I'll be able to leave this area and make a new start somewhere, but now, I have to stay. If you don't want to stay with me, I'll send you where you want to go—"

"No, of course I want to stay with you." Remorseful, she went to him and knelt at his side. He reached out after a moment, put a hand on her head to caress her hair, and smiled faintly when she said, "I just don't want to lose you again, now that we're together at last."

"No, Amie. I don't want that either."

It was quiet in the courtyard, the noises outside the wooden gates muted and distant; here, in the familiar security of the house, it was comfortable and reassuring, a reminder of what life could be.

Kit studied his sister with a pang of regret; she was right, but he'd never admit it to her. It was dangerous for him, more so now that Governor Claiborne had renewed his efforts to clear Barataria of pirates and Jean Lafitte by public proclamations of his intentions.

Typical of the pirate leader, Lafitte had returned to New Orleans and embarked upon enthusiastic entertainment, securing the attendance of some of the most prominent merchants at his private dinner parties, and boldly visiting public cafés surrounded by influential friends. Even more boldly, he had announced the dates he planned to sell slaves and other merchandise looted from his raids on merchant ships.

When Claiborne had initiated criminal proceedings, the Grand Jury had returned indictments against Jean Lafitte and all the other Baratarians, charging them with piracy. Pierre was indicted as an "aider and abettor" and tossed into the Calaboose without bail. Of course, Jean Lafitte immediately retained the services of two of the Louisiana Bar's most prominent attorneys, John Grymes and Edward Livingston—the latter was brother to the Chancellor Livingston who had administered the oath of office to George Washington.

Greed was a powerful motivation, and Grymes resigned his office as District Attorney of the Parish of Orleans to accept the case and the promised fat fee of twenty thousand dollars to defend Pierre Lafitte.

But even had Pierre been acquitted, the end was too closely signalled. No, Kit had done the right thing to build a house on a sandy island in the Gulf of Mexico. He could keep Amie safe there until enough time passed to quietly relocate and start life over as a wealthy business owner. He thought of Virginia, and pictured the coves and inlets he had loved as a boy, the green fields and sloping hills farther inland where a man could make his fortune raising tobacco or cotton. It would not be a bad life for him.

Or for Amie.

She had changed so much, a distant sorrow lurking in her eyes when she thought he wasn't watching closely, and he wondered again the exact nature of the events that had led her to be on a ship to Spain with an impoverished Spanish nobleman. He was certain it was not a love match; she had never voiced more than casual concern for the fate of Don Carlos, her betrothed.

But he was not as inexperienced as he might be in the ways of females, having observed much in the past years, and he knew that despite her outward indifference, she nursed a broken heart. Twice, he had come upon her unawares and caught the glint of tears in her eyes, her expression anguished, and recognized that all too female despair over a man as the cause. It only remained to him to learn who had hurt her.

Rising, he pulled Amie to her feet with him, slid an arm affectionately around her waist. She'd lost weight, was as slight as a child now, and her face thinner, so that her eyes were much too large for her face.

"Therese will feed you gumbo and fatten you up once you are settled in. It's not a big house, but comfortable. It may not be exciting like New Orleans, but you can come back whenever you like. You'll learn to love Belle Terre."

"I know I will, Kit."

She looked up at him with a smile that did not reach her eyes. Silent again, he held her loosely against him, and cursed the man who had done this to her. If ever he saw him, he would take great pleasure in running him through with a cutlass.

~

Belle Terre was, Amalie assured Kit, everything he had promised, a sprawling house of cypress and shingles. Wood-shuttered windows from floor to ceiling let in light and salty breeze from the Gulf of Mexico. The island was unnamed, though Lafitte called it Campeachy, an uninhabited strip of beach over thirty miles long off the coast of New Spain.

It was far enough away from New Orleans and Barataria to be safe from revenue cutters, yet close enough that they could be back in the city with only a day's voyage by sea. The *Cacafuega* was a swift sloop, low and sleek and bristling with so many guns that Amalie had expressed alarm.

"I've not forgotten the lessons I learned aboard the *Success* or even Captain Jack's ship," Kit told her wryly, "and don't intend to be caught again."

He stayed on Belle Terre nearly a month before telling her he must leave once more.

"I've got to go back," he said vaguely, and saw from the sudden shadows in her eyes that she knew where he went and why. It was unavoidable, but he refused to apologize for it or explain. It was a choice that had been thrust upon him, and he was making the best he could of it. It wouldn't be long before he had enough money tucked away to take them far from Louisiana and any taint of piracy.

"When do you leave?" she asked quietly, and he ignored the slight quaver in her voice.

"In the morning. But tonight there is a feast on the beach. Some of the men and their women have been cooking all day, and there will be roast pig and boiled crabs. You like crabs. Remember tending your crab floats?"

"Yes, and I remember how the other crabs would pull any that tried to escape back into the trap. It will be the same when you try to leave Barataria."

He fell silent, frowning at the obvious significance. She would have to accept this for now; neither of them had other choices.

Fires dotted the damp stretch of beach that curved like a scythe below the house. Tall bunches of oatgrass feathered over sloping dunes, and ropes of bright flowers grew wild, patches of blue straggling over sandy hills. The late afternoon sun turned the Gulf waters orange and yellow, a wide swathe that seemed to swallow the burning sphere like some giant aquatic predator.

A strange thumping rhythm undulated above the incessant wash of waves against the shore, the beat of drums a relentless, visceral pulse, familiar now to Kit, but foreign to Amalie, who stayed close to him.

She stared at the dark-skinned figures around the fires, green eyes reflecting the glow of flames and interest as she watched quietly. Kit introduced her to new members of his crew, his harsh gaze a reminder of his warning against offending his sister in any way.

They were polite—rough for the most part, but unwilling to incur his anger. He retained control by the art of intimidation, and had no intention of relinquishing his rank. He had fought too fiercely to gain it.

But no one insulted Amie, and soon she even seemed to be enjoying it, smiling and tapping her feet to the music. The tempting smell of roasting pig filled the air, turned on a spit over a fire to one side, sizzling as grease dripped into the low flames. Wine plundered from a French merchantman was shared liberally. Torches were lit as the sun sank into the gulf, shedding light in wavering pools.

Some of the pirates' women began to dance, long, loose hair flying about their faces and bodies as bare feet dug into sand. Bonfire flames licked the wind, beacons in the night, gleaming on bare skin as the women moved gracefully to the pounding rhythm of drums and guitars.

Kit saw Rosa glance at him, her mouth pursed in a sultry pout that he recognized, and was not surprised when she came to Amie and said, "You will dance with us, yes?"

"Oh no, I don't think so." She glanced up at him with an uncertain frown, and when he shrugged, turned back to Rosa, her voice suddenly firm. "Yes, perhaps I will dance, after all. Will you show me?"

Delighted at the willingness of the lady she had once referred to as a timid mouse—until he had told her how Amie had nearly bludgeoned one of his men to death on an Arab dhow—Rosa flashed him a triumphant smile and took Amie by the arm to the circle of dancers.

Kit watched indulgently, smiling a little at Amie's first halting steps, her shoes sending up geysers of sand as she tried to mimic Rosa's sensuous grace. He thought of her as he'd seen her aboard that Arab dhow, her mindless fury that had shocked him in a woman, horrified him in his sister.

What had happened to her to change her so much? It wasn't just the pirates, terrifying as that had been for her. No, there was something else, an indefinable regret, perhaps, that lay beneath her outward tranquility, a deep distress. It was encouraging now to see her enjoy herself.

Laughing, breathless, Amalie paused to remove her shoes, casting her brother a mischievous glance as she peeled away stockings as well, throwing them to her maid, Solange, before returning to the bonfire. He returned her glance with a grin, leaned against a stout-boled tree with his arms crossed over his chest to watch in amusement as his sister became the hoyden he had known as a child. But as he watched, his smile began to fade.

As her feet found the rhythm at last, Amalie reached up to remove the bright Spanish combs from her long dark hair, freeing it to tumble over her shoulders and down her back. She wore a scoop-necked *camisa* like Rosa's, white and trimmed with red embroidery, thin muslin that was much cooler than the heavier garments required by etiquette in a city like New Orleans; her skirt was full, gathered around her waist with a simple cord to fall in soft folds to her ankles, swaying with every movement.

Now Amalie's feet kept time to the wild, fast beat of the music, the soaring throb of guitars. Someone passed her a glass of wine and she took it, drank it in a single toss, then handed it back, laughing.

The sensuous pulsebeat of guitars and drums grew louder, mingled with cries and clapping of hands, and more women joined the dancers. But it was his sister who drew the eyes of the men watching as she mimicked Rosa, drawing her skirts higher to reveal slender ankles and calves, a teasing twitch of muslin, a flirtatious glimpse, then a whirl away and toss of her head.

My God, he thought, caught between amazement and anger, *she really does look like one of them, a gypsy wench like Rosa. . . .*

With her full lips curved into a sensuous smile and her eyes half-closed, the sheen of perspiration making her face shine in the firelight, she danced with artlessly sexual movements of her body in the very center of the crowd. Every man there watched her with the same avid admiration and lust in his eyes as she moved sinuously, with complete abandon. Pale shoulders with only a hint of color gleamed, and the expression on her face was dreamy and teasing by turns, an invitation and rejection in her heavy-lashed eyes as she danced as only a woman who has known a man can dance.

It struck him then that the reason for her anguish was more than he had considered, that she pined for a lover more than she did for England. And he wondered angrily who the man had been, and why he had abandoned her.

Rage began to build inside him, impotent and strong, that any man would dare defile his sister and desert her.

"Amante," Rosa murmured at his side, divert-

ing his reluctant attention, "your sister is not the lady you thought her, heh? She dances like a gypsy, like one of us."

He glanced down at her, his tone sharp. "My sister has always been spirited."

"Spirited? *Ay! sin falta!* If that is what you prefer to call it, eh? Look at her—she dances now with Miguel, do you see? No, she is not the timid mouse, I thought . . . do you see the way she dances?"

He did, and was furious. As men clapped and stamped approval, crowding close to watch, Amalie accepted another cup of wine, a slender arm reaching out for it, tilting back her head and drinking it in a single swallow, then tossing the cup back with a laugh. Perspiration made the thin garments adhere to her body, damp against her skin, clinging seductively. With the fire behind her, her legs were outlined against the glow.

She looked brazen, passionate—provocative. He did not need for her to present herself in front of his crew this way, as available as the rest of the women who lived with the pirates, and pushed away from the tree with the intention of stopping her. Rosa caught his arm.

"Ah no, lover, you must leave her be, I think. She is a grown woman, yes? Besides, I only think it will be good for her to dance so that you and I can slip away and be alone for a time, yes?"

"No. Damn it, Rosa, let go of me!"

With an angry hiss, Rosa released his arm and burst into a tirade in Spanish that he answered in kind; he was too intent on reaching Amie to notice that some of his crew had come up from their guard posts on the beach until he pushed Rosa aside.

Then he saw them and paused, recognizing the man who accompanied the guards as Lafitte's newest client. Damn, what was he doing *here*, when he was supposed to wait in Grand Terre?

Kit strode forward to greet him. He saw Amalie turn and stumble to a halt in the dance, and the gay smile abruptly disappear from her face. Flushed, dark hair in tempestuous tangles on each side of her face, she stared at the late arrival with wide eyes glittering like green jewels.

Puzzled at the horror in her voice, he heard her say, *"You!"*

Chapter 20

"Hello, my green-eyed gypsy," Deverell said softly, "it's nice to see you again, too."

Some of the color drained from her face, and in the light of the leaping flames, he saw her eyes darken. What a contradictory little cat she was, dancing with abandon, a sensual creature with her garments hugging her curves like a second skin, thin enough so that all could see the pink pout of her nipples through the blouse, and the elegance of slender thighs curving gently from her hips.

He thought of another night and another fire's reflection, of bare thighs and sweet breasts beneath his hands and mouth. Apparently, she'd expanded her experience since then; no woman danced like that if they were not well accustomed to the rhythm of seduction. He should not be surprised. He'd always thought the veneer of propriety she wore like a damn badge of honor was far too thin to be genuine, for all her protestations about *respectability*. A masquerade devised to deceive Grandmère, and it had nearly fooled him as well. *Christ!* He'd even considered marrying her after all, just to keep her away from Don Carlos.

That would have been the ultimate folly.

Now here she was in front of him, when after he had escaped that hellhole of a ship, he'd spent six months searching for her in Spain and the Indian Ocean as well, tracking down the pirates who had taken her. She landed on her feet like a little cat, it seemed. A vicious little cat. . . .

"Braxton," Kit Silver said into the heavy silence that enveloped them, "I presume you know my sister."

Still holding her gaze, he said smoothly, "We have met before, a long time ago."

Silver asked abruptly, "Did Lafitte send you here? We were to meet on Grand Terre."

There was more than a hint of hostility in that tone, and he released Amalie and turned to the young man staring at him with hot suspicion in his eyes.

"There has been a change in plans, but we can discuss that later, when you have read the letter from Lafitte."

After a moment, Silver nodded stiffly. "Come up to the house. We can talk there."

Deverell glanced at Amalie, who had recovered from her shock well enough to hide it, a sidelong glance from beneath her lashes the only indication she noticed him at all as she turned away.

"You will join us, won't you?" he said, catching her again by the arm, lifting her hand to press to his mouth in a courtly gesture that he was certain she saw through; he looked up at her, a wicked glance as the pressure of his fingers on her wrist tightened, a reminder and a warning.

"I never involve myself in my brother's business affairs," she said stiffly. Her eyes narrowed slightly, like a cat's, aloof and appraising when he said:

"We can discuss—old times."

"Not all *old times* are good memories, sir."

Releasing her hand, he knew then that she had not told her brother about him and she did not want to now. It was a leverage of sorts to wield, but a double-edged sword if she chose to tell Silver of their past involvement at an inconvenient time. It was obvious he was protective of his sister, and any man who had lived nearly five years as a pirate would not be shy about retaliation.

Besides, tempting as vengeance could be—especially now—he had not come here just for that. There were other reasons, and the man known as Kit Silver was one of them.

"Your presence will be greatly missed," he murmured with just the right note of regret, and saw from the way her lips pressed tightly together that she was not fooled in the least by his gallantry.

On a knoll overlooking the bay, a natural inlet rimmed by a tree-choked coastline, the house blended into the surrounding brush. If not for lights shining from the windows, it would be impossible to see it at night, and difficult even during the day.

Deverell followed Silver up the narrow path, dim in the dark gloom that was barely illuminated by the torches and fires on the beach; a thin moon shed weak light.

It was surprisingly spacious inside the house, with the main room sweeping across the entire front, flanked by an open veranda. French doors opened outward, left ajar to allow in cooling breezes that belled gauzy draperies and filled the house with the salty tang of the sea. Elegant furniture graced the room, obviously plunder; apparently they stole only the best.

"What is your connection with my sister?" Silver asked abruptly, after he poured brandy into two crystal cups. "How do you know her?"

"We met in London right after she arrived several years ago. It has been a long time since I've seen her."

Silver stared at him over the rim of his snifter; his eyes were as green as his sister's, but hard, with none of her softness. He was young but did not look it; there was nothing youthful in that ruthless face.

His expression held a hint of familiar insolence, the same inbred arrogance his sister possessed—inherited, no doubt, from his illustrious ancestors, who had passed along arrogance and little else to these descendants. *Silver*, a sobriquet derived from Lord Silverage, for his grandfather had been a titled baron of the realm, while the grandson was an infamous pirate. A remarkable analogy.

Brusquely, Silver said, "Give me Lafitte's letter."

Deverell lifted a brow, handed him the letter, then sipped brandy as the pirate took it across the room to read in the light of a gold-trimmed lamp. Thick carpet lay underfoot, and he recognized a painting by a Dutch master hanging on the far wall. Apparently, piracy paid well.

When Silver looked up from the letter, he said, "Who authorized you to make this offer?"

"The British government."

"Christ, I told Bos that you were not the wealthy merchant you pretended to be."

Deverell lifted one shoulder in a slight shrug. "A small deception to test the waters, so to speak. Do you consider our offer?"

"Like Lafitte, I will think it over." He eyed him with cold deliberation. "It seems the British assume the victory when it is not yet won. Thirty thousand dollars and grants of American land are rather presumptuous, don't you think?"

"I prefer to think of it as farsighted."

Damn Bathurst, I told him this would not work. . . . New Orleans was vital to British victory, to secure the mouth of the Mississippi and deprive inland Americans access to the sea. It was a strategic position, but the Secretary of War had misjudged the mood of the people in Louisiana when he'd assumed they wanted independence or a return to Spanish rule.

Colonel Nicholls, fresh from taking Florida from the Spanish, had ordered his officers to go to Barataria and offer Lafitte land, protection, the rank of captain in the British Navy, and cash to join them. Deverell had argued against it, sensing the mood of the people, but had been overruled.

It was increasingly obvious he was right, for not only Silver, but Lafitte delayed an answer. With Pierre Lafitte in a New Orleans prison, it would be unlikely that his brother would risk betraying American authorities.

"Are you berthed for the night, Mister Braxton? Or as a commissioned officer, should I call you by your rank?"

"My ship lies in the bay with ample accommodation. Braxton is sufficient." No point in getting into titles and rank, especially not here and now. Until he'd come here, he'd wanted only to get it over with, impatient to return to New Orleans, where there was a degree of civilization for a man who spoke French and did not announce his nationality too loudly.

That was before he had seen Amalie Courtland, before he had proof that the pirate captain known as Kit Silver was her brother, Christian Courtland. It was a suspicion he had not shared with Nicholls or anyone else; he'd just not expected to find her *here,* dancing like Salome with the seven veils.

But he had learned that life was full of surprises, most of them inconvenient and often unpleasant.

With Napoleon's abdication in April, all energies were turned to this war with the United States. Cochrane's secret weapon was safe with Napoleon checked at last. A damned waste, as far as he was concerned; it could have ended the war much sooner and saved lives, but Parliament was notoriously chicken-hearted.

The seven months he'd spent aboard the *Fortune* as an impressed sailor were well entrenched in his memory, and when he was finally rescued by a British frigate, he was welcomed into the British Navy with a promotion in rank, a brass medal, and a commission on a frigate. It was not surprising that hard on the heels of Napoleon's abdication he had been asked to return to his commission. The answer, of course, was the need for more men in America, and he had come with Nicholls to take Florida from the Spaniards, not an easy task. But one that had brought him closer to his objective.

When the letter had arrived in London from America, his grandmother had wept with relief that her darling Amie was still alive, and shared the glad tidings with him. It had not taken long to weave the fragments of information he'd gathered into a comprehensive tapestry of events, and he had half-expected to find her in New Orleans, yet the name Courtland was unknown to all inquiries.

Instead, he'd found her here, dancing with careless unconcern for the havoc she had caused in his life. His months as a common seaman aboard the *Fortune* had been hellish; each passing day had brought more indignities, more hardships, and he had learned what it was to serve below decks.

It was a lesson he was unlikely to forget.

Kit Silver regarded him warily, tapping the letter thoughtfully against the table. "It is late, and much more comfortable here on Belle Terre. Stay the night, Braxton, and in the morning, we will leave together."

A thinly veiled command, but it suited him, and he accepted the offer. "You are very generous. I admit to a preference for dry land under my feet for a while."

"Join us on the beach, if you like. There's music and dancing, and wine taken from a French merchantman. Or it may have been a British ship, a clumsy tub of a brig that wallowed in the sea like a dog pissing in snow."

The icy gaze was slightly mocking, daring him to comment, and he said only, "I'll need to send a message to my first mate to tell him of my plans."

"René will take it out for you. Come with me, and you can give it to him, then join us on the beach."

Obviously cautious—but then, he would have to be in order to survive. It was no secret in New Orleans that Claiborne intended to rid the area of pirates.

It was a sentiment he heartily endorsed.

Shivering in the night air that had suddenly grown too cool, the muggy breezes chilling her now instead of barely cooling her, Amalie stared up at the lit windows of the house with dismay. *Deverell! Here!*

How had he found her? Or was it only coincidence that had brought him here to this island that until recently had been uninhabited? Of course, it had to do with Jean Lafitte, as did everything Kit did lately, but she could not help but wonder if the earl had come here deliberately to find her.

And he seemed so—different. Harder, somehow, when she had not thought that possible, and leaner, with another scar on his face, a long curve across his left cheek. He looked—piratical. As if he belonged with Jean Lafitte's scourge of the seas. Despite the way he'd held her hand, she'd seen something else in his eyes, a glitter of menace that had left her quivering.

Oh God, here he came, walking with Kit across the sand toward her, his stride loose, easy grace. She stood up, seized by the sudden urge to flee, wishing she had not drunk so much wine. Why was it she always seemed to be slightly intoxicated at the most inopportune times, when she rarely drank spirits of any kind?

"We meet again," Deverell said easily when they reached her, and the same gleam was in his eyes.

She straightened her shoulders, saw Kit looking at her with narrowed eyes, and managed to say coolly, "So it seems, sir."

"Braxton says you met a long time ago, Amie," Kit said then, his eyes still on her. "In London?"

"Yes. Yes, it was in London. He—is acquainted with Lady Winford, you could say."

"Well acquainted," Deverell said smoothly, "but it has been some time since I have been back to England."

"How pleasant for you, to travel about the world."

"Do you think so?" His eyes never left her, and though his tone was amiable, there was an undercurrent to it that made her uneasy. "Alas, it was not exactly the way I would recommend one to travel. But it was an education in survival."

"Then we come from the same school," Kit said into the brief silence that fell. "Impressment in a pirate ship is a harrowing institute, and frequently fatal."

Amalie stared at Deverell, while torchlight played over his face; it gave him a saturnine appearance, with his black brows and narrowed eyes, the cynical curl of his mouth so familiar even after nearly a year and a half.

What had he meant about survival? Oh, and why did she care, anyway? He had made it quite clear he cared about her only in a carnal sense, that he wanted her in his bed, but not in his life. It was foolish, to be frightened of him now, for this was her brother's domain.

It was easy when Miguel came to find her, and ask her to come back to the fire and dance, to pretend a gaiety she did not feel, and agree with a laugh.

"Yes, I feel like dancing more tonight, for it is a beautiful night, and it's been so long since I danced with such a handsome young man."

Aware of Kit's frowning gaze, she went with Miguel, not glancing toward Deverell, though she could feel his eyes on her, hot and intense. He made her remember things she wanted to forget, the months of anguish she had endured after leaving England. The night terrors had been caused by more than the pirates, painful memories crowding her fitful dreams.

Yet even as she danced, feet finding the steps of their own volition, the earlier gaiety of the night was gone. Now she longed only for the dancing and music to end, so that she could retreat to her room in solitary safety. For the first time since Kit had found her, she felt uncertain and insecure.

"Ay, Dios mio!" Miguel said, black eyes hot flames in his dark face as he raked them over her, "you dance like an angel, Señorita Cambre . . . so beautiful."

"I do not dance as well as Rosa or the others, of course."

"It is not true. You dance as if you were born to it, as if you are gypsy like Rosa . . . if your brother were not so fierce, I would teach you the *jarabe,* for it is a dance made for a woman like you."

She smiled, a slow, sensuous smile, more for the benefit of the blue eyes watching her so closely than for Miguel, who came much too close in the steps of the dance, so that the front of his shirt brushed against her breasts in a teasing question.

The music soared, a plaintive throb and pulsing beat, and she forced herself to ignore Deverell and concentrate only on the primitive rhythm, abandoning discretion as her feet found the cadence. Her body seemed to move by itself, bare feet stamping on soft sand as she found the rhythm of the *corrido,* heard Miguel's fervent admiration, and saw, as she whirled past, her brother's scowling face.

But it was Deverell's expression that stood out, the narrowed blue eyes like daggers, his face familiar to her even though changed, skin a dark brown that made him look harsher, the face of her dreams for so long now. He watched like the others, tall enough to stand out, a lean threat even among pirates.

And suddenly she felt powerful, knew that he was angry without knowing why, knew that this was vengeance of a sort, this flaunting of her body, a silent reminder that he had been careless enough to lose her. Oh yes, she recognized that taut set to his mouth, remembered too well the intensity in his eyes as he came to her, held her with fierce need, and knew, as all females know, that he wanted her now.

Deliberately, she flirted with Miguel, tossed her long dark hair as she had seen Rosa do, let it dip into her face in a seductive drape, then flung her head back so that it whipped across his chest as he came near. Miguel caught her hands, lifted them, and pressed his body close to hers, so close she felt his desire against her, knew that he wanted her as well.

A provocative smile curved her lips, sultry and promising more than she would ever deliver as she teased him with a lift of one bare shoulder, a twitch of her skirts high enough to bare her legs to the knees, then a whirl away from him when he drew too close. It was a mating ritual, a dance that proclaimed her independence and her availability.

Miguel turned in the steps of the dance, his back against hers, stamping his feet in the sand; she felt his heat along her spine, the flex of muscles in his shoulders as he pressed against her, not much taller than she was.

And when she turned, panting a little from her exertions and the heat, she whirled back to see that *he* had taken Miguel's place, and was staring down at her with a challenge in those dark blue eyes.

Silent, he met her startled gaze with a lifted brow and a mocking curve of his mouth.

Refusing to be intimidated, she answered his smile with a taunting curl of her lips before whirling away again, just out of reach. Deliberately she lifted her arms upward, slowly, a sinuous movement as she had seen Rosa do for Kit, an invitation and enticement as she raised the mass of dark hair from her neck, then let it fall again.

Light exploded behind his eyes, and his smile went rigid. "Little hellcat—you have learned a lot since last I saw you."

"I have learned to avoid certain men, Mister *Braxton,* or should I call you by your other name?"

"You'll do what you want."

"Yes. . . ." She half-closed her eyes, let him move closer, then stepped back again, feet sending up showers of sand as she danced away. His eyes were on her, narrowed and hard, a promise in them that made her shiver.

She could not elude the hand he put out to turn her, strong and determined, bringing her up hard against him as he put his other hand in the small of her back to hold her. He moved with easy agility, as if he had been dancing the *corrido* all his life, but ignored the sequence of the steps to press into her so closely that she could feel the sharp metal of his belt buckle against her ribs beneath her breasts. Heat from his hand was searing, demanding, and she stumbled slightly, breathless with anger and rising agitation.

The music ended with a crash, and she saw Kit glaring at her from across the circle of dancers. A log collapsed in the bonfire, sending up arcing sparks that flared into oblivion. Deverell released her, stood back, swept her a bow as gallant as if they had been dancing in the Beacon House ballroom, then left her standing there.

She stood, panting for breath, aware of curious

eyes, then accepted gratefully a cup of wine from Miguel.

The rest of the evening was spent avoiding Deverell, or *Braxton*, as Kit knew him, though she was more familiar with his title name than his surname. She resolved to tell Kit about him at the first opportunity, a succinct recital that would avoid any mention of her personal involvement with the earl.

The earl—he didn't look like a member of the peerage now, but more like one of the pirates, wearing an open white shirt, tight fawn breeches tucked into knee-high black boots, and a wicked cutlass at his side. If he had come ashore with pistols tucked into his belt, as did her brother, they had been relinquished.

And as if guessing she deliberately avoided him, he focused his attention on her maid, Solange, another insult and reason to ignore him. Solange flirted, danced with him by the fire, and teased him with lingering glances from beneath her lashes. She noticed, of course, when he danced with her, for Solange rubbed up against him in blatant invitation, and he seemed to enjoy it.

Of course he did—it was all that he wanted from a woman, that casual alliance without entanglement. She had not forgotten for a moment that he offered nothing else.

As the night wore on, the crew became rowdy; it was hot, even for September, the air humid and sticky. Her clothes stuck to her with clammy heat, and she longed for a cool bath and perhaps some fruit juice. She looked for Kit, but could not find him, and instead found Rosa.

"Rosa, tell my brother I have gone to bed. It's late and I'm tired, and besides, this heat is too much for me."

Rosa laughed, dark eyes crinkling with amusement. "It is not hot, but only warm. But then, I have not danced as you, and stirred the blood of the men. Who do you choose for your lover tonight, eh?"

"No one."

"Miguel, he looks for you with longing in his eyes, and would make a good lover. I know this, for once, he and I were lovers."

As it was not a conversation she desired to continue, Amalie made her excuses quickly and left the beach. She did not bother to summon Solange, for she had disappeared alone with Deverell some time ago, no doubt to some hidden copse for privacy.

It was cooler on the knoll overlooking the water, breezes washing in through the long windows, belling out the thin curtains in graceful wings like seagulls. She closed the doors with faint regret; she preferred privacy to the muted sounds of revelry from below. It was louder now, the throbbing music of guitar and fiddle drifting up the hill even through closed doors.

She missed New Orleans, wished she had stayed there despite Kit's assurances that she would be happy here. It was too far from everything, too remote and isolated for her to feel comfortable. But how could she tell him that, when she knew he had built this house only for her, so that they could be together, instead of needing the risky meetings in New Orleans? She could not, of course.

But she loved the excitement, the theaters and the galas, and since she was thought to be the genteel sister of a seafaring captain, no one had questioned her presence or status. Here she was lonely, even with Kit, and now he was leaving her to go off again, and she would worry the entire time he was gone, waiting for his safe return.

Perhaps this time when he came back, she would insist that he take her to New Orleans, for the late summer fever would wane with the cooler temperatures of September. Soon the theaters would be open again, and life would return as residents came back to their houses for the winter. It would be gay and lively, a vital city, even with the rumors of approaching British forces. But surely the British would not actually come this far, would they? The *New Orleans Picayune* printed articles about the war, and the conflict seemed to be concentrated along the East Coast and up near Canada and New York.

But a lot could happen in a month, and Kit had said that British forces threatened Florida and Mobile Bay.

Was that the reason Deverell had come? Fretful, she wished Kit would come back to the house. She had to tell him about Deverell, wanted to know the real reason he was here at Belle Terre.

He would not have come all this way to find her; she knew that much. He had not cared about her when she was in London, and he certainly would not go out of his way to find her half a world away.

Restless despite her weariness, she paced the

floor, thought about Deverell and all that had happened, fretted over his arrival. She could not escape the feeling that he brought trouble with him.

It grew late, and Kit had still not returned; she would talk to him tomorrow, before he left with the morning tide. She took a lamp to her bedroom, set it on the table across from her bed, not risking fire near the drapes of mosquito netting that flowed from the ceiling to puddle on the floor around the bed.

Stripping off her garments, she stood for a moment in the dense shadows before washing; outside, the faint drift of music on the air could still be heard, mixed with laughter and the pulsing sound of the Gulf. She washed thoroughly, using scented soap that Kit had brought her, "purchased with coin and not steel," he had assured her with a grin, knowing how she felt about his forays. But even purchased with coin, it was tainted, for silver and gold were obtained as dishonestly as the rest.

Oh God, if only he would listen to her, and they go could go away—back to Virginia, perhaps, or even to the Carolinas . . . anywhere he was not known. They could begin again, without waiting for the ax to fall, as they did here. It wasn't that she did not like Jean Lafitte, for he was quite handsome and gallant, a charming rogue who kissed her hand and declared her the most lovely woman in all Orleans Territory.

But Orleans Territory was part of the United States now, Louisiana, and things changed. People changed. She had certainly changed, and she hoped Kit would, too.

As the humid air dried her body, she wrung out the cloth she had used and hung it over the edge of the washbowl. It could be emptied in the morning; now she wanted only to go to bed, and slipped into a light muslin shift, pulled it over her head to let it flow to her ankles.

She blew out the light and crossed the room. Bed ropes creaked beneath her weight, mattress dipping as she pulled the netting closed. It was humid, stuffy even when she opened the window, and beyond, the familiar sounds of night birds and insects, the clamor of revelry, continued.

She tossed and turned, wondering vaguely if she could be coming down with the fever despite all precautions, and if she should close the window. But it was so hot, even in September, and the breezes were worth the intermittent noise. Besides, it was cooler here than in New Orleans, where the streets were stifling in the late summer before the rains swept up the river from the Gulf to cool the air and wash the city clean. It was one of her favorite times of year, for then it would be fresh and bright, with the gutters cleansed of refuse and the *banquettes* that lined the street high above the mud to keep feet relatively dry. Perhaps tomorrow she would urge Kit to take her back for a visit. It was too remote here on Belle Terre, the dense silence oppressing when there was not a celebration. She would have no distractions to keep her free of the memories. . . .

An occasional shout pierced the night, and she lay still for a long time, until finally the wine and exhaustion claimed her in uneasy sleep.

Chapter 21

Strange dreams hovered, a blur of images permeated throughout with a sense of foreboding: Deverell was in the dreams, his wicked blue eyes staring at her intently, his touch light on her body. Her arms were as lethargic as if she was moving through water, weighted, trapped in spiderwebs clinging to her as she tried to avoid his touch.

But it was no use, and she began to whimper.

A whisper of sound, warm breath against her cheek, someone telling her to be quiet, and she opened heavy lids with difficulty; her eyes were scratchy, her vision blurred, and as it cleared, she saw that it was not a dream after all, but Deverell at her side.

As her mouth opened, he put a hand over her lips, his tone harsh: "Don't scream unless you want to get someone killed. I'm in no mood to be charitable tonight. Do you understand me?"

She nodded after a moment, convinced that this was no dream, his palm too painful against her lips, crushing them against her teeth.

"Do you promise not to scream if I take my

hand away? I warn you, yours will be the first throat I cut."

Because of the menace in his tone, she believed him; it was so dark, his silhouette so vague, a mere shadow against shadows in the room, the only distinction the faint gleam of his eyes and teeth.

"Excellent," he said, when she nodded again, "obedient at last. What a surprise, finding you here. No one in New Orleans knew you, or your brother. Of course, I didn't use your new names. Cambre, I think Solange said. Yes? Ah, she is a good girl, your maid, very informative and quite lovely. I could almost lose myself in her for a while, if I didn't have other things that are more pressing."

When his hand left her mouth, she considered screaming anyway, then knew it would do no good. There was too much noise, with the music and laughter, and no one would hear her unless they were right outside the house. So she lay there, stiff and frightened, watching him warily as he got up to light the lamp. A warm glow leaped, spread.

At once the room took on a different character, became less frightening, and she slid a glance toward the door. It was so far away, and she would have to leap from the bed without becoming entangled in the netting. Impossible.

When he turned, the light behind cast his face in dark shadows; he came toward her, a graceful menace, making no noise even on the floor of cypress planks.

"I've thought about you for well over a year," he said softly, as he sat on the edge of the bed;

it dipped with his weight. "I'm sure you know why."

"No," she finally said through stiff lips. "I have no idea why you would think about me, when you never did while I was there in England."

"Ah, but you see, I had little else to do at times while I was scrubbing decks in a broiling sun, or picking oakum or tarring keels . . . my education has been extensively broadened since last we spoke. But you know that, too."

"How could I?" She put out a tongue, wet her lips, saw him watching her through narrowed eyes.

His eyes burned into her; he caught up her hand, held it in a tight grip, his fingers like a vise curled over her wrist. Slowly he raked a thumb across her open palm, from the heel to the pads of her fingertips, a slow, leisurely stroke.

"No calluses, I see. It would be different were you to sail on a British warship. They're most efficient at getting laggards to work."

"What are you—"

"No," he said, and put a finger over her lips, "don't talk. I've thought of this for months, during nights when the ship was becalmed and there was nothing to do but lie in a hammock or on the deck and wait, and I want to savor the moment. You look frightened, my love—are you?"

But he didn't really want an answer, because he kept his finger on her mouth, a light tracery over her lips and chin, then along the curve of her jaw. He touched her ear, teased a curl dangling there, then spread his hand through the thick hair on the nape of her neck, fisting it until she felt it pull against her scalp.

There was a purring menace about him, like that of a panther, dark and ominous, with vengeance in the shadowed blue eyes that bored a hole into her. She drew in a shallow breath, truly frightened now, aware of the tension in his taut muscles, of the way he held himself, as if to take flight at a moment's notice.

Where was Kit? And, oh God, what did Deverell intend to do with her? There was an intensity to his anger that went beyond reason; he must be insane, talking as if he blamed her for his years on a ship, when it had been his decision to leave London, made long before he even knew she existed. But this was so confusing, and she wished he would go away and leave her alone.

It quickly became obvious he had no intention of going away or of leaving her alone—with a swift, shocking motion, he yanked away the light cotton sheet from her body and pushed her backward into the yielding mattress, his forearm across her chest pressing her down when she tried to struggle upright.

"Ah no, little cat, I have decided to accept your invitation."

"I gave you no invitation to come here, and certainly not to do . . . do *this!*"

She pushed futilely at him, but he was inflexible, ignoring her efforts with humiliating ease as he curled his fingers into the neck of her shift; it tore easily, a rending sound that was loud in the abruptly suffocating shroud of netting.

"Oh yes, you did," he said, holding her down, his words mocking, "and every other man out there tonight. I could not be so inconsiderate as to ignore such a blatant invitation, could I?"

"No . . . you misunderstood—"

"Hardly likely. Even your brother understood it, though he is not so pleased with you at the moment. Such soft skin." A deliberate caress, brown hand dark against her white body as he splayed his fingers over her belly. "How many others have replaced me, I wonder."

"Take your hands off me!"

He only laughed, a soft sound in the gloom, a threat.

She tried to twist away, but he held her pinioned, his hand moving leisurely over her body, bared now, and vulnerable. He moved his hand slowly to her breasts, teasing the nipples to taut peaks, an erotic torment too easily recalled. Oh, why was he doing this? He did not love her, had never loved her. It was only revenge that made him come here like this, a desire to humiliate her for coming between him and Grandmamma.

"Leave me alone . . . go now, and I won't tell my brother about this."

His lip curled in contempt, voice growing harsh.

"Pauvre jeune fille—is it so frightening to you to be found out? I thought of you every day, every hour during those long months of imprisonment on that goddamn hell-ship you and your lover consigned me to—and I vowed then I would make you both pay."

She went still, stared up at him, began to comprehend what had brought him here. But would he listen to her? Then he shocked her, his words cruel:

"What a scheming bitch you've turned out to be, with not even the least concern for your betrothed. Or did you marry him? Not that it matters—he died cursing your name to the last."

"Don Carlos is dead?" she whispered through suddenly cold lips, as icy dread stole through her veins to render her immobile. "How? Did—"

"Did I kill him? Oh yes, little gypsy whore, I sent him to hell, and if there's any justice, it's as bad as my hell aboard the *Fortune.* But don't worry. I don't plan to challenge you to a duel as well. There are other methods of payment that I might find more . . . pleasant."

Still reeling from the shock of discovering that Don Carlos was dead, she lay still as he pulled away the shreds of her nightdress, watched with detachment as he unbuttoned his white trousers, a strange sense of distance leaving her pliable and even quiescent beneath his touch. It was her nightmare come to life, the danger and menace a tangible thing, a live beast that would devour her if she let it.

What had he said? Something about justice and a duel? Oh yes, and payment. . . .

Deverell brushed his hands over her rounded breasts, tugged the nipples to prominence with thumbs and fingers; his head bent, breath heated on her skin as he drew first one, then the other, into his mouth, strong pulls that ignited a curling fire in her belly, made the center of her begin to throb. She expected harshness, even cruelty, but in a way, this was worse, for he forced her to respond to him, to participate.

Oh God, he knew where to touch her, as if he had truly been in all her dreams, the ones that had left her so restless at night and aching when she awoke, with the hard insistent throbbing still between her legs.

She tried to twist away from him but he held her between his knees, straddling her naked body, his hands on her summoning shuddering response.

And then he wrenched her thighs apart, touched her there, his fingers sliding over damp curls with an arrant sensuality that made her arch up into his hand rather than away. For a moment she was back in the library again, where he had held her with much more tenderness, with soft words in her ear; when she had hoped for love.

That illusion was quickly shattered, splintered into a thousand pieces as he took her roughly, his hard body replacing the sensuous strokes of his hand, entering her with a searing thrust that made her cry out. She flung up her hands, palms against the bare skin of his chest where his shirt was open, shoved hard at him.

He caught her by the wrists, fingers a cruel vise as he held her arms over her head, pressed down into the fat feather pillows shrouded in white lace.

"What did you expect, little gypsy?" he asked, bent over her, his eyes a dark glitter beneath his lashes, "a sweet reunion? This is no reunion, but vengeance, and I think you are more than familiar with that."

She opened her mouth to scream, with rage and grief and frustration, but he was too quick, and put a hand over her mouth, hard against her lips. It was all wrong, so horribly wrong . . . her protests against his violation of her were muffled, and his weight held her immobile as he took his hand from her mouth only to kiss her with savage anger while he took his time.

It was useless to struggle; logic bade her conserve her strength; but it was impossible not to resist. It was against her nature to submit quietly to injustice, but the ending was inevitable, for he was far bigger and stronger, and held her down easily until she exhausted her strength in futile resistance.

"Such a predictable creature," he muttered, but his hand moved slowly over her breasts in a caress that was surprisingly gentle. It was subtle torture, erotic teasing that exacted unwilling response.

A sharp breath caught in her throat, trapped there when he deliberately moved deeper inside her, an invasion that was almost unbearable, yet exquisitely seductive. In surrender, she arched her hips up to meet his thrusts, shuddered at the raw friction that sent chills down her spine. He drove into her endlessly, demandingly, until everything faded away but the need to reach the elusive promise that lingered just out of reach, that shattering release he had given her once before. And then it was there, a violent crashing in her ears like the relentless wash of waves against the shore, gathering power and cresting before crashing into oblivion.

As she collapsed, shivering with the release, she said on a half-sob of frustration, "Damn you!"

He laughed softly, his mouth against her ear. "You shouldn't have teased me if you didn't want to show me what I've been missing, little cat. But then, you didn't really expect me to be so uncivilized as to accept your invitation, did you . . . ?"

Scalding humiliation, to know that he was right in his assessment of her motives. She didn't stop to think, but curled a fist into his shirt, tugged hard to pull him away from her, and heard it rip; her fingers spread over bare skin on his shoulder, nails digging in until she felt blood.

He swore softly, grabbed her arm in a brutal vise, and held it, his tone vicious. "Goddamn it, don't you think you've done enough? Wasn't it enough to have me abducted, taken away so that my grandmother thought I was dead?"

"Why won't you listen?" she protested angrily. "I had no part in what was done to you . . . but you're still alive and look healthy enough, so it can't have been so bad. . . ."

"Can't it? Here, feel my back, and you may get an idea of what was done, though it might not be enough to satisfy you."

He forced her quivering hand to his back and she scraped her fingertips over hard ridges, long weals that crisscrossed his skin. Horrified, she curled her fingers into the palm of her hand, making a fist of revulsion.

Holding her gaze, he said softly, "The 'cat' leaves its mark on a man, and if he's lucky, he might survive it. A lot of men die under the lash, but that shouldn't matter to you."

It took supreme effort not to cringe from the savage lights in his eyes; she forced herself to lie still, to refuse to give him the satisfaction of seeing her cower.

"I had nothing to do with your forced service aboard a ship, but I cannot speak for what Don Carlos may have done," she said, her tone remarkably calm, under the circumstances. "You can believe me or not, but until you arrived on this island tonight, I thought you were still in London, as always."

His hands tightened painfully on her shoulders, a bruising force as his eyes stabbed into hers like dark blue daggers.

"What a consummate little actress you are. You would make your fortune on stage if you ever decided to return to England." His words were harsh, but there was a trace of uncertainty in his voice that made her try again.

"It's true, you know. But of course, I have no way of proving my innocence."

"Christ! I would have to be ten different kinds of a fool to believe you."

She looked at him and said simply, "Yes, I suppose you would."

Silence fell; abruptly he rolled away from her and tossed a corner of sheet over her body, then fastened his pants. A sudden chill made her shiver, and she clutched wads of cotton sheet to her chest. Lamplight sprayed walls with a faint rose glow; it illuminated one side of his face, left the other in shadow. He looked remote, impassive; impulsively she put out a hand to touch his shoulder.

He flinched away from her touch, his eyes hard as he raked her with a glance. "No need to come over all sympathetic now. It's a bit late for that. Bloody hell, I must be a sorry bastard as well as a fool. What is it about you that makes me believe you—even now, when I know what you've become?"

"What do you think I've become?" She rose to her knees with the sheet held in front of her, faced him with a level gaze. "A whore? Is that what you think? But then, you thought that of me before, didn't you, in London, when you came to Beacon House—it was in your eyes, your tone of voice, even your touch. That's why you were surprised that I was virgin. You expected me to be like the others you had known, eager and not too fastidious about my lovers. What a shock it must have been for you."

A cynical smile pressed one corner of his mouth. "It was indeed a shock. Christ, you were not the gypsy whore I wanted you to be at all."

"*Wanted*—!"

"Yes, *wanted*. Bloody hell, do you think I make it a habit to ruin virgins? I don't, despite your low opinion of me."

She sat quietly, staring at him in the shadows that painted walls in gloom. Had she not wanted him as well? He had been in her dreams for so long, a constant presence even when she thought she hated him—but perhaps there was more to his feelings for her than even he knew.

Softly, tentatively, she said, "Yet I yielded to you freely, for I thought you meant to give me something in return."

"Payment, as always, for services rendered, little gypsy?" he mocked, and she stiffened.

"It was never money I needed, but something you don't possess. You were right when you told me that—'*I cannot give you what I do not have to give. Don't expect it. I offer you a place, but not my name. . . .'* You see, I've never forgotten your words."

"So it seems."

Silence fell, fraught with tension; in the dim light of the lamp, he looked suddenly weary. Deep grooves etched each side of his mouth, and the scar on his cheek—a token of his impressment?—was a stark white curve against darkly tanned skin. He looked up at her, eyes fathomless and unreadable beneath black lashes.

"You didn't tell your brother who I am."

"No, but I will. If you have any sense of self-preservation, you'll be gone before he remembers you're here."

One corner of his mouth pressed inward; he put out a hand to touch her cheek, a light caress. "Vicious little cat. You will, won't you?"

"Of course I will. Do you think I won't do anything to protect Kit?" She faltered at the glitter in his eyes, then said firmly, "If you leave now, I won't tell him until morning. You can be safely away by then. If you stay, he'll kill you."

He rose to his feet, stared down at her, the lamp behind leaving his face in shadow. "He might find it more difficult than you believe to manage that."

"He might. Do you want to test him?"

"I've never run from a challenge before, and I doubt I'd start at this late date." He bent, grasped her by the arms, and pulled her up as the sheet fell away to leave her bare and shivering in his arms. "Christ, I should take you with me. You're a problem, a threat, and if I leave you here. . . ." His voice trailed into silence, then he laughed, a harsh sound. "But I won't. Your hell-spawned brother can take care of you."

Deliberately, he raked a hand down her bare back, his fingers digging into her flesh, palm cupping her buttocks to pull her hard against him, so that she could feel the rigid evidence of his need, knew that he wanted her again, that he would take her if he wanted, and she couldn't stop him.

Breathless, afraid, excited, and confused, she felt the rapid thump of her heart increase, her breasts scrape against the soft cotton of his open shirt, the buttons pressing almost painfully into her skin.

Then he groaned, a sound of surrender and frustration as he buried his face into the angle of her neck and shoulder, and she heard him mutter, "Christ, I must be insane, but I don't want to leave you here. You're trouble, do you understand? Nothing but trouble, and if I had any goddamn sense, I'd go back out to my ship and forget you even exist. . . ."

But he was pushing her back onto the bed, his body following hers, weight heavy as he kissed her face, brow, and temples, his hands urgent as he uncovered himself and slid inside her again, rocking in the now familiar motion that she had come to expect.

This time, she opened willingly for him, her arms lifting to curl around his neck, a surrender to emotion and need, to the sweep of hope that burned away everything but the driving desire to love him.

This time, she was certain he loved her, as well.

And when passion was spent at last, and the lamp had burned low to plunge the room into velvety darkness, she thought drowsily that she'd had to come halfway around the world to have him love her; then sleep claimed her, deep and dreamless.

Chapter 22

Morning, when it came, prodded her with sharp fingers of light through the open shutters, and she flung out a hand to encounter emptiness beside her. She sat up, naked, her body bearing faint marks of his hands on her, but he was gone.

There was no note, no words of farewell, nothing but this silent emptiness, and when she dressed and went down to the shore, she saw that his ship was gone. He had sailed away on the early tide, leaving her with only the memory of the night.

Kit looked at her sharply, his eyes narrowed, but made no comment when she said dully that she had only drunk too much wine the night before.

"I won't be gone but a few days," he said, and folded his arms around her. "Paturzo and Miguel are staying here to watch over you."

"You'll be careful?"

He laughed softly, tucked a loose strand of her hair behind her ear, drew the backs of his fingers along her cheek. "I'm always careful."

But it would not be enough, she thought, if the

governor of Louisiana was still intent upon ridding the parish of pirates. Yet they had discussed that too many times, and there was no point in arguing just before he left.

So she forced a smile, her eyes heavy and scratchy with the need for more sleep, and stood on the beach and watched while the sleek lines of the *Cacafuego* rode the swells of the Gulf, sails slowly filing with wind.

The days passed slowly, stretched into nearly a week before Kit returned; there was laughter and celebration among his crew. They had taken a Spanish galleon off the coast of Cuba, laden with silver from the mines in Mexico.

"There's enough to buy us an entire plantation with my share," Kit told her, elation in his eyes. "We can go to Virginia, or wherever you want—the Carolinas, maybe. I can find us a house much bigger than this one, Amie, and you can be a fine lady again. . . ."

As night fell, she went with him down to the beach, where bonfires were lit and the crew were already half-drunk on rum and plundered wine.

"Spanish wine," Kit said, a note of satisfaction in his voice, "and Spanish silver." Reflected light from the fires danced across his face, glinted in his eyes. He slid an arm around her, coaxed her into the circle of laughing dancers, where Rosa caught her hand. And when she slipped away from them, Kit and Rosa did not even notice.

Despite the promise of a new life, an end to the constant worry that Kit would be arrested or killed, there was a heaviness inside that had nothing to do with pirates or Spanish plunder.

How could she have been so wrong? Deverell

had not come back, nor had he sent her a message. She should tell Kit that he was not a wealthy merchant at all, but the moment had not presented itself. And since he was gone now, and soon they would be leaving as well, there was no need. Oh, she had been such a fool to think that he might care for her, when he had only wanted her silence!

Well, it had worked, for he was gone, and her brother knew nothing about him.

It was late when she finally went to bed, the noise from the beach a distracting chaos that mirrored her inner turmoil. In a few days they would leave Belle Terre behind for good, abandon the house that still smelled of new wood and paint. It would probably not be deserted long; just across the bay, the coast of New Spain had a thriving port. This island had been inhabited before, evidenced by old Spanish buttons she had found, and would no doubt be settled again soon.

Mid-September was still warm, and she left her shutters open over the window; a light breeze belled out the gauzy curtains, whispered over her body as she washed. It was humid, and she didn't bother with a shift when she went to bed. For a long time, she lay beneath the netting, gazed at the reflected silvery glow of a half-moon through her window.

Things changed so swiftly now; tomorrow, she would ask Kit to take her back to New Orleans while he made his arrangements to leave Belle Terre. She did not think she could stay here another day without remembering that she had been a fool again.

She must have slept; it was the silence that woke her, a heavy absence of sound as if a huge blanket lay over the island. As her eyes adjusted, and the thin shaft of moonlight lit only the far wall now, she listened for the noise of celebration. Only the wash of surf against the beach and the constant hum of frogs and insects disturbed the hush that had fallen.

Then there was a slight sound, a faint scrape that alerted her just before a hand clamped down over her mouth and pressed hard.

"Don't scream," came the husky warning, in a voice she knew only too well, and she nodded to show she understood.

Black against the sliver of moonlight, Deverell took away his hand, his voice harsh. "Get up, Amie. You have to leave Belle Terre."

"Leave?" Anger sparked. "I have no intention of leaving just because you—"

He flicked back the sheet, laughed softly when he saw she was naked, and pulled her to her feet with a hand around her wrist. "An unconventional nightdress, madam, but I approve."

He did not give her time to dress, grabbing her by the arm to shove her toward the window.

"What are you—"

"Here, take your clothes and you can dress later."

Despite her angry protests and horrified objections, he dragged her out the window and onto the veranda, then across soft dirt that still bore signs of construction. When she stumbled, bare feet catching on a loose board left behind, he swore viciously and scooped her into his arms.

Urgency seeped into her anger, then grew into

fear as she saw over his shoulder a nightmarish vision.

Black against a bright glare of flames, a burning ship bore down on Belle Terre, flanked by two more that looked like deadly birds of prey in the night. And as she watched, a tiny white puff, beautiful and deadly, spat fire toward shore. A heavy whistling sound cut through silence, then the night exploded into deafening noise and balls of flame as the new house disintegrated in a shower of cypress and gunpowder.

The force of the explosion knocked them down; dirt spattered them like rain, clods stinging where they struck her bare skin. He was lying over her, his body shielding her torso, so that only her arms and legs were vulnerable.

Dazed, she felt him get up, smelled the stench of sulphur thick in the air, heard his harsh command to dress as he shoved her clothes at her.

"*Now*, Amie, unless you have no aversion to showing off your ample charms."

Clumsily, she pulled on her thin shift, and pulled the blouse over her head. Her hands were shaking so that she could not tie the cords to her skirts, and with an impatient oath, he knelt swiftly beside her, his hands efficient and brisk as he tied the skirt around her waist.

Bewildered, she looked down at him in the hellish collage of flame and shadows. "But who—are those British ships firing on us?"

"No, my sweet. Those are Americans. It seems that Governor Claiborne is making good on his promise to clear pirates from Louisiana."

As horror struck her, she stared at him with

mounting realization. "You brought the revenue cutters. . . ."

"I didn't have to. They found their own way without my help." He stood up, eyes flinty in reflected light. "Come on, we don't have time to stand here and talk about it. Damm you, *come on!*"

She jerked away from him, pivoted on her heel, and started back down the slope. "I have to find Kit. . . ."

A harsh hand clamped down on her shoulder, and even though she struggled frantically, he ignored her efforts as he slung her over his back and bore her back up the slope and into the trees. Dangling over his back, she saw in the bay the ships belch fire again.

She sobbed helplessly, shuddered as another barrage of heavy guns pelted the island with flaming destruction.

"Oh my God—*Kit!*"

Kit lay in a hammock slung between two trees with Rosa beside him; when the first gun fired, he was nearly asleep after another tempestuous bout with the passionate little gypsy left him exhausted and spent. His head came up just before the grinding *boom* split the air, his eyes struggling to focus on the strange crimson light. A fire ship . . . the *Cacafuego* must be burning as well. Then came the familiar report of a thirty-pounder, blasting away from the bay.

Leaping from the hammock, he snatched up his cutlass and pistols as Rosa tumbled to the sand in a naked heap, blinking up at him as she sprawled on her hands and knees.

"Amante—"

"Come on. Run!" He picked her up, ducked as a shell burst close to them, grabbed her by the hand, and shoved her toward the line of trees. "Run!" he said over his shoulder, then raced across the beach where pirates were scrambling for their lives, intent upon the knoll where his house and sister were in danger.

As he crested a sandy dune, he saw the leaping flames and smoke erupting in huge clouds. Eerie light spread outward like hellfire, dancing red and gold shadows across sand and trees, reflected in the waters of the bay. Beyond the house, trees were black lace against the softer sky, lit by the blazing ruins. Cypress walls collapsed as he watched, imploding in a fiery shower of sparks that rose high into the air like thousands of tiny shooting stars.

With an anguished howl, he scaled the knoll, but the heat drove him back, searing his skin, and he went to his knees in the dirt, sprawled in boneless shock. Nothing could live through that inferno.

Amie. . . .

A crescendo of blasts reverberated in the night, shaking the ground, finally bringing him to his feet. If she was asleep when it hit, she was beyond his help now. If not—he would find her in the woods where the others were fleeing.

"Capítan!" Miguel found him, face streaked with soot, eyes huge and black in a face pale with fear. "They land on the beach. . . ."

He looked toward the bay, saw the outline of

two warships, and the burning masts of the *Cacafuego*. Nearing shore, the unmistakable shadow of a pinnace bobbed in the water. His mouth tightened.

"What ships are those?"

"United States—Patterson and Ross. . . ."

He'd warned Lafitte, dammit. Now Claiborne had sent Colonel Ross and Commodore Patterson against them. He'd bet a Spanish doubloon that Barataria was next.

Amie huddled in the marshy swamp, apprehensive as she stared at Deverell. What did he mean to do? He frightened her, with his cold eyes and grim expression, the rough, almost brutal way he pulled her along with him until she was nearly fainting with weariness.

The sandy waste that formed the island of Belle Terre had scattered stands of trees and brush, salty pools that were useless for water. Deverell had found a freshwater spring, more of a seep in the rocks beneath a copse of scraggly trees. It was light now, the sun a blazing ball in the sky overhead.

"Where are you taking me?" she asked finally, and he looked up at her impatiently.

"There aren't many choices on an island that's nearly deserted, I'd think. My boat is moored on the other side. Unless someone else found it first." He stood up, stared down at her. "In which case, you had best hope that it's Silver's men who find us, because if you're caught with a British spy, I doubt the American Navy will be as lenient. But then, I may be wrong."

"Why?" she asked dully, staring at him when he came to kneel beside her. "Why did you destroy it all?"

"It was Claiborne who sent Patterson. I had nothing to do with it. Do you think he'd listen to me if I even suggested it? Hardly practical, my love, when I'm on the other side of the fight."

His derision seeped into her exhausted brain, and she flared, "But you knew about it! You could have warned us."

"Why would I do that?" Cold blue eyes regarded her narrowly. "It was obvious neither Lafitte nor your brother had any intention of siding with us, and it just got them out of the way without wasting our gunpowder."

There was an element of logic that escaped her, and she tucked bare feet under her as she tried to find the thread of reasoning. "Then why are you here?" she asked finally, "If you knew Claiborne meant to fire on us, why did you come back?"

"Damned if I know." He stabbed a stick viciously into the dirt, looked up at her with brooding eyes. "It's a stupid thing to do. Christ! If you want the truth of it, I was told it was only Barataria that would be bombarded. It wasn't until yesterday that I knew they meant to destroy Belle Terre as well. When I got here, Patterson was ahead of me. I didn't have time to do more than get you out of the house."

"You could have warned Kit. . . ."

"When he already suspects me of deceit? I'd end up being cannon fodder as well," he said brutally, and she winced at the image his words conjured. He grabbed her wrist, forced her to look at him. "Dammit, Amie, it's treason if I'm caught here by my commanding officer. And it's damned doubtful Patterson would be so generous as to believe me if I tried to convince him I'm not one of the Baratarians."

As she tried to absorb the implications behind his angry words, he said softly, "Let's just say that I have my own reasons for being here, and they have nothing to do with pirates, or even with you."

She looked away from him; gray smudges still rose above the island, smoke from the bombardment. Had her brother survived? Grief welled, almost choking her. She wanted to scream, to flee back down the wooded slope to the beach, to search for Kit among the bodies and wreckage that would be there, but knew it was futile.

If he was alive, he would be angry with her for taking such a risk, and if he wasn't—she veered away from even the thought.

Useless, so useless. . . .

"We were leaving soon," she said abruptly, looked back at Deverell where he crouched beside her. "Did you know that? It was a celebration . . . last night, on the beach, when he returned. He meant to stop now, and we were going back to Virginia. . . ."

Her voice trailed into silence; she felt his eyes on her even when she looked away again. He would only say something trite, such as that men who lived by the sword died by the sword, an escapable truth, but unwelcome now.

But he didn't say any of that, didn't say anything as he reached out, took her by the arm, and held her when she fell blindly against him, her face against his chest and the hot tears streaming over her cheeks.

It seemed only natural for him to hold her, to let her weep into his shirt while the hot sun beat down and the acrid bite of destruction still hung in the air over the island. His heartbeat was a strong, steady thud, his hand gentle against her back.

And when he kissed her, it was gentle, too, a soft brush of his lips against her face and then her mouth, tasting of her salty tears. She clung to him, and when he lay her back on the cushion of grass and sand, she gazed up at the bright blue of the sky overhead with blurred eyes, her body arching to meet his, until she could blot out the pain with only *this,* the feel of him inside her and the rhythm of mutual need.

The shrill cry of sea-birds floated above them, a cascade of sound, white white against blinding blue, and she closed her eyes and gave herself up to the exquisite distraction.

And then it was over too soon. He lifted her to her feet, brushed sand from her hair and helped her straighten her clothes. Cupping her chin in his palm, he tilted her face up to look into her eyes, his thumb a rough caress against her mouth. He sounded suddenly tired.

"You know that I have to go back, Amie. It won't be what I want, but it's what has to be—and you're going to hate me for it."

Bewildered, she shook her head. "No, I won't—"

"Yes. You will. God help us, you'll hate me almost as much as I'll hate myself for it."

She couldn't help but shiver, even under the burning heat of the sun overhead, and long after they were aboard the pinnace he had stowed in a shallow inlet along the shore, she was perplexed.

It wasn't until they reached New Orleans that she began to understand.

Chapter 23

Barataria was leveled. Jean Lafitte's fine two-story brick house was a pile of ruins, still smoldering. The full warehouses had been emptied and burned, taverns and houses destroyed by Patterson's forces. On Lafitte's orders, the pirates retreated to the swamps rather than make a stand.

Kit found them at a large camp in the swamp, morose and sullen, for the most part, wet from a recent rain.

Lafitte greeted him with a cheerful grin that was strangely contradictory to his circumstances. "Ah, you are here at last. I see that you escaped Patterson's barrage."

"Barely. There was no way to warn you in time before he struck Barataria. When my ship burned, we were marooned until yesterday."

"Ah, then René was successful. It was he who brought you here, yes? *Bon*. As you see, we had very little warning ourselves." His shoulders lifted in a fatalistic Gallic shrug. "Patterson was most thorough, I fear. But I have a plan, now that the British have been so obliging as to be a distraction for Claiborne."

Abruptly, Kit said, "My sister is in the hands of the enemy."

Lafitte's black brow rose high. "How is this so? Was she not with you?"

"She was. When Patterson's first broadside hit Belle Terre, it destroyed my house. One of my crew saw her being taken into the woods by the British officer you sent with their letter offering protection for our help."

"Me? No, *mon ami*, I sent no letter to you, but the British were here as well, with the same offer. But I say to them that I must think it over, then I wrote to the governor in New Orleans to offer our help in exchange for pardons. I sent him the proof, but this was his answer." He waved a hand to encompass the camp. "I do not accept his reply."

"Then Braxton lied when he said you sent him."

"It is so." Lafitte glanced at the men huddled around the fire; mist crawled through knobby knees that studded the cypress swamp, thin tendrils like smoke curled around tree trunks and tangled brush. He glanced back at Kit and smiled. "If this Braxton has your sister, we will find them. But now, we must go to New Orleans, for I think perhaps that Claiborne may be more willing to listen. He has managed to release Pierre from jail, though he will not admit to it, calling it an escape. But still—I think we may yet come to terms."

"Why do you think he will listen now?"

"Because, my young friend, the British have burned Washington and taken Pensacola from the Spaniards, and they threaten Mobile Bay.

Now their Colonel Nicholls has issued a proclamation calling on all those he thinks to be dissatisfied with American rule, such as Creoles and Kentuckians, to support the British. General Jackson has appealed to President Monroe for more men and supplies, but since Washington has burned, it is impossible." A sly smile curved his mouth, and he stroked a hand along his chin in satisfaction. "Jackson has issued his own proclamation, urging all inhabitants of Louisiana to resist these British invaders. And we, as you know, are residents of Louisiana who happen to be experienced in resistance and warfare. Do you join us?"

After a moment, Kit said softly, "Yes, I'll join you, but I have my own ideas of how I can be useful. Now that everything I own has been destroyed, I've nothing left to lose. Tell me, does Daniel Clark still have a shipping depot at the junction of Esplanade and Bayou Road?"

"Ah, Clark . . . yes, he does, *mon ami,* on the banks of the stream there. And a most profitable alliance it has been for us all, as it is much easier to take our goods from the sea down the Bayou Sauvage when the revenue cutters are too close. What do you intend?"

"I intend," he said softly, "to become a wealthy merchant from Virginia. No one in New Orleans will know me, as I've been very careful because of Amie."

Lafitte laughed, a booming gust that earned the attention of Dominique You, who came to learn the cause. Grinning, Lafitte clapped a hand upon Kit's shoulder.

"Dominique, my good friend, we will have our

very own spy in Claiborne's circle, to tell us how the wind blows for our fortunes. It is better than we hoped!"

Kit smiled. It was not Claiborne who warranted his interest now, but Holt Braxton, who had taken Amie into his custody. He had seen them on Belle Terre, his sister in Braxton's arms, lying under the sun where anyone could see. It was then he'd felt a hot, burning rage begin to build inside.

He meant to find her, to take her back, and then he would kill Braxton.

Chapter 24

At night, Maspero's was a coffeehouse, bar, and meeting place for those who enjoyed gambling. The main entrance of the two-story wooden building was on Rue Chartres, and Deverell entered with a nod for the black servant who greeted him at the door.

"Evenin', *monsieur.* You are here to play?"

It was a prearranged code between them, and he gave the doorman a gold coin, pressed discreetly into his palm as he paused.

"Only if the play is steep."

"Ah, and in the far corner is just such a player, *monsieur.*"

Noise and laughter assaulted his ears as he made his way to the indicated corner, where shadows provided just the right mood for privacy. Smoke stung his eyes, lying in gauzy layers, dissipating as he passed through the room.

Above the clamor of voices and hired musicians, he heard a familiar voice: "You took your time getting here."

Chair legs scraped against the sand floor, and he sat down before saying, "I was unavoidably detained."

"Ah, another woman, I presume. You have not changed that much since last I saw you."

"Nor you."

Hazel eyes stared back at him from beneath lazy lids, and the faint smile plying Stanfill's mouth was the same cynical curve it had always been. "I must retract that last comment, I believe," he said suddenly, "for you have changed, after all. In this instance, it is most convenient that you have, as you greatly resemble a Creole."

"Yes, I fit in quite well here." He waited, patient now when once he would not have been; he'd learned much in the past years about patience, about the value of time and freedom. Oddly, he felt a kind of affinity for these crude Americans who clung so stubbornly to their independence and liberty. They were willing to die for the right to make their own laws, to elect their own leaders.

He thought of the Regent, spoiled and willful, with a petulant nature at times, but a great regard for beauty. He was bankrupting England, along with his wastrel brother, the Duke of York, whose military career was a joke. Out of the six younger brothers to the Regent, only two avoided draining royal coffers. He wondered what the Americans would do if their elected president dipped too heavily into the national treasury.

"Have you been successful?" Stanfill asked at last, a lift of his brow signalling his true meaning.

"The eagle has taken wing."

It was the information Nicholls needed, the knowledge that General Andrew Jackson had begun his offensive and was on the way to New Orleans to defend the city against the constant threat of British invasion. Already, Jackson had managed to drive British forces out of Pensacola, and was keeping Fort Bowyer at the entrance to Mobile Bay well garrisoned.

"What of the local guides?"

Another oblique question; he answered with a shrug. "It is still uncertain. They meet tonight with General Humbert."

That one sentence held ominous meaning, for Humbert was a fierce enemy of the English and known to be friendly with Lafitte.

"Does Claiborne waver?"

"I think their services will be acceptable to the governor when the time is right."

That was true enough as well: Lafitte and his men were still not enlisted to defend New Orleans, but Claiborne accepted their presence in the city without comment. He feared that New Orleans would be invaded, and needed defenders. It was at the governor's urging that Jackson was finally on his way to Louisiana.

"Do have some cognac," Stanfill said, indicating that he was satisfied for the moment, and pushed forward a small glass. "It is very good, named for Napoleon, if you will, a French vintage straight from Paris."

Amber liquid sloshed up the concave sides of the glass in a thick glide. He sipped it slowly, watching the viscount over the rim. There was a constraint between them now that had not always been there, a wariness that he could not explain. Nothing had changed—except him.

Unexpectedly, Stanfill said, "An old acquaintance has arrived in New Orleans, I understand. You may recall Sir Alex Maitland."

"Maitland? Good God. What is he doing here? He doesn't seem the sort to be involved in conflict."

"So I thought." A lift of one shoulder indicated outward indifference, but there was a hard gleam in the hazel eyes that belied the gesture. "I thought perhaps he had come to renew his acquaintance with your protégée."

"Protégée?" Amused, Deverell sat back in his chair and smiled. "An interesting term for her, though I'm not sure how close to the truth it is."

"She *is* under your protection. A valuable pawn. Bring her with you this evening."

With slow emphasis, he said, "If she is to be used, it will be at my discretion."

Stanfill glanced up, held his gaze while he rubbed a thumb around the edge of his glass in an idle motion. "You might keep in mind," he said at last, "that you are still an officer of the Royal Navy."

"Only when it suits his Royal Highness to acknowledge that fact," Deverell said dryly. He stood up, saw the surprise in the viscount's eyes as he added softly, "She is still my responsibility, and my *protégée,* as you so euphemistically refer to her. I intend to keep it that way."

It was raining when he left Maspero's; streets would be mud by the time he reached the small house on Rampart Street where he had installed Amie as his *amour,* or *fille de joie.* The significance of the location could not have escaped her, for it was on Rampart Street that so many Creole gentlemen provided their quadroon mistresses with lodgings, the small white houses discreet and convenient.

"You're not dressed, my love," he said when he entered to find her still in her dressing gown. "We're to attend the farewell banquet for the Chevalier in an hour."

She shot him a resentful glance. "I have no intention of going with you and being presented as your mistress!"

"Ah, that is not your choice. You will go with me, or must I remind you that I have Claiborne's ear? He believes me to be Monsieur le comte d'Avril, and values my advice and presence at his little affairs."

"It might be amusing to see his reaction should I tell him who you really are," she said then, eyes narrowed like an angry cat's. "How would he take the news that the man he has been entertaining in his home is actually a British spy?"

"Probably better than the information that the man he seeks to arrest for piracy is your brother, the infamous Captain Kit Silver, and not Christian Courtland, the merchant visiting from Virginia. But perhaps it will not be necessary to disillusion Claiborne, as long as you are cooperative."

Glaring at him, she said softly, "You really are the most reprehensible man I have ever known!"

He didn't dispute it. This farewell party for the Chevalier, who was returning to his native France now that Napoleon had been defeated and was in exile, provided an excuse to mingle with Creoles who might yet waver to the British cause if it was seen that the Americans might lose the city. After all, Stanfill stubbornly insisted, they were French and Spanish in origin, with few ties of loyalty to this new government, only to the land. But he had seen beneath their outward complacence to the fierce loyalty for this brash, energetic country, and did not have the same belief as the viscount.

Perhaps it was because he was so closely acquainted with the Americans, and one in particular. Amalie was staring at him angrily, and he wondered if she recalled that he had warned her she would soon hate him.

"Do you dress willingly, or shall I play the part of your maid tonight?" He crossed the room to her, saw the wariness spring into her eyes, and his mouth tightened. "Dammit, Amie, don't tempt me to be cruel. You know I have to take you with me."

"I know what you *say*, but I think you just fear that I will escape your tender trap. You're worried about what I might say, and to whom. . . ." Flinging back her head, her gaze defied him to deny it, but of course, he couldn't.

Goaded as much by her defiance as by the knowledge that he was caught in a trap just as she was, he grabbed her by the arms, shook her slightly. "I don't find subterfuge all that enjoyable, but this is war. I'm committed to a cause and I'll do what must be done—if you've no loyalty to England, which I can understand, you might think of it as saving lives on both sides. Wouldn't you rather that a battle be averted? It can be done."

"That's not at all what you're doing! I know what you intend, and avoiding battle is not your concern. You want only to seize New Orleans for the British, to defeat the American forces. I was born in this country, and while I admit to being torn because of my loyalty to Grandmamma, I cannot bear to stand idly by while you plot to destroy my native land!"

"Not destroy—occupy. Christ, why do I bother with any defense? I owe you no explanations. Get dressed, or I'll begin to think you're being coy and only want me in your bed."

Angrily, she obeyed, but he wondered wryly if he had really won this battle at all. Damn Nicholls and his idea of espionage; it would be far easier and probably much more efficient to focus his energies on plotting ways to invade New Orleans than this masquerade as a Creole to learn what he could about American plans. Using Amie had been the colonel's notion, and one that he had heartily resisted at first.

But then he had thought of what could happen to her if he let her go back to her brother, and how she had so narrowly escaped death on Belle Terre because of Silver's alliance with Lafitte, and knew that he would not be able to let her go. Perhaps Lafitte and the Baratarians were accepted in New Orleans at the moment, but the day would come when they would be pursued again, and to leave her in that kind of danger was unacceptable.

And he still wasn't certain why. He should be glad to be rid of her, of her accusing eyes and her resistance; even in bed, when he could no longer restrain the need he felt for her, and took her, she struggled at first, but in the end yielded to him with soft sighs and an abandon that was arousing and contradictory.

Damn her. He couldn't escape his own need for her and had begun to suspect that was the real reason he had no intention of letting her go. If the war ended tomorrow and America surrendered, he still would not give her up.

Bernard de Marigny, whose fine mansion had housed the Duke of Orleans and his brothers during their visit to New Orleans several years before, had already arrived at the St. Philip Theatre when they entered.

A handsome man, with the huge dark eyes and aquiline nose of his race, Marigny admired the young lady on Deverell's arm, his curiosity at her attendance without a chaperon politely stifled but obvious.

"I am honored, madame, to make your acquaintance," Marigny said, bending over her hand with easy gallantry. "It is not often we enjoy such beauty in our midst."

Amalie, clad in a diaphanous style of gown still popular with the ladies, returned the Creole's courtesy with a smile that did not reach her eyes.

"You flatter me, *monsieur*."

"Perhaps Monsieur d'Avril will not mind sharing your graceful beauty with me in a dance?"

Deverell gave his expected permission, an ironic bow of consent that earned him a flash of anger from Amie. But what had she expected? Besides, she was beautiful tonight, the gown a whisper of rose silk around her slender body, a thin veil of material that did nothing to hide her curves.

The low bodice was edged with ribbon that drew his attention to her firm, high breasts and the tempting shadow between them, and when she danced, the filmy skirts flowed around long legs in a seductive shimmer. With dark hair piled atop her head and entwined with sprays of roses, tiny wisps dangling over her forehead, at her temples, and at the nape of her neck, she emanated an air of tarnished respectability.

She stood out even in an auditorium crowded with fine Creole ladies dressed in the height of fashion, bright-colored silks, transparent taffetas, and richly embroidered velvets. Two rows of boxes flanked the walls, and a floor had been laid over the parquet for dancing. Potted plants waved delicate fronds along one wall, and framed an arched opening with slender columns.

He saw through the opening that Stanfill had arrived, and was not surprised to see in his company Sir Alex Maitland. The latter was in elegant dress, his blond hair a halo beneath glittering chandeliers. His presence in the company of the viscount sparked instant suspicion that Stanfill was plotting again.

Before he could cross to them, Marigny returned with Amalie at his side, to ask if he was enjoying himself.

"It is always enjoyable when you are present, Monsieur Marigny. I presume there will be a game of dice later tonight."

Marigny grinned. "It is a small passion of mine, the throwing of dice. There have been many fortunes won on the luck of the play."

"And lost."

"Ah so, and lost, of course. But that is not so great a concern with some men, I think. Not when there are higher stakes than money at risk."

"I bow to your exceptional knowledge of good fortune. Mine has not been so prosperous of late."

"A pity. Perhaps you only play in the wrong game, Monsieur d'Avril."

"That is entirely possible." His smile was smooth and practiced, and if Marigny meant more, he did not reveal it with his returning smile and observation: "Ah, I see that the Chevalier has arrived at last, and you must be introduced, if you have not met him."

"We met when I first arrived in New Orleans. He was good enough to take me into his confidence, and explain the differences between the customs of France and of the Creoles. There are great differences, you will admit, between the two."

Marigny laughed. "It is so! Now come, let us go and greet the old fire-eater."

The old gentleman known only as the Chevalier ignored current fashions, and wore a powdered wig and queue, knee breeches, silk stockings, frizzled cuffs and shirt-front, and bright silver buckles on his slippers. He greeted Amie with grave courtesy, then looked up at Deverell with dark, gleaming eyes.

"You have come to see me off, eh? It is a time of great happiness for me, and perhaps even for de Marigny, who has deigned to attend my celebration. And it is good to be where there are no *Americains* about!"

Well known for hating Americans, the exiled Frenchman frequently voiced his abhorrence of the radical ideas of equality which permeated even Creole ranks since the Terror. He expounded upon them now, a diatribe which took up the better part of a quarter hour, uninterrupted until Stanfill approached with Maitland in tow.

A glance of suspicion from the Chevalier was quickly banished when the viscount was introduced as a British merchant, but there was still a grudging acceptance.

A strange war, that allowed for convenience' sake the mingling of enemies at social functions when it was likely that soon they would meet across fixed bayonets. Deverell regarded Sir Alex with a cynical eye, wondered again at his reason for being in New Orleans.

Maitland bowed low over Amie's hand, glanced up at her through long feminine lashes, gray eyes regarding her with a thoroughness that brought a flush to her cheeks.

"We meet again, Madame Cambre," he said softly, and Deverell felt her tension in the slight quiver of her body next to his. Damn her, did she still yearn for this foppish coxcomb?

He lay a casual hand upon her arm, an act that stated his possession of her, met Maitland's startled glance with a hard smile. His silent warning was too obvious to ignore, and Maitland released her hand with a shrug, and turned to the Chevalier.

"My mother," Maitland said in perfect French, his comments addressed to the Chevalier, but obviously meant for Deverell, "was born here, and her French family still owns land out along the River Road beyond St. John Bayou. It is my duty, as younger son, to visit from time to time."

There ensued a spate of lively comments from the Chevalier about France, Louisiana, and Napoleon; Amie did not speak, but stood beside him with only the taut set of her mouth betraying her tension. Just how close had she been to Maitland, he wondered, and could that be part of the reason he was here? It was too great a coincidence, and he began to recall unanswered questions from his past, when his association with Cochrane had been watched and no doubt reported, a scrutiny that ended with his impressment onto the Dutch merchantman. Another coincidence?

Whigs and Tories were always at odds, Parliament feeding on its own at times, doing more damage to England than even Bonaparte. But that was ended now, too, and while there were rumors rampant in New Orleans that a house was being prepared here for Napoleon, the imminent danger of the British on their shores took precedence.

Deverell caught Stanfill's eye, and in a moment, they both drifted away to stand beside a small alcove between two giant potted palms, leaving Amalie with Maitland and the Chevalier.

"Is Maitland why you wanted her here tonight? It occurs to me to wonder how much of his tale is true," Deverell murmured, and the viscount gave a careless shrug.

"We are concerned only with his close ties, and how they may benefit our cause. Maitland has his uses."

"As do the rest of us." He saw agreement gleam in Stanfill's eyes, then the viscount glanced away, as if watching the dancers.

"The eagle we spoke of earlier flies more swiftly than one thought possible." Stanfill's lips moved in an almost inaudible murmur.

When he leaned closer as if inspecting a leafy frond of the palm, the viscount added softly, "He arrives even as we speak. You are recalled to your ship."

All the subterfuge was for naught, for when Jackson arrived in New Orleans, a battle would be inevitable.

Glancing past Stanfill, he saw Amie with Maitland, her smile strained but intact, the lovely flowing silk like a caress around her. It would no doubt be very satisfactory to her that he would be leaving New Orleans.

But he had no intention of leaving her to the likes of Sir Alex Maitland.

Music provided fodder for conversation for several minutes after the Chevalier took his leave of them, but it quickly palled as Amalie floundered beneath the clear gray gaze.

"Let us dispense with the niceties, shall we?" Sir Alex murmured, and took her arm to lead her onto the dance floor, ignoring her slight resistance. "You are here under false pretenses, and with Deverell, when London thinks you wed to Don Carlos and living in Spain. It would be very intriguing to discover how events led you to New Orleans."

"No doubt." She smiled when he glanced at her, felt his hand tighten on hers as he led her in the steps of a waltz. Her head hurt, and she wished she could go back to the little house on

Rampart where at least she had privacy from probing questions and curious eyes.

It was intolerable of Deverell to bring her here, for everyone to know that she was his mistress now. And oh God, why could she not hate him for it? Whether she would admit it to him or not, she had to admit to herself that he was only being loyal to his country. It was a cruel twist of fate that put them on opposite sides.

As the music changed and Maitland led her in the steps of a French *contre-danse,* she had the thought that he seemed so insipid next to Deverell, a pale imitation of the man who tormented her with hopeless dreams of a life that would never be, a happiness that would never exist for her. Not even when the dance ended and Maitland led her to a secluded corner, pressing a glass of punch in her hand and smiling at her as she had once thought she wanted him to, did she think for a moment of what might have been with him.

Since the night Belle Terre was destroyed, she had known that she was in love with Holt Braxton, the man who had haunted her dreams since she was only seventeen.

And she hoped that Kit would forgive her for it one day, for she knew he blamed Deverell for the destruction of all that he had accomplished.

That was the hardest—the estrangement from her brother. She knew he was in New Orleans, for Deverell had told her, and told her, too, that he was passing himself off as a wealthy Virginia merchant.

"But why?" she'd asked, bewildered, and the response had been an ugly laugh.

"Because, my sweet," he'd said, coming to her with a gleam in his eye to touch her face, then her breasts, "he can travel in the same circles now. It will make it easier for him to kill me."

"Kill you!"

"Yes, but if you're worried about me, it is not necessary. I don't intend to make it so easy for him."

"Perhaps," she'd said tartly, "I'm worried about *him!*"

Her anger always seemed to amuse him lately, and it was just as well, because she could not help being angry with him most of the time. The necessity of subterfuge, the house on Rampart Street, and the way he kept her now at arm's length were infuriating. Why could he not hold her again, as he had on Belle Terre—with tenderness, and a concern that was close to love?

It was as if he was afraid to get too close, afraid that she might see through the barrier he'd put up around himself, and know that he cared for her. But God, it would be so wonderful if he would let down his guard, and let her inside again.

"Madame Cambre," Maitland murmured, and she looked up at him with a lifted brow as he held out his hand. "Do me the honor, if you will, of another dance."

"I must decline, Sir Alex, as I find I am very tired tonight."

His smile did not waver. "It will be the last dance. And after all, you thought enough of me once to visit me at home."

"Ah yes, to borrow a book."

Cryptically, "Was that the reason? Somehow, I always thought it was more."

She shrugged carelessly, and allowed him to put his hand on her arm. "I cannot imagine why you would think so, Sir Alex."

"Can you not?" He laughed softly, leaned close, and in his gray eyes she saw a cold glitter that was disturbing. "I think you are not admitting the truth. But perhaps I understand. It is Devil's influence—an apt name for him, don't you think? He seems to have a way with fair ladies that can be quite—inconvenient."

There was a note of controlled violence in his tone that increased her uneasiness, and she shook free the hand he still had on her arm. "Really, Sir Alex, you are far too forward in your manner, and—"

"Forward? Come, come, *madame,* you are no longer the naive girl you were in London. Surely you must realize that you are hardly regarded as an innocent here, when all of New Orleans knows that you are kept in a house on Rampart Street. But do not look so angry, for it doesn't matter to me. My tastes do not run in that direction."

She remembered what Deverell had said of him once, and said coldly, "I cannot imagine why you think I care about your *tastes,* Sir Alex. This is not the place or the time to have such a discussion, nor do I care to ever hear of it again."

"But you should—your lover is a vicious murderer and you should know what he is capable of doing."

A chill shivered down her spine at the malice in his voice and eyes, and the intensity of his narrowed stare. "I do not want to hear this—"

"No, I imagine you don't. But it's true. Ask him, if you will, about Roger Wickham." He put out a hand, touched her cheek lightly, a caress that was more menacing than a fist, and added softly, "He cannot deny that he killed him as surely as if he had pulled the trigger himself. Such a waste of life, a promising life . . . but you look so pale, madame. Surely, he would not harm *you*."

As Sir Alex smiled at her with narrowed eyes, she saw over his shoulder that Deverell was leaving the auditorium with the viscount, and her mouth tightened furiously. How dare he go off and leave her with Maitland! It was as if he had forgotten she was with him tonight, when he had insisted she come . . . oh, he made her so angry, and Sir Alex was so frightening, saying these horrible things when she remembered that Roger Wickham had shot himself in his own library. A terrible scandal that happened before she even arrived in London, so long ago now.

"Excuse me, Sir Alex," she said stiffly, and ignored the hand he put out to stop her as she pushed past him. It was growing late, and her head began to throb unmercifully with tension and anger when she could not find Deverell. He was gone, vanished with Lord Stanfill, and she abruptly decided to leave without him.

Pleading a headache, she asked Monsieur de Marigny to call a hansom for her.

"Please, I do not want to bother Monsieur d'Avril, and it is only a small headache. . . ."

Concerned, Marigny insisted upon sending her home in one of his own carriages, and when it came, he tucked her inside with warm bricks at her feet, solicitous as he gave instructions to his driver.

Then he smiled into the carriage, and said softly, "I trust you will recover quickly from your ailment, Madame."

But she wouldn't, she thought, as the vehicle lurched forward and the sound of hooves on wet road was loud in the rainy night, because she had an ailment that could not be cured.

Tilly helped her undress, her light chatter annoying but distracting, then she brought her some chocolate and helped her into bed.

"It is not a good night for you to be out, *madame,*" the pretty mulatto girl scolded, "especially alone. This Monsieur Marigny, he is very kind to send you home, yes?"

"Yes, of course. You may go to bed now, Tilly. It is late, and I am very tired."

It was true, and after a last survey of the room, clucking over the bedclothes and fussing that she might not be warm enough, Tilly left a hot brick wrapped in cloth for her feet, and put out the light. Shadows claimed the room, broken only by the faint glow of a lamp in the hall.

Much later, she heard Deverell come in, the front door slamming behind him with a loud thud. He stood for a moment in the open doorway of the bedroom, leaning against it. Light from the hall lamp was soft behind him, outlined his lean frame against the glow. She lay still, remembered Sir Alex's words—*murderer*—and shivered. He was capable of it, she knew. But had he? No, of course not. . . .

Sir Roger had killed himself, she remembered

the tale well, remembered that Grandmamma had been quite indignant at the rumors that persisted. But still, there were times, like now, when she couldn't help but wonder.

"How is your headache, my love?" he asked, and beneath the mockery, she heard his anger.

Testily, she said, "It is worse *now*. Please . . . I will be better in the morning."

"I don't doubt that." He crossed to the bed in three long strides, stood over her. "Damn you, why didn't you tell me that you were leaving?"

"You were busy." She tried not to look at him, too aware of him so near, his anger just beneath the surface. "Monsieur Marigny sent me home in his own carriage."

"So I discovered, after I'd spent the better part of an hour looking for you. *Christ*, I thought you'd been abducted."

She rolled to her back, staring up at him in the dim light from the lamp in the hallway. "*Abducted*! By whom? Who would want to do that—and why?"

His reply was a soft, angry laugh. "Any man with blood still flowing in his veins, my love, or are you really so unaware of how you looked tonight? Damn you, do you think I didn't see you with Maitland? Or that I don't remember how you wanted to marry him?"

For a moment, she could not reply; she *felt* his anger in his words, in the husky grate of his tone, and saw that behind it lay much more than he wanted to admit.

She put out a hand to touch him, tentative, uncertain whether he would allow it, or even acknowledge it. Beneath his sleeve, the muscles of his arm were corded, tense, and she worked her fingers over his wrist, marveling at the strength she found there in hands capable of brutality or tenderness, of harsh retaliation or bringing puppies into the world. Her breath came unevenly, and her anger faded into nothing.

Softly she asked, "Were you worried about me?"

"If it would make you happy to hear me say yes, I suppose I was, dammit. Is that what you want to hear?"

"Not unless you mean it."

There was a long silence; she caught the fragrance of cognac on his breath, then heard his soft laughter. He put a hand out, stroked her loose hair.

"I mean it, little gypsy. I mean it."

This time when he came to her, she did not struggle, but went into his arms with an eagerness that surprised them both. His response was instant and fierce, and he did not pause to remove his clothes. It was only later, when they were exhausted, that he undressed and came back to the bed to hold her hard against him, his arms around her as he fell asleep.

For a long time, she lay quietly in his embrace. She knew that he must love her, but despaired of ever hearing him say it. But perhaps he hadn't said it because she had never dared to say it either.

She twisted to face him, put her hand against his jaw in a light caress, and whispered, "I love you," but her only answer was the soft cadence of his breathing.

Chapter 25

Jean Robert Marie Humbert, born in France and a veteran of wars in France and Ireland, had risen from humble beginnings to become a general under Napoleon; it was that autocrat who had also effected Humbert's downfall before meeting his own, but had not succeeded in tamping his spirit. The former general barely escaped arrest, and had arrived in New Orleans as an exile right after its purchase by the United States.

Tall, with a prepossessing demeanor, he commanded respect from those who knew him, avoided society as a whole, and preferred cafés and cabarets, where he had made the acquaintance of the Baratarians some years before.

Kit Silver sat in a corner of Turpin's cabaret at the corner of Marigny and the levee, a house that was still a rendezvous for Lafitte and his men. He had arrived earlier to preserve his pose of American merchant, discussed with Monsieur Turpin over a game of piquet the situation with the threat of British invasion, and was now tacitly ignored by the men he had known for the past four years. They all waited, however, for the arrival of Humbert. At small square tables nearby, Jean and Pierre Lafitte were in the company of Beluche, Dominique You, their banker, Jean Baptiste Sauvinet, and Vincent Gambie, who was called *Nez coupé* because of the partial loss of his nose in a fierce fight.

Tension was rife, the rumors of Jackson's approach both welcome and resented. When Humbert arrived, his imposing frame towering over the shorter Creoles, he sat down with Lafitte's table. A glass of *petit gouave* was given him, and as he sipped it, he glanced round the room.

"We are all patriots here, I think," he said, "and must give General Jackson our respect. He will see that we are capable of defending our city, for every man has been assigned a position. While we are few in numbers compared to the numbers of our enemy—" He paused for effect, swept his glance around the crowded room. "—We are greater in loyalty and bravery."

A resounding cheer erupted, deafening in the small room. Kit smiled; Humbert had the gift of motivating men. Now he could understand how a man of such humble origins rose to a high position under Napoleon.

And when he met General Jackson, he understood even more how this man had earned the admiration of redoubtable warriors like Humbert and St. Gêmes, both veterans of countless campaigns. Arriving in New Orleans ill with the lingering effects of fever, Jackson dictated preparations for battle from a couch in his hotel room on Royal Street.

The British had been victorious at Lake Borgne, and now had control of the lakes and water approaches to New Orleans. Martial law existed, while Jackson issued a call to duty of every able-bodied man in the city, British subjects excepted.

For the third and final time, Jean Lafitte and his Baratarians volunteered. Jackson accepted their offer, and assigned artillery detachments to Dominique You and Renato Beluche, men he had once referred to as *hellish banditti*.

Humbert was assigned to duty on his personal staff with the rank of brigadier general. His appointment was no sinecure, or sop to an old veteran. Humbert was to direct the mounted scouts, a special corps of observation responsible for checking the near approaches of the enemy's advanced pickets. For Humbert, who hated all the English, it was a chance to settle old grievances.

For Christian Courtland, who hated one Englishman in particular, it was an opportunity for vengeance.

Despite all their precautions, British scouts found the one waterway unguarded by the Americans, and slipped up the muddy bayou under cover of darkness. After much hardship, they captured a small American detachment at the mouth of Bayou Bienvenue, on the night of December twenty-second. Then the British advanced along the bayous until they reached firm ground at the edge of the Villeré plantation. Here, they surprised and captured a militia detachment the next morning, and news reached New Orleans at last that the enemy had achieved landing at a spot only nine miles from their goal—the city itself.

By chance, Kit was with Jackson when Augustin Rousseau and Philippe Villeré arrived muddy and breathless to inform the general of the British invasion.

Lying on a sofa in his headquarters, Jackson leaped up and smashed a fist upon the table at his side. "By the eternal, they shall not sleep on our soil!"

Then, calming, he called his aides to him, and said, "Gentlemen, the British are below. We must fight them tonight."

It was welcome news to Kit, who was sent out with dispatches. Freezing rain had turned to ice on the roads, chewed to impassable mire in places by wagon wheels and horses. He turned his mount up and along a bank, detouring around the worst of it, finally reaching his destination muddied and shivering.

"Major Plauché," he said, and held out the dispatch, "you are recalled to New Orleans as soon as possible. The British have landed."

Startled, Plauché swept out an arm to indicate the warm fire to him, while he opened the dispatch and scanned it swiftly, then turned and gave the order to his aide for a march from Fort St. John to New Orleans. "We will run all the way, if we must," he added harshly.

By mid-afternoon, Plauché's battalion had arrived in the city, having run the entire way. They were soon joined by other American commanders, filling the Place d'Armes.

With the advantage of surprise and approaching darkness, the small army divided after nightfall, when the only light was from a fragment moon. The opening salvo was from the American schooner, *Carolina,* positioned opposite the British encampment, a broadside that sent them scurrying.

The American advance was met with a discharge of musketry, hot balls of lead flying past Kit's face and shoulders, and he heard the man beside him scream as he was hit. It was a familiar scene to him, transferred from the deck of a ship to solid land, but no less dangerous.

In the darkness, both armies broke into small fights as men were separated from their troops. As the Americans drove back the invaders, British reinforcements arrived and combat escalated, the night illuminated by flashes of gunfire and flickering images that disappeared as quickly as they were seen.

Bitter cold seeped into his bones as Kit fought his way forward, slogging through icy mud chewed to sludge under his boots; he slipped once, brought up his sword in an instinctive motion to ward off the slash of a bayonet, saw in the erratic glow of gunfire and cannonades that men around him were engaged in the same close combat.

Vicious, desperate fighting surged like sea tides, an endless wave that carried him forward on its crest, until he found himself at the edge of the battle somehow, standing in field of trampled sugar cane, with stalks crushed and brittle beneath his feet. Panting, slightly disoriented, he looked around him as there was a break in the fighting, combatants receding farther down the field.

Nearby, just to his left in the darkness, he heard the unmistakable sound of struggle. Breath frosted in front of his face, but he was sweating, and swiped a hand over his eyes to clear his vision. Then he gave a soft laugh, recognizing one of the two men engaged in fierce conflict on frozen ground.

Slowly, he let his empty, useless rifle slide to the ground, and tightened his grip on the bloodied cutlass in his fist. It could not be a more perfect opportunity.

He moved forward, waited until the clash of steel swords paused as they moved apart, and said into the night, "Sir, you are my prisoner. Throw down your sword."

A sudden burst of cannon illuminated the darkness and the face of the man who looked up at him with grim mockery. "If you want my sword, Courtland, you'll have to take it from me."

Kit smiled viciously. "I would like nothing better."

A burst of laughter came from Braxton's opponent, who stood with heaving chest, his sword a bright glitter. It was startling to hear him say in a British accent, "I see that I am not your worst enemy tonight, my lord Deverell, but that can change."

Before Kit could react, the man was gone, disappearing into black shadows that stretched beyond the sugar cane field. Then he was alone with Braxton—Lord Deverell—and held him at the point of his sword.

"It seems," he drawled, "that you British cannot even keep peace among yourselves. And you call Americans quarrelsome."

"An apt observation, if the point of that sword at my chest is any indication." Coolly, he regarded Kit in the flickering light. "Now, if you intend to use it, be quick, for I have other business to attend to. . . ."

Kit stepped back and brought up his sword, saw that Braxton did the same, and the brittle clang of clashing blades was lost in resounding cannonades from the ship offshore. The ground vibrated from a nearby explosion, but neither man noticed.

Chapter 26

Echoes of thunder awakened her, and Amie opened her eyes, turned restlessly in the bed. More rain. December in New Orleans was always wet. Light from the hall lamp shone through the open door of the bedroom. She stared up at the shadowed ceiling, visible beyond the empty frame of the bed canopy. Netting was unnecessary in winter.

It was cold and damp, reminding her of England, and she thought again of Grandmamma, and wondered if she was well. Did she know that Derverell was in New Orleans? Or had been in New Orleans, she corrected herself, for he was gone, had not returned to the house on Rampart Street for over two weeks.

No explanation was given, save that he had business elsewhere, and she was to rely upon Georges for whatever she needed while he was gone. That was, after all, why he had hired him.

"But I'm sure you'll be fine, my love," he'd said, the familiar mockery back in his eyes when she'd protested at being left behind, "for you'll land on your feet, as you always do."

Disappointment was bitter that he had reverted to his aloof regard of her, keeping her distant again, when she had thought—hoped—that he might soften. Now she was alone, with only two servants as companions, and the man Georges gave her the shivers. There was nothing definite that she could say about him, only that he was so—attentive. Yes, that was the word, or maybe observant. He slept in the front room at night "as a precaution," he said calmly, when she told him he needn't be so vigilant, and nothing she said dissuaded him, for he had his orders. It was as if Deverell did not trust her to stay in New Orleans.

But where would she go? She had nowhere else to go, not even back to England, now that she knew everyone thought her married to Don Carlos and living in Spain.

Christmas Eve was tomorrow night, and she was so alone here, with not even Kit to console her.

Another clap of thunder reverberated in the night, distant and somehow ominous. She sat up, suddenly uneasy.

Then Tilly burst into her room, shaking, babbling in a high voice, "It is the guns, *madame!*"

"Guns?"

"Yes, yes, the guns . . . downriver, near Chalmette and the McCarthy plantation where I was born . . . oh, do come, *madame,* get up, get up, for I fear that the British will be in the city soon. . . ."

"Stop that," Amie said sharply, swinging her legs over the side of the bed and reaching for her wrapper, "or you will have the entire town hysterical. Where is Georges?"

"I do not know . . . oh, *madame,* I do not know. . . ." Wringing her hands, Tilly began to sob, her dark, pretty face contorted with fear.

To keep her busy and occupy her mind with something other than the booming guns, Amie sent her to light a lamp and look for Georges. "He is probably out back at the privy, or nearby somewhere. Well, do what I say, now, and find him. We may need to leave quickly, and he'll have to help."

While Tilly went to search for Georges, Amie pulled on some clothes, heedless of buttons or proper lacing, and ignoring altogether any undergarment other than warm wool stockings for her legs. She was buttoning her shoes when the little maid returned, her liquid eyes the warm color of tea wide and damp with apprehension.

"I cannot find Georges . . . what shall we do?"

"Witless man, always underfoot until I really need him—never mind. Get your cloak. We must be ready, should we have to flee. Oh, and don't just stand there looking at me as if it's the end of the world, for I assure you that it is not. I've survived worse than this."

It was true, she thought wryly. She'd survived pirate attacks, and bombardment by the United States government, and she intended to survive this.

Hurrying into the front room that seemed strangely empty without Georges occupying his usual place by the fire, she occupied her hands with stoking the gray embers to life while Tilly fetched their cloaks and hot drinks to take away the damp chill.

As the fire caught, blaze spreading out in a

warm pool to suck cold from the room, there was a noise at the front door, and Amie looked up.

"That must be Georges. Hurry, Tilly, and let him in before he freezes out there."

A cold blast of air swept into the parlor as Tilly unlocked and opened the door. But the man in the opening was not Georges, and as Amie looked up, her hand tightened on the poker with surprise.

"Sir Alex! What brings you here?"

Mud coated his boots to the knees, and there was a smear on his face that looked too dark to be dirt. He said abruptly, "Deverell sent me for you."

"Deverell?" She stood up, frowning. "Where is he?"

"Not far. He's hurt, and is asking for you. Do hurry, for I'm not sure how long he'll live."

It felt as if the blood drained from her body, so that she stood frozen with horror, heard Tilly cry out softly as if from a distance, but could not move. Sir Alex swore then, a harsh sound, and she blinked as he came toward her in two long strides.

"Damn you, I said we must hurry!"

Instinct, or perhaps the subliminal knowledge that of all the men Deverell knew, Sir Alex would not be trusted to bring her to him, made her back away.

"Tell me where he is. I'll have Georges take me—"

An ugly sound escaped Sir Alex. He grabbed her, his hand hard and hurting around her wrist. "Georges is in no condition to take you anywhere, I fear. Get your cloak. Or do I have to take you with me like this?"

Without pausing to think about it, she brought up the arm still holding the fire poker and lashed out at him. It caught him on the shoulder as he turned swiftly, and then he swung his arm to slap her viciously with the back of his hand, spinning her around so that she fell to the floor. Lights exploded in her head, and the world reeled.

"Stupid little bitch . . . give me that." He wrenched the poker from her hand, and dazed, she heard him snarl at Tilly to shut up her bloody screaming, then it stopped with an abrupt sound.

Still stunned, Amie was vaguely aware of him coming back to her where she sprawled on the floor. He yanked her up with a hand in her loose hair, bringing tears to her eyes at the sudden pain.

Cold air struck her forcibly, stealing her breath as she felt herself being lifted and carried away, the sound of Sir Alex's harsh breathing mingling with the noise of her own panting sobs. Darkness swallowed them, and mud and cold and the smell of the swamp that stretched behind the city boundaries. Marais Street was deemed the borderland, lying between *terra firma* and the swamps, an impenetrable morass beyond which none but experienced hunters or fugitives ventured.

In the darkest parts of these thickets and along the margin of a sluggish bayou or *coulée* a rude hut had been hastily constructed of willow branches, sheltered from wind and rain by latanier, or palmetto leaves worked into the roof. It was the habitat of outlaws or runaway slaves, beyond the jurisdiction of the police or rescue.

Noisome odors enveloped the hut, and furtive sounds of unknown origins. She thought of the alligators that lived in the swamps, dangerous reptiles with gaping maws lined with lethal teeth and a snapping force that could bite a thick log in two.

Shuddering, she watched Sir Alex as he crouched by the door to the hut, oblivious to the cold and damp.

"What do you intend to do with me?" she asked, and saw him turn in the faint light of a single candle.

He stood up, came to kneel beside her on the damp dirt floor of the hut. "Use you, of course. Not, perhaps, as you might normally think." He laughed, a harsh sound in the thick night. In the distance, the thunder was erratic now. "Deverell will come for you—if he has survived, and like the devil, he always survives. He'll know where I am, and where you are."

"Why are you doing this?"

"Why?" He put out a hand, drew it along her cheek, and she winced. "It has nothing to do with you. You're just caught in the middle. Providence, I suppose, delivered you to England and gave me a tool to use against him. He's got more lives than any man should have, or he'd be dead now instead of here. Another stroke of luck that I have connections here and could follow him without arousing suspicion. Or too mich suspicion—damn the viscount. He's another thorn in my side, always in the way, stepping in to muck it all up for me."

Confused, she stared up at him; it was so cold, and she was truly frightened now, for Sir Alex did not look sane. Maybe it was the dim light, or the ferocity in his voice, but she had the thought that he was more dangerous than any animal in the swamp.

Pale blond hair fell across his forehead, and she saw now that the streak on his face was not dirt, but blood. It was a long gash, marring the angelic perfection of his unholy countenance. A dark angel. . . .

He smiled, teeth white and feral. "Unless he's already dead, which I doubt, he'll be here soon, and we must be ready for him. I want him distracted, you see. An unfair advantage, perhaps, but I've learned that with Deverell, any advantage is best."

Before she could anticipate his action, he put a hand in the top of her dress and jerked, ripping it down the front. She gasped and tried to twist away, but he held her down, straddling her with his knees on each side of her squirming body, easily avoiding the clumsy, cold-numbed swings of her arms.

"A lively bit," he muttered, panting a little as he grabbed her by the wrists, "it is no wonder you've intrigued the earl. He's easily bored, I understand, but you seem to have retained his interest longer than most. Oh no, little bitch, none of that!"

Harsh fingers dug cruelly into her wrist when she aimed a blow at his head, her fingers dragging over his face to leave bloody furrows in his skin. He struck her, a closed hand against the side of her head that left her stunned for a few minutes.

Vaguely, she knew that he was tying her arms and legs, spread-eagled on the filthy mat covering the dirt floor of the hut, his hands efficient and impersonal. Cold air prickled her skin, and she realized that she was naked and lying in the tattered shreds of her gown. A sob of terror welled, but she held it back.

Still crouched beside her, Sir Alex ran a hand over her rib cage, light exploration that was all the more frightening for that it was so detached.

"I've never quite understood the attraction of the female form," he murmured, "save for the pristine beauty of statues. The Greeks mastered the art, I believe, but then, I have an affinity for Greek fashions."

His laughter was soft, derisive, and she shuddered as he stroked his open palm over her breasts, then down her torso to her belly. He looked up at her, gray eyes dark with his own demons, a brooding regard.

"He took something precious away from me, you know, and I mean to do the same to him. Regrettable, that you are the weapon I must use, for I have no quarrel with you. It's only Lord Deverell who I want to suffer, as I suffered."

His hand was warm where it rested on her abdomen, and curiously soft. Her teeth began to chatter with fear and cold and dread, and there was no pity in the gaze above her, nothing but abstract observation.

Then he turned, stared into the darkness beyond the hut, and rose to his feet. "Ah, I hear the avenging angel arrive now, I believe. The moment has come for vengeance."

He glanced down at her as he drew a pistol from the waist of his trousers. "You will pardon me, I trust, if I must insist upon your silence. Any unexpected sound, and I will be forced to kill him before I am ready."

Moving across the hut, he moved the flickering candle to a three-legged stool beside her, where it balanced precariously on the uneven surface. Light wavered over her body, gleaming on pale skin of her thighs, belly, and bare breasts. She shivered again, an involuntary tremor so hard it made her muscles spasm. Every breath was torture, every sound beyond the hut both anticipated and dreaded.

And then he was there, appearing in the open entrance with murder in his eyes, his gaze sweeping over the scene.

"A party, and I wasn't invited?" he said at last, and Sir Alex laughed softly.

"Oh, you were invited, Deverell. This is all for your benefit."

"Is it? How fortunate that I found you, then."

"I knew you'd find me. I took no trouble to hide."

"No," Deverell agreed, and stepped cautiously into the hut, his head brushing against the low ceiling, "you left an obvious trail."

His glance shifted slightly, surveyed Amie where she lay shivering and naked on the floor. His mouth tightened, but he made no comment. Leaning against the frame, he crossed his arms over his chest, regarded Sir Alex coolly.

Maitland lifted a brow, and waggled the end

of the pistol he held. "She's been waiting a bit impatiently for you, I fear. Perhaps she didn't have faith in your arrival as I did."

"That's entirely possible." He allowed a faint smile to curve his mouth, but was gauging the distance from the door to the pistol. At this range, Maitland could not miss him.

Damn the warped bastard. . . .

"Let her go, Maitland. I'm here, and that's what you wanted."

"Oh, not at all. I want much more than to merely kill you. I want you to suffer, just as I suffered."

"You don't need her to do that."

"Ah, but I think I do." Sir Alex moved warily toward Amie, and Deverell tensed as he knelt beside her, one hand holding the pistol steady while his other stroked over her quaking body. "See how she flinches when I touch her? What do you think she would do if I did much more than this?"

Cold rage surged, but he didn't move when Maitland put a hand on her breast. A faint sobbing sound like a whimper vibrated in Amie's throat, but she didn't cry out.

"If you hurt her," Deverell said calmly, "I'll kill you."

"You are in no position to make such threats." Pale eyes narrowed slightly, but neither the hand on Amie or holding the pistol wavered. "I am in charge here. There's not much time, so I intend to make it quick, and as painful as possible for you . . . I want you to feel as I felt when Roger died."

"Roger killed himself."

"No!" The hand on Amie clenched and she gasped; the pistol lifted slightly, the black bore of the muzzle pointed steadily at him. "He would never have killed himself if you hadn't destroyed him first. His life was over when you dishonored him in front of all of us—a public humiliation that he could not bear. God, how I've hated you all this time, how I hated you then and wanted to kill you as you'd killed him . . . he was the man I loved more than anything, and you ruined him."

"He ruined himself, Maitland." Watching the pistol, he shifted balance to his other foot, muscles tensed and ready, watching for an opportunity. "He fired before the signal."

"You were supposed to die, damn you! God above, you must have more lives than a cat, because you've survived it all, even the *Fortune!*"

Deverell went still; his eyes thinned, boring into Maitland. "You were responsible for that?"

"Oh yes, only they bungled it. That damn viscount—he found you, somehow, even after all my precautions. I thought when he wanted you out of the way because of that incident with Cochrane, that he would leave it at that, be glad you were out of it finally, and that Cochrane would stay in hiding and not dare to come out. But you had to interfere, and even then, it would have worked out if you had only had the decency to die as you were meant to do, a warning to Cochrane of what could happen to those involved with the weapon he'd invented."

"A weapon never used. So much trouble for nothing. It must have annoyed you excessively."

Watching Maitland's face, he moved slightly

to one side, but the pistol followed him, the warning sharp: "I would advise you to be very still, my lord. Bullet holes make such a mess." A mirthless smile curved the beautiful mouth. "Now, it is time you learned what it is to suffer for the pain of someone you love. . . ."

Tension stretched, wavered tautly, palpable as Sir Alex scraped his hand over Amie again, his intention all too obvious. Beyond, the rolling thunder of guns was sporadic, the battle falling off in intensity, but no one would pay attention to the sound of a shot.

Then he saw the knife in Maitland's hand, the edge of a razor-sharp blade pressed against Amie's bare breast, and knew there was no more time.

He lunged. The pistol spat flame and sulphur, the ball a burning pain as it struck him, but he felt Maitland beneath his reaching hands, heard his startled oath and Amie's scream, all blurred together.

It was close in the confines of the hut, too small to avoid the pale, naked body spread upon the mat, and he took Maitland down to the dirt with him, grasping his wrist with one hand, bending cruelly until he felt it snap and the knife fall away.

Sir Alex was stronger than he looked, his wiry frame lean and muscled as he fought back, and they grappled and strained, grunting as fists pounded into flesh. Finally, he pushed him back, felt Maitland's nose smash beneath his fist, blood spurting, and heard the soft choked cry. Atop him, he struck again and again, until there was no resistance, nothing but faint, garbled whimpers.

Then a scream pierced the haze that enveloped him, and he looked up through blood and sweat in his eyes, saw the dancing flames as the overturned candle licked at the walls of the hut, tongues of fire greedily devouring wood and palmetto. Sparks fell, peppered Amie's body where she lay tied to the framework, and he pushed away from Maitland to go to her.

Grunting with pain, he realized his left hand was nearly useless, and found Maitland's knife on the floor to sever the cords binding Amie. There was a *whoosh* of sound as flames gushed across the roof, and one of the posts made a shrieking sound as it began to collapse.

Half-dragging her with him, he pulled her from the hut outside, where cold air struck his lungs as he sucked in a breath. Coughing, he held Amie in one arm, wracked with spasms.

She was sobbing, but struggled upright, and somehow she was lifting him to his feet, urging him to run.

"Horses are coming . . . oh God, please get up. If you're caught, they'll hang you as the enemy. . . ."

Dazed, stumbling, he followed her into the thick night beyond the hut, deeper into the swamp.

Chapter 27

It was over. New Orleans had beat off the British invasion and their ships had sailed away. General Jackson was regarded as a hero, as were the men who had fought with him.

Amalie stood at the window of the small house on Rampart Street, staring into the gray January light. She heard the noise of celebrations still being conducted in the town, but could not find it in her to celebrate.

He was gone again, sailing with the British ships and Lord Stanfill. It was too dangerous for him to remain in New Orleans now, of course, and she understood that.

Yet she had thought that he would want her to go with him, or at least make arrangements for her to follow him. He had not, even when he recovered enough from his bullet wound to go with Stanfill.

"It's just as well," he had said, his tone remote, "for if your brother and I meet again, it may have a very different outcome."

That much she understood; Kit hated Deverell, and would have killed him, he said, if not for the shell that had knocked him unconscious.

"An American shell," he'd said wryly, "that was lucky for Braxton. When I came to, he was gone. And it was lucky for you that he knew where to go."

Shivering, she thought of the chain of events that had barely saved her, and was certain Sir Alex—to die like that, in a raging inferno!—would have killed her if Deverell had not come. It was Georges who'd told him where to look, half-conscious and tied to a post in the privy, where Tilly had not looked for him. She shuddered to think what might have happened if Deverell had not found him, or if Georges had not known where to look.

But again, nothing was quite the accident it seemed, for Georges was Lord Stanfill's spy, set to keep an eye on her, and on Maitland, as well.

He was gone, too, leaving with the rest of the British. But Kit was here, still angry, still not willing to understand.

He came into the parlor, and she turned, saw him give her a frustrated, brooding glance before he went to sit by the fire. Tension settled like fine mist in the room, pervasive and dampening.

Finally he looked up at her and said, "I've joined up with Jackson's forces. He's pardoned all the Baratarians, and I'm going with the general when New Orleans is secure and he leaves."

Tears stung her eyes; she nodded, aware of his bitterness. "I'm glad you've got a pardon now. This is a new chance for you, Kit. For both of us."

He rose to his feet, restless, raking a hand through his dark hair. "I don't know what to do with you. You can't stay here, Amie. Not now. Not after—"

When he halted, she smiled slightly. "No, not after I've been ruined. It's all over New Orleans, I suppose. I could always accept one of the offers made me to become a mistress. Odd, that men who once looked at me with respect and deference now treat me as one of the girls along the quay."

"It can't be too big a shock," Kit said harshly, "given that you let Braxton parade you around the city as his personal property. God, Amie, how could you do it?"

"I didn't have a lot of choices after Belle Terre, you know," she retorted, stung by his disgust, "and how was it so different from being the sister of a pirate? Of course, I guess the difference to you is that no one knew about it, and that made it all right."

His eyes narrowed slightly, then he shook his head with a resigned sigh. "You're right. God, you're right. Ah, Amie, I'm sorry. It's just that when I think of you with *him*—and you never told me about him, what he did, or even who he was."

"I knew you wouldn't understand."

"And you were right—I don't understand. I've tried, but I just can't get the picture of you with him out of my mind. . . ."

Jerking to a halt, he looked away, back at the fire, and she went to him after a moment, put a hand on his shoulder. "I'm sorry, Kit. I should have told you, perhaps, but it never seemed like the right time."

He pushed away from the mantel, turned, and

took her in his arms, a light embrace that was so different from his former exuberant hugs. "I've got some money put away. I'll leave it with you. It should be enough to keep you for a while, at least until all this is over and I can get back to New Orleans. We'll go away, to Virginia, and I'll see if I can sail on a merchantman. It won't be much at first, but one day I can earn enough to provide for us." He smiled slightly. "Then you really *will* be the sister of a sea captain, maybe."

After he'd gone and Tilly had banked the fires for the evening, she went into the bedroom she had shared with Deverell. It looked the same, the bed they had lain in together still there, the neat spread over it, and the simple lines of the furniture all familiar. But it felt so cold now, and empty.

Like she did.

There was an emptiness inside her that nothing could warm, nothing could fill. She wondered if it would have been better never to have loved him than to know that he had never loved her. Which was more cruel? The lack, or the loss?

Rain beat against the windowpanes, and she blew out the lamp finally and went to bed, heard it gust against the glass with tiny *pings*, like sleet. A foul night.

She lay in bed, listening to the wind moan outside the house, and the clacking of bare tree limbs scrape against the roof.

A soft noise penetrated the gloom, and she turned, squinting through shadows, heart leaping with fear when she saw a silhouette against the hall light.

"Tilly?"

"No," a familiar voice said softly, and she sat up with a soft gasp, blinking as the tall shadow coalesced into a shape she knew so well.

"Deverell. . . ."

"You know," he said, as casually as if he had only been gone an hour instead of weeks, "we don't always have to be so bloody polite. My name is Holt. Do you think you could use it?"

Laughing, she put her arms around him, felt the icy crystals that clung to him, his skin chilled and yet warm beneath her hands, and said on a half-sob, "Yes, I think I can do that, Holt. What would you like to call me?"

He kissed her, mouth hot and urgent and seeking, stealing her breath, and when he finally lifted his head, she saw the faint gleam of his eyes as he said softly, "My love, my heart, my wife—I want to call you all of it, and I want to call you that forever."

Hardly daring to hope, she stared into his face. "Do you mean—?"

"Come with me, Amie, my love. I've resigned my commission and I'm going home—and I want you with me. Do you think you could bear to live in England again?"

"Yes! Oh God, yes . . . I can live anywhere you are!"

Slowly, he pushed her back into the mattress, his arms around her comforting and warm and safe, and she knew then that she would never feel alone again. . . .